A
Moonlit Knight

Jocelyn Kelley

A SIGNET ECLIPSE BOOK

SIGNET ECLIPSE
Published by New American Library, a division of
Penguin Group (USA) Inc., 375 Hudson Street,
New York, New York 10014, USA
Penguin Group (Canada), 90 Eglinton Avenue East, Suite 700, Toronto,
Ontario M4P 2Y3, Canada (a division of Pearson Penguin Canada Inc.)
Penguin Books Ltd., 80 Strand, London WC2R 0RL, England
Penguin Ireland, 25 St. Stephen's Green, Dublin 2,
Ireland (a division of Penguin Books Ltd.)
Penguin Group (Australia), 250 Camberwell Road, Camberwell, Victoria 3124,
Australia (a division of Pearson Australia Group Pty. Ltd.)
Penguin Books India Pvt. Ltd., 11 Community Centre, Panchsheel Park,
New Delhi - 110 017, India
Penguin Group (NZ), cnr Airborne and Rosedale Roads, Albany,
Auckland 1310, New Zealand (a division of Pearson New Zealand Ltd.)
Penguin Books (South Africa) (Pty.) Ltd., 24 Sturdee Avenue,
Rosebank, Johannesburg 2196, South Africa

Penguin Books Ltd., Registered Offices:
80 Strand, London WC2R 0RL, England

First published by Signet Eclipse, an imprint of New American Library,
a division of Penguin Group (USA) Inc.

First Printing, May 2006
10 9 8 7 6 5 4 3 2 1

For the members of the RomVets,
who know what it means to be a woman warrior.
You inspire me and make me proud to be counted among you.

Acknowledgments

I would like to thank the many experts who helped me with archery questions for this book. You gave me so much wonderful information to make Mallory's work with a bow seem real.

Thanks to Mark and Karen Dennen, Lisa Manuel, Conquest.-Soc, Tom Epstein, Steve Wibberley, Richard Kordos, Ron Trenka, Hugh D. Hewitt Soar, and my uncle Gordon Loveland.

I appreciate your taking the time to answer my questions and go the extra mile to provide more information that made the story richer. You are all worthy of the title of Knight Extraordinaire.

Chapter 1

She woke and instantly knew something was wrong.

Sitting, Mallory de Saint-Sebastian looked around the small cell. The sisters of St. Jude's Abbey did not live as spartanly as those in other religious houses . . . or so she had heard. She had never been within an abbey until she came here only a few days after her mother's death.

Moonlight was a slender finger across the stone floor before it crept up over the chest by the door. Mallory knew the room and the shape of every shadow within it well after more than five years at the Abbey. She could not see anything wrong.

Not in her room.

But something *was* wrong.

She stood. The thin coverlet had already fallen to the floor because the night was almost as hot as midday had been. A slimy drop of sweat slithered down her spine when she inched toward the wooden door. It was ajar in hopes of inviting in any wisp of cool air.

She held her breath and strained to hear what had alerted her. From across the hall lit by a single sputtering candle came one of the sisters' snores. Another was mumbling in her sleep. Something skittered among the rushes on the floor. It would be either a mouse or a cat in search of one of the rodents that refused to be banished from the Abbey.

All those sounds were familiar.

What had roused her from her sleep? She had been deep in an odd dream that was melting away with every beat of her heart.

Then she heard it again.

Iron on stone. Horseshoes! There must be horses entering the Abbey. Who would be arriving in the middle of the night? Honest travelers sought shelter before the summer sun dropped past the western horizon a few hours before midnight. Only thieves and miscreants were abroad after dark.

She reached back into her cell. Easily she found the bow and quiver that she kept close at all times. Tossing the quiver's strap over her shoulder, she left the bow unstrung as she hurried to the stairs that curved inside the tower at the end of the corridor. Windows that were too narrow for her to slip through were set along the stairwell. Beyond them, she heard voices. Male voices.

Pausing on one of the landings, she put the bottom of the bow against the side of her foot. She bent the bow and slipped the loop at the string's end into the notch at the top. It would be harder to move along the cramped stairwell with the bow strung, but she must be ready.

Chirps from frogs came from the direction of the pond behind the Abbey, distorting the words spoken in the courtyard. She paused in the doorway that opened into the night as she lashed the leather guard over her left arm. Without moving, she surveyed the grassy area.

The light from the quarter moon was dim, but she could see at least four horses. More might be hidden behind the abbess's house. The riders were concealed by darkness. One man stepped out into the light, but scurried back into the shadows like a beast seeking its lair.

She looked toward the abbess's house. No lamps were lit, only the candles that burned in the window over her prie-dieu. If these men had announced themselves to the sister in the gatehouse, the abbess would have been alerted by now.

Reaching behind her, she lifted an arrow out of her quiver.

She set it against the string, one finger on the string above it, two below, but kept the bow at hip level. As she eased out the door, she pressed her back to the tower's uneven stone wall. She could use the shadows to her advantage, too. Beneath her bare feet, the courtyard stones were still warm with heat absorbed during the day.

"Where are the women?" one of the men asked, taking no pains to lower his voice. "Imagine so many maidens dreaming of a virile man coming to save them from dying as virgins."

"A chivalrous man would make their dreams come true," another added.

Laughter met his words.

As she raised the bow, she could hear her own voice echoing in her head, the stern tones she used when instructing the younger sisters in archery.

See how my arm and the arrow are both straight? My arm is straight, but not stiff. Do not grip the bow too hard. That changes the route of your arrow when you release it.

Pulling the string toward her until it touched her lips and chin, she frowned for a moment. Footsteps came from her right. More intruders? She pushed the sound from her mind as she focused on a man who had stepped out into the moonlight. The arrow was aimed at the narrow-brimmed cap on the man's head. As soon as she relaxed her string hand, the arrow would fly forward, up and toward the man.

The targeted man glanced toward her and punched the man beside him on the arm. The laughter ceased as the men turned to discover her aiming at them. Even in the poor light, she was able to see the shock and horror on the faces of the two standing in front of the others.

A man pushed past them, but remained in the shadows.

"Put down the bow, sister," he said quietly, but his deep voice resonated through the courtyard as if he had plucked the taut bowstring. "If you loose the arrow by mistake—"

"If I loose the arrow, it will not be in error," Mallory retorted, annoyed by his condescending tone. When the men exchanged anxious looks, she added, "Tell me why you are sneaking through St. Jude's Abbey."

"Hold your fire, Lady Mallory!" came a command. The authority in the woman's voice suggested she was accustomed to being obeyed immediately and without question. Yet it was how the woman addressed her that shocked Mallory into motionlessness.

She had renounced the title of lady when she came to St. Jude's Abbey. Gladly she had embraced being called sister, because being a part of the family at the Abbey allowed her to sever any connection with the father who had sired her. He had not come for her when she left home to journey to St. Jude's Abbey. After five years, had he decided to tear her from the life she loved? But why would *he* allow a woman . . .

Two women stepped out into light now cascading from windows as other sisters awoke to discover who was in the courtyard before matins. At once, she recognized the abbess, short and round, carrying a brand. With her came a taller woman Mallory had not seen since her last visit two years ago. Time had lined the face that was so smooth in the portrait in the abbess's office, but Eleanor d'Aquitaine remained beautiful and elegant and every inch the queen of England and all its domains across the Channel.

Dropping to her knees, Mallory kept the arrow to the string in case the queen ordered her to fire at the men. She would do whatever the queen asked of her, even though the thought of aiming an arrow at a man's heart made her stomach cramp. Twice during the years Mallory had lived at the Abbey, the queen had come to St. Jude's Abbey seeking the assistance of one of the sisters who had been trained to serve her. After the first visit, each sister had wondered when it might be her turn to serve the queen during a time of great need.

How wise Queen Eleanor had been to have the foresight to see a need for the Abbey! Mallory wished she could aspire to even a portion of that wisdom. Then she might be as wondrous as Queen Eleanor was, a woman who had married two kings and given birth to another.

"Rise, Lady Mallory," the queen ordered.

Obeying, Mallory kept the bow lowered. Her fingers were trembling, something they had not done since she had found a home at the Abbey, and she did not want to chance the arrow flying off the string. She slowly lessened the tension on the string, so the arrow could do nothing more than fall to the ground directly below the bow.

"Were you about to slay one of these men?" Queen Eleanor asked. The men began to protest that no woman armed with only a bow would have succeeded in killing them, but she waved them to silence. "Answer me, Lady Mallory."

"I wished only to give them cause to regret skulking about the Abbey."

"And that is a crime warranting death?"

She shook her head, then, unsure if the queen could see her motion, said, "I was aiming at his hat." She gestured toward the man who glowered at her.

"You could have missed."

"I could have, but I seldom do."

"Bragging?" The queen's brows rose toward the dusty veil covering her hair. "Pride is something I do not expect among the sisters at this Abbey."

"It is a fact."

The queen smiled coolly but again waved the men, who were muttering among themselves, to silence. "A fact yet to be proved to my satisfaction."

Mallory swallowed hard. What test was the queen about to suggest?

"Although," Queen Eleanor continued, "I am well pleased you are as vigilant and courageous as I have been led to believe." She swiveled her head toward the abbess.

The motion must have been some sort of command, because the abbess hurried forward. She was plump, but the softness was an illusion. She expected much of herself and everyone who lived within the Abbey, and she answered only to Queen Eleanor and God.

In that order.

"This lady has been taught well to heed anything unusual in the Abbey," the queen said.

The abbess put a gentle hand on Mallory's arm. "Lady Mallory has used her few years with us to hone every skill she brought with her, and she has eagerly learned all her other lessons."

"I assume my most trusted companions are welcome in the Abbey," the queen said with perfect courtesy.

Mallory could not hide her awe at how easily Queen Eleanor was handling the peculiar circumstances. The queen acted as if they were standing in her hall, being received while she sat on a throne. If Mallory had half that much poise, she might have been able to remain in her father's house and watch as he married the mistress he had kept openly, even before her mother died. But then she would have missed the opportunities that had come to her at St. Jude's Abbey.

Again she swallowed hard. That the queen was here and addressing her as "Lady Mallory" could only mean that Queen Eleanor had a task that required the assistance of one of St. Jude's Abbey's sisters . . . that required *Mallory's* assistance.

"We welcome everyone who comes in peace to the Abbey," the abbess replied with a smile. "If you hunger or thirst, gentlemen, you need only ask, and food and wine will be brought to you."

"You are generous, as always." The queen's face eased into a more sincere smile as she motioned to the men lingering in the shadows. "Come and make yourselves known to the abbess of St. Jude's Abbey."

One by one, the men stepped forward into the light of the brand. The first four were muscular and dark-haired and as alike in appearance as countrymen could be. Their clothing, more elegant than what was worn in England, identified them as the queen's subjects from Poitou, the site of Aquitaine's capital. One by one, the four introduced themselves.

"Porteclie de Mauzé."

"Folques de Matha."

"Guillaume Mangot."

"Hervé le Pantier."

Each one bowed his head toward the abbess, at the same time stealing a glance in Mallory's direction, ogling her when they thought the queen would not take notice.

The last man waited until the others were finished greeting the abbess before he emerged from the shadows into the light of the brand. He was the man who had stepped forward to tell her to put down the bow, so she was curious why he had hung back while the other men spoke their names. He wore a tunic of the red wool only a fine lord could afford. His cloak, which like the other men's was ingrained with dirt from his journey, was edged with gilt threads, and she wondered if one of the king's sons was standing in front of her. She had never seen any of them, but it was said that both Henry the Younger King and Geoffrey had hair as tawny as this man's. A closely trimmed beard and mustache were only a shade darker than his sunbronzed skin. His face appeared to have been sculpted by strong hands, and his beard could not smooth its sharp planes.

"Saxon Fitz-Juste," he said with a polished bow, revealing that the strap across his chest was connected to a lute. Unlike the others, he did not look at anyone but the abbess.

Mallory was astonished. His name was not Poitevin. It was not even Norman. Saxon was an old name from the time before William of Normandy conquered England and claimed it for his own. Why would the queen have a man of such lineage among her loyal companions?

She could not ask, because the queen said, "Saxon, I believe you can do what is needed while I speak with the abbess."

He bowed his head again, standing still while the other men hurried forward to remain at the queen's side as she walked across the cloister's yard. The four men jostled like children trying to get closest to their mother, each one glowering at the others, yet smiling if the queen chanced to look in their direction.

"Are they always so silly?" Mallory did not realize she had asked the question aloud until Saxon turned toward her.

"Are you always so quick to judge? I thought a cloistered sister was eager to forgive weaknesses in others, as well as praying to put aside her own shortcomings."

She rested her bow against her foot, but did not unstring it. "Forgive me. I did not intend to let my thoughts leave my mind."

His dark brown eyes narrowed as he appraised her with cool disdain. Only now did she recall that she wore her sleeping robe, a sleeveless garment that did not reach her ankles. She shifted the bow in front of her, but it was no shield to conceal her from his steady stare.

"*You* are the most accomplished woman in the Abbey?" he asked, and she realized she had been worrying needlessly about her state of undress. His thoughts, unlike those of the other men, seemed to be focused on the bow rather than on her. "The abbess must be jesting."

Mallory was glad she was holding her bow and quiver. Otherwise she doubted she could have resisted the temptation to grasp his arm and throw him to the ground with one of the moves she had learned from Nariko, the woman who taught the unarmed combat of her homeland at the far edge of the world. She would not slow the motion to ease his fall to the stones. Maybe the blow would knock some courtesy into him.

"We do not jest about such matters," she said.

"I would beg to differ." An icy smile pulled at his lips. "I cannot believe that *you* are the one the queen has come seeking."

Mallory drew in a quick breath to keep anger from tinting her voice. "The queen trusts the abbess to make that decision. As her man, you should do the same."

"You are right. However, as the queen's man, it behooves me

to serve as her eyes. You do not have the stance of a skilled warrior. If *you* are the best in St. Jude's Abbey, maybe the queen's faith in the Abbey is misplaced."

Was he trying to make her despise him? If so, he need not try so hard. She already loathed his arrogance. He could look down his aquiline nose at her all he wished. That did not do more than vex her, but she was furious at his disdain of her beloved Abbey.

"If you wish," she said, "I will be very glad to show you the extent of my training."

"That exhibition must wait for the queen." Again his gaze slid up and down her. "She must see something in you that I do not."

"I agree."

"You do?"

She smiled as she set her quiver back on her shoulder. "She must see something in *you* that I do not."

He said nothing, and she wondered if she had shocked him speechless. Maybe he had not expected a cloistered sister to speak her mind, but she could not allow him to denigrate the Abbey . . . and the queen! Queen Eleanor deserved their respect and more.

When he turned and went back toward the horses, she smiled. That smile vanished when he pulled a quiver off the saddle and withdrew two arrows. They were several inches longer than her arrows. To use them would mean readjusting her stance and draw, and even that might not be enough. She had never practiced with arrows of that length.

"You would do well," Fitz-Juste said, "to guard that whetted tongue in the queen's presence. She is unlikely to have patience with your attempts at wit, considering what is going on."

Mallory's brow ruffled with bafflement. What was occurring beyond the Abbey that would distress the queen?

As if she had asked the question aloud, he focused his dark eyes on her and said, "Surely you are not so isolated here that you are unaware of how the young king and two of his brothers have risen up against King Henry the Senior."

"We are aware of the revolt." She tried to put as much haughtiness in her voice as he had in his. "If the king had not been determined to guarantee his heir the throne and had not coronated him three years ago, his son might have enough patience to wait until the throne is rightfully his with his father's death."

"Sister Mallory," said the abbess.

Mallory turned, horrified, to see the abbess's scowl. Not wanting to know what was on the queen's face, she lowered her eyes, for what she had spoken could bring shame on the Abbey. Heat scored her face, and she was glad the moonlight would bleach any color from her cheeks.

When Queen Eleanor spoke, there was no hint she had heard anything said by either Mallory or the abbess. "Where do you teach others, milady?"

Her finger shook as she pointed beyond the abbess's house.

The abbess frowned at her again before gesturing more graciously for the queen to come with her. As they walked away, the four dark-haired men fell in line behind them with practiced precision.

Fitz-Juste copied the abbess's motion toward Mallory. He said nothing, but he did not need to. In addition to speaking of the king's demise, she had been rude not to answer the queen aloud. She could not openly accuse Fitz-Juste of infuriating her to the point that she did not guard her words. It had taken her five years to learn to control her temper, which had flared too often at her father's indifference to her mother's suffering. Five years of restraint that had been negated within minutes by Saxon Fitz-Juste's taunts.

She flinched as she hurried to follow the queen and the abbess. The queen had suggested he knew what to do. Had his words been a test of some sort? If so, she had failed completely, shaming herself and, more important, the Abbey.

The familiar targets that were set against short stacks of hay offered Mallory no comfort as she rounded the corner of the abbess's house. Other footfalls came from behind her, and she knew the sisters awakened by the voices were coming to watch. Hadn't she done the same, peering over the kitchen garden wall, the first time the queen came to St. Jude's Abbey and challenged Sister Avisa to prove her skills? Mallory had wished then that she could have been chosen. Now she would have gladly traded places with any of the sisters following quietly behind to see what the queen proposed.

"There," Queen Eleanor said. "The target farthest to the right, Saxon."

He gave Mallory a smug smile before crossing the open area to the target half-concealed by darkness. Easily he drove one arrow and then the other into the white sheet before stepping aside.

"There is your target, Lady Mallory," the queen said.

Mallory stared in disbelief. The moonlight and shadow dappled across the yard made more difficult a shot that would have been challenging in the sunlight. The arrows were barely the breadth of her arrow apart. For so long she had been training others in the Abbey, and she had not spent much time in practice.

Silence filled the courtyard, but she was aware of everyone looking at her, waiting to see if she could accomplish the task given to her by the queen. Setting the arrow to the string again, she turned so her left side was to the target and raised the bow, then lowered it. She heard whispers all around, but neither the queen nor Fitz-Juste spoke. He simply watched her with that same self-satisfied smile. She wanted to warn him that he would not be wearing it long.

She slid her quiver off her back, leaning it against her right leg. The murmurs vanished when she lifted the bow to aim the arrow again. Slowly she drew the string back until it touched her lips and the middle of her chin. As she had hundreds of times, she let her fingers ease off the string and the arrow fly.

It arched at what seemed an impossibly slow pace. She held

her breath, not wanting to disappoint the queen and the abbess, even as she reached for two more arrows, sending them one after the other in the wake of the first. As the first arrow reached the top of its arc, it seemed to speed toward the target. It struck with a dull thud, directly between the two arrows. Right after it, the second, then the third arrows hit, one on the outside of each of the arrows jammed into the target. All five arrows quivered with the impact.

Mallory lowered her bow and bent to pick up her quiver, so nobody would see her relief. Or, she had to admit, her own smug smile if she looked toward Saxon Fitz-Juste.

"Well-done, Lady Mallory," the queen said.

Straightening, Mallory delighted in the queen's praise. "I have been taught well."

Queen Eleanor continued, as if Mallory had not spoken, "You shall travel to my court in Poitiers, where I have a task that you are well-suited for."

Excitement and uncertainty battled within her, but she kept her face serene. "I am eager to serve, my queen."

"You will travel separately from us."

"As you wish."

"I would wish that you could journey with me, so you could tell me how you learned to be so accomplished." The queen's smile wavered for only a moment. "One must be cautious not to show one's hand in these perilous times." She motioned to her men to return to their horses.

As the four dark-haired men obeyed, Queen Eleanor expressed her thanks to the abbess. Neither woman could have noticed the lecherous smiles the four men wore as they eyed Mallory anew.

She raised her chin and looked away, dismissing them with the dignity the queen had shown. Her composure was threatened when Fitz-Juste walked toward her, carrying all five arrows. He held out the three shorter ones to her.

"Thank you," she said quietly.

"You would have been wiser to miss." He walked away without giving her a chance to answer.

Which was just as well, because she had no idea what she might have said.

Chapter 2

Saxon Fitz-Juste prowled the wooden quay on the River Clain. Odors of mud and dead fish could not cover the stench of other refuse thrown into the shallow river. Above him, on higher ground, the roofs of Poitiers were gilded by the setting sun. The river was drifting into thicker shadow, and the narrow-keeled boats navigating it were seeking a place to spend the night.

How many more days would he need to wait here, pretending to be drunk and recovering from a lost love? Even the true drunkards were beginning to question why he continued to loiter there. He had seen their heads tilt toward one another and heard the whispers as he lurched from one plank to the next. The boards beneath him creaked, so he hurried along the quay that was shadowed by the trees marching in perfect order along the bank. The quay was in need of repair, but, like so much else this summer, it had been overlooked as the countryside prepared for victory in the revolt against King Henry the Senior.

He had not guessed he would be waiting for so long. The boat he was supposed to meet must have been delayed somewhere along the river. Although that was to be expected when battles were waging between the king and his sons not too many leagues north of Poitiers.

He would wait. That was his duty, and he was determined to prove that even a second son could prove his worth to his king.

"A drink, friend?" called an intoxicated man who held out a filthy bottle.

"Thanks." He did not want to add to anyone's suspicions by refusing. Seeing the man was sitting with two other men, he dropped to join them on the side of the quay and held out his hand. The bottle was shoved into it.

Saxon hoped the men were blind with the sour wine in the bottle. Holding it close to his mouth, he acted as if he had taken a deep drink. He swallowed, wiped his mouth with the back of his hand, then burped before handing the bottle back. He shifted when the boards gave a warning groan. The whole quay was going to fall into the river.

"Thank you, friend," he said. "I keep hoping something will take away the pain of her betrayal."

"Women," the man grumbled.

"Women," he answered, as if that explained everything.

"Pass it along, Jacques," one of the other men ordered. "We are thirsty, too."

"Shut your mouth! I am talking to my new friend. Friend, you looked as if you were about to wear your feet off with your pacing." The man laughed drunkenly before tipping the bottle back to his mouth, then peered at Saxon's feet. "You have shoes!"

"Found them."

One of the other men leaned forward. "Where?"

"On the feet of a man who did not need them in his grave."

The men chortled at the thought of robbing a corpse. Saxon guessed they had done it themselves on more than one occasion, and he vowed anew to keep these drunkards from relieving him of his shoes or anything else.

When one of the men began singing, the others nudged him to halt and pointed toward the river.

Saxon hid his frown when he saw the expressions exchanged by the men. Their faces, for the briefest moment, were completely lucid. They were playing a role, as he was. What or whom were they waiting for? He would be stupid to ask. If they discovered he was acting too, they might try to silence him. He had no interest in seeing his blood flowing on the river's lazy currents.

"Another drink," he ordered in the thick tone he had used before.

The man, the one the others had called Jacques, absently handed him the bottle as he and the other two continued to watch a boat with a square sail slipping out of the center of the river and moving toward the quay.

Tilting the bottle back, Saxon let the disgusting wine pour down the side of his mouth and onto his mud-encrusted tunic. He grumbled as the other men came to their feet. They rushed along the quay. They went to the very end, pushing aside another man, who glowered at them and shook his fist. When Jacques scowled, the man hastily looked away.

That single exchange told Saxon a lot. Jacques must be Jacques Malcoeur, a notorious thief who haunted the river-banks. Tales were whispered about his wicked deeds and his insatiable greed. Were he and his fellows about to attack the incoming ship and rob it right under the windows of the towers of Poitiers's city wall on the steep hill above the river?

He had no intention of trying to foil their atrocious scheme. The queen had guards who were supposed to oversee and protect commerce on the river. He was here for another reason.

Raising the bottle again, he looked around it to scan the deck of the ship. Its prow and bow were plain. Maybe paint had decorated the boards along the side, but he saw no sign of it. Even the sweet water in the river was uncompromisingly cruel, thwarting any attempts to decorate ships.

On the deck were stacked cases and barrels. He wondered how many were empty. The younger king, his brothers, and the French king were laying waste to sections of Normandy to the north, destroying everything belonging to the barons who did not join them in their uprising.

But he was interested in neither the boat nor its cargo. He was waiting for someone. As the boat came to the quay and a plank was put against its side, he could see people on the deck among the cargo. The men showed the wear of their travels. He squinted to make out their faces, hoping one was the man he awaited. His eyes widened again when he saw a woman standing among them, her gaze focused on the shore.

The woman was covered with the dirt and filth that came from a long journey, but he could not mistake the curve of her face or those remarkable purple eyes that had cut into him like one of her arrows when they stood in the light of the torches in the courtyard at St. Jude's Abbey. She was wearing a short blade at her side. It was longer than a knife, but lacked the length of a broadsword. She carried an unstrung bow beneath her black cloak that must be suffocating on the summer evening. A dark brown sack dropping from a strap over her left shoulder concealed all but the top of the bow. He wondered where she carried her arrows. The thought of searching that slender body that he had seen in silhouette, outlined by a thin shift, to find the quiver sent a tightening pulse along him.

He groaned back a curse. No. Fate could not be so cruel. It could not be bringing Sister Mallory of St. Jude's Abbey back into his life *now*. If she had delayed another few weeks arriving in Poitiers, it would have been better. He had a job to do here, and she was certain to interfere in it. Maybe not intentionally, but already thoughts of her had distracted him from the task he had vowed to complete. He wanted to shout out his frustration as he saw her scramble down the plank as if she had traveled on French boats her whole life and were the master of this one.

His groan became a muttered curse when Jacques stepped forward to block her way. How had such a simple assignment— all he needed to do was come here and meet a man who must be arriving on another boat—become so complicated?

"Welcome to Poitiers," Jacques said, bending from the waist.

Sister Mallory started to walk past him without a response. When he shifted slightly to box her in between his filthy clothes and the boat, she paused. Her hand settled on the blade at her side. Would she be foolish and draw it? She would be over-whelmed by Jacques and his comrades before she had a chance to swing it. That is, if the men did not fall down laughing at the idea of a woman challenging them with a shortened sword.

Saxon took a single step forward, then paused when Jacques ordered, "You may pay me the tax, milady." He cleaned a tooth with his nail, then, holding out the same hand, said, "Now!"

"Are you charging all the passengers your tax?" Her voice was empty of any emotion, just as it had been at St. Jude's Abbey. What was she hiding behind her studied mask of serenity?

"That is not your concern."

"I think it is if you are asking me to pay."

One of Jacques's men chortled out, "'Tis a lady tax. Only paid by ladies who come to Poitiers."

"I see," she answered. "Then my answer is no. I shall not pay your extortion. Move aside."

"Listen to the fancy lady telling us we cannot have the tax each lady arriving in Poitiers must pay." While his men laughed, Jacques pushed closer to her. "Pay."

"I do not have any coins to give you."

"Then I will take that blade."

"No."

"Take it, Jacques!" crowed one of his men.

Knowing that he had to put an end to the confrontation be-fore Sister Mallory was hurt, Saxon reeled along the quay while he sang the bawdiest tune he knew. He tossed the bottle aside. When it shattered, the three men's heads swiveled to look at it. He bounced off one of Jacques's men, then another. He hit the second harder, and the man tumbled into the water with a splash. Laughter came from every side, and Saxon used it as the diversion he needed.

Stretching his hand past Jacques, he grabbed Sister Mal-lory's arm and yanked her along the quay toward shore while Jacques and his comrade were trying to fish their friend out of the water before he was crushed by the boat's prow. She tried to tug away, but he halted her attempts with a single snapped curse.

"Then lead us to the left at the end of the quay!" she ordered.

"To the left? Why?"

"Stop wasting time with questions. Do as I ask."

He acquiesced, because going to the left or the right made no difference to him. He simply wanted to get her somewhere safe. He looked in the direction she was pointing. On the far side of an open field edging the river was a gate in the high city wall. He was amazed that Sister Mallory remained so clear-sighted when she was in danger of losing any money she might carry and more.

His arm was grabbed. He released Sister Mallory, shouting to her to run to safety, as he was whirled to face Jacques. The thief's mouth was twisted with fury as he raised a fist to drive it into Saxon's face.

Ducking, Saxon wondered how he had lost control of the situation so quickly. He heard a thud, but no pain exploded through him. Jacques suddenly let him go. Saxon jumped back as the thief toppled toward him. As Jacques hit the ground, there was another dull thump, followed by a splash.

He stared in disbelief as Sister Mallory swung again what must be a broken board from the quay. The third thief scurried out of her way. She gave chase, and, with the end of the board, pushed at him. He grasped it, trying to yank it from her hand. She released the board, and he tumbled with an astounded expression into the water on the opposite side of the quay from his comrade who was trying to climb out of the mud. Spinning, she raised her foot and shoved him away from the quay with the cool poise of a seasoned warrior.

A woman warrior? Yes, the queen had revealed that the sisters behind the walls of St. Jude's Abbey were taught a knight's skills, but he had not guessed those skills were so well honed. He wondered what the shadows within the Abbey's walls had hidden from him and the other men.

"What are you waiting for?" Sister Mallory cried as she

jumped off the end of the quay and ran toward him. She leaped over Jacques's prone form without pausing. She scrambled up the steep bank.

Saxon followed and grasped her hand as she ran across the empty field toward the city wall. Matching her steps, he led her to the closest gate. He looked back down the bank to see the two men climbing out of the water and heading to where their leader remained facedown on the ground. The rest of the boat's passengers and crew were going about their business as if nothing out of the ordinary had taken place. He guessed none of them wanted to become mired in someone else's fight.

The heat seemed heavier when they stepped through the gate in the city wall and onto the narrow street leading up toward Poitiers's center. The houses were set almost atop each other on either side of the street, and only the strongest breezes off the river could navigate the twisting tunnel between them.

As Saxon slowed the pace, he was shocked when Sister Mallory asked, "Are you all right?"

"Me? I am not the one who took on three thieves by myself." He frowned as he led her around a puddle in the middle of the street. It had not rained for several days, so he knew it was not water. An odor reeked from it. "Especially Jacques Malcoeur."

"Who is Jacques Malcoeur?" she asked, faintly breathless.

That she was not completely out of breath vexed Saxon more. He did not need one of the queen's Amazons coming to Poitiers when the situation between the king and his sons and erstwhile allies was precarious. That anger honed his voice when he snarled, "He is a thief. Don't you have the wits God gave a goose? You should not have tried to infuriate him."

"I do not believe I had to try."

In spite of himself, he smiled. Her voice, prim and reserved, masked the humor in her answer. Was that intentional, or was she trying to make him laugh? Or could she truly be as naïve as she sounded? It was an astonishing thought, but then everything he had witnessed about Sister Mallory was astonishing.

"But you are safe," she continued.

"Me?" he asked as he had before, incredulous.

"Didn't you see the men on the ship?"

He did not want to admit that he had taken note of nothing but her from the moment he saw her among the other passengers on the crowded ship. "There were more than a dozen."

"Almost a score." She drew back the hood on her cloak, and her dark hair, braided with strips of silk, glistened with red fire in the last rays of the day's sunlight. "Some were the crew, but there were several who seem to have come from Brabant." She lowered her voice as she looked at the houses edging the street that contorted like a madman with a fever. "Mercenaries who are seeking King Henry the Senior so they can fight for him in exchange for the gold and prominence such battles can bring the victors."

"Mercenaries? I had not heard that the king was hiring mercenaries."

She laughed without humor, but kept her voice to a near whisper as they passed people walking in the other direction. "What choice does he have? His sons have the French king's help and allies they have gained among King Henry's own subjects. They are defeating him on every front. If you were noticed and seen as one of the queen's men, you could have been slain."

"I should be grateful for your concern."

"I would be as concerned for any ally of the queen's." She looked back toward the river that was a glittering ribbon beyond the wall. "The queen must be informed without delay. I assume you are taking me to her."

"We are going directly to her palace. There, with the moat and her guards to offer protection, you can take the time to discover if she wishes to see you."

"Why would she *not* want to see me? She came to St. Jude's Abbey to order me to come here."

"That was a fortnight ago."

"It took longer than I had guessed to reach Poitiers." She looked up at him as she stepped around some broken cobbles. "How long have you been here?"

"Almost a full week."

"Because you took the easiest, most direct route. I could not because I needed to travel a different way."

He laughed. He was unable to halt himself. Some of the passersby looked at him, but most went about their business, wanting to be done and home before night fell. "That was not what the queen meant when she said we must not travel together."

"If that is so," she said, her voice quieter, "then I will apologize for my lack of understanding. I hope I am not too late to do what she wished to ask of me."

Wanting to tell her how the queen had been asking with less patience every day if Sister Mallory had arrived in Poitiers, he did not. Making her feel worse would not do anything to make him feel better about being unable to return to the quay in his role as an intoxicated, heartbroken lover. He must choose another way to watch each arriving ship without garnering attention.

"I am sure," he said instead, "that she can find some task for a woman who halted three thieves alone."

"You sound peeved."

"Peeved?" That was exactly the way he felt, but he had thought he was hiding his emotions. Her arrival was going to complicate matters far more than he had guessed, because a woman with such insight was certain to see what others had failed to.

"That I halted the thieves by myself."

"I can assure you that I am quite capable—"

A scream came from behind them.

"It looks as if you are going to have your chance to prove that now, Fitz-Juste," she said as he turned to see Jacques Malcoeur and his furious comrades racing toward them, pushing past others on the darkening street. Jacques held a brand high, and the light sparked off the edge of the well-honed blades he and his men carried.

Saxon heard Sister Mallory draw the small sword. In these close, twisting streets, her bow would give her no advantage.

Any arrow fired would strike a building within a few feet of where they stood, if it did not hit a passerby first. Another sign that she had been well trained. If his older brother had even half of her courage . . . By God's teeth, he was not going to let Godard's ineptitude distract him now.

He reached for his own sword, then remembered that he had left it behind. No drunkard wore a knight's weapon. He had only a dagger. It would have to do.

The thieves surged toward them. He met a sword with his dagger. Luck was with him, because the thief was no expert with the sword. A quick motion, and the thief's sword went flying while the thief clutched his hand where a thin red line of blood was widening across his palm.

Saxon shoved the shrieking man away and turned to help Sister Mallory. She needed his help, because she was falling back before another of the thieves. Jacques was attempting to slip around to surround her, but she slashed at him whenever he took a step toward her. At the same time, she was trying to counter the other man's attack.

With a curse, Saxon rushed forward and snaked his arm around Jacques's neck. "Drop the brand!" he shouted.

Someone screamed as the thief obeyed. Saxon risked a look toward Sister Mallory, even though the scream had not been hers, and saw her tripping backward over another loose cobble. Her sword bounced away from her fingers. He heard a crack, and he wondered if her bow was ruined. The third thief ran toward her, triumph in his wide grin.

He spun Jacques about and slammed his fist into the thief's face. The man crumpled into a heap on the stones.

To Sister Mallory, he called, "Get up!"

She lay there. Was she knocked senseless? He started toward her, knowing with a sickness deep in him as the man leaped at her that he could not reach her in time.

He halted in midstep when she put her feet against the thief's belly and, with a motion so fast that Saxon's eyes blurred, sent the man soaring over her head and slamming into the street. The man struggled to get to his feet, then collapsed.

She jumped up, grabbing her bow from the street, and notched the string, so she could fire if she must. She seized Saxon's arm and ordered, "Run!"

So many questions exploded through his head, but now was not the time to get answers. He saw, as she had, that the man he had fought was recovering his sword, and Jacques, shaking his head, was trying to stand.

He ran with her, pausing only to pick up her sword. When he led the way first to the right and then to the left and then another left through the maze of the streets, she was silent. He glanced at her when she did not run as quickly as she had when they rushed from the river to the city's gate. Fighting off the thieves twice must have sapped her. He felt no satisfaction at that thought, for he had to admit she was a worthy ally.

Footsteps were coming ever nearer behind them.

"How close are we to the queen's palace?" she asked softly.

"Not close enough. Even if we were, to cross the moat would make us easy targets."

"The queen's archers—"

"Will not know if we are the victims or the villains who are trying to flee from our own victims."

She considered that for a moment, then nodded. "That makes sense. We need to find a place to hide."

He could not argue with that. Nor did he wish to. All he wanted now was to put an end to the chase. He looked both ways along the street and smiled.

"This way," he said.

Again she was silent as he led her beneath another arch and down a side street toward the hulk of Ste. Radegonde's Church. Just past where the street turned into the one where cows were brought for slaughtering, an iron-and-wood gate blocked their way. When he was able to push it aside without a squeak, he wanted to shout with relief, but the battle was not yet won.

Saxon drew Sister Mallory into the narrow street and closed the gate behind them. Paying no attention to the rats scurrying about their feet and the foul odors rising from the bloodstained stones, he put his hand on her shoulder and guided her around a broken crate. He pushed her down to sit. He was only partly surprised that she obeyed, her bow leaning against the crate, ready if she needed it. She might argue about which direction to take, but she seemed to have a finely tuned sense of what she needed to do to keep her heart beating within her skin.

He knelt beside her. Dampness soaked up from the stones, and he tried not to think about what he was kneeling in.

Shouts and the flash of a burning brand erupted up the street, echoing off the low arch. For a moment, the light paused outside the gate. It swept toward the ground as someone swore.

"What is it?" called someone beyond the gate.

"A rat!"

"Hurry! We need to catch them!"

"If they went behind this gate . . ." The light from the torch oozed over the top of the gate and across the damp ground. With squeaks, the rats scurried in every direction, eager to be in the darkness once more.

"A woman will not go where there are rats!" said someone else.

"But she is not like other women. She—"

Another shout sent the man carrying the torch rushing after the others.

Beside Saxon, Sister Mallory did not move. She was being wise again. They needed to give the thieves enough time to wander away through the streets so far that Jacques Malcoeur and his men would not have enough time to cut them off again from reaching the palace grounds.

When her head leaned against his shoulder, he was astonished.

She was lovely, but this was the first time he had witnessed anything soft about her.

"Are they gone?" she whispered.

"Yes," he answered as quietly.

"Good." She closed her eyes. "Are you unhurt?"

"Yes. And you?"

"We must alert the queen about the mercenaries."

"As soon as we can leave this hiding place."

"All right," she whispered with an acceptance he had not expected.

He put his fingers under her chin and tilted her face toward him. The day's last light played off its gentle contours and seemed to be highlighting her barely parted lips. He bent forward, wondering if the lips of one of the queen's female warriors would be as luscious as those of her ladies-in-waiting. His arm slipped around her waist, and she slanted toward him, her brown sack striking his leg. Eagerness burst through him at her surprising submission, which was more intoxicating than any cheap wine he had pretended to drink on the quay.

Pressing his mouth to hers, he pulled back when he heard her moan. Not with pleasure, but with pain. He drew his arm away, and she folded up like a sail on a boat. He caught her before she could fall into the wet and filth. Her head lolled against his thigh, her swift breath warming his skin through his tunic.

He kept one arm around her, but lifted his other hand to see it covered with liquid that appeared to be black in the dim light.

Blood. Sister Mallory's blood.

He put his fingers to the base of her neck. Her heart still beat strongly. She should live, but would she be able to serve as she had been asked to? Queen Eleanor was not a patient woman or one who was understanding of mistakes. She would not be pleased that a woman, especially one trained to serve her, was wounded. Even more, she would be furious that one of her own men had not been able to protect that woman from three thieves.

So how *was* he going to explain what had happened to the queen and still retain her favor? If he failed, everything he had worked for would be ruined.

Chapter 3

S he woke and knew immediately something was wrong.

Mallory blinked her eyes open, then squeezed them shut as strong sunshine battered them. But they were open long enough for her to see she was not in her familiar cell at St. Jude's Abbey. Nor was she in the bedchamber that had been hers at Castle Saint-Sebastian. A single glance revealed that this one was more than quadruple the size of the room at her father's estate.

Pain cascaded through her, rippling out from a spot on the back of her head. It surged to her toes and fingertips, then ebbed back to focus where her head was lying on a pillow redolent with herbs. Someone must have struck her skull. Who? When? Where?

She focused on the "where" question, because she had no idea where she was.

Forcing her eyes to slit open, she saw she was lying in an elegant bed. The curtains, pulled back to allow in the morning light, were made of velvet, and the uprights carved with images of birds about to take flight. She reached out a hand to touch them, then groaned as pain ricocheted through her head again. It nearly silenced the soft music.

Music?

She forced her eyes open again and looked past the curtains. Where was the music coming from?

"Awake, milady fair," sang a deep voice.

"For the sun has risen with the morn
And sweeps across the light-drenched field
Awake, milady fair,
As you have each dawn since you were born
And let the light sweep over you now healed."

Mallory stared in disbelief at the foot of the bed. There, leaning against one of the posts holding up the wooden canopy, sat Saxon Fitz-Juste. He rested his lute on his knee, its curved neck dropping toward the bed, and smiled at her.

She pulled the pillow from beneath her. Pain swirled through her head, but she paid it no mind as she flung the pillow at him. He laughed as he ducked, letting it fly across the room.

"Get out!" she ordered.

He bowed his head again before swinging his feet over the side of the bed and standing. "How do you fare? I assume your head is aching."

"It is, and your caterwauling does nothing to help it."

He rested the shoulder of his red tunic on the upright again. Running a quill across the strings of his lute, he wore a sad expression. "I thought my song would bring you back to your senses. Despite your protestations, it seems it has done exactly that. You are just as ill-natured as you were before you were knocked senseless on the street."

She touched the back of her head. "Is that what happened?"

"You collapsed like a tower undermined by sappers." He chuckled. "Now there is an image that needs a song—the brave woman warrior being cut down by evil ones."

"Will you go?"

"I have left your bed, as you requested. I thought I would—"

"Take your leave," interrupted a woman in the open doorway. The woman, whose hair was hidden beneath a wimple, was not tall. She was fleshy but not fat. She had the appearance of a well-fed hedgehog, for her clothing was the same brown.

Fitz-Juste gave her a deep bow. "Your command I cannot disobey."

The woman stepped aside to let him walk out. As he passed, he tweaked her cheek. She giggled as if she were no older than a girl, but quickly frowned. "Off with you and your charming ways. If I find you in this room again—"

"It will be because Sister Mallory has invited me in an attempt to salvage my immortal soul." He looked back and winked at Mallory. "Or in an attempt to damn hers."

The woman pushed him out, closing the door behind him and coming to the bed. Mallory forced her attention onto the woman. Too many questions careened through her mind. Fitz-Juste. The pain in her head. What had happened? Her journey to—

"Poitiers!" She gasped, memory rushing back and creating a renewed pulse of pain.

"Yes, you are in Poitiers." The woman's voice was soothing. "How do you feel?"

"All right." It was not exactly the truth, but if she had reached the queen's palace, she needed to go to Queen Eleanor and offer her services. "Where is my bow?"

"It is here, along with the other weapons you were wearing." Uncertainty heightened the woman's voice. "Or so I was told."

"Where is it?" She tried to sit up, but fell back onto the bed. Everything whirled in a drunken dance. She hated her own weakness. Queen Eleanor had commanded her to come here to do the queen's bidding. How could she do anything if she could not get out of bed?

She *had* thrown the pillow at Fitz-Juste, but anger and shock had strengthened her arm. Now she was completely sapped.

"It is here," the woman said.

"Where?" She sounded petulant, but she did not care. She had been training with the bow for so long that she felt oddly naked and vulnerable without it in sight.

The bed-curtains were pulled back slightly, and the woman wearing servant's clothing leaned toward her. The woman's face was lost in the glare of the bright light beyond the bed.

Mallory blinked several times, then rubbed her eyes that were caked with sand from sleep. How long had she been asleep?

As if she had asked the question aloud, the woman said, "It is the morning after your arrival, milady. There is your bow."

Mallory forced her eyes to focus as she looked in the direction the woman was pointing. Her bow, still strung, leaned against the stone wall beside a window. Relief slipped through her, and she relaxed back against the mattress again.

"Food is waiting for you," the serving woman continued. "I have called for warm water to be brought so you may bathe." Drawing back, she wrinkled her long nose. "We usually ask travelers to clean themselves upon their arrival, so the linens will need to be changed on your bed now as well."

Mallory wondered if an apology was what the woman was seeking. If so, the serving woman gave her no time to offer one, because she bustled off to draw back the shutters on the windows, which were wider than the ones Mallory was accustomed to at the Abbey and her father's house. The builders must have assumed that, within a city surrounded by a wall, the palace would not need many defenses against its enemies.

When she asked if Mallory needed help getting out of bed, Mallory pushed herself up to sit. Everything in the room spun wildly for a moment while dark spots danced in front of her eyes; then the world righted itself. As she edged her legs toward the side of the bed, she took care to blink slowly. Any quick motion threatened to send the room spiraling into darkness again.

"Sit here." The woman patted a chair at a small table beside the hearth. Other than the bed and a large chest, the table and chair were the only furniture in the room. "My name is Ruby, and I am here to serve you, milady."

"Here?"

"The queen's palace. In Poitiers." Ruby, who was about the age Mallory's mother would have been if she still lived, wore a matronly expression of dismay. "Your head was injured badly, milady. Have you lost your memories?"

"No, I am fine." She decided to prove that by getting off

the bed. As soon as her feet touched the uneven stone floor, she locked her knees in place. A long shift drifted down, but reached only as far as her calves.

Mallory did her best while eating the fresh bread topped with honey to show she was feeling well enough to be up and preparing to leave the room. When Ruby's back was turned while Mallory enjoyed the opportunity to soak the ingrained dirt from her skin, she did close her eyes and stopped fighting the pain. She was careful to hide the anguish as soon as Ruby came back with some clean clothes for her.

As Mallory sat by the window, which gave her a view of a lush garden below and the moat beyond it, she ran a comb through her hair, loosening the tangles left after washing it. The city was crammed between the walls of the palace and the fortifications that King Henry the Senior had had built to replace the crumbling ones left by the Romans. Rooftops jutted at all angles as if determined to capture every drop of sunshine that glistened on the river that edged the wall to the north and to the east. She knew it also followed the west side of the city, but she could not see that from where she sat. Steeples of the city's many churches threw shadows across the roofs.

The curve of the palace gave her a view of the round towers that edged out into the street. Statues were carved near the top of each one. She wondered if they represented the queen's family. Crenelations near the top were not tall, and there were few arrow slits. No wonder King Henry the Senior had strengthened the city walls. The palace had too few defenses.

Ruby said quietly, "Maybe you should spend the rest of the day recovering. You have no more color in your face than in that linen shift."

"Some sunshine will add color to my face." Looking away from a garden where people wandered by on errands she could not imagine, Mallory pulled a purple gown over her head and stood to let Ruby lace up the back. The dress was a bit short, too, because it reached only as far as her ankles. Long drapes of fabric dropped from the bottom of her sleeves to just below her knees. Once she had spoken with the queen, she would return to her room and let down the gown's hem.

"Do you think anyone would be bothered if I trimmed the sleeves?" she asked.

"If you wish some lace, milady . . ." Ruby began, confusion filling her voice.

"No, I did not mean trimming the sleeves that way." She wiggled her arms. "These absurd sleeves hamper every motion."

"But, milady, everyone in the court wears such sleeves. Not to be dressed so would be an insult to the queen, who takes such pride in the elegance of her court."

With a sigh, Mallory acquiesced. "Do you have some silk strips to weave into my hair?"

"Braiding your hair will be painful. You should wear it loose until you are healed."

She considered arguing, but the set of Ruby's mouth warned that the servant was not willing to compromise on this matter. And that, Mallory admitted silently, was fine with her. She needed to have all her wits focused on the meeting with the queen, not on the anguish pounding in her head.

When the serving woman gave her a white veil, Mallory settled it carefully over her hair. She fought not to wince when Ruby set a silver circlet over the silk to hold it in place, and she was glad when Ruby knelt to help her slip into the low shoes that fit better than Mallory had dared to hope.

Standing, she latched the sword belt around her waist and set her sword and a shorter dagger in it. She picked up her quiver and frowned. Two of the arrows were cracked. They must have been broken when she was shoved to the street. Plucking them out, she tossed them onto the table. They were ruined, but she might be able to reuse the feathers and the tips if she could find some wood to carve into thin shafts.

She put the bow over her shoulder, then shrugged on the quiver. Now, at last, she felt ready to go to the queen and offer her services.

"Are you sure you wish to leave the room so soon?" Ruby asked when Mallory wobbled on her first step toward the door.

"I am here to serve the queen, and I must not make her wait any longer."

"The queen surely knows you were injured."

"Who—? Fitz-Juste." Another wave of memories swept over her, flooding her with scenes from the Abbey and the quay and the streets of Poitiers. In each one, Saxon Fitz-Juste was trying to show that he was her better. In many of them, she could recall his amazement when she succeeded where he had obviously guessed she would fail.

"Fitz-Juste? Oh, you mean Saxon." Ruby's smile widened. "He *is* very skilled with the lute and in other ways."

"He is skilled?" That astonished her until she remembered that he had injured one of the thieves. She did not recall how. "With which weapon?"

Ruby laughed and winked. "With a man's favorite weapon. The one he carries between his legs."

Heat swelled through Mallory, and she quickly looked away.

"Forgive me," Ruby said. "I did not mean for my words to embarrass you."

"They did not." Mallory went to the door, threw it open, and went out into the hall before the rest of the words lying bitterly on her tongue burst forth. She closed the door behind her and strode along the hall at the best speed her unsteady legs could grant her.

She was not embarrassed by such words. She was furious! All too well she knew how a man could be ruled by what Ruby called a man's favorite weapon and his lusts. Her father, the esteemed Lord de Saint-Sebastian, had thought nothing of bringing his mistress to live beneath the same roof as his wife. Nor did having two women to bed halt him from casting a roving eye on other women within his fief. He believed in the droit du seigneur, and no virginal bride went to her husband's bed without first spending time in the earl's. He took great pride in the number of children in the fief who bore his features, and he gave a silver coin to each of them on their tenth birthday. She was surprised he had not bankrupted his estate with so many gifts.

Mallory was halfway down a wide staircase before she realized she had no idea where the queen's apartment was. She turned to go back and ask Ruby, but the idea of climbing up the stairs daunted her as nothing else had since she had left her father's castle to go to St. Jude's Abbey. She would find someone to direct her on the floors below.

At the bottom of the stone stairs, an archway opened into the garden she had seen from her bedchamber. The flowers, heavy with blossoms of every imaginable color, were even more inviting from this view. She had seldom had time to wander through the small gardens at the Abbey. While growing up, she had often gone with her mother to the gardens at Castle Saint-Sebastian. There, her mother had told her stories of the splendid woman who was queen of England and duchess of distant Aquitaine.

Mallory had been sure no one could be more magnificent than Queen Eleanor, and, even as a child, she had vowed to pattern her life after the queen's. That statement had always brought a laugh from her father, but her mother must have heeded the truth coming from a child's heart. Why else would her mother's dying wish have been for Mallory to go to the abbey established by the queen?

Pushing aside the memories, she looked along the corridor. More arches led out into the garden. She had seen people in the garden from her room above. One of them could show her the way to the queen's chambers.

She frowned with frustration when every view made the garden appear deserted. Had those strolling through it returned inside to complete their daily tasks? All of them? All at once? How odd! But her sisters at the Abbey had warned her that she would find the Poitevins strange, for they preferred their story-telling and songs to honing the skills needed to protect their queen. Maybe the honest ones were busy with poetry and music, but the thieves had fought well yesterday.

Mallory was about to give up on finding someone in the garden when she saw motions near a fountain. She walked beneath the arch and saw several steps leading down among the flowers. As she started down them, one of the people moved enough for her to see his face.

Saxon Fitz-Juste! He appeared as if he had no concerns about anything as he leaned back against a fountain that splattered water in a lyrical pattern into the lower pool. His tunic was particolored, plain red on one side and, she noticed as she had not in her room, decorated with gold embroidery on the other with a short cape attached to it. If he were standing, the tunic would have reached no lower than midthigh. Dark green stockings ended in the rolled tops of calf-high leather boots. Plucking the strings of his lute, he was smiling warmly at the four women sitting around him. Another was draped across his right leg, gazing up at him with obvious ardor.

There had been many whispers about Queen Eleanor's Court of Love in Poitiers, but nobody at the Abbey had openly spoken about the candid sensuality rumored to abound in the queen's palace. Mallory had given the stories no thought until seeing Fitz-Juste surrounded by his bevy of admirers.

She would find her way to the queen's chambers on her own. She wanted no part of such wanton behavior. Even as she thought that, her lips tingled as if something had brushed them. But what? A memory, uncertain and indistinct, teased her. A memory of Fitz-Juste's face near hers, strong emotions filling his eyes that were closing as his mouth lowered toward hers.

She shook her head to banish the image. A memory or a wisp of nightmare from when she had been lying in that grand bed?

Instantly she wished she had not moved her head without thinking. Everything whirled about. She groped for the arch. When she gasped as everything caved into blackness, she swayed like a sapling in a strong wind.

A hand caught hers while another propped up her elbow to keep her from falling. Her fingers curled around the broad palm as she waited to be free of the ebony abyss. When she was guided down to sit on the steps, every motion threatened to shatter her. She gripped the edge of the stones and breathed in deeply.

Light returned slowly; then, as she became aware of her eyes blinking, it exploded around her. Sound came from every direction: birds singing, people talking, the splatter of water. She closed her eyes and took a deep breath as she reopened them. Everything tilted slightly, then righted itself.

Realizing she was still holding the hand of the person who had come to her assistance, she said, "Thank . . . *You!*"

Fitz-Juste smiled coolly. "By your tone, I assume you are once more yourself."

She yanked her hand out of his and stood. As she had upstairs, she made sure her knees would not falter beneath her. To fall on her face in front of Fitz-Juste would be humiliating. She adjusted her bow over her shoulder.

He came to his feet as she did. She was amazed that she had to look up at him. She was accustomed to being the tallest in the Abbey, where there were few men beyond the priest and the laborers who came to work the fields.

"Can it be?" he asked, walking around her with slow, measured steps. "Can you be the same woman I saw on the quay? Where is the dirt on your face?"

"Stop this silliness! I need to—"

"What is silly about admiring a woman? You are no longer hiding your pleasing curves beneath a thick cloak. You are no longer wearing the memory of every mile of your long trip. You look as if you belong right here in Queen Eleanor's court with your black hair hanging straight and as smooth as a raven feather, almost to your waist."

"I do not need your pretty words. I need your help in finding the queen's chambers."

He smiled, but added as if she had said nothing, "Such a

simple gown enhances your beauty, while the engraved haft of your blade draws a man's gaze down over your breasts to your waist, a very pleasant exploration any man would enjoy savoring more than once. Your gown's fabric is the exact same shade as your eyes." He stepped up another riser. "And they are only a hand's breadth below mine. A very pleasing arrangement. With your face freshly washed and lacking the cosmetics other women don, you appear surprisingly delicate."

"Appearances can be misleading," she said. She was letting him draw her into his games of words that meant less than a donkey's braying. "For example, I cannot help wondering, is something stuck in your eyes?"

He frowned. "No. Why do you ask?"

"You seem unable to move them."

"Do you find it so difficult to believe that you are a pleasing sight?"

"I find it difficult to believe you would be thinking of that now."

"Then you know nothing of men."

Mallory had to put an end to the conversation at once. She *did* know about men. She knew about their lusts and how those lusts could destroy a family. Telling Fitz-Juste the truth would reveal the secret pain she refused to let take over her life again.

"I know enough," she said, "to realize you are hiding something behind your babble."

He recoiled, but she felt no sense of victory when his tawny brows lowered. "The abbess chose you as the most accomplished at St. Jude's Abbey. Was it only with weapons that you are skilled? Are you equally adept at gauging the thoughts of those around you?"

"Excuse me," she said in her primmest tone. "I have kept the queen waiting too long."

"Stop!" he called as she turned to leave.

She would have kept walking if Fitz-Juste had not stepped in front of her, blocking her way. Quietly, she said, "The queen is waiting for me."

"You are not in your abbey. You are in Poitiers, where the queen oversees the most glittering and glorious court ever known in history. The queen might not have been disturbed by your appearing before her in your sleeping shift when you were at St. Jude's Abbey, but here she will expect you to look your best." He tugged on the veil.

She put her hand up to halt the veil from moving, then winced. "I look fine."

"Your veil was crooked." His smile faded. "Are you sure you feel well enough to meet with the queen? You took quite a bump to your head. You were babbling nonsense while I brought you here."

"Nonsense? What did I say?"

He shrugged. "Nonsense."

"What sort of nonsense?"

"Mumblings that either made no sense or were unintelligible or both." His chuckle was icy. "You did not divulge any past sins or secrets that would turn the world upside down."

"How do I know you are being honest?" She could not keep from wondering what she had revealed. That he was vehement that she had said nothing suggested that she had, indeed, said some things that he could understand.

"Have I ever lied to you?" He leaned forward until his eyes were only a finger's breadth from hers. "I was honest when I said you would have been wiser to fail the test the queen set for you at your Abbey."

"I serve the queen." Her voice remained steady, but she drew back from him, halting when her heels found the edge of the step.

"No question of that, but I thought you might be smart enough to stay at St. Jude's Abbey."

"You doubted I would obey the queen's request?"

One side of his mouth quirked. "I thought you might be willing to listen to advice, Sister Mallory."

"I am now properly addressed as Lady Mallory."

"Lady?"

"It is what the queen called me."

He laughed shortly. "The queen may address a lamb as 'mi-lady,' but that does not change the truth."

"My father is an earl, so the title of Lady Mallory de Saint-Sebastian is rightfully mine."

"You are the daughter of Lord de Saint-Sebastian?"

She nodded, wishing she had not mentioned that. Yet her name was her own, and the abbess had reminded her before Mallory left St. Jude's Abbey that the queen expected her to use it.

"I have met your father several times," he said. "The last time, de Saint-Sebastian was boasting about his young wife and the fine set of twin boys she had given him. Not once did the earl mention having a daughter."

Mallory said nothing as she stepped around him, but did not turn her back to him. Her father was a man eager for gold and power, but he let his own pleasures divert him far too often. Once he had discovered that she intended to fulfill her mother's dying wish to cloister herself at the Abbey, he had made every effort to act as if she had never been born. He had told her before she left Castle Saint-Sebastian that her only use was to bring him more of the riches and influence he craved.

"I will tell you this one last time, *milady,* that you would be wise to scamper back to England immediately. The intrigues of the queen's court and the revolt sweeping through the lands on this side of the Channel are no place for an earl's daughter, be she a cloistered sister or a lady."

"Why are you so eager for me to leave?" Her eyes narrowed as her hand settled on the hilt of the blade she wore. "What reason would *you* have to see me fail in my duty to the queen?"

Before he could answer, his name was called. A woman rushed up the garden steps. "Saxon, how much longer are you going to be away from me?" the blonde cooed from behind him. She rested her cheek against his back as her slender arms, covered in pale blue silk, curved up the front of his tunic.

"I told you I would return, Elita." He peeled her possessive fingers off and turned to fold them together between the two of them.

"When? I am lonely without you."

Mallory tried to halt herself, but a muffled laugh pushed past her lips. When Fitz-Juste glanced over his shoulder, she made sure her face was composed and calm.

"Who is *she?*" Venom dripped from the blonde's words.

"Elita," he said with more patience than he had ever shown Mallory, "go back to the others. I will return to you as soon as I can. What I have to discuss with Sis—with Lady Mallory is very important."

"Being with me is important, too." She leaned against him, her hand slipping along his abdomen.

Mallory had seen enough. She turned on her heel and walked away. Or she meant to. The quick motion almost undid her again. She did not want to admit Ruby had been right when she suggested Mallory wait. Yet, Mallory would not be having such trouble if she had first encountered someone other than Fitz-Juste.

Again his strong hand under her elbow kept her from embarrassing herself by collapsing. She pushed his fingers aside as soon as she could stand alone.

"You should go back to bed," he said. "You lost a lot of blood."

"I did?"

"I would be glad to show you my ruined tunic, if you have to be convinced."

She did not need to be persuaded about the truth. Every unsteady motion revealed that. She needed to put an end to this conversation and present herself to the queen. Saying the latter, she added, "You are busy. I shall ask someone else how to reach the queen's apartment."

"I will take you to the queen." He held out his arm so she might put her hand on it.

She hesitated only a moment. Pride must not keep her from

doing as she had vowed. She put her fingers on his arm. "Thank you, Fitz—"

"The ladies call me Saxon."

She looked back toward where the woman he had addressed as Elita was watching them closely from the bottom of the steps. "I am sure they do. I am sure they call you regularly."

"Your sarcasm will not serve you well here," he growled. "Here, people would rather speak of love and chivalry and great deeds."

"Speaking of them rather than doing them? If that is the pastime you prefer, do not let me keep you from it and your ladies." She lifted her hand off his arm. "I do not need your help."

"You don't?" He matched her steps as she continued along the corridor. "What a misguided innocent you are! Subterfuge is widespread here, and those who are allies today are enemies on the morrow. Liege promises are being obliterated throughout the lands ruled by King Henry the Senior. To trust anyone now is foolish."

"Even you?"

"I will never break my vow of fealty once it is sworn."

"Nor will I. I will do whatever I must to serve the queen." She motioned along the corridor. "Are we going in the right direction?"

Instead of answering, he led her up another flight of stairs. He kept his steps slow, so she could climb without stumbling. At the top, he drew her toward more stairs. They kept climbing until she was sure they were about to reach the clouds.

The door he paused before was simple, like the rest she had seen. When he knocked, it was opened quickly. A maidservant bowed them into a room with no furniture and asked them to wait while she announced them to the queen.

"How does she know who I am?" Mallory asked.

"How many other women in this palace carry a bow and quiver?" Saxon returned with the cool smile she was coming to despise.

Mallory was grateful for the maid's return so she did not have to answer. They were ushered through a door.

Her breath caught as she stared at the glorious chamber. Every piece of furniture, from a chair to a vast cupboard, was intricately carved, and silk was draped in front of windows and across chairs. Pillows were scattered in front of a wide hearth where a group of women sat as they worked on embroidery.

When one of the women stood, Mallory knelt and watched in silence as the queen walked toward them. Everything about Queen Eleanor was perfection, from her aura of authority to her beauty that lingered at an age when most women were wrinkled and worn. Her voice when she greeted them and bade them to rise was like a favorite song upon Mallory's ears.

"How do you fare, Lady Mallory?" She smiled warmly. "I understand you have shown your skills already by defeating some thieves."

"With the help of Saxon Fitz-Juste." She hated having to admit that, but she would never lie to the queen.

"You two make a good team, it would seem. That is well, for I shall need the skills both of you possess to protect my life."

"Your life is in danger?" Mallory gasped. She had not guessed that the queen had come to St. Jude's Abbey because someone wished her dead. Why hadn't the queen remained behind the Abbey's walls, where every sister would sacrifice her life for her? Mallory could not ask such an impertinent question.

"There have been threats, and if—"

The door from the antechamber crashed open. A man exploded into the room. The queen's ladies screamed. The queen gasped as the man rushed toward her, his quiver of arrows bouncing on his back.

Saxon reached for his sword, but Mallory, forcing her eyes to focus, had arrow to string and flying before the man could take another step. It struck him in the sleeve, pinning him to the cupboard behind him. He reached to pull the arrow out, but froze when she aimed a second arrow at him.

Her stomach curdled in horror as she saw the terror in his eyes. He believed she was about to kill him. Could she? Could she do as she had boasted? Could she do anything to serve the queen?

She steadied her bow hand, which was trembling, and called, hoping she would be able to obey the queen's order, "Say the word, Queen Eleanor, and he is dead."

Chapter 4

Behind Mallory, Saxon whistled a single note of amazement. Did he doubt her threat? Or, worse, did he doubt her skills with the bow? She resisted the temptation to look at him and demand an answer. She stared at the man pinned to the cupboard by her arrow. He was regarding her with a mixture of fury and fear. His hand rose toward the arrow, but he froze when she drew back farther on the bow.

Something poked her leg.

She did not look down.

It poked her again; then she heard a sniffing sound as something moved along her foot.

"Go away, dog," she ordered through gritted teeth.

The dog, which could not be very big, sat on her right foot and gave a soft whine.

Was it the intruder's dog? What sort of thief brought a *dog* with him? A cur would increase his chances of being discovered.

She pushed the dog out of her mind, which was not easy when it was perched half on and half off her foot and continuing to whimper. She had learned to focus amidst more troublesome distractions.

No one else moved for the length of a trio of heartbeats.

Soft footsteps rustled the rushes on the floor, and again Mallory kept herself from peeking over her shoulder. Who was approaching?

Her breath burst from her with relief when she heard the queen say, "Well-done, Lady Mallory."

"Thank you." She was unsure what else she should say as she continued to aim the arrow at the man.

"Who are you that you intrude into my private chambers?" the queen asked the man.

"Bertram de Paris, a messenger." His teeth continued to chatter with fear, distorting his words.

"From whom?"

"The king of France."

Mallory sucked in another sharp breath, then clamped her lips closed before the soft sound could betray her shock. She had never held the firing stance for so long. Her shoulder was beginning to cramp, and she could not guess what the queen's next command would be. The king of France was her husband's enemy, but the ally of both the young king and her favorite son, Richard.

"Allow him to pass, Lady Mallory," the queen said.

"As you wish." She lowered her bow as she relaxed the tension on the string. The arrow flopped uselessly against her leg. The dog tried to catch it in its teeth, but she lifted the arrow away and slid it back in her quiver. In a whisper, she added, "Shoo, dog."

The yellow-and-brown dog, which appeared to be no more than a puppy, wagged its tail and gave her a canine grin. It did not seem bothered when she gave it a gentle shove with her toe as she shifted her foot from beneath it. A titter of laughter came from the other end of the room as the dog sat on her foot again.

"Lady Mallory," the queen said quietly.

Hoping she was not turning red with embarrassment at being caught in a battle of wills with a dog—an apparently *losing* battle—Mallory looked back at the queen. When Queen Eleanor motioned toward Bertram de Paris, Mallory stepped forward to pull the arrow out of the man's sleeve. The dog trotted right at her heels and yipped eagerly when she stopped in front of the messenger.

"You will be sorry for this," he muttered.

"For protecting the queen from someone who entered her chambers without waiting to obtain her permission?" Mallory smiled coolly. "I would never be sorry for that."

Bertram looked away and grumbled something else.

She paid him no mind as she grasped the arrow. It was stuck deeply into the cupboard door, and she had to put her foot against the door and tug with all her strength. She reeled back when it popped loose, and, as the dog barked in excitement, she hit something firm.

An arm surrounded her, an arm as rigid as the hard body behind her. When she struggled to escape it, the brawny arm gentled and encircled her waist as Saxon whispered, "The battle is over. You won."

Her hair fluttered with his words, letting the heat of his breath slip along her nape. His broad hand slid along the arrow to cover hers. Drawing it down, he took it from her abruptly numb fingers. No, not numb, for they tingled where his skin had brushed hers.

The dog ran around them, barking wildly.

Saxon released her and bent to calm the dog. Mallory smoothed her dress back into place and wished she could regain her aplomb as readily. Since she had found a place in St. Jude's Abbey, she had forgotten how horrible it felt to lose control of her emotions. How familiar she had been with that while living in her father's house! Her father had never let an opportunity pass to point out that she was clumsy or made the wrong decision for the food for their evening meal, or simply that she was a disappointment because she had not been born a son. Her temper had flared, and her father had laughed that he again had goaded her into a fiery reaction.

Now another man was doing the same. Saxon had not galled her into anger, but he had incited within her an emotion even more heated. She would never let a man take command of her emotions as her mother had done. Then, when he betrayed her—as her father had betrayed her mother—she would be left with nothing, not even her self-respect.

"You come from King Louis?" asked the queen with a frown, and Mallory looked back at the messenger, who was pushing himself away from the cupboard. "Why is he sending me a message *here* in Poitiers?"

As he adjusted the quiver with its collection of white feathers on his shoulder, Bertram swallowed so hard that Mallory could hear him gulp. "I was told only to deliver the message into your hand, your majesty."

"This makes no sense." Lines furrowed in the queen's forehead beneath her veil. "I never expected him to do such a thing. Why did he send you *here*?"

"I was told only to deliver the message—"

"Yes, yes, so you said, but I still have no understanding of why he sent you *here*."

Mallory glanced at Saxon in spite of herself. She saw that his face was blank. She wished hers were. Every tale she had heard of the queen had praised Eleanor as a woman who was decisive and always saw the solution to every issue with a clear insight that most men would envy.

But the queen had not been worried at other times about someone wanting to kill her, argued a small voice in Mallory's head.

The queen motioned, and Bertram, picking up the bow he had dropped, followed her across the large room. He fired one more glare in Mallory's direction, but she paid it no mind as she bent to pet the head of the dog who was again bumping against her. She was not unsettled by a glower, for she had endured many in her father's house. The harsh words that followed were what had lacerated her soul.

"Lady Mallory?"

She raised her head to see a woman who was dressed almost as elegantly as the queen. A gold-edged silk veil hid her hair, but her face resembled the queen's. Not certain of the woman's identity, Mallory dipped in a half curtsy.

"Your fervor for my mother's safety is exemplary, Lady Mallory," the woman said with a gentle smile.

Mother! The woman must be one of the queen's daughters, but which one?

As if she had asked that question aloud, Mallory heard Saxon murmur, "Marie, Comtesse de Champagne." Marie was not King Henry's daughter, because she had been the queen's firstborn when Eleanor was wed to the French king.

He turned and walked in the direction of the queen before Mallory could do as much as nod. His steps were a stroll, suggesting he had no cares beyond what poem he would devise next. Was there no more to him than a man who enjoyed the pleasant life at the Poitiers court? It would be simpler if that were the truth, but she had seen him battle Jacques Malcoeur's men. She knew there was more to him than the troubadour who played the lute for the ladies' entertainment. He had handled their attackers with the skills of a trained man-at-arms. But why would such a man be here singing songs instead of serving with his liege lord? What else was he trying to hide behind his façade?

"Take care that you do not allow my mother's anxiety to mislead you," continued Comtesse Marie.

Mallory looked back at the queen's daughter. "She is not in danger?"

The comtesse's eyes hardened. "We all are in danger, while the two King Henrys battle to see which one rightfully holds the English throne and controls the destinies of all who live within their realm. That is why she had you come from your abbey. There are times when her guards cannot be with her. For those times, she needs a lady who can protect her."

"That is true, so why are you urging me not to be misled by the queen's anxiety?"

"I speak not of King Henry the Senior's fight with his son, but of his mistress."

An acrid taste filled Mallory's mouth, and she clenched her hands by her sides. Mistress! She wished the word had never been invented, for such an innocuous term could not begin to describe the pain and grief that a family suffered when a husband took another woman to his bed. In St. Jude's Abbey, Rosamund de Clifford's name was never spoken. The young woman could not be forgiven for stealing the king's heart and taking his rightful wife's place in his bed.

"I understand," she said; knowing she must reply to the comtesse.

"I am not surprised. Now, Lady Mallory, you should rest from your long journey. The morrow will be soon enough to begin your duties for the queen." With a gentle smile, Marie walked back to where Queen Eleanor was talking to the king's messenger.

Heat flamed up Mallory's face as ice sliced through her center. The comtesse had excused herself graciously without saying what must truly have been in her thoughts. Any daughter of Lord de Saint-Sebastian would be well familiar with her father's adultery.

Loosening the string on her bow, Mallory pushed her father from her mind. She could not let thoughts of the past distract her now, when the queen needed her assistance. She looked across the room to discover that Saxon and the other Poitevins who had traveled with the queen to St. Jude's Abbey were gathered around King Louis's messenger, the queen, and her daughter.

A sudden pang ached across Mallory's head as the spirit of battle washed out of her like a spring downpour across a road. She saw Saxon standing close to the queen, as he should, to guard her. *He* had not pinned the French king's messenger to a cupboard. *He* had not heard the queen's stern request to release the man. Beside her the dog whined. Glancing down, she absently patted its head.

"Lady Mallory?"

At the call of her name, she looked up, hoping the queen spoke to her. Instead she saw a half dozen young women clustered together, staring at her with wide-eyed expectation. Expectation? Of what?

"Yes," Mallory said when she realized the women were waiting for an answer. She wished there were not so many. She was unaccustomed to crowds, for she had kept to herself in her father's keep. Even at St. Jude's Abbey, she always preferred the open fields, where she could practice alone, to the gatherings within the Abbey's walls.

"We have never seen any woman so skilled with a bow," replied a petite blonde. She was the one who had called Mallory's name. "Who taught you?"

"I learned the basics of archery at my father's castle; then I learned more at . . ." Heat flashed up her face again. The other sisters at St. Jude's Abbey whispered that only by remaining out of sight and out of people's minds could the Abbey best serve the queen. Mallory was unsure what she should say, a most uncomfortable and uncommon reaction. Maybe the queen had told everyone at her court about the Abbey. Maybe she had told no one but the men who had ridden with her to England. Until Mallory knew for sure, she must guard her tongue.

"Can you teach me—us?" asked the blonde, and Mallory could not help wondering if she always spoke for the group of women.

"Teach you to use a bow?" She inched back as the short woman moved toward her, excitement on her pretty face.

"As you do." The blonde turned to the others, who nodded eagerly as they all moved closer. "We hear stories every day of the wondrous deeds of chivalrous knights, and we adore the stories, but think how much more we would relish them if we knew the difficulties such brave men face upon the field of battle. Isn't that true?"

Mallory started to answer, then realized the question had not been posed to her. Edging away a bit more, she grimaced when she struck the cupboard where the messenger had been pinned only minutes ago.

A brunette who was tall and rangy frowned. "Of course it is true, Yolanda. We agreed to that before we came to speak with Lady Mallory."

"Oh, Lady Violet, do not take everything so seriously," chided the blonde. Without taking a breath, she whirled back to look at Mallory. Surprise filled her eyes when she noted how Mallory had moved. Closing the distance between them again, she asked, "Can you teach us?"

"Yes," Mallory replied, surprised. Were they trying to smother her with their attention? She should have guessed she would be in the company of many others at the queen's court, but she had not given the matter any thought . . . until now. "I would be glad to teach you when my duties allow."

She was not sure if the women had heard her whole reply, because they began to giggle in an excited chorus, and one squealed with excitement, startling her. The sisters at the Abbey did not act thusly.

From the other side of the room, Saxon listened to the commotion. He tore his attention from the queen and Bertram de Paris long enough to make sure Mallory had not found some new way to get herself into another complicated situation. Not complicated for her, but for him. She had intruded too often in the past day into his plans, but he had to be grateful that she had needed his assistance to find where the queen gathered with her ladies. Otherwise, he would be on the pier by the Clain instead of hearing what the French king's messenger had to say.

He smiled when he saw her surrounded by a flock of women in the glorious costumes that they wore in the queen's company. Mallory was dressed simply. Yet there was something about her that drew his eyes away from the women who were adorned far more beautifully. A confidence in her skills, perhaps. Or maybe it was the graceful movements of her hands as she spoke, hands that had moved with the speed of a lightning bolt searing the sky when she had whipped an arrow from her quiver and sent it flying. Or maybe it was the memory of how soft her mouth had been beneath his.

By God's teeth, he was letting her distract him again, even when she was halfway across the room. He had no right to be thinking of her. He was a second son, and she was a landless lady who, until a short time ago, had been cloistered.

"The young king and young Richard are excited by the victories," Bertram was saying when Saxon forced his attention back to the conversation. "They believe they will defeat their father soon."

"Others have been as confident and found that confidence misplaced," the queen replied. She was rubbing her hands together in a nervous habit she had developed since her sons had risen up against her husband. "Tell them to be careful and to recall well the cost of failure. That message is to be taken to King Louis as well."

"They will be pleased with your counsel, your majesty," the messenger hastened to say, even as his expression, quickly hidden, suggested his thoughts suggested quite the opposite.

"Warn them twice over that my husband is not to be underestimated. He has battled with allies before, and he proved to them that he was their better. The Earl of Clare might have claimed the name of Strongbow in Ireland, but he was easily defeated by my husband when he dared to claim to be the king's equal."

Bertram gulped something that Saxon could not understand. If the queen even took note of his half-spoken words, she showed no sign of it as she turned to speak with her daughter Marie.

"Come," Saxon said to Bertram before one of the queen's Poitevin guards could speak. "I will tell you where to get something to eat before you return to King Louis."

"I know where the kitchens are," Bertram de Paris replied coolly. "I have been here before."

"But the queen did not recognize you."

"I was not instructed previously to place the message only in her hand." The messenger's brow rutted with concentration. "But I have seen you. You are Saxon Fitz-Juste, are you not?"

"I am."

"Why are you still here? Your family has been unwavering in their loyalty to the elder King Henry."

"How do you know that?"

Bertram recoiled, and Saxon knew his question had been too pointed. After months at the Court of Love, he should have known better than to ask such a direct question of anyone attached to any court.

Recovering himself, the messenger frowned. "A wise man always knows about his king's enemies. I suspect you have seen that while you entertain the queen as her jongleur." Bertram gave him a condescending smile that suggested no real man would be content to sit by the queen's side and act as her troubadour to entertain her with song and tale while the rebellion was taking place to the north.

"Yes." He would not be baited when he was trying to lure information out of the messenger. "I suspect you have seen many great events that would be worthy of song."

Bertram smiled coldly. "Many. As well I listen to those in the countryside while I travel on my king's business."

"I am sure everyone is eager for the rebellion to be over." He would offer trite answers in hopes that the messenger would grow more arrogant and reveal something that would be valuable to Saxon and his allies.

"Not everyone. There are lands to be divided when King Louis is victorious."

"The lands that will belong to King Henry the Younger."

Bertram's smile became even colder as he ran his fingers along the smooth length of his bow that was leaning against his foot. "Who will be deeply beholden to his liege King Louis and to King Louis's men who have come to his service. Comte du Fresne has been very helpful to the young king."

"His exploits have reached our ears even here," Saxon said in the same cheerful tone. He glanced back to where the queen was now talking earnestly with her daughter. He did not want to give Bertram an opportunity to see any amazement on his face or in his eyes.

Comte du Fresne! The man was playing a treacherous game of offering his allegiance to both sides, switching his alliances as he judged one king stronger than the other. He had pledged his loyalty to King Henry the Senior less than a year ago in this very palace. He had vowed to raise troops if ever the rightful lord of Aquitaine were threatened. Others had made a similar vow, and, when they had risen against King Henry the Senior, they had spoken publicly of supporting young Richard, who was his mother's choice as the next Duc d'Aquitaine. Unlike the others, the comte had been specific in naming King Henry the Senior while taking that pledge of fealty.

Saxon let Bertram continue to prattle, taking note of which names the messenger spoke and which ones he did not. Wondering if the messenger was always as careless with showing his opinions of the men who had come to fight for his king, Saxon said only what was necessary to keep Bertram talking.

A cascade of giggles came from the other side of the chamber, and the messenger clamped his lips closed as he fired a scowl at the group of women. Not at all of them, but at Mallory, for he demanded, "Who is the she-cur who dared to do this?" He held up his sleeve, and the material ripped farther.

"Why are you distressed by a woman who happened to miss your heart when she let an arrow fly?"

Bertram's face became gray. "I did not think . . . That is, I assumed she missed on purpose."

Saxon laughed and pointed at the women gathered around Mallory, still twittering and chattering like a group of squirrels fighting over the same branch in a tree. "Look at them! Lovely on the eyes and delightful to spend an hour with in a very private bower."

"And it would appear from Lady Mallory's expression that the queen's ladies are making her more uncomfortable than I ever could." Bertram laughed so hard his belly bounced.

"So it appears." Saxon watched as Mallory seemed to be drawing herself into as small a space as possible. What was amiss? She should be at ease among the queen's ladies, for she lived a life surrounded by women at the Abbey. The answer to that question would have to wait. For now, he asked, "True, but do you see one among them who could even pretend to have a warrior's skills?"

"If that is so, why does the queen allow Lady Mallory to wear a quiver and carry a bow in her presence?"

"I do not question the queen's decisions. Why are you?"

The messenger hastened to assure Saxon that he would never cast aspersions on anything the queen said or did, adding that the queen was very knowledgeable for a woman and had the trust of the younger king and Prince Richard as well as King Louis.

Again Saxon let the man gabble on and on while he listened with half an ear. In his mind, he was repeating the names Bertram had spoken in addition to Philippe du Fresne. He did not want to forget a single one when he repeated them to friends who would be as interested in them as he was. It was becoming a very intriguing rebellion.

Chapter 5

The dog was persistent.

Mallory had tried to shoo her back to the queen's chamber with the side of her foot and the edge of her bow. Each gentle push seemed to persuade the dog to be more stubborn. She even attempted pretending to ignore her, but she rushed ahead of Mallory through the long, curving passage, pausing to sniff some odor that enticed her nose. As soon as Mallory walked past, the dog would give chase to catch up with her. The dog would match her steps for a few paces and then take off again to find a new smell.

"Where is your master?" she asked the dog.

She faced Mallory, giving her a lolling-tongue look of expectation.

"Sneaking out so soon?" came Saxon's voice from behind her. "I had not guessed you would abandon your duty to protect the queen so quickly."

Mallory transferred her irritation with the dog to Saxon, who was even more vexing. "The comtesse excused me, telling me to rest so I am ready to begin my duties tomorrow."

"But you stayed after she returned to speak with the queen."

"I would have left the chamber immediately if I had not been asked questions by the queen's ladies." She frowned as she kept walking. She did not need him *and* the dog following her. It had taken her too long to excuse herself from the ladies, who acted as if they expected her to begin their lessons with the bow right in the queen's presence.

"Questions? What sort of questions?"

"Must you know *everything* that happens in the queen's palace?"

"I like to know what is taking place."

"Then ask one of the queen's ladies. I do not owe you any explanation."

"No, but you owe one to the king's messenger, who is furious that you put a hole in his sleeve."

"The *French* king."

He caught up with her and matched her step for step along the hallway that led toward a tower at the far end. Over one shoulder, he had set the strap of his lute. She noticed that he reached behind him every few paces to make sure it was balanced across his back. That surprised her, for, if she had given the matter any thought, she would have guessed that he was as accustomed to wearing his lute as she was her quiver.

"I should warn you," he said with a cool smile, "not to use that condescending tone here when speaking of King Louis."

"He is our king's enemy."

"And our king's ally."

Her steps faltered as she wondered how many more mistakes she could make during her first day in Poitiers. As the dog bounded away down the stairs at the right, she faced Saxon. "That is true. I doubt there ever has been or ever will be as much confusion as there is now when both King Henry the Senior and King Henry the Younger claim to be the only one holding the English throne and its lands."

"I have to agree with you."

She was about to fire back another retort but halted when she saw his easy grin. It was completely different from the practiced smile that he had worn in the queen's chamber and much warmer than the one she had seen moments ago. And his gaze . . . She knew she should look away from those dark eyes that suggested he hid so much. To stare into them brought forth thoughts that she must not have while serving the queen. Thoughts of putting other obligations aside until she discovered if his secrets were somehow connected to the extraordinary buzz that flitted across her skin whenever he was close.

His hand slowly rose toward her face. Was he as curious as she was to learn the cause of the strange, disarming sensations? She slanted toward him, wanting to know the answer. His eyes narrowed ever so slightly as he brushed a vagrant strand of her hair back, his fingers lingering on the sensitive skin behind her ear. As his face lowered toward hers, she was swept with the feeling that they had been close like this—and closer—before.

With a gasp, Mallory drew back. How many times had she vowed—as fervently as she had made her vow to serve St. Jude's Abbey—that she would not let herself be beguiled by a man's lusts? Her mother had made that mistake, as she had told Mallory over and over. Just as many times, her mother had warned Mallory never to fall into the same trap.

Even though her feet wanted to speed her along the passage, she kept her pace slow enough so that she did not risk falling on her nose. With each step, numbness climbed higher up her legs until she felt as if she were walking on wooden limbs. She put one hand on the wall, sliding it along, but did not use her bow as a cane. She did not want to have it twist out of its proper shape.

The dog yelped when Mallory bumped into her.

She halted. "Begone back to where you belong, dog," she said, exasperation slicing through each word.

"The dog's name is Chance," Saxon said as he stepped around her, and she knew he was as unwilling to give up his pursuit of her as the dog was.

"That is an odd name for a dog."

"Not one that is left to her own purposes. Her life is up to herself. Up to chance." He bent and scratched the dog behind her floppy ear. "I have seen her wandering through the gardens, and she does not seem to belong to anyone. Until now, because it appears that she has decided she wants to belong to you."

"I have no time for a dog."

"She can help you in your duties for the queen."

"Chance would be more likely to interfere."

"I find that chance often interferes with my plans."

At his absurd jest, Mallory closed her eyes and shook her head. It was the wrong thing to do, she realized, when her head felt as light as one of the clouds floating in the sky. He was not touching her, so the weakness had to be all her own. The anticipation of meeting the queen and the focus of battle that had strengthened her arm when she drew her bow had melted away, leaving her with no more vigor than a damp rag.

"Chance is not the only thing interfering with my plans," she replied, opening her eyes. She wished her voice did not sound so breathless. "The comtesse sent me to rest, so I must ask you to excuse me."

"I assume you can find your way back to your room."

"Of course. I . . ." She looked around and realized they were in a different corridor from the one Saxon had led her through to reach the queen's rooms. This corridor had one wall that was punctured by windows, which, like the one in her room, were bigger than any she had seen in England. The other corridor had contained only a single window. Where had she gotten turned around? It did not matter. She was not sure where she was, and she was going to have to admit that.

When she did, Saxon continued to smile. "The interior of the palace is confusing until you have had an opportunity to wander about and learn which passage leads where. If you wish, I will be glad to show you where you can find the staircase that is closest to your own chambers."

"Thank you." She set her bow on her shoulder as if it were a quarterstaff and followed him along the narrow corridor.

"I am relieved to see that you have unstrung your bow," he said as he paused at the top of a curving set of stairs. "Now I don't need to warn everyone in the palace to shout out their identities before they come into any chamber where you might be."

Mallory regarded him with the icy expression that had worked best with her father, but inside, her stomach contracted. Did he have the devil's power to see within her and pinpoint her greatest shortcomings? To cover the discomfort that thought elicited, she snapped, "Is that supposed to be funny?"

"I had thought so."

"*You* would." She was further annoyed that her never-fail frown had no effect on Saxon.

He stepped in front of her before she could put her hand on the rope railing curving down into the dusk. "Did you consider that an insult?"

"I considered it the truth." She motioned for him to move aside. She was unsure whether she could walk around him without falling on her face. She did not want him to see her so feeble. As well, she needed to regain her wits after the debacle in the queen's chamber. "Go away!"

"Mallory, are you sure you can—"

"I have neither time nor interest in continuing this conversation. I am surprised that you do, when your ladies are eager for your return to the garden to entertain them once more."

"They will wait."

"Breathlessly, no doubt."

He chuckled. "My dear Lady Mallory, you use words with the skill of a trouvère."

"What?"

"A traveling jongleur." He smiled. "*Troubadour* may be the word you are most familiar with. Have you ever considered creating songs and stories to share with others?"

"My skills lie elsewhere."

"You can be skilled at more than one thing."

"Stop belittling me!" she snarled.

He recoiled, clearly astounded by the venom in her voice. "I was not belittling you."

"No?"

"I thought I was showing my admiration for you."

"I don't want your admiration or anything else." She pushed

past him and went down the steeply curving stairs with the dog
bounding in front of her.

Why couldn't Saxon have accepted her request to leave?
Why couldn't he depart as willingly as he had from the queen's
presence? She wobbled. Gripping the railing, she slowed her
pace. She could not let her vexation cause her to tumble off her
feet. If she were injured, she would fail in her service to the
queen and to the Abbey.

Before she could take another step, strong arms caught her
at the waist and knees. She was swung up against a hard chest.
Her bow fell out of her hand and bounced down the quartet of
remaining stairs as she grasped the fine fabric stretched across
the muscles beneath it.

She raised her eyes past Saxon's chin, where his neatly
trimmed beard followed each severely carved line of his jaw.
She had never seen anyone other than a peasant who wore a
beard, and she wondered how those short hairs would feel if she
ran her finger along them.

Sharp and contrary.

"That tickles," he said softly.

She jerked back her hand, realizing that she had put her
wayward thoughts into action. "Forgive me."

"Why?"

Could this man be any more exasperating? She did not want
to linger in his arms to discover the answer to that question.
Twice, in quick succession, his brazen attentions had bewitched
her into doing as she had vowed never to do. She knew about
men and their attempts to seduce a woman into giving them
what they wanted before they became bored with their conquest
and went on to the next woman. The mistress her father had
brought into the castle had not been his first nor his last.

"I can walk," Mallory said in her primmest tone as he
stepped off the bottommost riser.

"You have proven that. You do not need to prove it again."
He gave her a grin. "Hold tight."

Before she could ask what he intended, he bent toward

where her bow had come to a stop. She stretched out to grasp it before he could tip her onto the floor. With a grunt that suggested she weighed as much as a millstone, he stood straighter, drawing her back against his chest.

"If I am too much of a burden, you may put me down posthaste," she said.

"You are a burden."

"Then put me down."

"You misunderstand me, Mallory. Carrying you is not an onerous task. Trying to figure out what you will do next is."

Mallory hoped he did not feel her start at his words that were as cold as a slap across the face. Not that she could fault him when she had spit at him like a furious cat moments before she stroked his face. Explaining was impossible, because then she would have to recount how her father had taunted her until she lost her temper. She had struggled to hold her emotions in check and had succeeded at St. Jude's Abbey. Until she had met Saxon Fitz-Juste, she had believed she had put that part of her past behind her, but his half-jesting derision had blinded her anew with icy rage.

She would not give in to it again. Quietly, she replied, "I could say the same about not knowing what you might do next."

"Then let me put your mind to rest. Here's what I intend to do next."

His mouth covered hers before she could draw in another breath. Then *his* breath was mingling with hers as he deepened the kiss. She never had imagined anyone's skin could feel as hot as his lips or as searing as the delight swirling through her like a summer wind, powerful and gathering into a storm.

Her hand edged around his nape, and her fingers sifted up through his hair. She had no idea if he was still walking or if he stood still. All of her was craving motion, to be closer, closer, ever closer to him. She shifted, but he held her between his brawny arm and his lips. As he sprinkled kisses across her face, her skin sparked as if each spot he touched glistened with starlight. His beard brushed against her skin when he tilted her head back to trace the flame along her neck before recapturing her lips once more. His tongue caressed hers, and she moaned with a longing she could not name, a longing that urged her to surrender herself to him, to give him . . .

"No!" She gasped, drawing back.

"Don't say no before I even ask you anything," he whispered against her ear.

Shivers, heated with the force of that summer storm brewing within her, cascaded along her spine. She fought them as she ordered him to put her down.

"I like holding you." He gave her an easy grin.

It was exactly the grin she had seen her father give his mistress—the she-beast who had come into her mother's house and her father's bed.

"Put me down!"

"Mallory, it was only a kiss."

"Only a kiss?" Her fury refocused on how he denigrated her precious feelings. She was not being reasonable, but every nerve within her throbbed with the memory of his touch and the yearning for him to kiss her again. Her mind was warning her not to be more foolish. She must listen to her mind, not to her body. "Put me down!"

"Nonsense. The fact that you have not sent me flying halfway across the palace shows how weak you are. I am carrying you up to your room." His smile became icy. "And I am going to enjoy doing so."

She decided she was wasting her breath trying to reason with him. She did not look at him as he carried her along another corridor and then up the stairs she recognized.

Saxon kicked at the door. She opened her mouth to scold him, but closed it when he cocked a single brow at her. Was he trying to infuriate her, hoping to arouse more than annoyance within her? If he had any idea how he had succeeded with his kisses . . .

"What has happened *now*?" demanded Ruby as he walked into the room.

He pushed past the serving woman, who was holding a half-folded blanket, without speaking.

"Did you allow her to be hurt again?" Ruby called after him.

"No, she is suffering still from her encounter with Malcoeur and his cronies. And if you give it a moment's thought, you will recall that I did not *allow* her to be hurt the first time. I could not keep her from throwing herself into the fray in some misguided attempt to show she could better some common thieves." He gave Ruby a scowl that she seemed as immune to as Saxon had been to Mallory's frown.

If Mallory had not been distressed, she would have laughed at his amazement that Ruby was not daunted by his expression. She wisely decided to say nothing. Maybe if she were silent, he would leave more quickly.

With a barked greeting to Ruby, the dog pranced into the room like a fine warhorse. Chance wagged her tail.

"You may as well make Chance welcome," Saxon said, dropping Mallory not very gently on the bed. "The dog has decided she belongs to Lady Mallory, so you two should become acquainted."

Ruby patted the dog's head and was rewarded with a friendly bark. She stepped around Chance as she shook a finger at Saxon, who remained by the bed. "You may sit on the bench. Not on milady's bed."

"I would never *sit* on the lady's bed without her invitation."

"Nor do anything else on it."

"I always ask a lady's permission." His smile was the calculated one Mallory had seen in the queen's chambers, and she could not keep from wondering what he was trying to conceal beneath such an insipid expression. Whatever it was, she had no interest in satisfying her curiosity. Her head ached, and the events with the *French* king's messenger flitted through her mind over and over, reminding her of every error she had made.

Clasping her hands on her lap, she said, "Ruby, I can deal with him. Don't worry."

"From what is being said, milady, I should be worrying about *his* safety."

"Tales travel fast in the palace."

Ruby smiled. "Always, but most quickly when someone new comes amidst us. If that someone has an amazing talent like yours with that bow, milady, the news races even more swiftly along the corridors." She turned away to go back to her laundry.

Mallory shifted on the bed. "Ouch!"

Ruby whirled and rushed back to the bed. "What are you doing now? Don't hurt milady."

"I did not hurt her," Saxon said at the same time as Mallory replied, "He did not hurt me."

"Thank you, milady, for coming to my defense." He bowed toward her.

She paid him no mind as she shifted so her bow was not under her leg. Drawing it off the bed, she leaned it against the pole rising from the headboard. She slid her quiver from her shoulder and stretched to put it on the floor. Dizziness flooded anew through her head.

Saxon took the quiver from her and put a steadying hand on her shoulder before she could tumble on her face. His touch threatened to undo her completely, because the sensation that had no name resonated outward from his fingers. It vibrated along her as if it were within her blood, reaching every bit of her.

"Be careful," he said. "Think about what you are doing before you move."

She wanted to repeat the warning back to him, but then she would have to explain why. She must avoid doing that, because he seemed unaffected by the frisson surging through her. So she said nothing.

As she settled into the pillows with her back against the headboard, Chance jumped up on the chest at the foot of the bed, wagging her tail eagerly. The dog turned around in the narrow space three times and then curled up, her nose on her paws and her gaze focused on Mallory. Even when Chance closed her eyes, Mallory guessed the dog was on alert.

"You have a faithful guardian," Saxon said as he sat on the bench Ruby had pointed to. He set his lute on the floor beside him.

"It seems that I do."

"Now that you know you are well guarded, you should rest, Mallory."

"I shall once you take your leave, unless you intend to sit there and stare at me as Chance did."

"I shall take my leave as soon as you answer a question for me."

"And what is that?" She was torn between telling him he should go and asking him to remain. If he went, the scenes of the messenger's shock and the queen's face would haunt her. If he stayed, he would continue to pelt her with questions. She was certain he would never ask only one. If he went, she guessed Ruby would want a complete accounting of what had happened to sort the truth from rumor. If he stayed, the serving woman's questions could be postponed. If he went, his thrilling touch would not tempt her to put aside her vow to let no man delude her. If he stayed, he might draw her to him and he might . . .

She silenced the yearnings from her traitorous body. She needed to think of him sitting with Lady Elita and the other women in the garden as they played at games of love at which she had no skill and which she must not want to learn.

"I saw," Saxon said so quietly that Ruby's ear would hear only a murmur, not the actual words, "that you were discomfited by the queen's ladies who came to congratulate you on your quick thinking. Why? You must be accustomed to being surrounded by women."

"I do not like being the center of attention."

His brows lowered, and she saw the intensity bursting past his jovial exterior. "You must be the focus of every eye when you fire an arrow with such skill at the Abbey."

"That is different."

"Why?"

"You already asked a question. You should go."

Saxon leaned forward, his fingers resting on the lute so he did not reach out to keep Mallory from edging away. Each time he touched her, whether inadvertently or with his intentions clear as in the corridor below, she reacted like a mouse fleeing a prowling cat. Even a mouse would turn and attack when backed into a corner, and he did not want to force her to do that. Not yet, anyhow. He needed to discover how she fit into the small community within the palace moat. Then he would decide what to do with the unexpected complication she presented.

"True," he said, "but I was astonished to see that you, a woman who is brave enough to fight off two attackers at once and skilled enough to pin a man to a cupboard with a single shot that drew no blood, were overwhelmed by a group of admiring women whose only weapons are flirtatious smiles and giggles."

"I do not like being praised when I erred in firing."

"Erred?" His voice rose on the single word, and both Ruby and the dog glanced in his direction. By now, he should have known that Mallory would never give him the answer he anticipated. Even so, he was amazed. "How did you err? You did as you pledged to the queen seconds before the door opened."

"Don't you see?" She looked down at her hands clasped tightly in her lap. "I overreacted."

"You simply acted more rapidly than anyone else. That pleased the queen."

"Do you think so?"

Saxon was taken back by the sudden burst of hope in her voice. It shone in her violet eyes, which regarded him with earnestness. She truly yearned for his reassurances, astonishing him because she had been so sure of herself before. Choosing his words with care, he said, "I would not have said so if I did not believe that I was speaking the truth."

"I am glad to hear that." She took a deep breath and released it slowly.

He struggled to keep his gaze on her face and not the steady rise and fall of her enticing breasts. Pushing himself away from the bench—and her bed—before he could no longer fight the need to hold her again, he stood and picked up her bow and quiver. He set them beside the window in an effort to regain control of his body, which was reacting to such a beguiling sight.

Since his arrival in Poitiers, he had enjoyed the company of some of the most beautiful women he had ever seen. Some of them had eyes that snapped as Mallory's did, and a few had her razor-sharp wit. There were alluring blondes and women whose hair had an ebony sheen like Mallory's. One or two had finer features than hers, along with curves that were guaranteed to give even a monk lascivious thoughts. Several were eager to fulfill every fantasy a man could devise.

But none of them intrigued him as Mallory de Saint-Sebastian did. She was annoying and possessed a strength of will he had seldom encountered. Yet there was a vulnerability about her that was fascinating. How had such a fragile spirit grown so strong?

"You did nothing for which you should be ashamed," he said as he faced her again. He was glad he had spoken before he caught sight of her regarding him with such wistfulness on her delicate features. An answering craving burst through him, even as he reminded himself that she probably did not intend to show him any desire but the need for assurance that she had not made a potentially horrible mistake.

Would that be the only need she would feel if he swept her into his arms as he ordered Ruby from the room? His lips ached for hers as he remembered their flavor and softness, not only today, but in the alley when they were eluding Malcoeur and his men. She had shown no sign that she recalled that kiss. He could not forget it. Kissing her again had been the only way, he had believed, that he could persuade himself that the first kiss was nothing but emotion heightened by the threat from the chase. He had proved just the opposite, and he could think of little but how much he wanted her in his arms while they shared more than a few stolen kisses.

"Thank you, Saxon," she said quietly. "I must make no mistakes, for what I do here reflects on the Abbey."

"As did the actions of those who have served her previously."

"The two sisters who were called forth to do her bidding before me did not have the responsibility of safeguarding the queen's life."

"Two? Did they come to France, too?"

"No, but one went to Wales."

"I wonder if she was sent because the queen had heard of the prophecy."

"Which prophecy?"

"One spoken by a hermit in Cardiff when the king was returning from his battles in Ireland."

"I have not heard of that one. The only prophecy I know is the tale of the stone named *Llech-lafar* and how King Henry would die if he were to step on it after defeating Strongbow in Ireland. A silly tale about a curse that supposedly was spoken by Merlin circulated through the Abbey about a year or so ago."

His eyes lit with amusement. "I do not mean that prophecy, but it sounds interesting. Someday, you must tell me more about it, for the little you have told me already suggests the tale of Merlin's stone could become an intriguing story to entertain the queen."

"One she knows well."

"She does?"

Mallory looked away. She had said too much, almost revealing a secret that needed to be kept within the walls of St. Jude's Abbey. No one should speak of journeys other sisters had been sent upon by the queen.

"So the abbess mentioned to me," she said, speaking enough of the truth so she did not have to spill the whole of it.

Leaning toward her, he whispered, "There are many strange stories from Wales. Some probably are not true, but who can say which? Is the prophecy spoken to King Henry the Senior in Wales the portent of events yet to unfold, or have they come to pass even now?"

"You act as if you believe such stories."

"A troubadour learns to heed well everything that is said, for in every tale there is a seed of truth. Otherwise the story would never be repeated."

Mallory fought to keep her aggravation hidden, but it burst from her. "How can you talk so much and say so little? You told me about a prophecy, and now you chatter on and on about everything but it. What is the prophecy?"

"It begins on Easter morn when the king went to Mass in Cardiff. King Henry did not take communion that holy day."

She nodded. "Because he would have needed to confess, and it was said he had not since the murder of Archbishop Thomas à Becket in Canterbury during the Christmas season two years ago."

"Yes," he said with impatience. At her interruption or for some other reason? "King Henry went out to the church's porch and saw an old man there. The old man greeted him with words he could barely understand."

"In Welsh?"

"No, in English. Do you speak it?"

She leaned back against the pillows, wishing she had never asked him a question. Her head hurt, and she was exhausted, and she still had no idea how to safeguard the queen when Queen Eleanor's daughter had sent her away to rest. She clenched her hands. Because the comtesse did not want to chance Mallory's overhearing what the French king's messenger had to say? That made no sense, because Bertram the messenger had said he was to deliver the message into the queen's hand. It must be a written missive.

Nothing made sense now. She had been brought to the queen's side to offer protection and then been sent away before she could make another horrendous blunder.

"Mallory?" Saxon prompted. When she looked at him, he asked again, "Do you speak English?"

"Just a few phrases," she said as she closed her eyes. "Some of my father's tenants speak Saxon." Opening her eyes, she frowned. More pain rippled across her forehead. "Why do you have the same name as the old language of England?"

He waved aside her question as he asked, "Do you know what is meant by *'God houlde dhe, Cuning'*?"

"Yes, I have heard that said by some of the tenants on my father's fief. It is a benediction asking for God to watch over the king."

"That is how the old man by the church porch greeted King Henry and Sir Philip de Mark, the lone knight who had accompanied him to Mass. Fortunately"—his lips tilted in an ironic grin—"or maybe not fortunately, Sir Philip could translate the old man's words, which were a warning for King Henry to keep Sunday as a day free of work and to change what the old man deemed a life of evil. If he did not, the old man cautioned that the ones King Henry loved best would bring him great pain."

"And now his wife and sons have risen in rebellion against him."

He pushed away from the window and opened his mouth to reply.

A dull thud sounded behind him. Ruby screamed in horror, and Chance jumped to the floor, barking. He whirled to see an arrow driven deep into one of the wood shutters. A piece of parchment fluttered from it. Several lines were written on the page.

As he reached for the arrow, Mallory pushed past him. Her slender fingers grasped it first and ripped the still-vibrating shaft from the shutter. She rocked back on her feet as she had in the queen's chamber when she pulled the arrow out of Bertram's sleeve. Saxon caught her when she bumped into him again.

She started to push away from him, but he halted her by sliding his arm around her slender waist. He marveled how such a lithe form could use a bow with such power. A scent from her hair, a fresh, enticing aroma, filled the single breath he took before he seemed unable to draw in another.

Slowly he turned her to face him. When she was standing, her eyes were almost even with his. He was unsure why that was so pleasing. Maybe because he needed only to shift slightly and her lips would be beneath his. Every shallow breath she took stroked her breasts against him, a rapid rhythm that set his heart to pounding in an answering echo. He was amazed she could breathe when her eyes were filled with amethyst fire that lilted like a glorious song through a still afternoon.

His fingers coursed up her back, and she quivered, her lips parting. Was she offering them to him? He did not wait for an answer as he tilted her mouth to his. He had barely brushed her lips with his before another frantic cry and more barking erupted through the room.

Saxon cursed when Mallory yanked herself away from him. Another chance to sample her lips ruined! A man could talk only so often about love with the queen's ladies or sing only so many songs about beautiful maidens before he needed to use his mouth in other, far more intimate ways. When Ruby erupted into more shrieks, he started to order her to be quiet long enough for him to kiss—really kiss—Mallory's delicious lips again.

He silenced his retort when the serving woman cried, "Who would fire an arrow into your window, milady?"

The arrow! He saw that Mallory still held it. How could he have forgotten . . . even for a moment?

"Maybe the note will explain," Mallory said, her voice trembling as she had in his arms.

Note! By God's teeth, he had been bewitched by his craving for her. There was no other way he could explain overlooking something so important.

He was surprised when Mallory handed him the arrow. Was she fearful of what the piece of parchment might contain? When she tore the page from the shaft, almost jerking the arrow out of his hand, he realized he was mistaken again. She was not afraid. She was impatient to read it.

"What does it say?" He could not keep his vexation out of his voice. She might be one of the queen's warriors, but the arrow had come close to piercing *him*.

Her face was ashen as she looked up from the slip of paper. "It says," she whispered, " 'Leave now. This will be your only warning. If you remain and try to halt us, you and the queen will die.' "

Chapter 6

Mallory watched the queen pace from one side of the small chamber to the other. At her request to speak with the queen, Mallory had been brought to a room no bigger than the abbess's office at St. Jude's Abbey. Like the abbess's office, the room had little furniture—a table, a chair, a pair of benches, and a prie-dieu. She wondered if the abbess had patterned her office after the queen's private chamber.

From beyond the thick door, she heard the murmur of voices in the great hall where the Court of Love met. She had noticed nothing but its vast space when she was escorted through it to the much smaller room.

"No, I did not see who fired the arrow," Mallory said quietly. The queen had asked her the same question a few minutes before, so the queen must be more unsettled than she appeared. That bothered Mallory. She had expected the queen to be focused as she had been at St. Jude's Abbey. Again, she reminded herself that Queen Eleanor had not been worried about a murderer within the Abbey's walls. "Nor did Saxon or Ruby, who was working on the other side of the room." She hesitated, then asked, "The messenger from King Louis said he was going to the kitchen, but—"

"It could not be Bertram de Paris, for he represents the French king within these walls, and he has no reason to threaten one of my ladies." The queen's mouth was taut, revealing lines that showed the many difficult years she had lived, years of wars and divorce and rumors and betrayal and more war.

"But he is the only stranger within these walls," Mallory protested.

"You are new here, too."

"I—or Saxon—was the target! If you would call Bertram de Paris to speak with you, you—"

The queen's eyes drilled her, and Mallory lowered her own. How foolish could she be to question the queen?

As if she had asked the question aloud, Queen Eleanor said, "Lady Mallory, you *are* recently arrived within my palace, so I will excuse your outburst that is based, I know, solely on your fears for my safety. Bertram de Paris serves King Louis of France, who is my sons' ally. You understand what that means, don't you?"

"Yes." Mallory bit her lower lip before more words could spew out. She must not say the wrong thing . . . again! Taking a moment to compose herself, she added quietly, "I understand, as well, that someone is making no secret that he or she wishes me to be gone."

"I expected nothing less." The queen seemed almost pleased that her enemy had done exactly as she had anticipated. "Someone wishes me dead, and you are here to protect me. If you can be frightened away, I will be left with fewer defenses. That must not be allowed to happen."

Mallory fought the urge to smile with relief. *This* decisive woman was the queen she had admired. Rising, she bowed her head toward the queen. She realized her foolishness when dizziness swept over her like a rogue wave. Taking a deep breath, she locked her knees to keep from tipping onto her face as she straightened.

"I am here to serve you, my queen," she said in the strongest voice she could manage. "You may rest assured that I will not leave until you order me to do so."

"That is pleasing to hear, Lady Mallory."

"Could you tell me about previous threats? Knowing what has happened will help me better serve you now."

The queen's brows lowered beneath her veil. "I would have guessed that Saxon Fitz-Juste had regaled you with all sorts of tales."

"He has, but I was not sure which were the truth and which were fancy."

"Unless he is playing his lute or sharing a poem, you can be certain that he is being honest."

Mallory bit her tongue before she could ask, *Are you truly certain?* She simply nodded. The queen was more trusting than Mallory was. Maybe it was because the queen had never stood within his strong arms and gazed into his eyes, which promised so many pleasures that she suspected she would be a fool to sample even one. Yet, she could not resist when his mouth had grazed hers, his mustache tickling her skin in the moment before she was riveted by the heat of his lips. There had been a sense of knowing just how wondrous his kiss would feel as he held her to his broad chest. And that disturbed her, for how could she have such knowledge? In spite of the assurances, Saxon was not being completely honest with her.

The queen looked at the parchment that had been pierced by the arrow. "This is written in the language of the north."

"You do not think someone from Aquitaine would threaten you, do you?"

"I have no idea, when there are traitors everywhere, even in my own family." Giving Mallory no chance to react to the strong words, the queen went on, "You ask why I fear for my life. It is simple. Such a message as you have received is not the first to come to my attention. Each time, the threat is aimed at a specific person as well as myself." She gave Mallory a cool, steady gaze. "You are the first, Lady Mallory, not to come to me with a request to leave my court."

"If the intention is to strip your court of your allies, the plan must not be allowed to work."

"The intention *is* to leave me defenseless, but it will not succeed as long as I have my guards close. Now you can see why I have requested you to be nearby." She tapped her chin with her finger. "I shall have your things brought to a chamber within my apartment. That way, you will be close when the gentlemen cannot." A hint of a smile tipped her lips. "I am too vain to allow young men to see my aged form when I bathe."

"Ask of me what you wish." She was careful to bow her head slightly.

"I ask that you do everything to find the archer, Lady Mallory."

"I shall."

"Ask questions of anyone, for you are acting on my behalf."

"I shall." Again she hesitated, then asked, "Even of your other guards?"

The queen's eyes widened, revealing that Mallory had startled her with such a forthright question. "I trust those I have chosen to protect me, Lady Mallory."

"I understand, but I thought they might have seen or heard something that would help me discover the identity of the archer."

"If they had, they would have come to me posthaste with the information, just as you have."

Mallory said nothing, for the queen's voice was a rebuke that warned there should be no more questions about her guards. It seemed logical to Mallory to speak to them, for they would have the greatest opportunity to see anything out of the ordinary. But she would ask them nothing, as that was the queen's wish.

"I have heard," the queen said into the silence, "of the request of some of my ladies to study archery with you."

"Yes." She was not surprised that Queen Eleanor was aware of a conversation she could not have overheard. Nothing stayed a secret long within the walls of a palace . . . save for the identity of the person threatening the queen.

"What do you think of the idea?"

Now she was astounded. She had not anticipated the queen

to ask her opinion on such a subject. "I—I—I—" She swallowed hard and began anew. "I think it would be wise for you to have as many trained protectors as possible."

Queen Eleanor gave a soft laugh. "I do not expect you to make them into skilled archers. However, such lessons will offer you the opportunity to learn more about the residents of my court. That way, you will be more able to see if something seems amiss."

Or someone, Mallory added silently before saying, "That is a good idea. I will begin such lessons tomorrow afternoon, if that is agreeable to you."

"Very agreeable. One more thing, Lady Mallory."

"Yes."

"Keep yourself safe." Her voice became grim. "You are the first to ignore the threat, and I do not wish you to be the first to die at the hands of my enemy."

The fletcher's room brought the one at St. Jude's Abbey to mind. It had the same smells of planed wood and the polishes and waxes used to keep a bow dry. A bag of feathers, all from gray geese, was set beside a table where a man was fitting a single feather to a shaft. The other end held a lightly ribbed arrowhead. His dark hair had fallen forward to obscure his face, and Mallory doubted he had heard her enter.

She waited patiently. No one disturbed a fletcher at his work. It took a steady hand to set feathers into place on the arrow. The slightest motion could ruin the feather being attached to the shaft.

The dust from the feathers and the wood that had been sliced away to make the shafts tickled her nose. She wrinkled it, trying to stop the sneeze building up within her. It was impossible. She put her hand over her mouth as it burst out of her, but feathers fluttered across the table.

The fletcher looked up, scowling. He eyed her as his frown dug furrows in his forehead and dragged down his thick jowls. "What do you want . . . milady?" He added the last with an obvious reluctance that warned her that he could not imagine a single reason why a woman would enter his small fiefdom within these walls.

Mallory had faced such bigotry at her father's estate when she first sought to learn to use a bow. Old Claud, the fletcher there, had come to see how serious she was. She had persuaded that stubborn man to teach her what she needed to know. She must do the same with the fletcher in Queen Eleanor's palace. After all, she had managed to convince Saxon that she deserved the queen's confidence in her as an archer.

By St. Jude! She did not want to think of Saxon. She had been able to avoid him all day. She had seen him sitting in a garden, his lute balanced on his leg while he was talking with some young women. One she recognized as the blond woman Lady Elita, who had been draped over him yesterday.

"Forgive me, Master Fletcher," she said, lowering her eyes like a child seeking an apprenticeship, "for I did not mean to intrude on your work. I seek a great boon from you."

"A boon from me?" His frown eased into bafflement and curiosity.

"I am newly arrived in Poitiers," she answered in the same respectful tone, looking through her eyelashes to gauge his reaction, "and I would appreciate it if—"

He stood. He was almost a head shorter than she was and old enough to be her grandsire, but she saw determination in his light blue eyes that were narrowed from hours of squinting at his work. He grasped her bow, and she shrugged it off her shoulder before it snapped. Running his fingers along the shaft, he glanced from the bow to her.

"This is English ash," he said.

"Yes."

"Cut from beneath the bark toward the tree's center." He slid his finger across the variations in color that had appeared after she spent hours polishing the wood with wax. He focused his pale blue eyes on her. "Where did you get this, milady?"

"I made it."

"You?"

"Yes."

His eyes widened, rearranging the wrinkles along his full face. "Tell me your name."

"Mallory de Saint-Sebastian," she replied, knowing that no title, whether it be lady or sister or queen, would matter to him. A master fletcher respected only the wood he worked with and those who shared his admiration of it.

"*You* are Lady Mallory?" He looked her up and down as he had the shaft, then nodded. She was unsure what the nod meant until he handed her back her bow and asked, "What may I do to serve you, milady?"

She raised her head and smiled as she slipped her bow over her shoulder. "I wish to borrow some equipment, Master Fletcher."

"My name is Ivon."

"Master Ivon, the queen has requested that I teach archery to her ladies. I was hoping you had some bows I might borrow, bows that might have been made by an apprentice and not worthy of being drawn by a warrior." She had no idea if there were any apprentices working in the cluttered space, but she would never insult the fletcher by suggesting his work might fall short of perfection.

"Look along the wall." He pointed toward the back of the room where strips of wood were piled haphazardly. "You may find something there that may be useful." As she thanked him and turned to go scavenge through the stack of wood, he added, "Come back when you have time to talk, milady. I would like to hear about the master who taught you to make such an excellent bow."

"I would enjoy that." She smiled, relieved that—at last—circumstances were going as she had hoped when she traveled to Poitiers. She was doing the queen's bidding and could lose herself in teaching as she had at the Abbey.

As she reached for a piece of wood, Ivon called, "Not that pile, milady. I am saving those scraps for Saxon Fitz-Juste."

"Saxon!" She jerked her hand back as if someone had set the wood afire. "What use would he have for these strips of wood?"

Ivon was bent over his work once more. "What use any jongleur would have for them, I assume. The lute *is* a wooden instrument."

Chastised, she went to another jumble of wood to gather what she could use with her students. What she needed for herself was a chance to find some equilibrium that would not come undone each time she heard Saxon's voice or even his name.

I will not let my own cravings defeat me! she promised herself. *I will not let a man make a fool of me as my mother did.*

She must remember each lesson she was taught in the Abbey about cool poise in the face of great odds, but she had never guessed her greatest challenge would be subduing her yearning to be in Saxon's arms again.

By the end of the week, Mallory wished she had never agreed to teach archery to the ladies of the queen's court. At the time she had made that pledge—and now—it made sense that the women should learn to defend themselves and the queen. But few of the ladies seemed to be serious about the lessons she offered every afternoon on the empty field near the River Clain. Rather they saw the sessions in the sunshine as a continuation of the hours of flirting and conversation they enjoyed within the palace.

She suspected the reason the women were unfocused on their lessons was a group of men who had come to sit on the grass and watch. Flasks were being passed among the men, and their laughter grew more raucous each time a flask was tilted back to a mouth.

On the other side of the field, Chance lay with head on paws, watching everyone. Mallory wished she could give the dog a command to herd the men away like sheep. They did not act as if they had any more wits than newborn lambs.

Instead of giving in to that fantasy, she looked back at her students. Five women were attending the daily class now, although there had been almost a dozen at the first session. Lady Elita was among the ones who still came to each class, surprising her, because the blonde had been cold during their first meeting. When she first heard Lady Elita call Lady Yolanda "sister," she guessed Lady Yolanda had invited Lady Elita to join them. Lady Diamanta, whose brother was one of the queen's Poitevin guards, stood next to the tall brunette, Lady Violet. Lady Oriel, the fifth woman, never spoke unless one of the women addressed her, which they seldom did.

"Is today the day?" Lady Elita asked in the impatient tone she used with every woman except the queen.

Mallory looked at the short bow she held. The women were eager to use a strung bow instead of learning basic lessons such as how to hold it properly. The narrow branches that Mallory had collected as their "bows" were scattered around the women. She noticed Lady Violet stood on hers.

"Yes, today is the day," Mallory said.

Her words were met by cheers. Not from the women, but from the men who were watching. She tried to ignore them as Chance began to bark. That Saxon was not among the men helped, but she could not help wondering where he was. He often could be found sitting among them, laughing and playing his lute and telling amazing tales that could not be true.

She motioned for the dog to be silent. Turning back to the women, she held out the bow. "This is a weapon, and you must take care of it, so it will never fail you when you need it. As you can see, I have waxed the wood." She shifted it, so the wood gleamed in the sunshine that was filtering through thickening clouds. "The string is waxed, too, to keep it strong and pliant. You need to prevent both the wood and the string from getting wet."

"But in bloody battle . . ." Lady Yolanda gave a small shiver.

"In battle, archers are protected behind the shield wall of the foot soldiers," she replied. "They fire from that position." She lifted the bow as if to fire up into the sky. "The arrows go up and over the foot soldiers to strike the ones on the other side of the field." Lowering the bow, she added, "You will not have to worry about that, for you will not be in battle."

"We are being trained to safeguard the queen," Lady Elita argued, toying with the silver braid stitched along the front of her gown. "Who knows? We may be in glorious battle."

"Yes, glorious battle!" seconded Lady Yolanda, her voice rising in excitement. "We shall be sung about like the greatest heroes. Everyone will cheer for us."

"Huzzah! Huzzah!" called the men as they waved the flasks. Several fell back onto the grass and laughed drunkenly.

When Lady Elita blew a kiss toward the men, one jumped up as if to catch it. He pressed his hand over his heart and bowed deeply. Too deeply, because he tottered, falling to his knees. That brought more laughter and a low growl from the dog.

"Ladies!" Mallory frowned when she realized none of the women was paying attention. "Ladies, if I may . . ."

Lady Violet, wearing a guilty expression, turned to look at her. The others continued to bask in the attention from the men.

Mallory's hand clenched on the bow. When she heard the wood creak, she loosened her grip on it. The lesson was ruined. She would not allow the bow to be destroyed, too.

Not "too." She had promised the queen to teach her ladies to use a bow, and she would not be stopped from fulfilling that vow by a group of drunken oafs.

Although she was tempted to use the bow to push past the ladies who were now fawning on the men, she stepped around them and walked across the field. A drop of sweat slid between her shoulder blades, startling her. The day was warm, but a slight breeze from the river made it bearable. Yet she was perspiring. Was she unnerved at the thought of speaking to these men? She hoped not.

The man who had dropped to his knees bounced back up and tried to bow again. She put out a hand to steady him.

He grasped her arm. Tugging on her, he said, "I will kiss you as well, milady."

"I think not." She twisted her arm sharply, snapping it away from him.

His eyes grew wide with astonishment.

"Begone," she ordered before he could say something else stupid. Looking past him, she added, "All of you, begone."

The young men exchanged amazed glances, and she wondered when they last had been denied any entertainment.

One—dressed in a garish bright blue tunic—came to his feet to tower over her. She did not step back or shift her bow or put her hand on the knife at her waist. She simply kept her gaze locked with his.

The red-haired man's eyes shifted away, revealing that he was unsure what to do now that he had failed to rouse any reaction from her. Another man snorted a laugh, and the face of the man who had grabbed her arm grew as scarlet as his hair.

She still did not speak or move. Into her mind came the echo of Nariko's soft voice warning that a foe should never be further provoked. Not only would that increase the chance of her adversary's doing something foolish in anger, but vexing an antagonist took her own attention away from controlling her emotions and watching for the first signs of attack. Sensing that the dog had come to stand beside her, she put her hand on Chance's head and felt the low growl that did not reach her ears.

"L-L-L . . ." The man halted when laughter roared from the men on the grass. Clearing his throat, he said, "Lady Mallory, grant us the pleasure of learning from you as well."

"I teach the queen's ladies. No one else."

"You could teach everyone. Why not? Isn't that what you are supposed to do? Train us to protect the queen? Why should only the women have fun?"

Mallory forced down the rising pulse of fury boiling in her. The fool in front of her was not her father, even though he acted as selfishly and demanded his way with a petulance that brought Lord de Saint-Sebastian instantly to mind. She would not allow the man to goad her into reacting. She had learned to command her temper at St. Jude's Abbey, and she would not let this red-head make her forget those important lessons.

"I do not teach a warrior's skills," she said, pleased her voice was even. "I teach how to use a bow to protect oneself."

"Renoul is no warrior!" a dark-haired man said through another burst of laughter. "Maybe you can teach him what little you teach the women."

She gave the dark-haired man the same stern glare. He also looked away. Muttering something, he pushed himself to his feet and strode away. He went a few steps, then whirled to come back. Chance leaped forward, growling loudly. The dark-haired man inched forward and, never taking his eyes off the dog, bent to pick up a flask before he stamped toward the city wall.

Again the men glanced at each other. They got up and followed the dark-haired man.

Chance trotted in the opposite direction, then raced after a squirrel near the trees along the river. Barks echoed against the cliffs on the opposite bank.

Mallory let out a low sigh of relief. She had grown accustomed to the good sense of the women who lived within St. Jude's Abbey. She had let herself forget how idiotic both sexes could act when preening before each other.

"Well-done," came a deep voice behind her.

Saxon! He must have come onto the field while she was confronting the men.

"I asked the other men to leave," she said without looking at him. "They have agreed, and I hope you will do the same."

"They do not, together, have half the wits of a fish. I will sit here and speak nary a word."

Chance bounded past her, tail wagging, to greet Saxon before racing after something else in the grass. *Traitor!* she wanted to shout after the dog. Yet how could she blame the dog for reacting so when her own heart had begun pounding within her at his compliment?

She closed her eyes and took a deep breath, letting it sift slowly past her tight lips before she faced Saxon. It was impossible to imagine him being silent, for he seemed to have a comment about everything. She was about to say that as she turned, but found herself unable to draw in another breath. She could only stare at how the wind ran invisible fingers through his hair. She wanted to do the same while she slipped her arm up his back, pushing aside his lute as she brought him to her.

"I promise to be as silent as a mote of dust." His eyes sparkled.

She should look away. The men had been wise enough to do that when she confronted them, and Saxon was right, because while their minds were soaked in whatever they had been drinking, they did not have a bit of sense among them. She was not as goose-witted as they were. She did not have the excuse of being drunk. She should look away.

Yet, she did not as he put his finger to his lips and whispered, "Shhh." She watched, unable to stop herself, when he touched the same finger to her lips and repeated himself.

She grasped his hand, knowing she must push it aside before the tingle undulating across her skin erupted in her head and extinguished any thoughts she had left. Instead her fingers laced through his. He bent and pressed his mouth to the back of her hand as his gaze held hers.

When he released her hand, she did not lower it. She knew she looked silly, but she could not move. He gave her a slow-burning smile before he went to where the others had been sitting. Even before he could draw off his lute, Lady Elita rushed over to him and flung her arms around his neck.

"Oh, Saxon, how adorable of you to come to watch us!" She tickled him beneath his beard as she leaned over him. "Are you going to write a poem about us?"

Mallory did not wait to hear his answer. His easy grin spoke loudly enough of how he enjoyed Lady Elita's attentions. Why couldn't she recall that he was sure to be as faithless as every other man proved to be?

Squaring her shoulders, she raised her voice. "Ladies, your lesson has been interrupted long enough. Please come here."

She was unsure if Lady Elita would leave Saxon's side, but the blonde rushed to her and held out her hands for the bow Mallory still held. When Lady Elita looked over her shoulder and Saxon winked, Mallory realized the blonde was eager to show off for him.

"Not this one," Mallory said. "It is mine. I have others for you." She pointed to the stack of bows that she had created out of the scraps from Master Ivon's fletchery.

The women swarmed upon them. Something cracked, and a high-pitched voice rang out through the afternoon air, "You broke my bow!"

Lady Elita pushed past the others and lifted a bow. She put an arrow on the string, shocking Mallory. Where had she gotten an arrow? Seeing the tip of another poking from the cuff of Lady Elita's long sleeve, Mallory wondered how the blonde could be so unthinking and arrogant as to imagine she could fire off an arrow the first time she held a bow.

"No! Don't hold the bow that way!" Mallory ran to where Lady Elita was aiming the arrow at her own foot as she tried to get the arrow on the string.

"Look out!" called Saxon.

Shouts and barking came from everywhere as she grasped Lady Elita's arms and tilted them up just as the blonde released the arrow.

It arched high into the air. The women called out warnings and scattered, but the arrow tumbled to the ground, harmless.

"You made me miss!" cried Lady Elita.

"Yes, I did. I made you miss your foot."

"Don't be silly. I would not have hit my foot." Grabbing the other arrow, she fit it onto the string. She raised the bow.

Mallory drove her own arm down on Lady Elita's. The arrow skittered through the grass.

"You made me miss!" Lady Elita snarled again. She cried out more in surprise than pain when Mallory jerked the bow out of her hands.

"That is enough," Mallory said in the tone that had been a

warning to her students at the Abbey to heed her more closely. "If you care nothing for the safety of your companions, then consider the others around you."

"What others?"

"There." She pointed to where a woman and two men were strolling among the trees by the river.

Lady Elita rolled her eyes. "You worry too much!"

"A bow is no toy. It . . ." She paused when she saw the woman and the two men emerge from the shadows around the trees. Her stomach cramped as if someone had reached within her and clamped it in a vise.

The woman was Queen Eleanor!

Beside her, Lady Elita made a gurgling sound and hastily stepped away from Mallory. The other women froze where they were, and Mallory found she could not move either.

A hand touched her elbow. Heat flowed from the chaste touch, and she knew Saxon's fingers brushed her arm. Tearing her gaze from the queen, who was walking toward them with de Mauzé and Mangot, two of her Poitevin guards, she looked at Saxon. His face was grim, and she knew he was thinking, as she was, how easily the queen could have been slain by an errant arrow.

Dropping to her knees, Mallory stood when the queen said, "Rise, Lady Mallory, and tell me how the lessons with my ladies are going."

"They are attempting to gain a basic mastery of archery," she said, glad she was staring at the queen's hem. She did not want to meet Queen Eleanor's eyes while speaking half the truth. The women had less interest in archery than they did in taunting their admirers. She doubted most of her students would master anything but failure.

"You are a patient instructor."

"I am attempting to be." She frowned at Chance, who was growling as the dog stared at the trees farther along the river. She could not look over her shoulder to see what was bothering the dog, nor could she chide Chance while conversing with the queen. Putting her hand on the dog's head, she gave it a gentle pat, hoping that would distract the dog from the squirrel or rabbit probably hidden in the shadows.

The queen smiled. "I know you are finding the adjustment to Poitiers difficult, Lady Mallory, but your efforts are greatly appreciated."

"Thank you."

"Saxon, are you assisting—"

A soft whoosh came from behind Mallory. She reacted with instinct rather than thought. Tossing aside her bow and grabbing the queen's arm, she fell to the grass. Shouts and shrieks came from every direction as Queen Eleanor tumbled to the ground beside her.

Hands tore her away from the queen and jerked her to her feet as the women she had been teaching screamed and screamed. The dog barked wildly. A knife pressed against the underside of her chin. She drew in a breath to speak, and it pricked her throat.

"Don't!" shouted Saxon.

"Be silent, troubadour," snarled de Mauzé as he held his sword to Saxon's chest. "She attacked the queen, and now she will see the price of such treachery."

"I did not attack the queen," Mallory whispered. "I saved her life." She stared at Saxon, whose face was twisted with fury and frustration.

"You lying bitch!" spat the man behind her. "That is the last lie you will ever speak." He tilted the blade so she could see it, then shifted it to draw across her throat.

"Stop!" The voice was the queen's, and it sounded as enraged as Saxon's. "Release Lady Mallory. Release her at once."

The knife was lifted away from her, but Mangot gave her a sharp shove that knocked her back to her knees.

A hand reached out to her. The queen's hand, she realized, when she saw gold rings on the fingers. She put her own on it and came slowly to her feet. Dampness ran down her neck, and she knew she was bleeding, but she did not reach to wipe it away.

"Explain yourself, milady," the queen said in the same angry tone.

"If I may . . ." She motioned past the queen.

Queen Eleanor nodded, her mouth taut.

Mallory took a single step and wobbled. Silently cursing her weakness, she was relieved when Saxon said, "Allow me, Lady Mallory."

"Thank you." She watched as the others did when he sprinted across the grass toward two arrows.

One arrow had flown far off to the right, but the other arrow had come to a stop at a spot not far behind the queen. No one spoke until he returned and held out the arrows, one with a bent shaft, to her. She took them and straightened the crooked arrow with its white-tipped feathers before placing both arrows on the queen's hand.

"Two arrows." Queen Eleanor examined them closely, then said, "I don't understand, Lady Mallory, what you wish me to know about these arrows."

"My students were not yet ready to fire any arrows, so I did not bring any to the field today. One of my students in her enthusiasm had two, but both of them are on the ground here, and you can see they are of Master Ivon's making. The two you are holding are not, for they are not fletched with the gray goose feathers he uses. I heard the arrows flying toward us." She met the queen's eyes steadily. "Toward *you*. I did not have time to warn you, so I did the only thing I had time to do. If I have injured you in any way with my actions, I am deeply sorry."

"It appears you have saved my life, Lady Mallory. I will not forget that."

"If I may be so bold, Queen Eleanor, I would suggest you remain behind the city walls, where you will be safer."

"Wise advice." She handed the arrows back to Mallory. "I trust you will inform me of anything else you may discover about this incident." She motioned to her men, who were looking chagrined, and led them toward the city wall, walking as calmly as if nothing had happened. The women rushed after them.

Saxon turned the arrows over on her hand. "You *heard* the passage of these arrows?"

"I was alerted by Chance." She pointed to the dog, which was sniffing near the trees. "She was growling and looking in that direction. At first, I ignored her. Then, I heard a low sound that I have heard so many times."

"A sound only a skilled archer would recognize."

"And the archer who fired this arrow"—she held up the one that had been bent—"was not skilled, because the arrow went wide." She frowned. "Odd."

"What is odd?"

"The two arrows seemed to follow an identical path, as if they had been shot from the same bow."

"Is that possible?"

She ran her finger along the arrow. "I don't think so. When I was first mastering the bow, I tried to fire two arrows at the same time. I could not make it work."

"If you could not make it work, I doubt anyone could." He stared at the dog and sighed. "There is no sense in giving chase. The men who fired the arrows have certainly found a place to hide by now."

"Yes, but we have been warned. The ones who want the queen dead are very daring."

"They must be when the queen is so well guarded. I wonder who fired the arrows."

"The feathers are white-tipped. The French king's messenger had white-fletched arrows in his quiver."

"Are you accusing King Louis—the queen's ex-husband and current ally—of arranging to have her killed?"

She shook her head carefully, trying to pay no attention to the scorching pain from the cut on her neck. "I am saying only that Bertram's arrows and these were both fletched with white feathers. Someone may wish to point an accusatory finger at King Louis, or the French king might be involved."

"So we are no closer to an answer to the identity of the archers who let the arrows fly."

"No." She winced as she shook her head again.

His brow lowered. "That scratch is deep, Mallory. You should have a healer examine it before bad humors enter it."

"I will." She bent to pick up her bow.

Saxon's hand on her arm halted her. She stood straighter and met his gaze. When the arrows slid from her hand to tumble to the ground as his arm eased around her waist, he pulled her to him. His mouth covered hers before she could speak. His kiss was neither quick or cursory. He deepened it until her lips softened beneath his. When his tongue slid into her mouth, stroking her in ways she had never imagined, she curved her arms up his back, splaying her fingers across muscles that seemed too powerful for a troubadour. But she did not care if he sang for the queen or careened across a battlefield on a mighty steed. All she wanted was the kiss to go on and on while her fingertips combed up through his tawny hair.

His mouth left hers, and she started to protest. She halted when his tongue glided along the curve of her ear. His soft laugh at her gasp of delight erupted through her with the speed of an arrow striking a target. As she tilted her head to let him place kisses behind her ear, she stiffened with pain.

"I am sorry," she whispered, "but it hurts when I move my head like that."

"You have no need to apologize." He stepped back and picked up her bow and the arrows fired at the queen. Holding them in one hand and whistling for the dog, he offered his other hand to her. "Let me take you to the palace healer. Eudes will tend to your wound." He gave her a beguiling smile as he murmured, "And then I want to tend to the rest of you."

When he gave her a swift kiss, she could not halt the shiver sweeping along her. Nor could she decide if it was a shiver of anticipation at more of the pleasure they shared or a shiver of fear at allowing her life to become enmeshed with that of a man who, as her father had, flirted with every woman who crossed his path. She was brave enough to knock the queen from her feet to save her life, but she did not know if she had the courage to endure the humiliation and grief her mother had.

Putting every bit of coolness she could in her voice, she said, "I think you are forgetting why I am here, Saxon." Plucking the bow from his hand and pulling her fingers out of his grip, she walked away before she forgot, too.

Chapter 7

Saxon was again prowling the wooden quay on the River Clain. As each time he came there, odors of mud and dead fish mixed with the garbage and sewage that had flowed into the river. Above him, the steeples of Poitiers were silhouetted against the rising moon. The river emerged from thicker shadows, and sailors were asleep on decks or readying their boats for the next day's journey along the river.

How much longer would he need to wait? He had asked himself that question over and over in the past hour, even though he knew the answer just as he had the evening when he had watched Mallory step off the boat filled with mercenaries on their way to join King Henry's troops.

He heard some guttural oaths, and he looked over his shoulder, his fingers settling on the haft of the knife he had hidden beneath his well-worn cloak. He relaxed slightly when two men swung their fists at each other, one knocking the other onto the uneven planks. Neither was Jacques Malcoeur nor one of his cronies. Saxon stayed alert. Malcoeur and his gang were not the only thieves loitering near the pier in hopes of finding easy prey.

That he had learned yesterday when two archers had taken aim on the queen. If Mallory had not reacted quickly, there would be no need for him—or anyone else—to remain in Poitiers. Until he picked the scattered arrows up out of the grass, he had not believed the queen was in real danger. He had thought that

Queen Eleanor was overanxious because of the stress of her sons battling her husband, and he had dismissed the note on the arrow shot into Mallory's room as an empty threat.

He had been wrong. Mallory, fortunately, had taken the queen at her word, accepting the unseen menace as real. With her incredible ability to sense an arrow sent from a nearby bowstring, she had saved the queen's life.

"But how many other lives will be lost in the rebellion that now continues?" he murmured to himself, knowing that the queen's sons would lose heart in continuing the battle against their father if they were mourning their mother.

Two boats edging along the river caught his eye. One turned toward the pier. Even in the dim light it was obvious that the boat sat low in the water, and Saxon marveled at the captain's greed at filling the boat heavily on the shallow river. A single miscalculation could leave the boat stuck on a sandbar or aground, unable to move in any direction.

Just as Saxon was.

He snarled a curse under his breath that would have shocked even the low creatures gathered along the river. He was no closer to learning who was threatening the queen. There had been no trail to follow on the riverbank, save for a few footprints. He had to assume the men who had fired the arrows had an accomplice waiting with a boat. There must be something he was overlooking, but he could not guess what.

He had found no clue to the threat fired at Mallory's window. He had considered anyone with archery skills within the palace, but none of them seemed to have had the opportunity . . . or the interest in chasing Mallory from the palace to leave the queen vulnerable. When he had mentioned Bertram de Paris, who clearly had a grudge against Mallory, she had told him of the queen's reaction to the messenger's name.

"She was very adamant," Mallory had said. "She believes Bertram de Paris is a trusted ally, because he serves a trusted ally."

"Alliances change," had been his own response.

Mallory had given him no reply, which had told him much. She would not belittle the queen, even when Mallory did not agree with her.

But the arrow could have come from anywhere, from anyone, including those whom he had dismissed as having no archery skills. One did not need great skill to send an arrow flying upward, as Lady Elita had shown. That was especially true when the windows were as large as they were in the palace. Neither the ducs of Aquitaine nor King Henry had clearly ever imagined the palace coming under assault. The archer who had loosed the arrow into Mallory's window had not needed to do more than aim in the approximate direction and fire. If the arrow flew over the window and skidded across the chamber's floor, or if it had hit something—or someone—may not have mattered to the archer. Getting the message to Mallory had been what was important.

Saxon could have told the archer it was a waste of time. Such a message would not frighten Mallory de Saint-Sebastian.

Mallory had blanched at the threat, but she had quickly arranged to speak privately with Queen Eleanor. Even Saxon could not obtain an invitation to that discussion. And he had tried. Nor would Mallory say anything of the meeting other than that the queen had thanked her for letting her know of the incident.

Was Mallory de Saint-Sebastian always so closemouthed? He had discovered little about her. He knew more about her father than he did of her. Yet, he could tell from the way she avoided his eyes, even when he drew her into his arms, that she was hiding something.

That should be no surprise. He had never met anyone in the queen's circle who was not hiding something.

"Saxon Fitz-Juste? Is that you?" asked an impatient voice.

Saxon's hand was beneath his cloak on his knife as he whirled to face the man behind him.

"Are you just going to stand there, or are you going to welcome your brother to Poitiers?" asked Godard Fitz-Juste.

He did not lift his fingers away as he measured his brother, who stood in a pool of moonlight. Godard was not quite as tall as he was, but the angular features emphasized by a jagged scar across his forehead just beneath his mail cap and matted strands of light brown hair were almost identical to his own. The blow to the brow appeared to have been a glancing one, or done with the sword dulled by striking against other mail, but Saxon knew it had come from a tumble off a horse.

Saxon drew his hand off his knife, then clasped his fingers behind him, beneath the lute he always carried for his place in the palace as the queen's troubadour. Their father considered a man worthy only if he had proven himself on the tournament grounds or the battlefield. Godard, as their father's heir, probably shared the same shortsightedness. He would deem a troubadour a lamentable waste of Saxon's previous education. Saxon reminded himself that he did not have the luxury of showing his brother that such assumptions were dangerous . . . not while he remained at the queen's court.

Instead he asked in a voice as cool as Godard's, "Why are you here?"

"Weren't you told to await my arrival?"

"I was told to await the arrival of the king's man. I did not realize that man was my own brother."

"Here I am." He spread his empty hands wide and gave Saxon the superior grin he had often worn during their childhood.

"You were supposed to arrive a fortnight ago."

"There have been some changes."

Again Saxon nodded. Godard was not telling him anything he had not already guessed from how the French king's messenger had guarded his every word to Queen Eleanor.

"Such as you being here in the queen's court," Godard said as he glanced around the riverbank. "What caused you to throw your lot in with the queen? She has broken every vow she ever took. What makes you believe she will give you the reward for your allegiance that she has promised you?"

"That is not something I intend to speak of here," Saxon answered.

Godard often acted as if he were several years younger than Saxon, but he was his elder by less than a half hour, second-born of a set of triplets. The first had died within an hour of his birth, and their mother had lost her battle to hold on to her own life less than a day after giving birth to three babies. Doted on by their father and stepmother as the heir, Godard had been given everything he wished. He had had the best teachers—even though he had learned little more than how to read and sign his own name—and the most skilled instructors in weaponry and riding. Saxon had been fortunate that he had been allowed to join the lessons, but their father had not cared how his second surviving son did, refusing to acknowledge Saxon when his abilities surpassed Godard's.

"I was not sure whether I could trust you, but our foster brother always said you could be trusted," Godard continued.

"How is Bruno?"

"Dead."

This time, Saxon's curses rang along the river, but he lowered his voice when he saw heads turn toward them. He could not allow his grief at his foster brother's death to betray what Bruno had given his life to protect. Bruno Humphrey had been several years older than Saxon and Godard, and Bruno had challenged Saxon to hone every skill a man needed to serve his country and his king. When Saxon had not measured up to Bruno's expectations, the punishment was swift and usually ended in laughter. A bucket of icy water over his head or the task of finding a single marked stalk among the many in a haystack had been the penalty Saxon paid for not practicing or for failing to know the answers to his lessons. In every case, Bruno had set him to the task, then joined him to complete it as they laughed together over whatever mishap Saxon had found himself in that day.

Bruno Humphrey had been closer to him than either his own brother or his half brothers by birth, even Godard. Knowing that Bruno would never break his oath of loyalty, Saxon should have guessed that his foster brother would not hesitate to join the fighting where it was fiercest.

"I am sorry," he said, knowing his sorrow would be shared by Godard.

"He spoke of you often and always with the highest of emotion." Godard appraised him anew before adding, "I hope he was not mistaken in his faith in you, Saxon."

"As I do." He gestured toward the steep bank.

"I had not expected to arrive in Poitiers ahead of the armies." He grumbled an oath under his breath. "I had hoped the king would have cut through the traitors' lines by now."

Saxon did not let his brother's inflammatory words vex him. "How long do you plan to stay?"

Godard's thick brows, resembling two fuzzy worms, lowered toward each other. The brows and the expression he had inherited from their father. "You should know better than to ask me such a question. I will stay as long as I must to fulfill the orders given to me."

Saxon nodded as they crossed the open field toward the city wall. He understood the answer, for it was the same one he would have offered. Had his brother changed so much that he had been offered a sensitive task that would require guile instead of his customary bragging? He hoped so, or Godard could destroy the fragile façade of lies Saxon had created.

Motioning in the direction of the closest gate into the city, he scanned the riverbank. Men were gathered in clumps near the deepest shadows, but nobody seemed to be paying any attention to Godard and him. He saw one lad glance at them and quickly away.

It was all the warning he needed. Hearing a footfall close behind, he pulled his knife as he swiftly turned to see a quartet of men racing toward him.

"Godard!" he shouted, hoping his brother's skills had improved and were equal to an ambush. He had no chance to see as he held up his knife to meet the downswing of another blade.

Not a sword, he was relieved to see. The attackers wore filthy, tattered clothes. No one of such low class would have a sword. He heard metal clash behind him. Godard had a sword, so he should be able to protect himself. Saxon had to concentrate on keeping his own heart beating.

He slashed in a broad arc with the knife. The man in front of him jumped back, his tunic ripped more. With a growl, he raised his knife and ran forward again.

Saxon prepared to jump aside, out of his reach. Something whizzed over his head. The man fell backward, an arrow sticking out of his shoulder. The knife dropped, useless, to the ground that was already turning scarlet.

He noticed that in the moment before, moonlight glinted off something beneath the man's sleeve. Mail! The thief was wearing mail!

Running toward him, Saxon grasped him by the front of his tunic. He lifted the moaning man partway off the ground and demanded, "Who are you? Who sent you to attack us?"

Fists struck Saxon on the back, knocking him atop the wounded man. Clawing away from the man who was screeching his pain, Saxon swore. His knife! Where was it?

Before he could look for it, another knife cut through the darkness. He jumped back. The knife sliced through the air inches from his gut. He heard Godard shout something. He paid it no mind. He had to concentrate on his own attacker.

Where was his blade? There! On the ground just past the wounded man.

He took a step toward it, then leaped back as the knife tried to cut into him again. Pain scored his right arm, and blood burned a trail toward his elbow.

"What is . . . ?" His attacker gasped and looked past him, his eyes widening.

Mallory appeared out of the darkness. Her black hair was loosened, some of it falling around her shoulders, and her quiver was torn and empty. Before he could warn her to flee from these men wearing mail, she swung the bow as if it were a quarterstaff. He expected it would crack and shatter when it struck his attacker, then realized it would not hit the man at all. She had swung it in an arc too close to her.

But she had given Saxon the opening he needed. He ran toward his blade and heard a scream. He turned to see the loose string snap toward the man like the end of a whip, catching him on the cheek. The man shrieked again and turned to her. When he started to swing his knife, she gripped the bow with both hands.

"Don't try to strike him with the bow!" Saxon shouted. "His reach is longer than yours! He will—"

Her right foot rose as she jumped toward the man. Toward him? Had she lost her mind? Had she . . .

He watched in disbelief as the side of her foot struck the man in the chin. He crumpled to the ground, then leaped back up. She took another step toward him, but he bellowed like a wounded beast and ran.

"Are you all right?" she asked, panting.

Saxon started to answer, but a thick arm caught him around the throat. He wiggled, trying to escape before his neck was broken.

"Saxon!" she shouted.

He looked toward her as the arm tightened around him. He gasped for air, but nothing reached his lungs. She raised her right fist and slammed it down past her side.

"What?" he managed to choke out. The arm constricted farther.

"Like this!" She made the same motion, more emphatically. "Do it! Now!"

His strength was streaming out of him like blood from an open wound. He fisted his fingers and raised his hand as she had. Behind him, his captor growled. He knew he had only seconds left. He drove his hand down and back.

His captor screeched as Saxon's fist struck him. Between the legs, Saxon realized as the man's arm went limp and slid away. He whirled to see his captor bent over double. With a grim smile and inhaling deeply, he struck him in the face. Pain erupted up his arm, but he ignored it as the man hit the ground hard, moaning for a moment before becoming silent.

Saxon rushed to where Godard was waving his sword wildly and swearing at a pair of men who turned to flee along the river when they saw Saxon approach to even the odds. His brother took a single pace to give chase, then fell to one knee. He lifted his sword over his head as he continued to snarl at the men.

"I am fine," Godard said as Saxon reached him, even though the dark stream of blood along his side and left leg contradicted his words.

"You are hurt."

"I am fine." He wiped away the blood, and Saxon realized it was not his brother's. "Who were those miscreants?"

"I suspect they are Jacques Malcoeur's men," Mallory said quietly from behind Saxon.

Godard pushed himself to his feet, paying her no attention as he repeated the question.

Saxon replied, "She is right. They may be Jacques Malcoeur's men. He is a thief who hunts those who linger too long on the riverbank."

He was not going to speak openly of the glint of steel he had seen beneath the man's tatters. The mail could have been stolen, or the attack may not have been random. Until he had some answers, he was not going to let any eavesdroppers—or Mallory— learn of his suspicions. He was unsure what she would do, and he wanted his vengeance on the men who had dared to ambush them.

"They will not be so bold again," Godard said.

Saxon wished he could agree with his brother, but, if the men were Malcoeur's, they had not been deterred by the beating and humiliation they had received the last time Saxon had encountered them. If they were others . . . Then, as now, superior skills had saved them. Not his. Not Godard's, but . . .

"How do you fare?" asked Mallory as she leaned her bow against her leg. Her dark hair swirled about her face, but, unlike

Godard and himself, she no longer showed any signs of being winded. Her breathing was even and her face serene. If he had not witnessed her abilities himself, he would have guessed she had done no more than watch the fighting.

"Are you following me?" he demanded.

"Yes, for I thought you might be risking trouble when you left the palace with no weapon other than your lute. I did not realize that troubadours also carried daggers, but at least you showed some sense when you left the palace after dark. Were you expecting trouble?" Her chin rose slightly as she met his furious gaze with a tranquillity that seemed aimed at inciting a man to an even greater rage . . . or arousing other passions that he would find even more difficult to control.

"No trouble that we could not deal with ourselves," said Godard as he hobbled toward them, putting as little weight as possible on his left leg. "Who is this impertinent wench?"

"She is—"

"I am Lady Mallory de Saint-Sebastian, the impertinent wench who saved your life," she said, shrugging her torn quiver back over her shoulder.

Saxon chuckled, unable to halt himself. What a bizarre trio they made! Godard was limping, so he must have banged his knee when he fell to the ground, blood was running down Saxon's arm, and Mallory . . . All desire to laugh vanished as he looked back at her. Relief was like a potent wine coursing through him when he realized the only damage done to her, other than her ruined quiver, was a torn silken veil.

"Let me escort you back to the palace," Mallory went on. "The streets can be perilous, as Saxon and I discovered upon *my* arrival in Poitiers." She glanced at him again, and he saw the remnants of the cold fury that had burned in her eyes when she faced their attackers. "You should have warned your friend here, Saxon, of the dangers."

"I should have."

She faltered, amazing him. Did she expect every word that came out of his mouth to be a challenge? With a nod, she turned to walk toward the gate, where a guard was staring at her with his mouth wide open.

"Mallory de Saint-Sebastian," Godard sneered, "needs to be taught a lesson or two about how to address a knight properly."

"Do *you* want to be the one to suggest she change her ways? A poor recompense for her help in chasing off our attackers."

"She should not be strutting about as if she were the equal of a knight."

"She is not our equal." Saxon's head was aching, and he knew he should not be baiting his brother. Yet his frustration was as great as Godard's, even though it was aimed at a different target. Who were the men who had attacked them? He needed to discover where Malcoeur and his followers hid when not prowling about looking for victims.

"Then she should be taught to treat her betters with respect."

"Betters?" Saxon's laugh was so whetted it sliced through his throat. "We are not her betters. She is one of the queen's ladies."

Godard shuddered and then turned to stare toward where Mallory was now talking to the guard. In a choked voice, Godard asked, "The queen has a lady who wields a bow in her own defense?"

"Not solely a bow. You saw her." He added no more. The queen had demanded a vow from each of the men traveling with her to St. Jude's Abbey never to speak to anyone else of what they encountered or heard there.

"I may be here longer than I had guessed," the knight said glumly. "I had no idea the queen had ladies like Mallory de Saint-Sebastian."

"It has been a surprise to all of us." Saxon looked again to where Mallory stood. "A surprise in more ways than I could have guessed."

*   *   *

"Let me help," Mallory said as she entered the room where only a single candle was lit to drive back the darkness beyond the pool of moonlight on the uneven stone floor.

In the shadows, Saxon looked up from where he was wrapping bandages around Sir Godard's leg. "What are you doing here?"

"I wanted to be sure your wounds were bound." She held a bowl of steaming water. "Do you need more?"

"Yes, thank you."

Sir Godard shook his head. "Go away, woman! We can take care of ourselves." His lip curled in a sneer. "You already aspire to be a knight. Do you intend to act as a squire as well?"

Putting the bowl on a table by where Sir Godard sat, she walked out of the room. She bit her trembling lower lip and blinked back tears she thought long dried. Another sign of how hopeless it was to believe that she could ever escape the humiliations of her past. So easy it had been to flee them during her years in St. Jude's Abbey, but they had been waiting beyond the Abbey's walls to pounce on her again.

She had not expected to hear such abuse from the lips of Sir Godard. Once they had reached a pool of light within the palace, she had been startled to see the resemblance between the two men. When Saxon explained they were brothers, separated by just minutes in age, she had appraised both men anew. Saxon was taller and a bit broader in the shoulder. Sir Godard had a fiercer expression and was a bit wider in the belly, a sign that he was accustomed to a comfortable life where food always awaited him.

When she heard Saxon call her name, she wanted to keep walking, to avoid the questions he must intend to ask. To do so would arouse even more of his curiosity.

She turned to see Saxon walking toward her in the dusky hallway. She could not keep from thinking of how his eyes had narrowed ever so slightly when he had drawn her into his arms just before she walked away by the river. As if he were afraid of showing her how he truly felt, she had guessed, especially when he kissed her. The touch of his lips against hers had revealed little about him, but too much about herself.

She should not want to want a man's kisses. Men were faithless dogs. If a magnificent woman like the queen—or like Lady Beata de Saint-Sebastian—could not persuade a man to be constant in his affections, what hope was there for any woman? It would be better, she had decided at St. Jude's Abbey, to avoid men and their temptations.

Another vow that was being thrown back into her face, because she was aware of every motion Saxon made as if it were her own. She did not want any sort of connection between them, save for their duty to the queen. Yet her body no longer obeyed her. She tingled in anticipation of his touch, even when he was more than an arm's length away.

"Allow me to apologize for Godard's rude words," he said quietly, and she guessed he did not want his voice to carry to his brother's ears.

"It is not your place to apologize for your brother."

"True, but I thought you were due an apology from someone."

His expression threatened to undo her carefully constructed self-possession, because it suggested he was being honest with her. The queen's voice speaking of Saxon echoed in her head: *Unless he is playing his lute or sharing a poem, you can be certain that he is being honest.*

"I appreciate your sentiment," she said.

"But you will accept no apology from anyone but the perpetrator himself."

"An apology means nothing unless it is sincere."

"Then I will ask you to forgive Godard, because he is quite out of sorts."

"Out of sorts? He sounded furious. His tone reminded me of my father's when I displeased him." She clamped her lips closed. She had not wanted to mention the earl.

He lowered his voice and leaned toward her. "Don't repeat this to anyone. Godard can be an ass."

She laughed, jolted out of her melancholy by his teasing.

"You will not repeat that, will you?" he asked, still somber. "My brother would not be pleased to hear me speak so."

"No, but if someone else finds out . . ."

"Someone else *will* find out as soon as he opens his mouth, but then he can be angry with that person."

"As well as me."

"And me." He gave her a grin. "See? We have far more in common than either of us thought even a few days ago."

"Why didn't you tell me your brother was coming to Poitiers?"

"I was unsure he was."

"Was it he whom you were waiting for when I arrived?"

He nodded. "I had been told to await someone, but I had not been sure who it might be."

"Why is he here?"

"You need to ask him that." He put his crooked finger under her chin and whispered, "I have not had a chance while I watched your amazing defeat of our attackers."

"You don't know why Sir Godard is here?" She drew his hand down away from her and stepped back, wincing as the simple motion resonated painfully along her neck.

"Did I hurt you?" he asked. "How are you healing from that imbecile Mangot's knife?"

"I am fine." She focused her annoyance on him. It was much less complicated to be irritated at him than to let herself be wooed closer with his words that were probably well practiced. Yet, she had to ask, "How is your arm?"

"I am fine," he said as she had. "I have been injured worse in practice." He held up his hand as if about to swing a sword. "Even troubadours need to know how to protect themselves."

"Especially if they loiter near the river where rats crawl off the boats."

"Godard will not like being described that way."

"You know I did not mean your brother." She glanced along the corridor to make sure it was empty in both directions before saying, "I spoke of the ones who attacked you, the ones wearing mail beneath their rags."

"You saw that, too?" His eyes slitted, and she wondered what he was trying to hide now. "Then why did you mention Jacques Malcoeur by the river?"

"The men might still answer to him."

"Thieves wearing a knight's mail?" He snorted his disgust at the very idea.

She folded her hands in front of her so she did not grasp his arms and try to shake some good sense into his head. "If they are thieves, they could have stolen it."

"The battles are taking place far from Poitiers, so the corpse strippers would have scanty pickings here."

"Be that as it may, we have no idea if they are connected with Jacques Malcoeur."

"True." The single word was grudging, and she sensed his futility in it.

"There is nothing to link those men to the ones who shot at the queen," she said, unleashing some of her own frustration.

"Have you learned more about the archers?"

"I took the arrows to Master Ivon, hoping that he may be able to see something we could not. He told me to come back in a few days."

"A few days? The queen's life is at stake."

"He knows that, which is why he is busy making arrows for her archers. So we know nothing more about the archers now. Nor do we know," she continued before he could protest again, "if the men who attacked you and Sir Godard are connected to the threat shot into my chamber."

"*You* were not attacked."

"Maybe the threat was not aimed at me."

"It was fired into your room."

"But you were the one standing in full view of anyone aiming at the window."

He opened his mouth, then closed it. Astonishment filled his eyes, and he stared at her as if he had never seen her before.

Quietly, for she had no idea what ears might be listening within the palace, she said, "I did not give that idea any thought at the time, but the facts are clear, Saxon. The arrow was fired when you were visible through the window. The warning may have been meant for you rather than for me."

"Or for both of us." His voice was more disconcerted than she had ever heard it.

"I have not been within the palace for long. For someone to know that window opened into my room—"

"Would require only eyes, for you sat there the morning of your arrival."

"How did you know that?"

"*I* have eyes." He stepped closer to her.

Warnings exploded in her head, pleading with her to move back. She did not, because she did not want him to see her running away like a frightened child. Instead she raised her chin. "Were you watching me?"

"I happened to see you sitting in the window while I was in the garden." He edged a bit nearer. "Anyone else could have, too, including the one who fired the arrow which you believe was aimed at me. Is that the reason you followed me out of the city?"

She nodded. Speaking was impossible when his finger traced a lazy trail along her cheek, creating a melody that matched the eager beat of her heart.

"I had not guessed when you vowed to protect the queen that you had taken on the task of watching over everyone at her court."

Not everyone, she wanted to answer. *Just you.* She kept those traitorous words silent as she turned away before she could be as witless as her mother and let a man woo her into exposing her thoughts in exchange for his caresses.

"If something happens to you, the queen would be distressed," she said.

"Would she be the only one?"

She clenched her hands at her sides. By St. Jude, she did not want him to play flirtatious games with her. She preferred the straightforward speech of the Abbey.

"I would imagine Lady Elita and her friends would be shattered that you were no longer around to sing to them and fill their heads with pretty poetry."

"I don't fill your head with that, do I?"

Before she could answer, a bellow reverberated along the corridor. "Saxon! How much longer are you going to linger out there? I need some help!"

"It seems now that he thinks *you* are his squire," she said beneath the oaths spewing through the doorway. As he started back toward the door, she hurried after him. "Saxon, did Sir Godard see— Did he see what those men were wearing?"

"He said nothing of it, so I doubt he saw anything out of the ordinary."

"Saxon!" came another shout. "Where in perdition are you? Finish up with the harlot, give her a coin or two, and get back in here and help me."

Saxon smiled at Mallory. "Harlot? If Godard is that wrong about you—and I am certain if I were to tell him you have been a cloistered sister—"

"No! You must never reveal that! You promised the queen you would say nothing about St. Jude's Abbey."

"I was only jesting, Mallory." He ran his thumb along her jaw in a motion that seemed deliciously intimate. "But if he is so very mistaken about you, who knows what else he is wrong about?"

She did not smile in return. "What we saw those men wearing under their tattered tunics . . ."

When her voice faded away, he became somber, and his eyes sparked with the honest emotion she so seldom saw. "Tell me what you are thinking."

"I cannot. It is unspeakable."

"I agree." He scowled at the doorway as Sir Godard shouted his name again. "It *is* unspeakable to think that the queen is in more danger than any of us thought."

She wrapped her arms around herself as he went back into the room and closed the door after him. Hurrying toward her room within the queen's apartments, she knew she must devise something unexpected to protect Queen Eleanor. She had a few ideas and hoped she would choose the right one to thwart an enemy who might be close by, readying the next strike even now.

Chapter 8

"What have you discovered about the archer who fired at me?" Queen Eleanor asked. She sat in a chair by an unlit hearth in her private chamber. Rain splattered in the deep sill of the window overlooking the gardens that were so quiet each drop could be heard plopping on stone. The air was heavy, as if everyone in Poitiers had drawn in a deep breath and were not yet ready to release it, waiting to see what would happen next.

The queen wore heavy fabrics draped around her, but no perspiration marred her cheek. Beside her, Comtesse Marie was working on embroidery. Both acted nonchalant, but the queen's maid Amaria stood near the door, guarding it.

Mallory hated having to say, "I have learned nothing yet, your majesty."

"And the attack on Saxon and Godard Fitz-Juste by the riverbank . . . Have you uncovered anything more about that?"

Again, Mallory said the bitter-tasting words, "I have learned nothing yet, your majesty."

Queen Eleanor sighed and shook her head. "I know you are trying your best, Lady Mallory, but perhaps I have been expecting too much of you after the achievements of the other ladies of St. Jude's Abbey." She gave Mallory a gentle smile to ease the impact of her words. "I do not blame you. I blame myself, for I forget you are not familiar with Poitiers. It might be better if I handed the investigation of these incidents to someone who is better acquainted with the city."

"If that is your wish, I will step aside and allow someone else to continue to try to discover the truth," Mallory said, almost choking on the words she did not want to say. She had forgotten the acrid taste filling her mouth when she had to admit that she had disappointed someone she wished to prove her worth to. In Castle Saint-Sebastian, it had been a familiar flavor on her tongue, left each time she spoke with her father. Her years in St. Jude's Abbey had shown her that she did have some value, but now she was facing failure again. Looking steadily at the queen, she added, "However, I would ask that you allow me to continue in my attempt to find answers about these two events."

"As well as the attack on you when you first arrived."

"Yes." She was not surprised that, even though she had said nothing to the queen about Jacques Malcoeur and his men, she was aware of what had happened. She suspected the queen had eyes everywhere in the city, which added to her impatience—and Mallory's—with not being able to find the names of the archers who had fired the arrows at the queen and of the men in mail pretending to be river thieves.

The other sisters who had been called out of St. Jude's Abbey had done exactly as asked, succeeding so well that the stories of their adventures were already legendary behind the Abbey's walls. Every sister within yearned to have her opportunity to serve and join that pantheon of heroines.

And Mallory was failing horribly.

"I see no problem with your continuing, although I would remind you that I expect you to continue with your duties as one of my guards," the queen said with a glance at her daughter.

The comtesse raised her eyes from her embroidery and affixed her cool stare on Mallory. "Everyone deserves a chance to show that the faith put in him or her by the queen is justified. You have invested much of yourself in St. Jude's Abbey,

Mother, so I would hate to see the promise you have nurtured there come to an untimely end."

Mallory kept her head high as the comtesse's words stabbed at her. Not only were Mallory's abilities being called into question, but the future of the Abbey as well.

"Thank you, your majesty," she said, struggling to keep her voice from faltering. "I vow, Queen Eleanor, that I will find those who have attacked both yourself and those pledged to serve you."

The only answer she received was, "Thank you, Lady Mallory. I will need you to return after the midday meal to stand by while I tend to some personal matters."

Knowing she was dismissed, Mallory backed away from the chair where the queen sat. She bowed her head when she reached the door. She had to exert all her strength not to whirl and race out of the room before the tears in her eyes threatened to flood along her cheeks. She would not weep. She would not. Crying always had been proof that she was defeated. She was not defeated. She would not be. She *could* not be.

As she strode through the hallways, she did not pause to speak with anyone. It was shortly after dawn, so she had several hours before she needed to return to serve as the queen's personal guard. She was not going to waste a minute.

When Saxon knocked on the door, Ruby opened it and said, "Good morning."

Saxon gave the serving woman his most affable smile, but, as always recently, it had little effect on her. Before, Ruby had not been immune to his charm, giggling like a young girl whenever he teased her. That had changed when she had been given the duty of watching over Mallory. The two women were perfect together, because both took their duties to heart and never would be waylaid by something as simple as a suggestive smile.

"May I speak with Lady Mallory?" he asked.

"She is not here."

"Did she tell you where she was bound?"

Ruby burst into tears.

Astounded, Saxon stepped into the room. He put his arm around Ruby's shoulders and led her to a chair. Seating her, he went to where a bottle of wine was open. He poured a generous serving and brought it back to Ruby.

The serving woman mumbled something that might have been thanks before gulping the wine.

He clasped his hands behind his back as he scanned the room. As he had expected from seeing Ruby's bizarre reaction to a simple question, neither Mallory's bow nor her quiver was in sight. She was off somewhere trying to do as she had promised the queen. He should have persuaded Mallory to vow not to leave the palace unless he went with her.

Kneeling by the serving woman's chair, he folded her left hand between his. He waited until she had finished most of the wine before asking, "What is she determined to do now, Ruby?"

"She was called before the queen and Comtesse Marie this morning. She said little about the short audience, but I suspect the queen was not pleased that the archers who fired at her have not been found."

He nodded. Queen Eleanor had the highest standards for those serving her. That endeared her to some people, but it infuriated others. Many of the irritated people sought to undermine her with rumors and outright lies and repeating old stories—like her supposed affair with her uncle while she was on Crusade—that injured her reputation. In his own opinion, she was much like her husband. Both were assured of their right to rule and rule as they saw fit. Nobody who knew both of them had been surprised that their lives had come to the point of outright rebellion as both sought to have the upper hand. If Eleanor had been born a man, no doubt as Duc d'Aquitaine she would have declared war on the kings of both France and England, rather than marrying them.

"Lady Mallory has been doing her best," he said, guessing that was what Ruby wanted to hear.

He was wrong. The serving woman slammed the cup onto the table and came to her feet so suddenly she almost jerked him to his before he released her hand.

"Her best could get her killed."

He stood slowly. "Get her killed? What do you know, Ruby, that you are not telling me?"

"I promised to say nothing."

"You just said she could get herself killed. Now you tell me you have vowed to say nothing. That promise may lead to her death." He leaned forward to set his hands on the table and did not let Ruby escape his gaze. "You know as well as I do that she will do anything to prove her worthiness to the queen. She will not allow herself to fail. Not while she lives."

Ruby sucked in a fearful gasp and shuddered. "I promised her I would say nothing."

He pushed away from the table and went to the shivering woman. Putting his hands on her shoulders, he said, "I appreciate your dilemma, Ruby, because I do not want to keep Mallory from doing what she believes she must to serve the queen. I know, as well, that like me, you do not want to see her die in order to try to fulfill that vow of service."

The serving woman nodded with reluctance. "I would rather she dismissed me than to know that she died because I kept my mouth closed when I should not have. She mentioned going to the market near where they are building the new church."

"Why?"

"To find him."

"Him? Who?" he asked again.

"Jacques Malcoeur."

Saxon pushed past Ruby and headed for the door at a run. He heard her shout something to him, but he did not pause to heed what it was. He had to stop Mallory before she actually arranged a face-to-face meeting alone with the thief. Malcoeur would be eager to make her pay for humiliating him and his men, and the cost would be very high.

Mallory held the lantern higher as she heard the steady drip of water just beyond the light. Metallic odors mixed with the smell of damp earth. She could see a pool of water ahead of her, so she had no choice but to wade in or to turn around and go back out of the cave. It was one of the many beneath Poitiers. Holes, both large and small, pocked the cliffs on both sides of the river and opened into a vast maze of caverns decorated with white from where limestone had leached through the rock.

The click of a stone on another came from behind her. Turning from the pool, she drew her short sword and prepared to defend herself. Her bow would be useless in the twisting tunnel.

"Mallory?" The sound of her name echoed weirdly through the tunnel, but she recognized the voice.

A light bounced toward her along the wall. She put her sword back in its sheath as she raised the lantern again. "I am here, Saxon."

He appeared around a large rock that half blocked the tunnel. Above it was a hole where the boulder must once have been part of the tunnel's ceiling. Small icicles hung from the hole, but they were made of stone rather than water.

Saxon was wiping dust and cobwebs from his hair, and she guessed he had been in several of the caves that had daunted her when she saw the thick webs covering the openings. She could only stare as he brushed his hands down the front of his pale green tunic and pushed aside straggling dots of dust clinging to his dark green hose. How she wished her own fingers could follow that same path!

Holding up a blazing brand, he asked, "What in the name of Sainte Radegonde are you doing here?"

All her fantasies faded like plants too long denied the sun. "I am seeking—"

"I know whom you are seeking. Jacques Malcoeur and his men." He shook his head, dislodging more dust to drift in a gray powder onto his black cloak that was held at his left shoulder by a silver brooch. "And what did you plan to do if you encountered them beneath the earth?"

"I wanted to find where they hid during the day. Then I intended to come back and get you to help me arrange to talk with them."

He laughed tersely. It was more of a snort than a laugh, and it echoed oddly through the convoluted tunnel. Tossing his cloak back over his right shoulder to keep his arm free, he put his hand on the haft of the dagger he wore at his side. "Just like that?"

"Why not?"

"Because Malcoeur has no reason to talk with you. He would just as soon finish what Mangot started and slice you open." He stepped closer and ran his finger along her throat, drawing his hand back before he could touch the healing incision on her neck.

"But Jacques Malcoeur does have a reason to talk to me." She set her lantern on the rock. "If the men who attacked you and your brother were not his men, then he has competition for the already scanty pickings along the River Clain."

He was slow to respond, and, when he did, there was admiration in his voice. "I must admit that I did not give that possibility any thought."

"But I have not been successful in finding them. I asked several people in the marketplace, and I got no specific information. I thought maybe he and his men were seeking a haven in one of the caves, safe from the queen's guards and from the others who attacked you and Sir Godard." Looking over her shoulder, she added, "If Jacques Malcoeur and his men are hiding beyond the pool, then I shall not find them today."

He edged past her to peer across the pool. She clasped her hands behind her, so she did not reach up and remove the bit of web still sticking to his sun-streaked hair right where it fell over his ear. "I see no way to cross this expanse."

A low roar came from deep within the cave, and air puffed past them. Odors of things long dead and other things that had died recently struck her like a fist. She knew the rushing air must come from another opening in the cliff. Turning her face away, she picked up the lantern. To explore farther no longer appealed to her.

"If there is a way across the pool," she said, "we will not find it today. I want to get out before something else crawls in here and dies."

He held his brand in front of them as she followed him, carrying the lantern. "Do not worry about that, Mallory, unless you are afraid of spiders and bugs. I am sure there are many bats hiding up among the rocks over our heads."

"Spiders and bats do not bother me. I was thinking of something bigger."

"The monster that lived within these caves was killed long ago by Sainte Radegonde." Putting his hand at the back of her waist, he guided her toward the cavern's mouth. "The saint was then at Saint-Croix Abbey, which should be somewhere over our heads, and the people of Poitiers came to seek her help against La Grand'Goule, who was sneaking out at night and feasting on the citizens. Taking a piece of the true cross, Sainte Radegonde confronted the creature that was part dragon and part snake, and it died."

"We could use her help in dealing with our opponents, too," she said, clambering around some rocks that were at a spot where the tunnel diverged into two directions. Taking the left one to lead them back where she had entered, she smiled. "Now I understand the warning I received to be cautious about what might have been born within the caves."

"There are monsters that walk on two legs as well."

"I know," she whispered.

Bringing her to face him, he asked, "Who is it, Mallory? Who is the cause of that pain in your voice?"

She considered giving him a flippant answer. To do so might work with others, but Saxon never was satisfied with less than the truth. He would probe until she spoke it. And, she was surprised to realize, she wanted him to know the truth.

"My father," she said as softly. "He was unhappy that I failed to be the son he wanted. He never allowed me to forget that I had disappointed him from my first breath."

"I am sorry."

She was surprised how much she appreciated that he added nothing more. She did not want his sympathy, just his understanding. And his words showed that he knew exactly what she was feeling. Now it was her turn to be curious why.

Before she could ask anything, he said, "We need to get out of here." He walked toward the tunnel's exit.

"How did you find me?" Mallory asked as she crawled over another large stone near the entrance. "I asked Ruby not to tell you where I had gone."

"I can be very persuasive." He jumped down from the stone and grinned as they stood within the half circle of light that came through the opening in the cliff.

"That is no surprise."

"She is worried about you, Mallory. When I mentioned how much trouble you could find yourself in, she was less reluctant to hold back the truth. Once I learned you had gone to the market, I needed only to discover to whom you had talked and to follow your path from there."

Reaching up, she swatted dust from his hair. "It seems you were sent off course."

He caught her hand and drew her closer. "Mallory, don't be so reckless again."

She tried to yank her arm out of his grip, but he held it tightly. "Release me!" How could he be so understanding one moment and so insufferable the next?

"You are smart enough to know this is not the way to find Malcoeur. There must be dozens of caves under Poitiers. Even if he is in one, he can slip away before you find him. We have to devise a way to persuade him to come to us."

She stopped trying to escape him and faced him. His eyes were shadowed, but his expressive mouth beneath his mustache was lit by both the brand he held and the sunlight reaching into the adit. Silhouettes of the limestone fingers reaching down from the ceiling were lines across his cheeks. She imagined Jacques Malcoeur wearing those shadows as he waited behind bars for his trial before the queen's magistrates.

"What do you have in mind?" she asked.

"A trap."

"With what for bait?"

He grinned. "I considered asking Godard, but my brother avoids any situation where he might get hurt."

"So you are going to be the bait yourself."

"Unless you want to volunteer."

"I will."

"You know I am just jesting," he said quietly.

"And you know I am not."

He jammed the end of his brand into a crevice, then put his arm around her waist, bringing her to him. Releasing her arm, he took her lantern and set it on a shallow shelf. He cupped her chin in his hand as he kissed first her left cheek and then her right. She clasped his face between her hands and steered his mouth to hers, unable to wait any longer to taste the dangerous passions on his lips.

He pressed her back against the rough wall of the cave. She would have sworn that his chest was as hard as the rock behind her. She swept her hands up his back as she gave herself to the potent pleasure building between them. Warning bells clanged in her head, but she ignored them. He might be a faithless man, but right now he was the faithless man who kissed her with wild abandon.

When his hands slipped down to cup her bottom, he pressed his hips into hers, introducing her to his most masculine hardness. She gasped, and his tongue slipped into her mouth to capture every bit of her unsteady breathing.

He whispered her name, or she thought he did. She could not hear much beyond the frantic pounding of her heart and the steady click of small stones falling to the ground.

Stones falling?

She pulled away and shouted, "Saxon! The entrance! It is collapsing!"

His dazed eyes hardened when he glanced toward the light. She did not give him a chance to do more. Grabbing his hand, she pulled him toward the entrance. She threw herself headfirst through the opening. Rocks rained down around them. She winced when one struck her left arm a glancing blow. Pushing Saxon away from the entrance, she looked up to see a man shoving on a larger rock.

She rolled to her feet as she drew an arrow and set it to the bow. It arched up toward the man. He screeched at the same time the boulder came loose and crashed down the cliff.

An arm around her waist hauled her back out of its path as it bounced into the river with a great splash. She shook off Saxon's arm and reached for another arrow.

"No need," Saxon said, his voice laced with fury. "Someone pulled him up on a rope. By the time we get to the top of the cliff, they will be gone."

She was not going to accept defeat. Running to the stones around the edge of the entrance, she hoisted herself up the cliff, getting handholds where she could on the rock face. She heard Saxon swear, but he quickly caught up with her and then passed her as he climbed the wall like a spider on its web. When he reached the flat area where the man had set the rock falling, dirt tumbled down on her. She spit it out and took the hand he held out to her to help her scramble up the last few feet.

"Is there anything you will *not* attempt?" he asked, shaking his left hand, which was covered with bloody scratches.

"I promised—"

"Yes, I know you promised the queen to find the archers, but we could have climbed the path to the monastery and then come back down."

She paid him no mind as she knelt to look at the spot where the rock had been shoved out of its place on the cliff wall. "See the scratches on the other stones? He did not have an easy time bringing down that rock. If we had not halted by the entrance, he would not have had time to push it down and trap us inside."

"You cannot be sure of that. He was letting it go as we emerged. The scree tumbling down proves that." He kicked some of the loose dirt toward the water below.

"Your enemy is growing more desperate, Saxon."

"My enemy? You were within the cave, too."

"But the attack came after *you* entered the cave. If we assume the message on the arrow was for you, then it is clear that this attack was also aimed at you."

"I will not assume that." He kicked more of the dirt. Something glittered beneath his feet.

"What is that?" She edged around him in the narrow space and picked up something that had caught the sunlight. It was a mail gauntlet, well oiled and without any rust. "He must have dropped it."

Taking the glove, he turned it over in his hand to examine it. He blew out a low whistle before saying, "This mail is not Norman, Mallory. It is French."

"French? Could King Louis really be the queen's enemy?"

"I hope not. Even assuming the king has not changed his mind about allying himself with the young king and the queen, someone could be trying to drive a wedge into that uneasy alliance by making it appear as if King Louis is behind the attacks."

"We cannot know that for sure."

"No, we cannot. We cannot know anything for sure now."

She took the gauntlet from him and slipped it into her quiver. "We can know one thing. Those trying to frighten us are getting more desperate. Scaring us was one thing, but now they are trying to kill us. We must be getting closer to the truth."

Chapter 9

Mallory looked around the great hall. It was crowded, but, unlike in her father's castle, men were consigned to the lower seats along the wall while women claimed the spots at the table on the raised dais where the queen sat beside her daughter. Laughter sparkled through the hall, and sweet perfumes suggested they were gathered in some palace in Outremer where an eastern caliph ruled.

The immense room had been added by the queen's direction to the palace, and Queen Eleanor enjoyed spending time in the great hall with the members of her court. A grand window allowed light to spill in and accent the amusing faces carved beneath the arches. Smaller windows were open, and the sounds of masons working on the church beyond the palace walls could be heard under the rumble of conversation.

Shifting on the stone bench along one wall, Mallory wondered how long the discussions could continue. For too many hours during the afternoon, she had been sitting in the great hall. She had arrived with the queen after many had already chosen their places about the room. Most were gathered on the steps leading up toward the hearths beneath the grand window that grew darker as storm clouds gathered, as they had since morning. No one had left as the conversations went in endless circles about whether love could be truly love within marriage or if love could exist only when freely given between unmarried lovers.

She had never been so bored. What a ludicrous way to spend an afternoon! Only a few hours ago, she had been wandering through a cave seeking a criminal and his band of outlaws. She had dared bats and bugs and being buried alive. She had even dared to succumb to Saxon's eager kisses.

Now . . . boredom!

Annoyance at the waste of time and innocuous comments made her tingle like a lightly plucked bowstring. She listened to the debate and realized nobody was changing anyone else's opinions. Didn't these people have anything better to do with their time? They should be preparing for the unthinkable possibility of King Henry the Senior defeating his sons and the French king and turning his wrath on Poitiers. She would much prefer to be training every woman in the room how to defend herself and the queen.

The few she taught had made little progress, but even the most rudimentary skills might be enough to discourage the king's men if they stormed Poitiers. While King Henry the Senior might be willing to burn villages and fields to the north, he was reputed to love Poitiers as much as his queen did, so it was whispered that, even if the worst possible events unfolded and the king reached Poitiers, he would spare it. She hoped that was true, because her students were more likely to pierce one another with arrows than any attackers.

She leaned forward and propped her elbow on her knee. Her visit to the master fletcher yesterday had gained her nothing but an order to return the next day. How long did he require to examine two arrows?

Resting her chin on her hand, she looked around the room as she had every few minutes since her arrival. Nobody seemed interested in harming the queen, but she could not allow herself to become complacent as she fought not to yawn. She wished she could have brought her bow and quiver into the hall, but the queen had insisted on having no weapons

within her Court of Love. Without her bow, Mallory felt oddly
vulnerable.

"May I?" asked a man.

She sat straighter as he pointed at where she sat on the
stone bench running along the wall. He gave her a warm
smile that brightened his blue eyes. They were a startling
contrast to his black hair. His features, almost too perfect,
seemed more suited for a woman than a man, and she wondered why he did not grow a mustache like Saxon's.

"Of course," she said, motioning for him to sit next to her
and Lady Violet on the stone bench. The lady had put as
much distance as she could without being obvious between
herself and Mallory. She saw Lady Violet glance at the man
sitting on the bench. Lady Violet's lips tilted in the slightest
smile, and Mallory wondered what mischief the lady was
planning now.

She put the silly woman out of her head as she added,
"I am—"

"Lady Mallory de Saint-Sebastian." His voice had an accent that revealed that he was from the southern regions of
Aquitaine, where they spoke a language quite different from
the Norman used in Anjou and England. "I doubt there is
anyone in Poitiers who has not heard of you, milady."

"Is that so?"

He smiled, revealing even teeth. "Your courage in saving
our esteemed Queen Eleanor's life has been lauded on every
corner."

"I did only what anyone else would have done."

"That you believe that proves you are as modest as I have
heard." He slanted toward her and said in a conspiratorial
whisper, "I trust your courage will protect me as well."

"Are you in danger . . . ?"

"Landis D'Ambroise," he supplied with another nod of
his head. "I fear I am in the gravest peril, milady. When last
the Court of Love met here, I was too forthcoming in
my opinions, and I daresay I shall be the focus of several

vexed women. I could use a champion of their gender to safe-guard me."

Mallory struggled not to retort. How could anyone be caught up in such silliness when the queen's husband and sons were embroiled in a real war?

She was saved from having to answer when cheers rang up into the high ceiling. Saxon walked to stand near the queen's table. He bowed to her and then to the others as he slid his lute around to where he could play it.

"What tale will you share with us today, Saxon?" asked Queen Eleanor.

"I bring to you today the story of Garwaf, a baron well loved by his people." He gestured toward the steps, and the queen nodded. Sitting, he settled the lute on his lap and began to play while he sang in a rich baritone, "His wife was beautiful and adored him until the day she discovered where he spent half of each week. Because he loved her and trusted her, he told her that he was cursed. Three days each week, he wandered the woods as a werewolf. He had to spend those days hunting like the beast he became." His voice deepened as the lute took on a dire tone. "His lady was dismayed that she shared the bed of a man who spent half of each week as a four-legged beast. She asked if he wore his clothes while a wolf, and he said he did not. He refused to tell her where he hid his clothing while he was a beast, for, if he could not re-dress in his man's clothing, he was doomed to remain a beast."

The lute's notes lightened until they sounded like drops of rain upon lush leaves. "The lady was determined to end her marriage to such a creature, so she begged him to tell her where he hid his clothes. Because he loved her so well, he finally told her that he hid his garments in a chapel near the forest where he roamed as a wolf. He kissed his wife and thanked her for her love."

"But she was not worthy," came a woman's voice from amid the listeners.

Mallory did not see which woman had spoken. That shocked her. She had not realized that she had become so enrapt in Saxon's tale. She must focus on keeping watch. Sitting straighter, she folded her hands on her lap and looked away from where he was drawing the quill across the lute's strings, once more bringing forth a grim melody.

Lady Violet and D'Ambroise were now slanting toward each other, clearly discussing some aspect of Saxon's story. Mallory thought that was rude, but she paid them no further attention as she glanced around the room. Everyone seemed eager to hear the rest of Saxon's tale, and she could put a name to every face in the room. She did not allow that to comfort her, because the one trying to slay the queen could be part of her Court of Love..

"No," Saxon said with a sad smile, "Garwaf's lady was not worthy, for she sent for a knight who lived nearby. He had loved her from afar for many years, even though she was faithful to her husband. When he rushed to respond to her summons, she offered herself and her husband's lands to him if he would sneak into the forest and take her lord's clothing from its hiding place. He eagerly agreed to whatever she wished, for he had been tormented with yearning for her."

She almost gasped aloud when he looked across the room at her. In his eyes, she saw the craving she had tasted on his lips. An answering need gnawed through her. A pulse throbbed deep within her, and she could think only of his fingers lilting across her as the quill did on the strings.

"A man denied his lady's sweetest gift," he went on, his gaze still holding hers, "will do anything to obtain it, even if he knows he is a fool."

"So the knight," intruded a dark-haired woman sitting at the queen's table, "stole the baron's clothing."

Saxon looked at the woman, and Mallory slumped against the wall, as breathless as if she had rowed herself across the Channel slicing through King Henry the Senior's lands. His eyes had too much power over her, spellbinding her with ease. She must be careful and avoid them.

"Yes," he said as he plucked the lute again, "the knight stole the lord's clothing, and poor Garwaf was left to roam the forest as the beast he now was from dawn to dawn. His tenants sought him, but in vain. All believed him dead, save for the knight and the lady he married.

"It went on that way for several years, until one day the king and his favorite companions went on a hunt in that forest. Garwaf knew the king's dogs would tear him into pieces, so he went to where the king sat on his horse and pleaded in a beast's way for his life. He licked the king's foot. The king, amazed by the beast, spared Garwaf's life and took him back to his court, where the wolf was deemed a wonder because of its love for the king. An edict was issued that the wolf should be protected, for the beast was gentle and never did harm to any person."

He put the lute on his knees as he continued his tale. She marveled at the firm timbre of his voice, which commanded each ear in the vast chamber. The power in each word he spoke demanded everyone's attention. She was puzzled anew how such a forceful man could be content to consign himself to a troubadour's role.

Role! He was playing a role. Again she almost gasped aloud. Why hadn't she seen the truth before? She should have when she watched him battling Jacques Malcoeur's men. If not then, for she had not known him well that day, she should have recognized his skill when she saw him fighting beside Sir Godard.

Who was Saxon Fitz-Juste? More important, why was he at the queen's court? He must have some reason why he was playing such a part among her courtiers.

As Saxon went on with his story, telling how the king invited his liege lords to a festive court, including the knight who had taken Garwaf's clothing, Mallory stood. It was easier to slip out of the great hall than she had guessed, because the others were riveted by Saxon's story. The pulse of guilt at neglecting her duty to the queen—even for the short time she would be gone to sort out the many thoughts battering her mind—was pushed aside when she saw both de Matha and Mangot standing near the queen. Also Saxon was close by.

Or was that a bad thing? She could not guess when she had no idea what he was really doing within the palace walls.

Mallory walked into the main courtyard. Unlike within the queen's great chamber, where thick stones kept out summer's warmth, the air here was heated and heavy. A rumble of thunder seemed to follow the river around the city. She looked up. Clouds were black along the western horizon, but overhead the sky was still a pale gray. It might be hours before the storm reached Poitiers.

Habit more than anything else led her to the fletchery. She often had sought a sanctuary within the one at St. Jude's Abbey, and the sisters had learned not to disturb her if the door was not ajar. She hoped Master Ivon meant the same with the partially open door into the fletcher's room on the other side of the courtyard.

The old man nodded as she entered and then bent back over his work. With the soft click of his hammer, he was setting arrowheads over the end of a shaft. She wanted to ask him if he had learned anything from examining the arrows fired at the queen, but she waited for him to acknowledge her.

Going to the stacks of branches waiting to be made into shafts, Mallory sorted through to find the smallest ones. She might not know why Saxon was in Poitiers, but she did know how she wanted to halt the person trying to slay the queen. She was going to spring the unexpected on the murderer.

But the unexpected can work only once, so make sure you save your surprise for when it is most effective. She had often repeated to her students the lesson she learned from Nariko.

Sitting on a stool across from Master Ivon, she drew out her knife and went to work peeling bark off the narrow branches. She shaved the branches thinner, with each stroke recalling another instance when she should have noticed that Saxon had fighting skills that belonged to a trained warrior.

"What are you doing?" Master Ivon asked.

"Some of my shafts were broken during the journey to Poitiers, and I need to replace them," she said, wishing she could be honest with him. Until she discovered who wished the queen dead, she must be careful what she said.

"Have you made other arrows?"

"Yes." She hoped he did not ask her how many, because she had lost count of the number of arrows she had fletched to replace those cracked or lost by her students. "What did you discover about the arrows I brought you?"

"I did not make them."

Mallory struggled to restrain her frustration. Was that all he had discovered in the time he had had the arrows? Not wanting to vex him, because she needed his help, she said quietly, "I guessed that. Do you know who did?"

"Not by name," he said, setting the shaft he was working on back onto the table. He lifted one of the arrows. "This one was made by a master, for it is straight and the fletching well-done." He set it on the table and picked up the other one, the one that was still bent enough that it had not been able to lie flat. "The hands that created this one did not belong to a master, for the feathers are not all from the same bird's wing." He ran his finger along the feathers held on with silk thread. "See? This feather was put in backward in a foolish attempt to make it match the others and to allow someone to believe the arrow would fly true."

"So its intended target may not have been in the direction it flew?"

His tired eyes drilled into her as he handed her the arrows. "You need not mince words, milady. *I* know how you rescued the queen. Was she the actual target? Quite possibly, but you are missing an obvious reason for the feather to be put in as it was."

She set the arrows back on the table. "It was intentionally

made not to fly in a straight path. Was it made solely to frighten the queen?"

"Quite possibly," he repeated.

"Allowing the archers a chance to flee or blend in with the others on the field without anyone taking note because we were concentrating on making sure the queen was unhurt."

"Quite possibly."

"I don't understand how two archers could have gotten so close to the queen without any of us noticing."

"There may be many ways it could have been possible, but the only way to know for sure is to ask whoever set these arrows to string." He turned back to the arrow he was making.

Mallory stared at the white-feathered arrows in front of her. The invisible killers were far wilier than she had guessed. They had created panic with nothing more than faulty arrows. Sighing, she tossed the bent arrow on the table and went to work on the thinner arrows. She wanted to get at least a half dozen completed.

Master Ivon rose, came around the table, and peered over her shoulder. "Those are flimsy shafts, milady."

"They will serve my purpose."

He frowned. "I thought you were here to guard the queen. Those would do no more than prick a man through his sleeve. If he were wearing mail—"

She spun on the stool to face him. "What do you know about men wearing mail?"

"What do you mean? Warriors wear mail when they go onto the field for battle, both real and in a tournament. What else is there to know?"

"Not much," she said, silently chiding herself for pouncing on a simple comment. Master Ivon had made an observation, nothing more.

She was overreacting, as she had when she fired the arrow into the French king's messenger's sleeve. She would be worthless to the queen if she continued to act without thinking. Yet, there were times when she must. If she had paused to give thought to her actions when the arrows were fired by the river, Queen Eleanor might be dead.

"I am trying to learn more about everyone in the palace," she said, relieved to speak the truth.

"A silly lot for the most part." He sat and cleared his throat in disgust. "All they want to do is talk about love. Not real love, mind you, but what they call . . . um . . ."

"Courtly love."

"That is it. There is something unnatural about men letting women tell *them* what love should be. 'Tis even worse when they tell one another stories about men who love women from a distance and never do anything about it."

She held up the branch she was working on and gauged its width. It was still too thick. "Such stories do sound far-fetched."

"Not as far-fetched as those fools believing that such a love is better than holding a woman in your arms. Talking about love!" He spat on the floor. "It is like living in a palace filled with eunuchs. Hardly a real man among them. Ordinarily, I would warn a lovely lady like yourself to be careful around so many young men, but the only part of yourself that you need to worry about being assaulted is your ears, with their stories and songs and silly poems."

Mallory laughed. "So I have seen, but the ladies seem to like the attention."

"And why not? It is not often that women rule men. It is not natural." Again he spat as if warding off a curse. "I am glad they stay away from here."

"Not all of them do."

He regarded her with abrupt suspicion. "What do you mean? Have you seen someone sneaking in here?"

"No, but you told me that you were saving some pieces of wood for Saxon."

Master Ivon grumbled something under his breath. She understood only the word *lute*. She waited for him to say something else, but he remained silent while she worked. Even when she rose to leave, he said nothing.

She paused in the doorway. "Master Ivon, you said there could be many ways two archers would be able to skulk close to us, even though we did not see them. What did you mean?"

"I meant you should not assume the number of arrows fired matches the number of archers."

"Are you suggesting there was only one, and the arrows were fired simultaneously?"

"I am suggesting anything is possible."

Mallory stared at him as he went back to work, then stepped forward to pick up the two arrows she had brought him. He glanced at her as she tore the hanging fabric on her left sleeve and slipped the arrows within as Lady Elita had, but said nothing more. She went out into the courtyard. The sunshine had grown thinner, and the clouds had risen through the sky. Thunder thudded along the river as she went into the keep.

Could someone fire two arrows from one string at the same time? A single person could have slipped among the trees by the river unseen. Two might have caught their attention. One person firing two arrows at the same time? The two arrows *had* been on a closely parallel track until the bent one flew off in another direction. Was it truly possible? She and Saxon had agreed it was not, but she was no longer certain. She had to find out the truth.

As she hurried past the great hall, she saw the raised table was empty. The queen must have returned to her private rooms. Whirling toward the closest stairs, Mallory bumped into a hard form.

"Pardon me," she said, putting her hands behind her before the arrows were noticed. She frowned when she saw Saxon's easy smile. By St. Jude, she had not expected to find him loitering in the hall once his audience had dispersed.

"I was wondering when I might run into you, Mallory, but it appears you ran into me first." He put his hand on his chest, even as he shifted to see why she clasped her hands in back of her. "I was heartbroken when you did not stay to listen to my whole story. Had you heard the tale before?"

"No." She did not move, because that might reveal the truth. "If you will excuse me, I should go to the queen."

"She is well guarded right now, because she is doing some correspondence. Mangot would not allow even you to pass. He takes his obligations very seriously."

"As do I."

"But you vanished from the hall while the queen was enthralled by my *lai*."

"Your what?"

"A poem that tells a story. Jongleurs of the queen's court vie with one another to discover who can create the most amazing tale." His smile grew more taut. "But you left in the middle of my *lai*. Why?"

She had to tell him something, so she decided on the truth. "I left because I needed some fresh air. There is a lot I need to consider, and I found it difficult to think when the air was so stale."

"The scents were heavy in the hall today, even though the windows were thrown open. Accustomed as you were to thick incense in the chapel, I am surprised you find the air within not to your taste." He put one foot on the stone bench by the door and rested his elbow on it. "Or could there have been something or someone else? I saw D'Ambroise was honoring you with his attentions."

"Jealous?" She regretted the question as soon as it slipped past her lips.

"Of D'Ambroise?" He laughed. "If you had enjoyed his company, you would not have skulked out of the room before he had the opportunity to show you his renowned skill with women."

"He seems to think the women are furious with him."

Saxon laughed again, his eyes crinkling. "He tends to elicit high passions in women, sometimes to his detriment, because he believes a man should do more than admire a woman. He believes in consummated love, not courtly love, as so many others vow they do."

"As you vow you do?"

"As *you* vow you do?"

She frowned. "I asked you first, so you owe me the courtesy of an answer before I give you mine."

"Then I shall do you such a courtesy, milady." He put his foot back on the floor and took her hand. Bowing over it with the same smile she had seen when he began his story, he said, "It is said that there are rules of love, and one is that a man afflicted with too much passion seldom is in love. He simply wants what is denied him."

She drew her hand away. "I agree."

"You do?" Honest astonishment wiped away his practiced expression.

"Yes." She was not going to explain how she had learned to what lengths a man would go in order to obtain what he thought was his heart's desire, only to toss it—or his wife and daughter—aside to seek someone else. "That is why I do not understand how you can go on and on about unimportant matters."

"The topic is of love. Surely you don't consider love unimportant."

"I consider it a bothersome necessity, just as you are now when I have something I must do." She started to walk past him, then paused as she recalled that the queen had trusted him enough to make him one of her guards. She could not let her own disquiet whenever he was around endanger the queen. Hoping she was not doing the wrong thing, she said, "Come with me."

"Where? I am supposed to be meeting Godard here."

"This will take but a few minutes."

"What will take but a few minutes?"

"Don't ask questions where others may hear my answer."

He regarded her in silence for a long moment, then nodded. She went to get her bow and quiver. When she returned, he said nothing. That unsettled her, for he usually had a quick quip for everything she said. She could not keep from wondering what his silence meant. She hoped it was not more trouble.

Chapter 10

Thunder was still complaining to the west, but what Mallory had to do would not take long. She walked into the empty courtyard, glad the storm had chased the others inside. She had taken the two arrows out of her sleeve and put them in her quiver. As she wrapped the long fabric hanging from her sleeves around her wrists and strung her bow, Saxon remained quiet. His peculiar silence unsettled her more than the thunder erupting ever closer.

"Watch," she said.

He nodded.

Setting her quiver on the ground, she drew out one of her arrows and aimed at a pile of hay near the far end of the court-yard, more than fifty yards away. When she released the arrow, it flew straight into the hay. The sound of the impact told her it had hit as she wished.

"Now watch this." She carefully lifted out the two white-fletched arrows.

Setting them to her string and resisting the temptation to straighten the bent arrow, she held them between the fingers of her right hand. She had to shift her grip several times to get the arrows balanced. Once she had, she released the string. She heard Saxon's sharp intake of breath when both arrows flew. The straight one arced true and struck the hay right where she had aimed. The other wobbled and careened to the ground several feet to the right.

As she put one end of her bow against her instep and unstrung it, he whistled under his breath. "I would not have believed it was possible to shoot two arrows at once if I had not just witnessed this with my own two eyes."

"I guess I was wrong when I said I could not do it."

"I guess you were." He rubbed his chin. "But it is possible, as you have proven."

"Yes, and I believe a single archer fired at the queen. Two arrows were fired to make us think that there were two archers. One of those arrows, however, was misfletched, so it fell far short of its target, while the other went wide because the archer could not aim well."

"One arrow struck the hay when you fired it."

"I may be a better archer than he is." She smiled coldly. "Also I was not anxious that someone might see me taking aim on the queen. Even the smallest tremble can send an arrow in an unintended direction."

"I never guessed anyone could fire two arrows at once."

She picked up her quiver and shrugged it onto her shoulder. "Do you have much familiarity with a bow?"

"Why would a troubadour need a bow?" He gave her a self-deprecatory smile.

"Why would a troubadour need a fighting dagger?" she retorted.

"Not everyone likes my music." He wrapped a length of her hair around his finger. "You walked out on my story. Don't you want to know how it ends?"

"I am more concerned about keeping the queen alive." She loosened her hair from his finger. Crossing the courtyard, she dug into the prickly hay and pulled the arrows out. She put them in her quiver and turned to collect the other. She was not surprised Saxon had picked it up.

He handed her the arrow when she walked to where he stood. "A very interesting demonstration, but one that gives us little help in finding the person who fired at the queen."

Now it was her turn to nod mutely. Satisfying her curiosity

about the possibility of a single archer had been exciting, but Saxon was right. Nothing in discovering how the arrows had been fired offered a clue to the person who had set them to bowstring.

"May I try it?" he asked.

"I need to ask you again. How familiar are you with a bow?"

"I know I am capable of firing a single arrow, but I doubt I could fire two arrows and strike any target, no matter how large." He gave her a roguish wink. "And you will be here to make sure I take the proper stance and do not end up shooting through an open window by mistake."

"I doubt you do anything by mistake, Saxon." She gave him no chance to answer as she went through the fitful wind to where she had been standing when she fired the arrows. Turning to look at the haystack, she pretended not to see the astonishment on Saxon's face. She strung her bow and held it out to him. "It is not tuned to you."

"I could adjust the string—"

"Please don't, because then I will have to adjust it back. You are not much taller than I am, so the bowstring should not be troublesome for a single shot."

"And if I wish to try two arrows at once?"

"Don't be silly. I was only showing you that it could be done. Other than causing us to think there was more than one archer, I cannot guess why anyone would want to fire multiple arrows. The flight of one arrow would throw off the motion of the other, and neither would reach its target."

"As neither did when someone fired at the queen."

"If the aim for those arrows was creating fear, the archer succeeded brilliantly."

Saxon took the bow and plucked the string as if it were one on his lute.

"Don't do that!" She gasped.

"I wanted to hear how it sounded," he replied. "Sounds tell me much about the things around me." He put his hand on her shoulder, his fingers curving around it in a questing caress.

"Such as the sound of how your breathing quickens when I touch you."

"If you want to fire the bow before the storm reaches us, you need to do so now."

"Ah," he said with a broadening smile, "and there is the reproving sound you get in your voice whenever you want to avoid speaking the truth about how you feel."

"The truth is that I do not want to be seared by the lightning." She glanced over the wall as the sky lit with brilliant flares half-hidden by the low clouds. "Fire the arrow!"

He raised the bow, and she rushed forward to put her hand on his arm to shift him into the proper alignment with the pile of hay. He gave her another grin as she lowered his hand holding the bowstring so he did not fire over the wall.

"Draw the string back at least as far as your chin," she said, "then release it smoothly."

"Like this?" He looked at her as the arrow flew across the courtyard and struck the ground close to the tree. "How did I do, Master Archer Mallory? Or is it Mistress Archer Mallory?"

Trying not to roll her eyes, she took the bow. "I have seen worse."

"And better, I assume."

Before she could answer, lightning flashed, followed almost instantly by thunder. When Saxon grabbed her hand and pulled her to the closest door, Mallory did not hesitate. She ran as a bolt of lighting struck one tower, smashing one of the carvings and sending stone dropping to the ground. The crash following it threatened to burst her ears as rain fell in a thousand different blows to her head and arms.

Then she was inside. The rain chased after her, but vanished into darkness as a door slammed shut. She heard footfalls and then the ebony eased to gray as Saxon opened an inner door to a room against the outer wall. Its arrow slit allowed in the dim light sifting through the storm clouds. More thunder pounded the palace, but was muffled by the thick stone walls.

Water pelted her, striking her face, and she saw Saxon shaking rain from his hair like a dog.

"Stop it!" she ordered as she loosened the long strips of fabric hooked to her sleeves. With the left one, she wiped the water from her cheeks and eyes.

"I prefer not to have water drip on me for the next hour." He sat on a small bench beside an unlit hearth.

"That is fine, but don't splash me. I am too wet already."

"You are, aren't you?" That smile that always lured her closer tilted his lips. Folding his arms over his chest, he gave her a slow perusal from top to bottom and then back up again. "But on you it is a pleasing sight."

Mallory turned away before he could see how her face must be flushing with his candid admiration. She unstrung her bow and leaned it against the wall by the door to the courtyard. Slipping off her quiver, she sat and set it next to her on the stone floor. She leaned back against the wall, but not even the stones could cool the flame within her that had burst into life with his bold words.

"I am sorry if my appreciation of your loveliness makes you ill at ease," he said.

"It is nothing."

"Would you be more comfortable if I spoke of my respect for your skills as an archer?"

She knew she should not, but she looked at him. He was leaning forward from where he sat, his fingers locked together between his knees. The space was so cramped that she could have reached out, even from where she sat, and cupped his cheek. Her fingertips quivered with the yearning to do so, and she could not help wondering if he had laced his together to keep from touching her.

"Thank you," she said. "And you truly are a good troubadour, Saxon. Everyone in the hall was enjoying your story."

"Even you?"

"Yes."

"But you left in the middle of my *lai*."

"I wanted to speak to the master fletcher about the arrows fired at the queen. I thought that while the others were occupied was a good time, for I would not be missed."

"And?"

She smiled coolly. "And I wanted to consider why you are pretending to be a troubadour, Saxon."

"I am not pretending." His expression did not change. "I am a troubadour."

"And?" she asked as he had.

"I serve the queen as one of her guards."

Mallory shook her head and grimaced as water splattered her again. "But why would Queen Eleanor ask a troubadour to serve as one of her guards?"

"As a poet, I am accustomed to observing those around me, looking for foibles that will fit into my stories. At the same time, at her request, I have watched her court to determine if anyone is acting contrary to his or her nature. That might be the very clue to pinpoint someone who is ready to betray the queen. As you have seen, Queen Eleanor has many ideas that do not fit customary assumptions."

"Such as?"

"She founded St. Jude's Abbey and arranged for its sisters to be taught a knight's skills."

She sagged against the wall and nodded. She could not argue with that fact. "If my mind had not been blunted by the conversation in the great hall, I would not have overlooked that."

"You may be the sole person in Poitiers who believes that love is boring."

"I did not say that I found love boring. I said I found the conversation boring."

"True. You said love was . . ." He tapped his chin. "What did you call it? A bothersome necessity, I believe."

"What would you call it?"

"Glorious and soul-thrilling."

She laughed coolly. "As I would expect you to say, for you

delight the ladies and their companions with your tales of brave knights who are willing to give everything, save their honor, for a smile from their lady love."

"Sometimes, a smile is all a knight can aspire to possess."

"That is silly."

"Is it? I am a second son. Like all younger sons, I am denied marriage unless I can find a wealthy widow or win enough honor to gain the hand of a daughter with a generous dowry."

"But if a younger son were to marry, he might have a son who would wrongly challenge the claim of the rightful heir."

"Such challenges do not seem limited to the sons of younger sons, do they? They seem to afflict many families, common and royal."

She frowned. "You sound like the king's man."

"I am."

"King Henry the Senior, I mean."

"I know what you mean, and you know I have the queen's best interests at heart." He frowned. "You do, don't you?"

"Yes," she said as the queen's voice echoed in her mind. *Unless he is playing his lute or sharing a poem, you can be certain that he is being honest.*

"I am glad to hear that." He stood and turned to look out the arrow slit as more lightning laced its sharp thread through the sky. "It appears we shall be stuck here for a while." He lifted his lute off his back. "Shall I finish the tale for you?"

"I would like that," she said, realizing that she really would. Before disquiet had sent her from the hall, she had been enjoying the story of Garwaf, the werewolf baron. "Did the poor lord ever return to his human form?"

He knelt beside her and held out the lute. "Why don't you tell me what you think happened?"

"It is your story." She drew back from the lute. "I have no idea how to play that."

"It is simple." He took her left hand and folded down all but one finger. Letting the curved neck of the lute rest atop his shoulder, he ran her finger lightly along the strings. "You need only to learn to seek the music within it."

"Saxon—"

"Let me show you how to bring forth the music that comes from deep inside you."

At the raw emotion in his voice, she raised her gaze from the lute to his face. Her breath caught atop her fiercely beating heart when she saw the candid hunger in his eyes. As her fingers slid back up the strings and onto his shoulder, he drew the lute from between them. She did not see where he put it as his mouth slanted across hers.

With a moan, she returned his kiss with the craving that had been building, like the summer storm, in her. As he leaned her back onto the floor, her arms around his shoulders kept him close. She stroked down his back, savoring the reaction of every strong muscle beneath her fingertips. Running her tongue along his lips, she let it slip between them when he gasped for a breath. She delighted in the flavor of wine in his mouth and how she was giving him the pleasure he had offered her.

His hand glided upward from her waist to cup her breast, and she gave a soft sound that she had never heard from her throat before. Nor had she ever felt anything akin to the sensation billowing outward from where his finger toyed with the very tip of her breast. The heat coursed through her, curling her toes and flowing into her most intimate center.

He rolled over, bringing her to lie on top of him. He hooked a single finger in the laces holding the front of her gown closed. Slowly, as his gaze held hers, he loosened them. As the fabric gaped, he shoved it to one side to release her breasts into his cupped hands.

"Beautiful," he whispered.

She would have answered, but she seemed to have forgotten how to draw in another breath. Even so, when he raised his head to sear her bare skin with his heated mouth, she cried out in astonishment. No song, no poem, no whispers had ever hinted that a man's touch could be so wondrous, stripping her of every rational thought save that she wanted more. More of his kisses, more of his touch, more of her against him.

Bending forward, she slid her tongue along his ear. His eager panting burnished her breast with sweet fire, and the rough fabric of his tunic teased her to tear it aside so she could feel his naked chest. As his hands pressed her hips to his, she found his mouth and put all her longing into the kiss.

Then he pushed her off him.

Mallory hit the floor with a thump. "What is—?"

He put his finger to her lips even as his other hand was fumbling to draw her gown back into place. She shoved him away and bent to lace up her bodice.

"Will you explain?" she asked.

"Be quiet, Mallory."

"I—"

"Silence!" he hissed with a scowl that contradicted the desire that had been in his eyes only moments before. "Listen."

She did, and she heard what he must have while she was consumed by the rapture of his touch. Someone was calling his name from beyond the courtyard door.

It crashed open, almost striking her as she jumped to her feet. She pulled her dagger and balanced lightly, trying to focus her thoughts on attack instead of on how grateful she was that Saxon was fighting by her side.

She lowered her knife when she realized he had not drawn his. She understood why when she saw Sir Godard pushing into the small room.

The drenched man glanced at her, his lip curling in contempt, before turning to Saxon. "You were supposed to meet me a half hour ago. How long does it take to tumble your harlot?"

Mallory put her hand on Saxon's arm as she saw his fingers curl into a fist. "Don't strike him," she said softly.

"He insulted you."

"Yes, but he is your brother."

"And you are . . ." He looked amazed, and she guessed

that—for once—he could not find the word he wanted. She and Saxon were definitely not friends. So easily they could become lovers, but had Sir Godard's intrusion been a sign that doing so would be foolish?

She did not need any sign to know that. She had seen how uncontrolled passion brought pain as well as pleasure. Her father had not cared how many lives he tarnished with his lusts.

Taking her bow and quiver, she rushed out of the room. She hated fleeing like a frightened child, but the memories had turned her once more into the terrified little girl who never knew when angry words in her father's castle would explode into thrown furniture and shattered crockery.

The rain coursed down over her, soaking her before she had gone many steps. She paused in the middle of the courtyard and let the storm rage around her. The lightning would fade. The thunder would vanish back into the clouds. The rain would go away.

The painful memories never would.

"Mallory?"

At Saxon's voice, she turned to face him. He was as wet as she was, his clothes lathered to him, outlining each honed sinew in his arms and the muscles across his chest. More than ever, he did not look like a troubadour, but, more than ever, she wanted to forget her duties to the queen and St. Jude's Abbey as she sampled each delight they could discover together.

More than ever, she knew she would be a fool to surrender to her longings.

"Your brother needs to talk with you," she said in barely a whisper. She backed away one step, then another. If he touched her, she doubted she could resist.

"Mallory . . ."

"I need to be by the queen's side." She took another step away with each word. "I have been gone for too long."

"Mallory . . ." He closed his mouth and went to where Sir Godard was watching from the doorway.

Saxon looked back as he put his hand on the door to close it.

She met his gaze evenly as the rain flooded down over her. When he shut the door, she walked away in the opposite direction, telling herself she should be happy that both of them had come to their senses.

Maybe she should be happy, but she was as miserable as she had been in her father's castle. As miserable as she had vowed she never would be again.

Chapter 11

Saxon listened to Godard's complaints as they walked along one of Poitiers's narrow streets. His brother hated being at the queen's palace, and he wanted to put an end to his visit. Just as vehemently he wanted Saxon to leave Poitiers with him.

Stepping over a puddle in front of the small church of Saint-Jean several streets from the palace, Saxon said nothing. He was not going to persuade Godard to heed him. Godard Fitz-Juste acted as if Saxon were his page to be ordered about. And why shouldn't he? Their father had ignored his many offspring, save for his heir. Godard could do no wrong, and the rest of them could do nothing right to gain their father's attention.

But he could not fault Godard for their father's actions, just as Mallory must relinquish her rage with her father for dismissing her as a disappointment. If de Saint-Sebastian knew what his daughter was doing now . . . No, that did not matter. It was time for both of them to focus on the reasons they were in Poitiers.

He let Godard rant while they walked past the building that was almost as old as the stone walls built by the Roman invaders a millennium ago. "You are ignoring the truth," his brother said. "You have lost your concentration on your task. *She* has bewitched you."

"*She* has done no such thing," he replied, wondering how many times he was going to have to repeat himself before

Godard listened to him. "*She* is simply a complication I did not expect."

"You should have."

"How could I expect to find a woman with her skills in Poitiers?"

Godard sniffed with a derisive laugh. "You have heard the stories of her subterfuge and feminine wiles."

"How could I have heard such a story? I had no idea she—or her abbey—existed until a month ago."

"Abbey?" Godard turned to face him. "Is she thinking of retiring to an abbey?"

Saxon forced his face to remain calm. He could not let Godard suspect that he had revealed something he had pledged to keep secret. What was wrong with him? He knew how to hold his tongue. That was why he had been chosen to come to Poitiers.

"When she is finished here, I assume she will return to a cloistered life," he said with care. He must be cautious not to divulge more about St. Jude's Abbey.

"Return? When was she cloistered before?" Godard laughed sharply. "During the few weeks between her divorce from Louis and her marriage to Henry?"

"I misconstrued your words," Saxon said, startled to realize Godard had been talking about the queen. "I thought we were speaking of another woman."

"Your harlot?"

His hand settled on his knife. "Her name is *Lady* Mallory de Saint-Sebastian."

"Are you going to slay me for slighting your *lady*?"

"Don't be absurd." Saxon lifted his hand away from the knife and smiled coolly. "Forget Lady Mallory."

"Advice you should take for yourself. That woman is eager to twist you to do her bidding."

"Let me worry about that."

"And shall I worry about how the queen has bewitched you? I have seen you sitting at her feet like a favored pet. She is evil, inciting rebellion in the hearts of sons who have pledged their loyalty first to their father."

Saxon paused as a herd of cows appeared from down the hill. Two boys drove the mooing beasts toward a corner leading to the street where the butchers worked.

Turning back to Godard, he said, "Don't mistake my efforts to do as I vowed for being under a spell. I have not failed in my pledge of service, and I shall not."

"Then you need to get rid of your *Lady* Mallory."

"Why?" He paid no attention to Godard's insulting tone, too shocked by his words. Nothing had unfolded as it should have since Godard's arrival in Poitiers with the news of their foster brother's death.

Bruno's death haunted Saxon. If he had tried harder to persuade Bruno to come with him to Poitiers instead of seeking glory on the battlefield, his foster brother might still be alive. He could have used his help with Godard, who seemed so exasperated to have been rescued by a woman that he refused to think of her as anything but a harlot who dared to enter a world that should belong solely to men. Godard had received commiseration for his tarnished honor from the men in the queen's inner circle, who saw Mallory's skills and her lessons with the women as an affront to their manhood. One woman who was proficient with a bow was an entertaining oddity; having more women learn to handle weapons could upset the carefully contrived world of the Court of Love, where women should be adored and men had the honor of fighting all the battles.

Maybe if Mallory would act more like the other ladies, the undercurrent of alarm might disappear. He tried to imagine her sitting and listening to a man brag about deeds not yet done and rewarding that man with a glorious smile.

Impossible!

Her words were as pointed as the arrows she fired with skill, and her purple eyes snapped with sparks that could scald a man. How could he have imagined a sister who stood with a skilled archer's stance dressed in a simple linen garment that, reaching barely past her knees, revealed her shapely legs? It had been weeks since that night, but he remembered every detail of her during his visit to St. Jude's Abbey.

St. Jude's Abbey! Another story he would not have believed, save that he had seen the truth with his own eyes. What woman other than Queen Eleanor, who had ridden to the Holy Land on Crusade with her first husband before divorcing him to bind her destiny with the then-young Henry Plantagenet, would ever be bold enough to establish an abbey where young women were taught a knight's skills?

"Lady Mallory can interfere with our plans," Godard growled, breaking into his thoughts.

"She is readily distracted." He hated speaking the derogatory words, but he must find a way to change the subject. He had learned that agreeing with his brother often was the best way.

"So I have seen." Godard walked back toward the small church as more cattle came up the street. "But she could prevent you from doing what you came here to do."

"How?"

"You may believe her readily distracted, but she is also readily distracting. Too frequently you are watching her when you should be alert to other matters."

Saxon smiled icily. "Let me worry about Lady Mallory. You may be surprised how she may yet prove to be an able assistant to help us achieve our goals."

"But she is the queen's lady!"

"And because of that she is privy to many conversations we would not be able to listen to. As well, she would do anything to protect Queen Eleanor." Saxon's smile became sly as he lowered his voice to a conspiratorial whisper. "That is the key to obtaining her help, whether she wishes to offer it or not."

That answer seemed to satisfy Godard. He nodded, then said, "I wish you to be the first to know that I am being wed."

"Wed?" Saxon stared at his brother in amazement. Was

making such an announcement the reason his brother had come to Poitiers? "To whom?"

"Lady Violet, whose mother is cousin to Lord Bigod of East Anglia. The match was approved by her father and ours before I came to Poitiers. I will remain long enough to marry her before I return to my duties."

"Bigod?" Saxon arched an eyebrow, amazed as much at the family connection as he was that he had not heard about the impending nuptials. His attention had not been focused on anything but his work . . . and Mallory. She *was* too distracting. "Very impressive match, Godard. However, the earl has risen against King Henry the Senior. If you ally yourself with Lady Violet, you may lose Henry's favor."

"Henry knows our family's allegiance is unwavering, and he is pleased to have one of the ever-vacillating Bigods brought into our circle. With my influence, perhaps they will recall their sword-sworn oaths of fealty instead of switching sides whenever they deem it worthwhile." Slapping Saxon on the back, he said, "You will attend the wedding, won't you?"

"I would not miss it."

Godard bade Saxon a good day before leaving to watch the workmen raising the walls of the new church on the other side of the palace. As soon as his brother was out of view, Saxon strode across the street and into the church of Saint-Jean. He needed to be alone with his thoughts, and the little church was usually empty now, as the Poitevins went to the grander churches.

Acrid odors of paint assaulted his nose as he came down the few steps toward the baptism pool in the center of the small rotunda, and he looked up to see a man standing on a ladder and painting fresh frescoes on the recently plastered walls. Had the queen taken interest in the ancient church? Or was another rich patron eager to keep the tiny church from being overlooked as the grand new one was being raised?

Saxon considered leaving, but the painter was so absorbed by his work that he had not even looked up when Saxon entered. Sitting on one of the steps, Saxon watched the man dip his brush into a puddle of bright red on a board and run it along the wall. The man was whistling as he painted what were clearly the draped robes of a saint in conversation with another figure outlined to its right.

Saxon sighed. How he envied the painter his delight in his work that was for the benefit of everyone who entered Saint-Jean's! He leaned his forehead on his palms and set his elbows on his knees. He had had such enthusiasm when he first came to Poitiers to serve as King Henry the Senior's eyes and ears in the king's estranged wife's palace. Now he hated the subterfuge that consumed his life. He despised the lies and the half-truths and how he must hurt those who had come to trust him.

It had been easy. During his first months in Poitiers, he had had no trouble persuading everyone he was a troubadour who had sought out the Court of Love in order to practice his skills in every aspect of love. Even Queen Eleanor had believed his tale of being a discontented younger son who saw no future while he lived beneath King Henry the Senior's rule. She had welcomed him, enjoying his songs and poems, and even asking him to be part of her inner household that was separate from the rest of the court.

Then Mallory de Saint-Sebastian came to Poitiers. With her archer's clear eyes, she had seen aspects of him that nobody else had, and she began to question his place in the palace. He had deflected her questions—so far—by bringing her into his arms. Now all he could think of was bringing her into his bed.

He heard the painter snarl a curse that was out of place in the church. The painter was dabbing with his shirt at the wall where the red had streamed down in a bloody trail as if the saint were wounded.

Saxon stood and climbed the steps. He walked out the door, closing it behind him. Godard was right about one thing: Mallory *was* distracting him from his task. He needed to focus on what he must finish in Poitiers. The simplest way to do so was to remind her that the unseen archer who could have slain the queen still had not been captured. While she was busy chasing flimsy clues, he would gather the information King Henry the Senior was waiting for and send Godard back to the king. With luck, they both would succeed in what they had come to Poitiers to do.

Ruby had retired to the small chamber that opened off Mallory's. The room Mallory now used was even more magnificent than the first she had been given when she came to the palace. Cloth of gold draped the windows and served as curtains for the bed. A pair of tapestries of hunting scenes that hung on the wall would keep out the cold when winter arrived. The furniture— the bed, a chest, and two chairs set on either side of a small table—were intricately carved with birds and flowers. She had never been in such an elegant room, but in the past fortnight, she had grown accustomed to the grandeur.

She paid none of it any attention as she worked at the small table. The pieces of wood she had gotten from Master Ivon, but she had come to her room, where his knowledgeable eyes would not take note of what she was doing. The thin shafts of the arrows she had made in the master fletcher's room were piled on the table, but she was focused on gluing together the corners of a box. The noxious odor of the glue made in the still-room made her cough, but she kept working.

"What are you making?"

Startled by Saxon's question, Mallory dropped her brush on the table. "What are you doing here?"

"I was sharing a new poem with the queen."

"But that does not give you the right to burst into my room."

"I did not burst in. I knocked, and Ruby let me in." He glanced toward the door.

A shadow could have been the maid who was trying to avoid Mallory's dismay while still keeping a close eye on Saxon as long as he was in the room.

With a sigh, Mallory picked up the brush and put it back in

the bottle of glue. She set the pieces of wood aside as he asked again what she was making.

"I am only at the beginning of my project," she answered, "so let me discover if I can get it underway before I answer all your questions."

"*All* my questions?"

"All that I can answer."

He smiled. "That is more like the cautious Mallory de Saint-Sebastian I know." He bent to peer at the pieces of wood that were stacked neatly in the moonlight. "You seem to have the very good beginnings of a box."

"Then I have been successful so far."

"Is it a gift for someone? A wedding gift?"

"Wedding? Whose?"

"My brother informed me today that he is marrying Lady Violet."

Mallory bit back her laugh, but could not keep from saying, "We know who will be in charge in that household."

"Godard is eager to ally himself with a family as wealthy as the Bigods."

"And as controversial."

Saxon leaned a hip on the table and folded his arms in front of him. "My brother seems to think he will provide a positive influence on the family."

"The best of luck to him, but I am not sure how good his chances are."

A soft thump made Mallory smile as she looked toward the window where Chance was curled up on a blanket. The dog seldom slept when there was anyone in addition to Mallory in the room. Chance was clearly determined to protect her.

"Go to sleep, Chance," she called softly. As the dog lowered her head, she added, "I think that is good advice for us as well. It must be close to the middle of the night."

Saxon smiled. "Mallory, are you trying to get rid of me?"

"I told you I would not answer questions now." She stood and stretched as she pretended to yawn. Recalling that she wore nothing but a thin sleeping robe, she crossed her arms in front of her and asked, "What do you want?"

He gave her a lopsided grin. "I thought I had made that obvious during the thunderstorm." He came around the table in one smooth motion and drew her into his arms.

His lips, warm and eager, teased her to forget everything but the ecstasy they could share together. Her hands rose to curve around his shoulders as she sighed with eager delight into the inviting chamber of his mouth. When he brushed her throat with rapture, she moaned, the sound echoing in the depths of her body. As she swayed with the yearning flowing through her, his lips returned to burn so deeply into hers that she wondered if they would be blistered.

When his mouth slipped along her neck as he reached for the laces holding the back of her shift closed, she pressed to him. She did not want to think. She wanted only to feel—to feel him against her and to feel herself against him.

But she stepped back as she had so many times before. She saw shock and exasperation on his face.

"Good night, Saxon," she said quietly.

"It could be the very best night if you don't send me away."

"Good night," she repeated more firmly.

"Are you going to make me beg?" His smile grew warmer. "I am not very good at it, so do not ask that of me, sweetheart."

She recoiled as if he had struck her. "Don't call me that. Don't ever call me that!"

"Mallory—"

"Don't ever call me that!" She knew she sounded hysterical, but she could not halt the words pouring out of her mouth. "I don't want to hear your lies and the promises you have no intention of keeping just so you can get what you want from me before you go off to the next woman on your list."

"List?" Puzzlement furrowed his brow, but she could not guess if he was being sincere or just continuing to play the game men enjoyed at the expense of women who were stupid enough to listen to their pretty words.

She waved toward the door. "Get out! Get out and don't come back. Don't ever come back! I don't want to hear your lies and fake pledges."

"Mallory—"

She turned her back on him, unable to endure seeing the disappointment on his face when her own body was urging her to forget everything and enjoy what awaited her when she invited him into her bed.

He put his hands on her shoulders. She shrugged them off, but he set them there again. "I am not lying to you, sweet—" He halted when she stiffened beneath his touch. "I am being honest when I say I want to spend the night with you."

"I don't doubt that."

"And I am being honest when I say that I can promise you no more than this night of rapture, along with any other nights you welcome me in your bed."

Stepping away again, she faced him. "I appreciate your honesty, Saxon. If my father had been half as honest with my mother, my life might have been very different."

"Different how? Do you think he was less than honest with his disappointment that you were not a son?"

"No, he was very honest with that. I meant my life would be different because then I would not already know what it is like to be betrayed by a man who makes marital promises he has no idea of keeping."

"I thought you had never wed."

"I have not, but my mother did." Her lips tightened until her words had to be forced past them. "She had great devotion to my father, but he cared more for his mistress than he did for her."

"A woman he married when your mother died."

"A woman he brought into my mother's home while my mother still lived."

"He did?" His frown could not hide his astonishment. "Few men parade their mistresses before their wives, preferring as the king does to keep their lovers and their wives far apart. On that, no one doubts that King Henry the Senior is wise."

She went to the door and threw it open. "Good night, Saxon."

For a moment, she thought he was going to protest, but he said nothing as he walked out of the room. She closed the door and leaned against it. Every inch of her ached for his touch. If she called out his name, he would return and introduce her to the pleasures that filled the songs sung in the Court of Love.

Should she?

No, she must not. Congratulating herself for having been wise brought no surcease of the craving. She remained riveted with grief at losing what she could only imagine.

Chapter 12

Clouds obscured the night sky. On the riverbank, Mallory hid in the deepest shadows beneath a tree. She watched as Saxon walked along the shore, his hand on the sword he wore at his side. He had not seen her yet, and she intended to keep him from discovering where she was perched, her bow in one hand and an arrow in the other.

Since their quarrel in her room two nights before, he had spoken to her only if they chanced to pass each other in the palace. She had not realized before now how much she looked forward to spending time with him.

She should have had no time to worry about anything but getting answers for the queen. Each morning she had been called to the queen's side, where she was questioned about what else she had discovered about the incidents by the river. Other than when she could tell the queen that there may have been a single archer, she had had nothing to report. The queen's frustration matched her own.

Knowing she could not allow her personal problems with Saxon to interfere with her work for the queen, she had gone earlier this evening to speak with him. She had hoped a truce—a chaste truce—would allow her to center her thoughts on serving the queen. She had chanced to see him slipping out of the palace with a furtiveness that suggested he wanted no one to note his departure.

So she had followed. When he went to the river, she was not

surprised. He had been talking about setting a trap for the river thieves. She guessed he was using himself as the decoy, but who was assisting him?

Hours passed as Mallory squatted beneath the tree. Her leg muscles protested, but she did not move. Her eyes grew heavy. She forced them to remain open and scanned the riverbank in both directions. A yawn tickled her throat. She swallowed it as Saxon continued to walk back and forth by the river. She guessed he was struggling to remain awake, as she was.

As the night's darkness became less resolute with the impending dawn, Saxon paused and called, "I don't think anything is going to happen tonight, Mallory."

She stood, wincing as her cramped legs threatened to send her collapsing to her knees. Stepping from beneath the tree while she put the arrow back in her quiver, she asked, "How long have you known I was here?"

"Since I saw you following me down the street toward the river."

"And you let me lurk in the shadows all night?"

He chuckled as she slid down the bank toward him. "You could have been great help if I needed any. I have to admit I was shocked to discover you following me. I would have guessed you would be greatly pleased to see no more of me."

"You are one of the queen's guards."

"So that is the reason you came after me?"

"It is the one I will admit to."

His smile broadened. "Ah, there is the Mallory I have come to know. Never give a complete answer unless absolutely necessary."

"Something I learned from you." By St. Jude, he was almost as vexing as her father. But her father thought only of his pleasures, while Saxon concerned himself with protecting the queen and her court.

"Did you learn from me as well that there are times when giving up is the best course?" He looked at the river that was inky beneath the starless sky. "It appears that I have not lured our enemy out of his lair tonight."

"Which one?"

He motioned for her to climb with him up the bank. "Either one, assuming there are two different enemies. I have failed, so you will have to report to the queen that nothing new has been uncovered."

"I grow weary of telling her that." She scrambled to the top and held out her hand to help him up the last steep part of the bank.

He grasped her wrist and pulled down sharply. She let out a cry as she toppled to the ground. She slid headfirst down the bank, hitting the bottom hard. Rolling over to sit up, she heard the clash of steel.

At the top of the bank, Saxon was balanced awkwardly as he swung his sword. The man fighting him was a silhouette, but he had the advantage of standing above Saxon and on a flat surface. She reached for an arrow, but halted. The two men were moving in a wild dance accented by the clang of steel. She could hit Saxon. She had to think of another way.

Mallory slipped into the shadows and looked up the hill. Were there any others with the man? Before, several people had attacked them. She smiled coldly when she saw some forms moving across the field toward them.

Shrieking the queen's name, she ran up the hill as she pulled out the arrow and put it to string. She reached the top of the hill and set it flying toward the forms. They scattered as it struck the ground in front of them. In quick order, she sent more arrows flying. The forms turned and ran. She kept firing until they had disappeared into the darkness.

Only then did she whirl to run to where Saxon still was struggling to keep his footing while fighting his attacker. She drew her knife and put the point to the man's back.

"Stop!" she cried.

He ignored her.

She tried to jab him and realized he was wearing mail. Tossing aside the knife, she pulled the string off her bow. She dropped the bow and whipped the string around his neck.

"Stop!" she cried.

He choked, but obeyed when she told him to drop his sword.

Saxon surged over the top of the hill and picked up the sword. Raising the point of his own so it was beneath the mailed man's chin, he waited until she had withdrawn the string and stepped back.

"Who are you?" Saxon demanded.

"A dead man," he panted as he drew in deep breaths.

"There is no need for you to die if you will tell us what we need to know."

"I will not do that."

Mallory walked around the man to stand beside Saxon and asked, "Do you serve Jacques Malcoeur?"

The man laughed, then began coughing. He pointed to a flask he wore on his belt, and Saxon nodded. Lifting it to his lips, he drained it before tossing it aside.

"If you don't serve Malcoeur, then who?" Saxon asked.

"You would be very surprised if I told you the truth," the man said.

"Why don't you tell me the truth? Then I will see how surprised I am."

The man's face constricted as he shuddered. With a groan, he dropped to his knees.

Mallory took a step toward him, but Saxon put out an arm to block her way.

The man tumbled to the ground, quivering and shuddering. Spittle formed at the corners of his lips. He muttered something, then was silent. His legs and arms twitched several times before motion ceased.

Saxon walked over to the flask the man had emptied. As he picked it up, Mallory kept him from raising it to his nose to sniff.

"Take care," she said. "Some poisons can kill with a single breath."

"Do you know what it could be?"

She shook her head. "I have not studied much with Sister Arnetta and her assistant, Sister Isabella, who know more about herbs than anyone else in St. Jude's Abbey. One of them would know what was in the flask simply by watching the man's reaction."

"It must be some sort of flower. His last words thanked the flowers."

"Lily of the valley is very deadly, as is monkshood."

He turned to look at the corpse contorted in its death throes. "He was prepared to die rather than risk revealing the truth of whom he served. It seems the queen's enemies are more determined than we had guessed."

It did not take long to discover the man wore nothing to identify his liege lord. His mail was French, but his sword had a hilt of Norman design.

As the eastern sky grew pale, Mallory heard the sound of riders. She whispered to Saxon, but he was already drawing his sword. He lowered it when a half dozen men rode out of the dusk. She recognized Sir Godard and Landis D'Ambroise on the two lead horses. The other men were familiar from the queen's Court of Love. All the men were armed.

Sir Godard was the first to dismount. Coming over to the dead man, he asked, "What happened here?"

"We were attacked," Mallory said.

He ignored her. "Saxon, we heard there had been a fight by the river. I did not expect to find you involved."

"We were looking for the men who attacked us," Saxon said as the other men swung down to look at the dead man.

"He looks like a warrior." A short man chuckled. "But what sort of warrior is slain by a jongleur?"

"I did not slay him, Duby."

"Then you let Lady Mallory do it?" The men laughed, save for D'Ambroise, who knelt by the man.

"Neither of us slew him," Saxon said with more patience than Mallory could have shown while being derided. "He drank poison to keep us from questioning him."

D'Ambroise rose and shook his head. "What did you discover before he died?"

"Nothing," Mallory answered, her frustration bursting out in the one word, because, in a few hours, she would have to tell the queen the exact same thing.

Sunshine burned on Mallory's head as a thud echoed across the empty field near the River Clain. Birds fled out of the trees, screeching in dismay. She shielded her eyes and peered toward where the arrow still vibrated in a tree. She lowered her hand and tried to silence her sigh.

"Try again, Lady Violet," she said.

The dark-haired woman nodded, but blinked back tears. Only Lady Elita showed any promise as an archer, and she rubbed the noses of her friends in that fact whenever possible. Mallory was growing as exasperated as the women. At the Abbey, her students progressed quickly. Some, even in such a short time, had honed their skills to be as sharp as an arrow's tip.

But at the Abbey, they do not spend the rest of their time in flirtations and assignations, she reminded herself.

"At least I hit *something* this time," Lady Violet said with a superior smile at the other students.

"The wrong something," Lady Elita called with a laugh.

"But I did hit something. Won't Sir Godard be proud of his wife-to-be?"

Her smile vanished when Mallory frowned and pointed to where a blanket had been draped over a pile of straw about thirty yards closer to the river. "The arrow you fired is probably ruined, for the shaft may have cracked when it struck the tree. Retrieve it and check to see if it is still usable."

"How do I do that?"

"Roll it in your fingers near your ear. Listen for any crackling sound. That reveals it is broken within. After you pull it from the tree—"

"Pull it from the tree? You expect me to tug an arrow out of a tree?" Lady Violet's excitement became vexation. "I am not your servant."

"No, you are not my servant. You are my student, and you will obey if you wish to continue to study with me."

Tossing the bow onto the ground, then jumping aside as it bounced toward her, Lady Violet stormed away. She looked over her shoulder, and the other women in the class walked to Mallory. Each threw her bow at Mallory's feet before raising her chin and walking after their friend.

For the briefest second, Mallory considered calling them back. She had promised the queen to teach her ladies to use a bow. If she did not persuade them to stay, she would be failing in her vow to Queen Eleanor.

Then Lady Elita turned to give her a superior smile while saying loudly enough so Mallory could not fail to hear, "If we find Saxon, maybe he will sing the song he wrote especially for me."

Rage boiled in her as she imagined Saxon holding Lady Elita as he had wanted to hold her last night, and she almost spat the fiery retort searing her tongue. She halted herself, remembering the arguments between her mother and her father's mistresses. Forcing the anger back into the place where she usually kept it hidden, she did not respond.

Lady Elita lowered her eyes first, but Mallory felt no sense of victory. She would never allow herself to become a pawn in a battle that men seemed to enjoy watching women fight, even though no woman could be triumphant while a man played freely with her emotions. She would not let herself be drawn into a battle she could never win.

She bent to gather up the bows and tried not to think about never savoring Saxon's touch again. "He is a troubadour," she said to herself as she unstrung one, then the next. "He charms everyone. Letting him charm me more would prove I have no more sense than Mother." She reached for another bow.

"May I try?" came a soft voice.

Mallory was amazed to see a girl who had never come to

practice. Her hair was light brown, only a few shades darker than Lady Elita's. Her nose was sprinkled with freckles, but there was nothing childish about the expression in her dark green eyes. She had a strength in her gaze that Mallory had seldom seen since leaving the Abbey.

"Who are you?" she asked.

"My name is Fleurette D'Ambroise." She gave a shy grin, and abruptly looked even younger than what Mallory guessed were her dozen years. "I want to learn the skills you possess, Lady Mallory. Not only with a bow, but the other skills of fighting without a weapon that Lady Violet told my brother you possess."

"Your brother?" she asked, even though she suspected she already knew the answer.

"Landis D'Ambroise, a knight in our gracious queen's service."

Only with the greatest effort, Mallory kept her smile from falling away. The young man had hurried to her side each time she had come into the great hall the past three days. Each time, he had lathered her with excessive compliments about her calm demeanor during the most recent riverside attack. At the same time, he urged her to walk with him in the garden. She had deflected his invitations with excuses she doubted he believed, but he did not seem daunted in his attempts to seduce her. And Lady Violet, she had to admit, because she had seen him talking often to the lady, even though she was to marry Saxon's brother. He was as faithless as her father, and she wanted nothing to do with him.

Now his sister stood in front of Mallory.

"Why have you not attended my earlier classes?" Mallory asked.

"I thought I would not be able to complete them." Her eyes grew sad. "Landis had been hinting he would not remain long in Poitiers. When Lady Violet announced she was betrothed to Sir Godard, I was certain Landis would want to leave. I would have had to go with him."

"Why would you have to leave?"

"My brother professes a deep love for Lady Violet." She put her fingers to her lips. "I should not have said anything. It would be embarrassing for them to have that widely known when she has accepted Sir Godard's offer of marriage."

"I will say nothing." Mallory did not add that she cared little about the complex relationships in the palace. "Have you ever handled a bow?"

"Only a few times. Landis disapproves of a female using a weapon."

Mallory hid her surprise, because D'Ambroise had been ebullient in his admiration for her ability with a bow and how she was sharing that knowledge. Were all the men in Poitiers accomplished liars?

Unless he is playing his lute or sharing a poem, you can be certain that he is being honest. She wanted to tell the queen that statement was as false as everything Saxon spoke within the palace walls.

"Show me what you know," Mallory said, holding out a bow that was close to the proper size for the girl. It would not require much strength to draw it.

Lady Fleurette took the bow and strung it with an ease that suggested she had been modest about her experience. Glancing at Mallory, she reached for the quiver of practice arrows and drew out one. She balanced it in her hand, then put it aside. She lifted out another one, examined it, and then set it to the string. She held the bow straight out from her hip.

"At your command, milady," she said.

Mallory smiled. "I believe you have had more training than you wish your brother to know."

"A bit more." She smiled, but weakly.

"Raise your bow, Lady Fleurette."

The girl obeyed.

"Fire," she ordered.

Lady Fleurette drew the bowstring back to her chin, then

released it. The arrow arced into the air and hit the ground in front of the haystack.

Lady Fleurette lowered the bow, her eyes filling with dismay. "I missed."

"You did better than any of the queen's ladies."

"I did?" She smiled, then giggled at the praise. "But I know I can hit the target." Raising her bow again, she drew back on the string.

Mallory put her hand on Lady Fleurette's arm, halting her. "Never pull the string when there is no arrow on it."

"Why not? I cannot miss the target when there is no arrow nocked on the string."

"You will strain the string and the bow drawing it empty." Ruining the practice bow would mean Mallory's having to make a new one, and she had scars on her fingers from the last two she had carved out of ash at the Abbey. "You will hit the target next time you fire."

"How do you know?"

"Because you will hold the bow so your left arm and the arrow are on the same straight line." Bending, she picked up her bow. Unlike the bows she had brought for the ladies, there was nothing wrapped around the string to mark where the arrow should be set against it. "Watch."

Mallory turned so the target was to her left. She quickly looked around. The ladies had vanished behind the city wall, and Lady Fleurette was close to her side. Among the trees, no one was in sight, nor was anyone passing along the river. She did not expect her arrow to fly in that direction, but she never forgot the lesson of checking in every direction before she loosed an arrow from the string. Nobody else stood between her and the target. Reaching into the quiver she wore across her back, she selected an arrow. She set it to the string and fired.

She gasped as another arrow appeared, flying in a matching arc with hers, only a finger's breadth separating them. The arrows struck the very center of the target at the same moment, still less than an inch apart.

Whirling, she saw the field was empty save for her and Lady Fleurette. A cloud of dust struck her, and she coughed as she waved it away from her face in time to see several men riding at a reckless speed toward the gate into the city. Surcoats of bright red and blue and yellow covered their mail.

"Which of those men fired the arrow?" she asked.

Lady Fleurette shook her head, her eyes wide. "I don't know. I did not see it until just before it hit."

"Hurry to the palace." Mallory continued to stare at the gray cloud marking the route of the riders.

"Do you think they are a threat to the queen?"

"They are strangers."

Lady Fleurette nodded and ran toward the wall in the opposite direction of the riders.

Mallory knew there was no need to run. If those men were the vanguard of the king's army, they would not be welcomed into the city. Or so she assumed. The castellan at the gate had pledged his loyalty to the queen, but many who had vowed service to King Henry the Senior had risen up against him. Betrayal was everywhere.

Going to the target, she pulled her arrow from the hay. She put it in her quiver and reached for the arrow that had flown in perfect precision beside it.

The design of fletching and the bands of paint on the shaft identified its maker. Red and blue and yellow, like the men had worn. She set it with care into her quiver. She looked forward to returning it to its owner, along with a curt reminder that firing past her and Lady Fleurette had been worse than foolish. It had been dangerous. She intended to make sure whoever had let the arrow fly would never forget that again.

The excited voices reached out into the corridor to draw Mallory into the great hall. People milled about, chattering excitedly as if they had not seen one another in many months and could not wait to share everything that had happened since their last conversation. She glanced toward the raised table. Neither the queen nor the comtesse was sitting there.

"Have you heard the tidings?" asked D'Ambroise as he rushed up to her.

"What tidings?" She whispered a prayer that the rebellion was over, that both sides had agreed to cease fighting.

"Normandy is rising up against the king."

"Are you certain that is true? Normandy has stayed loyal to King Henry the Senior right from the beginning."

"So I was told." He grasped her hands, raising one, then the other to his lips. "We should celebrate such wondrous news."

"Maybe later." She withdrew her hands from his clasp and pushed her way through the crowd near the door. Looking past the others in the room, she saw another door open on the far side of the hall.

Cheers rang up into the rafters as the queen and Comtesse Marie entered the room. The queen climbed the steps to the platform beneath the grand window. Her daughter followed, but stood to one side. On the other side of the platform, the queen's guards were standing with their hands on the hilts of their swords.

Mallory pushed through the crowd, trying to reach the raised area. People were hesitant to move aside, so she used one end of her bow to edge them to the left or right. A few people snarled curses at her, but most said nothing as they stared after her. Going up the steps, she paused by the four men who had traveled with Queen Eleanor to St. Jude's Abbey. She balanced the end of her bow against the floor as she drew a single arrow from her quiver. She frowned when she realized it was the one with the bright decoration that matched the men's surcoats. Setting it on the bench by the table, she withdrew another, but did not set it to her string. She was ready if she needed to fire.

The queen motioned toward the crowd, and a trio of men stepped forward. All wore the garish surcoats that she had seen through the dust out on the practice field. As one, they knelt at the bottom of the steps.

As Queen Eleanor told them to rise, Mallory saw a motion near the doorway from the outer corridor. She instantly recognized the man coming through the press of people eager to see the queen greet the strangers.

Saxon glanced at her, then looked back at the men as he climbed the steps to stand beside her. She wondered if she had ever seen him look so handsome and powerful. His face was as rigid as she had ever seen it, and she guessed he had heard about the arrows fired past her and Lady Fleurette. Or was he distressed about the information D'Ambroise was spreading? His eyes became dark hearths of searing fury when one of the black-haired men in red, blue, and yellow, the shortest of the three, stepped away from his companions.

"Your majesty," he said, bowing his head again to the queen, "I am Comte Philippe du Fresne, here as an emissary from the court of King Louis, to bring you greetings from your sons and allies. I bring, as well, glorious tidings. Normandy is rising."

The room buzzed with amazement, surprising Mallory. D'Ambroise had told her much the same, but he looked as surprised as everyone else. Had he been engaging in conjecture and was shocked his words were being repeated by the French king's emissary?

"The old king will have no place to hide," the comte went on, "save behind a monk's robes. A just reward for a king who ordered the death of an archbishop."

As the room filled with cheers, Mallory heard Saxon curse under his breath and looked at him as the queen warmly welcomed the comte to the palace by letting him bow over her outstretched hands.

"What is it?" she whispered.

"Du Fresne is lying to the queen," he answered.

"How do you know?"

He put his hand on her arm. "I cannot tell you here, but, Mallory, if you have ever trusted anyone, trust me now. Du Fresne is lying to the queen."

Mallory had no chance to answer, even if she had known

what to say. Trust him? She could think of a hundred reasons not to trust him; the most important that he was a man who enjoyed flirtations—and she had no idea how much more—with every woman he met. But she nodded, for she could not doubt the low rumble in his voice. She had heard it only a few times before: both times when they were attacked by the river . . . and when his brother had interrupted them in the wall room. He was furious.

Saxon pushed past her and walked down the steps. With the practiced smile she despised, he greeted Comte du Fresne as if they were friends of long standing.

She could only stare. What was he doing? And why?

"Fitz-Juste, I am pleased to see you here," the comte said with a broad smile. "I should have known you, with your strong sense of self-preservation, would align yourself with the victorious side in the rebellion."

"I could say the same to you."

The comte laughed. "It takes a wise man to see the direction of the wind before it changes."

"You have always had such wisdom, my lord."

Mallory feared she was going to be ill. Saxon had asked her to trust him, but he was, once more, the smooth courtier she could not trust, for she was never sure which words he spoke with sincerity and which were aimed at getting him what he wanted. She had to wonder if he had been as obviously insincere when he came to her room. Wanting to run away, her hands over her ears so she did not have to listen to more of his half-truths, she had to remain where she was to be at ready in case the queen needed her.

"And this is Lady Mallory de Saint-Sebastian," she heard Saxon say.

Forcing herself to reveal none of her disgust, she looked from one man to the other.

Her vow to hide her feelings failed when the comte said, "De Saint-Sebastian? I know your father well, milady. He and

I have had many conversations in which we find we are in complete agreement about the events that surround us."

Horror bubbled up from within her, frothing loudly in her ears. Father was switching sides, too, to gain power and prestige from the rebellion? On one thing he had always been constant: A promise to his liege lord was sacrosanct. He could violate his vows to his wife without a second thought, but never to the king.

"It is a pleasure to meet you, milady," the comte was saying when the buzz in her head dimmed enough so she could make out his words.

"Thank you, milord," she managed to whisper.

"Maybe you and I can have a discussion of our own soon," the comte continued with a smile that suggested words played no part in the intercourse he was considering.

"My duties for the queen keep me busy." Her voice was stiff, for she wanted to give him no suggestion that she would ever consider his offer.

"Duties?" Comte du Fresne glanced at Saxon.

"Lady Mallory serves the queen as part of her personal household guard."

The comte laughed. Loud and hard. When neither Mallory nor Saxon joined in, he halted and muttered something, obviously embarrassed at what he had believed to be a joke.

As the comte hurried back to fawn on the queen, Saxon said, "You would be wise to avoid him for a while."

"I intend to avoid him forever." She raised her chin and met his eyes steadily. "And you, too. One minute you are speaking with loathing of the man. The next you are flattering him as if you were his best friend."

He put his hand on her arm as she was about to storm past him to stand close to the queen. When she scowled, he said, "Stay out of this, Mallory. The game we are playing is one that you have no experience with, and it is dangerous."

"I am here to guard the queen. Didn't you say as much to the comte?"

"Mallory, please trust me."

"Trust *you*?"

"I will explain when I can." He folded her hand between his. "Just trust me now."

She yanked her hand away. "Do you know how many times my father said those exact words to my mother? I would trust him as soon as I would trust you."

"I am not your father, Mallory. I have not betrayed you."

"Yet."

His mouth tightened into a straight line as she pushed past him to go and stand next to the queen. Only later, after the formalities were completed and the queen had retired for the night, did she realize that he had not challenged her comment.

Chapter 13

The fountain's water trickled to splash its song in the pool edged by blossoms that were brighter against the thickening twilight. As he watched the moon rise, Saxon tried to pick out the matching notes on his lute. It leaned against his left leg. His right leg was outstretched and serving as a pillow for Elita's head. As she gazed up at him with a smile that suggested she would enjoy a much more private concert, he absently smiled back.

His thoughts were not on his song or on Elita. Instead he tried to think about what could have brought Philippe du Fresne to Poitiers. The liar might be seeking a haven from the fighting, but why now? There had been no major battles between the forces of Henrys—father and son—in the past fortnight. Even Godard was hinting that he might return to the king's camp once his wedding was celebrated. Godard would not be going if he thought there was any chance he would be called into real battle, but he would see standing by the king's side as his best way to keep the family honor.

Not that their father would care. Juste Fitz-Juste cared only for the family lineage. He had his heir, and the rest of his offspring— his legitimate children by both wives and his bastards—were there only in case something happened to that heir. Not that anything would, when Godard stayed far from any events that could be dangerous.

Or was it that Godard was thinking of leaving Poitiers because King Henry the Senior was threatening in the wake of the rumored uprising in Normandy, as was whispered in the corridors, to move south and burn every field and village in his path until he reached his queen's palace? First, he would have to pass through the troops assembled by his sons and the French king and their allies, but it seemed as if both sides tired of the war.

As he tired of the war with Mallory.

He had never met anyone who was so afraid to trust others. Not others, he corrected himself. She was afraid of trusting men. She was afraid of trusting *him*. And she did not trust herself when she was close to him. He wanted to reassure her that she could never be a victim as her mother was. He doubted she would heed him, or that she would ever lower the walls of pain around herself enough to let herself relish the bliss they could find in each other's arms.

"That is horrible!" Elita bemoaned from where she was now lying across both his legs.

Saxon was about to agree, then reminded himself that Elita was not privy to his thoughts. He smiled at her. She was a beauty with golden hair and voluptuous curves draped in fabric so fine that the shadows of her body were visible beneath them. When he had left Poitiers with the queen to visit St. Jude's Abbey, she had been besotted by a jongleur who had come to court to trade entertainment for food and shelter. He had gotten far more, because Elita had taken him to her bed. They had been inseparable until the jongleur took his leave. If she had regretted his departure, Saxon had seen no sign of it since she had decided he should be the next to serenade her in her bed.

"What is horrible?" he asked, pausing in his strumming.

"Why are you playing such discordant music?" Her perfect nose wrinkled as her full lips became more lush with her pout. "Play that lovely tune you played for me last week, Saxon." She shifted so her full breasts brushed his thigh. "The one about the fair maiden who gave herself to her daring champion and the ecstasy they discovered together." Her finger trailed up his leg.

He moved the lute before her wandering touch made him forget that he had no interest in being the next in her long line of lovers. "That song does not sing for me today. Rather I am thinking of the unrequited love of a man who would die for his beloved, without knowing that she never thinks of him."

"What an appalling story!"

"I hope by the time I have finished writing it, you will enjoy it as much as you have my other songs."

"Oh, Saxon," she cooed, "you are the most— Look who is here!" She giggled as she stared past Saxon, but her expression gave her the appearance of a beast ready to leap on a defenseless creature.

He rested his arm lightly atop the lute's curved neck and turned to see what Elita found so enticing. The silly woman seemed to have no thoughts of anything beyond doing whatever she must to persuade a man to write a poem or a song in her honor. Honor? Whatever honor she once possessed had been traded long ago for the attention she sought. He almost laughed, but the sound faded when he saw who stood in the garden.

Philippe du Fresne had shoulders that suggested he could lift a cow with each hand without a single drop of sweat appearing on his brow. Dressed in his finest tunic with his family's colors of red, blue, and yellow, he looked every inch a lord of the realm.

Saxon came to his feet, ignoring Elita's protests. She grabbed his ankle. Bending, he lifted her perfumed hand away. He started to raise it to his lips, but paused when she whispered, "Will you introduce me to your friend?"

"Of course, my dear. I shall return with the comte as soon as I can."

"Each moment you are gone shall be an eternity."

"An eternity," he agreed, releasing her hand.

Before she could delay him with another comment, he climbed the steps to the doorway.

"I should have guessed I would find you in a garden playing your lute," du Fresne said with a sneer. "Hardly the pastime I would expect for someone of your blood, or have you gotten tired of hiding behind a woman's skirts, as your brother does?" His eyes focused on Elita. "Although I cannot find fault with your company."

"My *company* wishes to be introduced to you." He did not refute du Fresne's words about Godard. It was well-known that his brother had had to be routed from his mistress's bed on many occasions when he should have been training in the knightly arts. He would not allow the comte to bait him.

Bait! He still needed to trap Malcoeur, so they could find out what the thief knew. He kept thinking of how Mallory had volunteered to be the bait. He would not allow that . . . unless he could think of no way else to get the thief's attention.

"If she wishes to be introduced to me," du Fresne murmured, "then we should not keep her waiting." His tongue swept along his lips like a dog about to feast on scraps tossed to the floor.

Saxon put his hand on the comte's arm. "She is worth waiting for, so answer a few questions for me first."

"Your father is well, if that is what you want to know."

"That is good to hear, but how will your health remain when the king learns you have broken your pledge to him and come to Poitiers?"

Du Fresne's eyes flicked from Elita to Saxon and swiftly away, telling Saxon all he needed to know. The comte had not come to Poitiers to vow his allegiance to the queen. He had come for another reason. Saxon knew he had to discover what it was quickly.

Saxon glanced at Elita, who was running her fingers through her hair. She let her fingertips linger against her breast in an obvious invitation for du Fresne to do more than look. Saxon might have the very ally he needed to keep him apprised of du Fresne's plans. All he needed to do was figure out what Elita would want in exchange for keeping her ears and eyes open and her mouth shut.

"Brother! I thought I would find you here." Godard stepped out of the doorway behind the comte. With him was Lady Violet, who was hanging on to his arm with one hand while she had her other through D'Ambroise's arm. Godard drew his fiancée away from the other man and around the comte. "We wanted to let you know the arrangements are completed, and the queen has given us her permission to marry on the morrow."

"That is very good to hear." Saxon smiled at his brother and Lady Violet, but could not resist a glance at D'Ambroise, who wore a strained smile. There had been rumors that D'Ambroise wished to marry the lady himself, so it was surprising to see him with the soon-to-be newlyweds.

"You will come to the ceremony, won't you?" Godard asked.

"Most certainly. I would not miss it."

"Well, look at *that*!" the comte murmured, his voice taking on the predatory tone that Elita had used when she saw him.

Saxon watched as Mallory walked toward them. Her ebony hair was braided with white silk ribbons that matched the sleeves of her undergown visible beneath the drooping sleeves of her deep red gown. Every motion should have had music with it, for each seemed part of a seductive dance. That she seemed unaware of her effect on men made her even more alluring. Not even her bow and the arrows in the quiver over her shoulder or the dog trailing behind her could detract from the fantasies she created in a man's mind.

Holding out his hand, he smiled when she placed hers on it. His smile faltered as he sensed the tremor in her fingertips. What was upsetting her? Without hesitation, she had faced Jacques Malcoeur and the unknown men in mail. Yet now she was trembling. Did he dare to believe he caused her reaction? During the days since he had held her in the room within the wall and had been interrupted by Godard, he had imagined again and again having her in his arms. During the nights, he might have dreamed of her, if sleep had not been banished by his craving for her, even when he reminded himself how she would despise him if she discovered the truth he hid from her.

Godard gushed, "Lady Mallory, just the person I had hoped to see! You must attend our wedding ceremony tomorrow. Lady Violet has told me how much she learned in your little classes for the ladies."

"I am glad she feels the classes were worthwhile," Mallory replied.

Saxon recognized her emotionless tone and knew she was infuriated by his brother's condescension about the classes she believed so vital to protecting the queen. He folded his fingers over her hand. It was like no other woman's hand he had ever held. It was not soft and scented. Her skin revealed how hard she had worked to achieve the mastery of her bow. Yet, he could not imagine any skin he would rather caress.

"You will come, won't you?" Godard asked.

"You want me to come to your wedding?" Mallory's shock matched Saxon's, because he had not guessed Godard would forget his humiliation when Mallory saved him.

"Of course we want you to come. You will, won't you?" Godard repeated with a broadening smile as he looked at their clasped hands.

Saxon said nothing. Once, many years ago, he had given his brother the benefit of the doubt about failing to understand how their birth order gave Godard opportunities that were forever proscribed to a second son. That had changed the day Godard was praised for participating in a sword-fighting contest, and Saxon's victories were ignored—not just by his father, but by his brother, who accepted the praise as his due. Saxon had grown accustomed to such behavior, no longer hurt as he had been when he learned he was necessary only if the cherished heir failed to survive.

"I will try," Mallory replied. "If the queen needs me, I will not be able to leave the palace."

Before Godard could spout more, Saxon looked at the comte, who was listening with a superior smile. "You remember Lady Mallory de Saint-Sebastian, I am sure, Comte du Fresne."

"Milady," the comte murmured, bowing over her other hand, as Godard and the lady and D'Ambroise wandered out into the garden. "A fair creature to add to the beauty of this fair night."

"It is a pleasure to meet you, my lord." Looking at Saxon, she said, "I must speak to you of an urgent matter forthwith."

Saxon saw the comte's shock that any woman would turn from him so quickly, especially to speak with a younger son. "I promised the comte that I would introduce him to Lady Elita, who is eager to make his acquaintance. May I postpone our conversation for a short time?"

"Most certainly." Her answer was calm, but, even in the thickening shadows, he could see the disquiet in her eyes. Dipping her head toward the comte, she added, "I trust I shall have another opportunity to talk with you, Comte du Fresne. As you can see, I have a great interest in archery. I look forward to chatting with you about the art of the bow."

The comte barely waited until Mallory was out of earshot, her dog Chance at her heels, before he asked, "Archery? What did she mean? Bows are for peasants who cannot afford a fine sword."

"Haven't you learned that women are often incomprehensible?" Saxon chuckled as he motioned for the comte to come with him. Once Mallory spent more time with du Fresne, she would come to see rapidly that the comte was not much more competent with any weapon than his brother was. Therefore, he must find ways to prevent her from spending much time with the comte.

As he introduced a simpering Elita to the comte, Saxon could not help wondering if Mallory's learning about du Fresne's ineptitude was the real reason he wanted to keep the comte from her side. The comte had both title and lands and could marry where he wished. Even though du Fresne seemed much taken with Elita, he might quickly become bored with her. Mallory was a tempting woman, and no man would suffer boredom with her, because it was impossible to guess how she would react.

Saxon forced himself to focus. He had come to sit by the fountain, waiting for exactly the opportunity he now had. He presented the comte to Elita, then stood to one side, pretending to tune his lute while the comte and Elita began the game of courtship with teasing words and looks that both had honed to perfection.

When the comte bowed over Elita's hand, he vowed to meet her later when the garden was "less crowded," he said with a glance at Saxon.

Elita waited until the comte was walking back into the castle before she turned on Saxon. "Why did you remain here? Couldn't you tell that we wanted to be alone?"

"You will be alone." He did not hesitate as he added, "And you should remember who brought you two together."

She waved at him and laughed. "I can get any man I want. I did not need your help, Saxon."

"But I could use yours."

Her smile became the cold one he had seen each time she set her eyes on a prize. She swayed closer to him. "Is that so? You should know by now that my help does not come cheaply."

"I know that."

"What do you want me to do?"

"I want you to get du Fresne talking about why he is here in Poitiers and what his plans are."

She laughed, but the sound was as calculated as her expression. "I was not planning on talking that much to him."

"I am sure you can change your plans slightly."

"I could if it was worth my time."

"What do you want?" he asked.

She walked her fingers up his arm. "You know what I want, Saxon."

"A song?"

"Only if you sing it to me in bed." Her eyes grew hard. "Kick that she-knight out of your bed. I know you are fasci-

JOCELYN KELLEY

nated with her because she is one of a kind." She ran her hands
along her gown, pulling it tight to her curves. "But you will see
that I, too, am one of a kind, and I am the kind of woman a
man truly appreciates. I would never bring my weapons to bed
with me."

"Just your charm," he said, knowing that was what she expected him to say.

"I have many." She gave him a simpering smile. "Get rid
of that she-knight, and I will join you within the fortnight. It
should not take longer than that to learn why the comte is here."
She laughed. "Indeed, I may well have the information for you
on the morrow."

"I trust you to do whatever is necessary."

"And I trust you to get rid of that *woman*. I do not want her
in your bed another night longer."

"I can guarantee you that she will not be in my bed tonight."
He almost laughed at the idea of how furious Elita would be if
she discovered that he and Mallory were not lovers, that Elita
was bargaining for nothing. But it was no laughing matter when
he ached to hold Mallory.

"One more thing."

"If I can." He hoped her request would not cost him dearly.

"I want her bow. I want it broken in half."

"What?"

She slithered toward him, suddenly resembling a snake.
"I want Lady Mallory's bow brought to me broken in half.
That will prove that you have severed all ties with her, because she would never forgive you for breaking her treasured
weapon."

"Breaking her bow will break her heart."

"That is her problem and yours. I can get you what you
want, Saxon, but it shall not be yours until you give me what I
want."

"I understand."

"Good." She walked away, her hips swaying in the rhythm
meant to spellbind a man.

Into Saxon's mind came the words to a song Elita's jongleur had performed several times in the queen's hall.

> *La li jura ceo que ele quist—*
> *E plus asez qu'il I mist.*
> *Pur ceo dit hum en repruver*
> *Que femmes seivent enginner;*
> *Les vezïez e li nunverrable*
> *Unt un art plus ke deable.*

Aloud, he repeated, *"Unt un art plus ke deable."* The ending of the old fable about a woman and her husband and her lover warned against a woman's treachery—"more artifice than the devil."

He sat on the edge of the fountain. The information he had waited for months to obtain might be his if he complied with Elita's demands. He had worked hard to get to the point where he could bring an end to the rebellion before more people died, as his foster brother had, but how could he take Mallory's bow and break it in two?

He hung his head as he stared at the moon's wavering reflection in the pool. The answers had seemed straightforward when he had offered to come to Poitiers. He would find what the traitors had planned and report back to the King Henry the Senior. It had appeared to be a simple task that would bring peace and protect the Norman lands from the greedy influence of the French king. Then he would be lauded by the king. Even his father could not have ignored the honors heaped on his younger son.

Everything he wanted was within his grasp. All he needed to do was betray Mallory as heartlessly as her father had.

Chapter 14

Mallory had paced from one side of her chamber to the other for the past two hours. Even Ruby's suggestion that she sit and work on the project—"your strange box and sticks," as the serving woman called it—had been futile. Mallory had tried to sit, but she had shot back to her feet within seconds, unable to remain still while she waited for Saxon to come to her room, as he had promised once he was finished with introducing the comte to Lady Elita.

How long could that possibly take? She tried not to think that the comte might have received a cool welcome from the lady, who wanted to continue her pursuit of Saxon. If the comte had left and Saxon had stayed with Lady Elita and . . .

No, she did not want to think of *that*!

"Your fretting will not bring him here a minute quicker," Ruby said as she opened the lid of the chest at the bottom of the bed. The dry scent of herbs wafted out.

"What could be keeping him?"

"I warned you that he is a busy man when women are around."

Mallory halted in midstep and faced Ruby, who was putting a blanket in the chest. "Ruby, you should not speak so of him."

"I am not suggesting an insult to him, milady." Closing the lid, the serving woman went to sit on a chair by the window where moonlight bleached the gray stones to a pale cream. "He is a virile, handsome man, and women appreciate such a man, and such men appreciate women in return."

"He may appreciate their admiration, but that does not mean he acts upon it every time." She thought of how he had wooed her with tender patience and a restraint her father had never shown around women. Did she dare to believe Saxon might be different, that he could be honest when he said he wanted her, even though he could not promise her forever? Her father had vowed unending faithfulness to each of his women. That she knew, for she had heard him say as much many times when he insisted his daughter meet his newest "very special lady."

"Milady, my concerns are solely for you, because you have not participated in the games of love practiced here. I do not want to see you hurt, so when you said he was with Lady Elita in the garden, I wanted you to know what that could mean."

"It means," said Saxon from the doorway, "that I would be delayed while introducing her to the comte, exactly as I told Lady Mallory."

Ruby's face became as fiery red as her name. Mallory patted the serving woman on the shoulder before nodding as Ruby excused herself to go to her room.

Closing the door behind her maid, Mallory returned to where she had been standing. Saxon had not moved, and she could not help wondering what he had overheard. Her sudden shyness about asking shocked her, but she reminded herself that she had invited him to discuss the arrow and unknown archer.

"We need to talk, Saxon," she said, hoping her voice gave no clue to the tempest within her.

"Yes." His gaze settled on the unstrung bow she had left by the window.

She went to it and drew the quiver from behind it. Lifting out the arrow with the blue, yellow, and red threads holding on the feathers, she said, "These colors belong to Comte du Fresne."

"Yes."

Even though she was amazed at his terse answer, she told

him about the arrow that had matched the flight of hers while she was teaching Fleurette D'Ambroise. His expression did not change.

"Why do you care who shot it?" he asked when she finished what she had considered an amazing tale.

"The archer was skilled, and I want to be certain that neither the comte nor one of his companions is the archer who fired two arrows at the queen."

He took the arrow, glanced at it, and threw it on the table. "It was not the comte or one of his men."

"How do you know?"

"Du Fresne was insulted that you suggested he is involved in archery. He deems using a bow far below his status as a knight in the service of the king or the queen or whomever he is claiming to support at the moment."

She picked up the arrow and slid it back in the quiver. "We have too many questions and no answers, Saxon."

Walking over to where she stood, he ran a finger along the top of her bow. "Maybe it is time we stopped looking for answers and accepted what is right in front of us."

"How can you say that? We are here to serve the queen. If we do not find the answers to why someone is trying to kill her—"

"We know the answer to that, Mallory. She is a strong woman, and people fear strong women." He slid his finger along the bow, his face becoming pensive. "Those who fear strong women are determined to destroy them."

"Saxon . . ."

He looked at her without any expression and turned. "I should go."

"I wish you would stay."

He paused, but did not face her. "Mallory, be careful what you wish for."

"I wish you would stay."

"To talk about setting another trap for Malcoeur?"

"If you want."

He continued to face the door. "What do *you* want?"

She went to him and leaned her cheek against his shoulder. Slipping her arms past his lute and around his chest, she whispered, "I want you to stay."

"I must not. I have told you that I cannot offer you the lifetime commitment you yearn for."

"That is not what I yearn for tonight."

"But on the morrow, will you change your mind?"

She closed her eyes as she drew her arms away and stepped back. He was right. He had no reason to stay when she had accused him of being little better than a liar only a few hours ago. As he walked out the door, closing it behind him, she watched in silence. She had not believed he would go.

As Mallory turned toward her empty bed, the door opened again. Her shoulders were grabbed, and she was twisted into Saxon's embrace. He kicked the door closed as he whispered, "It is not *my* bed. It is yours."

"What are you talking about?"

"About a pledge I made and must keep."

She regarded him with bafflement. "A pledge about my bed?"

"No, mine."

"You are making no sense."

"You are right. It makes no sense to stand here talking when we could be . . ." His mouth claimed hers.

She reached to put her arms around his shoulders, but he bent and scooped her into his arms. When she gave a small cry of astonishment, the door to Ruby's room flew open.

The serving woman rushed in, but stopped as a broad smile creased her wrinkled face. Without a word, she walked past them and threw the bolt on the door to the corridor. She called to Chance. When the dog ran to her, she led Chance back to her room and closed her door, but not before Mallory heard her say, "It is about time."

Saxon looked at Mallory, and they both began to laugh at once.

"Do you think I am in her good graces again?" he asked.

"I don't think you were ever truly out of them." She combed her fingers up through his golden hair. "She enjoys your teasing."

"But she is protective of her lady." He drew her earlobe into his mouth and nibbled gently as his mustache brushed it with soft bristles. When she gave a soft cry at the thrill erupting within her, he whispered, "But tonight I want you to be *my* lady." He kissed her eagerly.

Her need for him spun through her. "Saxon—"

"Hush. Listen to your heart. Let it heed mine that says tonight is ours." He pushed aside her hair and found the swift pulse at the base of her throat.

When he pressed his mouth to it, she shivered in excitement at what awaited them. He carried her to the bed and set her gently on it. Turning, he went to the door to Ruby's room. He grasped the bolt. Looking over his shoulder, he winked as he slid it to lock them in where nobody, not even the queen, could intrude.

He sat on the bed and drew his lute over his head. She reached forward and plucked a string. It made a sharp sound. Pushing her fingers away, he ran his along the strings, bringing forth a melody that she knew she would never forget. It contained both longing and joy, the emotions rushing madly through her.

"What is that song?" she whispered.

"I don't know. I am making up the notes as I play."

"It has the sound of *tsurune*," she whispered.

"What is *tsurune*?"

"The perfect sound of a bowstring when the arrow is set on its flight." She smiled. "More accurately, the sound when the archer forgets herself and the target and the arrow."

"That is nonsense."

"Not really." She ran her hand up his back and over his shoulder to explore the firm muscles of his chest. Bending close to him, she whispered, "If the archer forgets herself and the target and the arrow, then they are not separate. They are one."

He set the lute aside and frowned at her. "Now I know you are trying hard to confuse me."

"One does not have to exert much energy to confuse you, Saxon." She laughed and kissed his cheek before she added, "However, I am not trying to do anything now but tell you what I learned from my instructor at St. Jude's Abbey. She is from the distant East, even beyond the realm of the Persians. In her country, there is a belief that the mind can dominate the body, but it is best when the mind and the body work in concert to release the archer from the confines of both."

He shook his head. "Every word you speak leaves me more baffled."

Shifting so she faced him, she framed his face with her hands. "Maybe I can show you more easily. Close your eyes and kiss me."

"Gladly."

When he leaned toward her, she shifted slightly.

He opened his eyes and scowled. "You moved."

"Yes, but you can still kiss me."

"When you are avoiding me and my eyes are closed? How can I find you?"

She stroked his face. "Because I am here just as you have longed for me to be. You have imagined this moment so often that you know exactly how it should go."

"How do you know that?"

"Because I have imagined it myself often. Try again. You have wanted this. You want it now. Perceive what is, and let your senses take you beyond what you can see."

Closing his eyes, he sat silently for a long moment. Then he slanted forward. She moved again, but he found her lips. His fingers coursed up through her hair, loosening her braids to let her black hair stream around them, as he held her mouth to his. He deepened the kiss until she was gasping.

Only then did he raise his head enough to whisper, "I perceive that *you* can take my senses beyond what I can see."

"Saxon . . ." Her voice faded as his lips covered hers again.

Her hands gripped his strong arms as he leaned her back
onto the bed. He pressed her into its softness, but there was
nothing soft about his male body. She wrapped her arms around
his shoulders and closed her eyes to savor what could not be
seen, only felt. When he cupped her breast, the craving grew
into a need like she had never known.

He laughed, low and deep in his throat, as he drew her up to
sit between his knees. "I like your gown that is laced in the front
better," he whispered into her hair as he reached behind her to
loosen the back.

"This one is more stylish."

"To hell with style." He drew down one sleeve and ran his
tongue along her shoulder.

She sighed and tilted her head back to allow him to trace that
line up her neck. As she reclined back into her pillow, she
brought him with her. His finger hooked in the front of her
gown, lowering it and her undergown in one swift motion down
to her waist. Entwining his fingers with hers, he pinned her
hands to the bed as he slid his tongue down between her breasts
before drawing the tip of the left one into his mouth. His mustache and beard tickled her like hundreds of miniature fingers.
Her own fingers curled tightly over his as sensation battered
her, and his laugh was a heated storm across her damp skin.
With his knee between her legs, her gown kept her against the
bed. She strained against his gentle imprisonment, fearing her
mind was going to shatter beneath the sensual assault.

She needed to touch him. When she tried to pull her hands
out of his, he pressed them more firmly into the bed.

"Let me go," she ordered.

"Not yet." He smiled down at her. "I have waited so long for
this that I want to drive you mad with longing as you have me
since you threatened to skewer me with your arrow."

"Let me go."

He laughed again and shifted his knee higher against her.
She quivered as an even more powerful need surged through
her. With a cry, she ripped her hands from beneath his and

seized the front of his tunic. She pushed him onto his back. Grasping his hands, she held him down as he had her. Instantly she knew everything she did only accelerated the pulse of desire further, because the rough fabric of his tunic stroked her naked breasts on every quick breath.

He reached beneath her loosened gown and slid his hands over her bottom. He held her hips against his, but her body would not remain still. It wanted to move, to stroke his, to invite him to join her in the song that had no music but swirled wondrously through her. She gave in to the craving as he loosened the rest of her clothes, pushing them lower and lower as his fingers glided along her.

When her clothes lay in a jumble at her feet, she had no chance to kick them aside. He, in a quick motion, pushed her onto her back and beneath him again. She felt small and vulnerable, being naked while he remained dressed, but at the same time she realized how powerful the passion growing between them was.

She knew nothing about men's clothing, but it did not take her long to find out what pieces came off over his head and which must be pushed over his feet. Every piece, as it fell away, revealed new expanses of muscle that urged her fingers to explore. She did not hesitate. As she stroked his broad chest, he gave a soft purr of pleasure before he claimed her lips anew. That sound aroused needs she had never imagined, even in her most carnal fantasies.

She ran her fingers up his sides. When she felt puckered skin just below his right ribs, she gasped and drew back. She stared at a scar the length of her hand from her palm to the tip of her longest finger.

He tilted his face back toward hers. "It is nothing, dearest."

"Nothing? You were nearly split in half. What happened?"

"My brother needed someone to practice with before his first tournament. I learned why no one would ride against him."

"Because he is so good?"

He laughed. "Because he is so bad. He did not run me

through while we faced each other. He drove his lance into me when I was trying to help steady him on his horse."

She stared in astonishment, then laughed. Not because the story was funny. He could have died from such a wound. She laughed because she was happy that he had survived to hold her.

Then, when he kissed her again, she forgot about the past—his as well as hers. All she wanted was this moment with him as she learned about every angle of his male body. Growing more brazen, she lowered her hands to his hips. The varied textures of his body enticed her. When she touched the smooth hardness that pulsated with yearning for her, he moaned and caressed her inner thigh. He edged his hand higher until he was stroking the focus of her pulsing need.

She gasped as his finger delved into her as his mouth explored across her abdomen. She was lost in a splendor she was certain could never be bettered until his mouth slid down over her to stroke her with the same rhythm his finger had. Clutching his shoulders, she writhed as the passion became an exquisite pleasure. Every thought burst into dazzling delight. From a distance somewhere, she heard herself cry out.

She opened her eyes to see him above her, his gaze focused on her face. He was straining to breathe, as she had been moments before, and when his knee slipped between her legs, she opened them with what energy she had remaining. She was about to tell him how she felt, but her words became another gasp as he drove himself into her.

Everything that had happened before was a prelude to him sliding in and out of her, each motion inciting the craving to sweet desperation. She reached down to caress the hard shaft as it moved against her, and he moaned her name. She grasped his shoulders when the rapture escalated within her as his motions became faster. She had only a moment to bring his lips down to hers before he shuddered within her. She thought she heard him cry out something but could not understand because she exploded once more into ecstasy, an ecstasy that was all the more glorious because she shared it with him.

Mallory woke to the sound of soft music. Opening her eyes, she saw the first light of dawn crawling across the windowsill, where Saxon was sitting, dressed only in his tunic. He had one bare foot on the sill and was playing his lute.

"Good morning," he sang as he continued playing.

"It is a very good morning." She leaned on one elbow, not caring that the covers slid down her. During the night, Saxon had learned every inch of her, and she could not imagine hiding herself from his appreciative gaze. "To follow an amazing night."

He stood, not pausing in the song that was the same one he had picked out on the strings last night before he taught her the incredible music two bodies could make together. She listened until he reached its end.

"You finished it," she whispered. "I am in awe of the music you create."

"I write music only when I am inspired." He kissed her bare shoulder. "And you are a true inspiration, dearest."

She liked when he called her *dearest.* Lying back into the pillows, she smiled when he set the lute next to her bow and stretched out beside her.

"I cannot linger as long as I would like," he said. "I must go and ready myself for my brother's wedding."

"You can do that here." She draped her arm lazily over his shoulder. "Have your things brought here."

"So I can watch you hide your beautiful form beneath heavy silk and embroidery?" He shook his head. "I don't know if I could endure witnessing that."

"But then you can undress me later."

"Now *that* is a very good idea." He gave her a rakish grin as he reached under the covers to pull her closer. "I wish we had a few minutes more before I have to go and meet my brother, who is sure to be nervous. I do not want to hurry with you."

"I like how you think, Saxon Fitz-Juste." Running her finger along his nose, she said, "One thing you have never explained is why you are named Saxon."

He nestled his head onto her shoulder and said, "I think there is enough time for the tale."

"For anyone else to tell it, but a troubadour . . ."

Chuckling, he kissed her neck. "Keep chattering, and we will not have time for the story. My name goes back into my family's history to the times before the Norsemen first attacked the shores across the Channel. In my grandfather's grandfather's grandfather's grandfather's time, the scourge of the north preyed. The Vikings came every year with the lengthening days, sailing up rivers to demand gold and women from men who quailed before them. But one man was wiser than those around him."

"Your ancestor?"

"How did you guess?"

She smiled and wrapped her arms around him. "It is your family's story, isn't it?"

"It is, and my grandfather's grandfather's grandfather's grandfather saw how the Norsemen took what they wished, letting their bare axes and honed blades speak for them. My grandfather's grandfather's grandfather's grandfather was old and had seen his wife and all their children and even most of his grandchildren die before him when winter fevers tore through his fief with even less mercy than the Viking warriors. Only a single granddaughter survived. He did not want her to die, but how could an old man protect her? He had an idea that he knew others would call insane. What did he have left to lose?

"When the Vikings arrived to attack, he went to speak with the Viking chief, taking with him a flag of truce. He was unsure if the Vikings would honor it, but they did. He was greeted by the Viking chief, who listened to his offer. My grandfather's grandfather's grandfather's grandfather would give his daughter and his lands to the Viking chief, if the Viking chief accepted his terms. They were simple. First, the Vikings must no longer raid that section of the English shore. Second, the Viking chief must marry my grandfather's grandfather's grandfather's grandfather's granddaughter in a Christian ceremony and agree to treat her well the rest of her days. When the old man died, as he would soon, the lands and the Anglo-Saxon title of jarl would be bestowed upon the Viking chief.

"The Viking chief agreed, for upon seeing my grandfather's grandfather's grandfather's grandfather's granddaughter, he lost his heart to her beauty and gentle love and wisdom that matched her grandfather's. The raids stopped on the shore after they were wed. When the old man died, the Viking became a respected jarl who guided his lands with compassion and good sense. In honor of the old man, he named their firstborn son Saxon and decreed that in every successive generation there must be a son named Saxon in order to guarantee the prosperity and respect due the family."

"But you are a second son."

"I had an older brother who was given the name, but he died after Godard was born. When I arrived, I was given the name."

"Your eldest brother died between the time of your birth and Godard's? If you are twins—"

"We were three born at the same time. Triplets." He turned his head to look out the window, and pain slipped into his voice. "My oldest brother died that day and our mother the next. It was her wish that the old tradition be continued, so I was called Saxon. She loved that story, I have been told."

She tipped his chin toward hers. "It is a wonderful story, Saxon. You should set it to music as a tribute to your mother and your ancestors."

"Maybe I will someday." He paused when church bells rang in the morning's light. "But for now, in spite of what I said earlier, I think there is another story I want to continue to enjoy, a story I do not want to end. There may just be enough time for . . ." His roguish grin returned.

She answered it with a kiss, understanding what he had not said. When they left the bower of her bed, the magic of the night would be submerged beneath by the peril surrounding the queen and her court. They could not be sure when they could again escape those duties to savor each other. She vowed to make sure it was soon.

Chapter 15

Joyous voices climbed to the tower where Mallory was adjusting the veil covering her hair. It was of a pale cream silk that accented her yellow gown. Beneath her veil, her dark braids were loosely wrapped around her head. Ruby had worked for more than an hour on her hair, but stubborn wisps already curled about her face. Blue and yellow embroidery accented the neckline and the silk dropping from her sleeves.

She could not help recalling the last time she had worn a silk gown. It had been a dreary gray color, and she had been standing beside her mother's grave as rain blew in sheets across the flat fields of her father's lands. In the polished silver shield on the wall, she could see the girl she had been that day: frightened and alone and facing a betrayal that she had tried to ignore for the past two years.

But she was not that child any longer. She was one of the queen's ladies of St. Jude's Abbey, and she had spent the night in the arms of a man who wanted her, a man who had made her no promises other than to spend another night with her as soon as he could.

"I love weddings," Ruby announced from behind her.

Mallory turned and smiled. "Maybe there will be a wedding for you soon. I have been hearing you are finding excuses to visit the wall and talk to one of the guards there."

"You are making too much of a simple friendship." The color rising on her face contradicted her words.

"Who knows? Maybe it will become more, and you will find yourself standing by the church door as you speak your vows to become man and wife."

Ruby picked up a pillow and began to plump it. "At the church door . . ." She held the pillow close to her. "I remember my great-grandmother telling me about weddings in her day. Back then, no one went to the church to be wed. The priest would come and witness the couple agreeing to be married, just as family and friends did. Now a wedding must be blessed at the church door and celebrated with a Mass by the altar before the wedding feast can begin." She tossed the pillow onto the bed and chuckled. "As well as all the other things a newly married couple wish to do."

Looking back at the polished shield, Mallory saw herself smile. Gone was the reflection of the hurt, scared child. In its place was a woman who had learned about rapture last night.

"You look perfect!" Ruby assured her. "What a lovely wedding it shall be."

"She does look perfect," said Saxon as he came into the room, once more wearing his lute around his back.

Mallory wondered if she would ever grow tired of looking at him. Until last night, she had not noticed a dimple in his left cheek or how one corner of his mouth tilted more than the other when he smiled. Now dressed in a tunic of red embroidered with green threads, he had a sedate brown belt around his waist. From it hung the sheath with his dagger, and a much longer sword hung below it on his left side.

She rushed to him, paying no attention to Ruby's call to be careful so her hair did not fall out of its braid, and grasped his hands. "I thought you needed to be at Godard's side to calm him."

"A few bottles of wine have done what I failed to do." He smiled. "When I left his chamber, his servants were trying to keep him on his feet, so he did not tumble on his nose."

"Neither Lady Violet nor the priest will be pleased if he is drunk at the wedding."

"That," he said, slipping his arm around her waist, "is soon to be their problem, not mine." He looked past her. "Ruby, do you want to join us for the wedding?"

The serving woman beamed at the invitation. "That is kind of you."

"Hurry, Ruby, and make yourself more beautiful," he urged with a playful wink at Mallory. "We will find something to do while we are waiting."

Ruby wagged a finger at him. "I expect, when I return, that milady's hair will look as unmussed as it does now."

"You know how to ruin a man's fun!" He laughed.

Mallory joined in as she wondered if she had ever been so happy. She knew, in spite of her attempts to believe otherwise, that a few nights with Saxon would not be enough. Even though she had vowed never to put her heart at risk, it had intentions of its own. She had fallen in love with him. She did not want to wonder how long it would be before her joy was replaced by pain.

She did not want to wonder about that today.

Or ever.

The church was not far from the palace, but it had taken almost an hour to reach it. Mallory had been unsure why Sir Godard had chosen to be wed at the door of Saint-Porchaire Church instead of at the chapel on their father's estate, and Saxon told her that his brother seemed unable to wait any longer to have his Lady Violet as his bride. They walked slowly behind the bridal cart inching through the narrow street lined with shops and houses.

The wedding guests further clogged the street. It seemed as if everyone from the Court of Love, save the queen herself, had gathered on the street to try to push closer to witness the wedding. Mallory wondered if the queen had chosen not to come because she feared for her life in such a crowd or because Queen Eleanor was furious with the church leaders, who were insisting she be a dutiful wife and surrender to her husband.

As the wagon threaded its way through the guests dressed in a rainbow of silk and wool, shouts of congratulations echoed off the simple stone buildings. Lady Violet waved, clearly enjoying being the center of attention. Beside her, Lady Elita ignored the bride. All her smiles were aimed at the comte, who was riding next to the cart.

When they reached the church, the comte helped the women from the cart and offered his arms to both the bride and Lady Elita. Their giggles as they accepted his assistance echoed against the stone fronts of the buildings.

"Odd," Mallory said as she watched the threesome.

"What is odd?" Saxon asked.

"I thought Landis D'Ambroise would be here. He and Lady Violet seem to be good friends."

"He may be waiting inside in order to get a good seat for the Mass."

Smiling as Saxon led her and Ruby through the crowd toward the church door, charming people in order to get them to step aside for the groom's brother, she forgot about the other guests, friends and strangers alike. Her gaze focused on Saxon. He kissed her hand, then went to stand beside his brother at the arched church door.

The columns on either side of the door were decorated with carvings of animals and people, both real and imaginary. The church's great wooden door was closed, and she knew it would not be thrown open until the ceremony was completed and the guests went into the church for the celebratory Mass.

Lady Violet was led to the door by an elderly man Mallory did not recognize. When she heard someone whisper it was the lady's father, she wondered why Saxon's had not come to the ceremony. Saxon had not spoken of his father often. Could it be that his father had sided with King Henry the Senior? Maybe the king was not the only one whose offspring had turned away from him.

Mallory pushed those uncomfortable thoughts aside. The ceremony was about to begin. She tried to watch the priest as he smiled benevolently at the bride and groom, but she kept looking at Saxon. He glanced at her as he put his hand on his brother's back to steady him when Sir Godard tilted to one side. She stared into Saxon's eyes as the priest spoke of how it was always special for two people to announce their love for each other and their desire to spend the rest of their days together. For the first time, she wanted that promise of forever with a man. She wanted it with Saxon, because she dared to believe that the love they could share was worth trusting him.

She hoped they would not spend too long at the wedding feast in the queen's great hall. She wanted to be alone with Saxon, to taste his slow, luscious kisses, to stroke his skin, to thrill in the ecstasy with him again.

Noise along the street tore through her fantasy. Hoofbeats. Mallory heard shrieks. As the priest choked on his words, she looked over her shoulder to see a trio of men riding at top speed along the street. People scattered before them, but someone was going to be trampled.

Steel flashed. The riders were carrying bare swords! When she saw them cutting down those who would not or could not get out of the way fast enough, she reached for her bow. Her fingers found nothing, and she remembered she had left it at the palace.

"Get inside the church!" Saxon shouted as he tugged the tall, thick door open.

Ruby!

As her maid threw open the door of a nearby house and pulled two small children in with her, she looked at Mallory, motioning wildly.

Mallory knew she could not push through the panicked people in time to reach the door before the riders did. She leaped forward and grabbed Lady Violet's and Lady Elita's arms. The ladies seemed too shocked to move, but Mallory urged them toward the church doorway.

"No!" Lady Violet cried.

"Saxon will bring Sir Godard," Mallory said, pushing the

priest into the church because he seemed as frozen as the ladies. "Father, hurry before you are hurt."

"No! Father!"

Realizing that Lady Violet was not calling to the priest, but her own father, Mallory looked back in time to see the older man climb into the cart. It bounced away, fleeing the riders. He used a hand whip to push people out of his way. He was abandoning his daughter? Rage struck Mallory. She could too easily imagine her father leaving her the same way.

The anger strengthened her, and she seized Lady Violet's arm and swung her into church. The lady crumpled onto the floor, but tried to crawl toward the open door. Mallory halted her by taking her arm again.

The interior of the church was dark and cool. A single lamp burned by the steps going down into the crypt near the altar. The sounds from the street echoed strangely among the rafters.

Saxon waved wildly as he ran into the church, his brother lurching after him. "They are coming!"

"Into the sanctuary?" gasped the priest.

Taking the priest by the arm, Saxon ordered him to run along with him and Sir Godard. "Mallory, hurry!" he shouted over his shoulder.

Mallory once more took Lady Elita's arm as well as Lady Violet's. "We need to go."

Lady Elita gathered up her skirt and fled after Saxon, but Lady Violet refused to move.

"Lady Violet, you must come with me." She punctuated each word with another tug on the lady's arm. "You are in danger."

She feared Lady Violet was suffering some sort of nervous fit that left her paralyzed. There was no time to find out. Whirling the woman around, she shoved her after the others.

"No!" Lady Violet shrieked.

Mallory did not slow. As Saxon came running back up the stairs from the crypt, she kept pushing Lady Violet forward. He shouted to Mallory to hide in the crypt as he took the lady at the waist and tipped her over his shoulder. Running by his side and trying to keep the woman's flailing hands and feet from striking her or Saxon, Mallory paused at the top of the stairs and motioned for Saxon to go down first.

"Protect Lady Violet," she said when he halted.

He nodded and stepped past her on the narrow, steeply curving stairs. As he did, she pulled his sword from his belt. She raised it and backed down the stairs, not wanting to give anyone the chance to leap upon Saxon and the lady.

A flood of men flowed into the church. Several people by the door tried to halt them, but the men refused to be stopped. The glare of sunlight through the doorway burned eye-scorchingly bright off the bare steel in their hands.

Mallory went as quickly as she could down the stairs. The light had been doused, so she had to feel for each step with her toes as the darkness swallowed her. Damp odors tainted each breath. She had just reached the bottom when she heard footsteps overhead.

A hand reached out of the dark and pulled her away from the stairs and behind a stone sarcophagus that must be the memorial for Saint Porchaire. She dropped to her knees, scraping her hand on the rough stone. She held tightly to the sword, not wanting it to strike the memorial and alert the men chasing them.

"Who are they?" she heard Saxon whisper.

She was about to answer that she had no idea, then realized the question was not for her, because his brother said, "I don't know."

Light bounced down the stairs and, for a second, streamed over the sarcophagus. She saw the priest on his knees praying silently. Beside him, Sir Godard was sitting with his arms clasped around his knees. Lady Elita was clutching Saxon's shoulder, and he had his arm around Lady Violet and his hand over her mouth.

Mallory was sure the brief spurt of light had fooled her. Why would Saxon be trying to keep the lady silent?

She got her answer when a voice called, "My beloved Violet, are you down here?"

Light bounced off the low ceiling, and Mallory glanced at Saxon as she recognized the voice. Landis D'Ambroise! Why . . . ? She stared at Lady Violet, who was struggling to free herself from Saxon. The lady must *want* to go to D'Ambroise, but if she wanted him, why had she agreed to marry Sir Godard?

The sword was yanked from her hand as a shout was roared in her ears. She stared at Sir Godard, who was brandishing the sword as he drunkenly lurched around the tomb to stand in front of a low table that must serve as an altar.

Jumping to her feet, she saw that D'Ambroise held a sword out in front of his mail tunic. She put her hands on the top of the sarcophagus. She prayed that Saint Porchaire, whoever he had been, would forgive her as she swung her feet up and over the memorial. She landed in the narrow space between Sir Godard and D'Ambroise, who was flanked by three men holding their swords at the ready. Both Saxon's brother and D'Ambroise snarled for her to move as they edged toward each other, circling like two beasts ready to pounce.

"I am not moving," she said in her sternest voice, "until you both put down your swords. Do you want to damn yourselves by spilling blood on holy ground?"

Neither man looked at her.

"Think of your immortal souls," she pleaded.

D'Ambroise reached out and shoved her aside, knocking her into the stone tomb. She tried to get between them, but the swords struck, the sound resonating through the crypt.

"Where is she?" D'Ambroise snarled.

Sir Godard swung his sword, missing the other man and striking the altar. Sparks bounced off the stone.

"Mallory!" Saxon called. "Move away!"

Standing, he released Lady Violet. He pushed her toward D'Ambroise and seized Mallory's hand in the same motion. He jerked her roughly around the stone sarcophagus toward him. She saw him draw his dagger, but he gave her no time to ask questions as he led her toward where his brother stood once more by the altar. Lady Elita scurried after them, her eyes wide with disbelief as Lady Violet threw her arms around D'Ambroise. Their embrace was quick, but its intimacy revealed they had shared far more.

"You have Lady Violet," Saxon said. "Go, if that is the lady's wish."

"Is it your wish, my beloved Violet?" D'Ambroise cooed.

"You know it is." She turned and spat at Sir Godard's feet. "Listen to your brother sing of this day's events when I gave myself to my chivalrous knight."

"Go then, D'Ambroise," ordered Saxon. "Take your lady and leave."

"She is mine!" cried Sir Godard as the two lovers began to climb the stairs after D'Ambroise's men. He raced toward them.

Mallory ran to stop him. She watched in horror when D'Ambroise turned and drove his sword into Sir Godard. Lady Elita screamed. Lady Violet may have, too, but Lady Elita's screech echoed from every direction, so Mallory could not tell as she tried to catch Sir Godard as he fell backward. His weight pressed her to her knees, sending pain up through her.

Saxon slipped his arms between her and his brother. She scrambled away as he brought his brother down with care to the stone floor. Blood pooled beneath Sir Godard.

"Elita, go to the palace and bring help!" he ordered. "We must take him to the healer immediately."

Hearing a thump behind them, Mallory saw Elita in a pile on the floor.

The priest went to Elita, checked her, and looked up. "She has fainted."

"I will go and get help," Mallory said.

Saxon picked up his sword and pressed the hilt into her hand. "Be careful."

She nodded, then ran up the stairs. She listened, but the church was silent except for the rumble of the priest's voice from behind her. Hoping he was not giving Sir Godard last rites, she hurried out into the street. People cried out in horror and pointed at her. Only then did she look down at herself to discover her gown was covered with blood. As she ran toward the palace, she wondered how much a man could lose and still live.

Mallory had no answer by the next morning. Sir Godard clung to life with a tenacity she had never seen in him before. On one side of his bed, Saxon paced, while on the other side, the priest sat, his face glum. The wound had been stitched closed, but so much blood had been left on the crypt's floor.

When the physician arrived, he ordered them from the room. Saxon protested, and the squat man agreed that he, as the wounded man's brother, could stay, but the others, including the priest, must leave.

Saxon went to the door with Mallory. Folding her hands in his, he said, "I will send for you if there is a change, dearest."

"I want to stay here with you."

"I want you to stay here with me." He curved his other hand along her face. "But go and change. I do not like to see you covered with blood."

Her face grew cold. "Oh, Saxon, I am sorry. I did not think how my gown would remind you of . . ." She glanced toward the bed.

His fingers turned her face back toward him. "I do not like to see blood on *you*. I will send for you as soon as I can."

"I will be in my room."

"Isn't this the morning you teach your archery class?"

"Yes, but Lady Fleurette D'Ambroise is my only student. I doubt she will be there today."

"Go, dearest, and see if she comes. If she does, teach your class. It will make the time go more quickly for you."

She put her hand over his on her face. "We will be by the river, as we always are."

"Do not go alone."

"I will take Ruby and Chance with me."

"Two good guardians." He released her as a groan came from the bed.

Mallory closed the door, then hurried along the corridor. Each person she met averted their eyes. She could not blame them. Nobody wanted to think about what had happened.

There were whispered rumors that D'Ambroise would be outlawed, and if he married Lady Violet, the marriage would be annulled because it had not received the queen's permission. She was unsure if either story were true.

An hour later, as Mallory crossed the field by the river, her maid and Chance both walked close to her. A lone figure stood by the pile of hay that served as the target for her students.

"Wait here," she said to Ruby.

"As you wish, milady." The maid could not hide her distrust of the young woman waiting by the hay.

Mallory glanced toward Chance and repeated, "Wait here."

Ruby put her hand on the dog's head, and Chance sat with doleful eyes focused on Mallory. Giving them both a bolstering smile, Mallory walked across the field.

Lady Fleurette raised her head as Mallory approached. The scars of heated tears glistened on her cheeks in the sunshine. She held out her unstrung bow.

"I am sorry, Lady Mallory," she whispered. "I wish I could have continued our lessons, but I can understand if you never wish to teach me again."

"Our lessons can continue, if *you* wish," Mallory replied, not taking the proffered bow.

"I would like that, but I must leave Poitiers. My family has been shamed by my brother's actions, and I will not be welcome at the queen's court any longer. It has even been whispered that Landis is the one who has tried to kill the queen. I know that is not true, but I cannot prove it because I have to leave."

"The queen has banished you?"

Lady Fleurette shook her head. "She did not need to, for I

offered to leave. I wanted you to know, Lady Mallory, that my brother is no murderer."

"Sir Godard—"

"I know of that," she said, her face ashen. "I know, as well, that my brother would not have intended to slay him, only to halt him long enough to allow Landis to slip away with his lady."

Mallory nodded. She believed Lady Fleurette was right, because Landis had been completely focused on Lady Violet. He was simply a fool in love, who had made a horrendous mistake that was going to cost him and his family much.

"Are you going home, Lady Fleurette?" she asked.

"I am not sure. My father died two years ago, and my mother has remarried. My stepfather was very happy to have me come to Poitiers with Landis."

Mallory dampened her lips, then said, "If I may, Lady Fleurette, I have a suggestion for a place where you will find welcome and can continue your lessons."

"Where?"

"St. Jude's Abbey in England."

"An abbey?" The tears filled her eyes again. "I know my mother would like me to join a convent, but I have resisted."

"St. Jude's Abbey is not like the holy houses you are familiar with here in Poitou and Aquitaine." She lifted her bow off her shoulder and, setting an arrow to it, shot it directly into the center of the hay. "It is where I learned to do that and much more."

"At an abbey?"

"At St. Jude's Abbey, where I live. When I return . . ." She almost choked on the commonplace words as she thought of going back to St. Jude's Abbey and never seeing Saxon again. He knew how to reach the Abbey, so he might make the long journey to visit her. But, even then, they would be within the Abbey walls, and the joy she had discovered in his arms would be denied them. She had not given any thought last night to the future, and even when he had spoken of how he might not be able to be with her always, she had never considered that she would be returning to St. Jude's Abbey without him.

"Lady Mallory?"

Realizing she had become lost in her dreary thoughts, Mallory said, "When I return to St. Jude's Abbey, I will be glad to take you with me."

"You? Return to an abbey?"

Mallory sat down in the grass and motioned for Lady Fleurette to do the same. Quickly, she explained what was behind the walls of the Abbey. Lady Fleurette's eyes cleared of tears and grew bright with hope as Mallory spoke of the instructors, especially Nariko, who had taught unarmed combat.

The girl listened, rapt, until Mallory mentioned how Nariko had come to St. Jude's Abbey along with her late father from some land farther east than Jerusalem. With a gasp, she asked, "Are you saying your instructor Nariko traveled from somewhere beyond the farthest borders of Persia?"

Mallory smiled. "When you go to St. Jude's Abbey, you can ask her yourself about her journeys with the queen. We are fortunate that she came to St. Jude's Abbey to train us in the ways of combat in the distant East."

"But how can Nariko be real? You say she lived on an island where fiery rock bursts forth from mountains."

"She is real, and such mountains exist in Outremer between Rome and Jerusalem. I was told often at St. Jude's Abbey, as you will be, that you must learn to make your own judgments based on what you observe, not what rumor suggests."

Fleurette nodded. "I will try."

"Do you want to go to St. Jude's Abbey?"

"I do," she said fervently. "There is nothing left for me here, and I have enjoyed our lessons. I wish to continue. When do we leave?"

"I am not sure." She glanced up at the city wall, so the girl could not see her pain at the idea of bidding Saxon farewell. "I am here, as I told you, in the service of Queen Eleanor. Until she releases me from that service, I must remain. I . . ."

Someone walked through the city gate. Saxon! Her heart contracted with dread as she imagined the reasons he might leave his brother's bedside. None of them were good.

"I should go," Lady Fleurette said, standing.

"Saxon will not blame you for your brother's misdeeds." She got up and put her hand on the girl's shoulder. "But I understand if you are uncomfortable. Return to the palace."

"The queen—"

"I will tell her of our conversation and your plans to go to St. Jude's Abbey."

"But you would be wise," Saxon said as he came to stand beside them, "to remain out of Queen Eleanor's sight."

"Saxon, I am sorry." Bright tears flooded her eyes again.

"As I am, because I know that you are suffering, too. I am sure Mallory can provide you with a letter of introduction. You should leave posthaste."

Mallory bit her lower lip as Lady Fleurette stared at him in disbelief. His compassion undid the girl, and she began to weep. As Mallory put her arms around her, she saw the tension on Saxon's face. He wanted to talk with her, but not when Lady Fleurette could overhear. She motioned with her head toward Ruby.

The serving maid came when Saxon called to her. Letting Lady Fleurette lean on her, Ruby guided the girl back toward the gate. Mallory motioned for Chance to go with them. The dog's eager antics would help cheer the girl.

"Lady Fleurette is lucky she began lessons with you," Saxon said as he walked with Mallory to collect her arrow from the target on the hay. "St. Jude's Abbey may be the perfect place for her."

"How is your brother?"

"He still lives, but the surgeon insisted I leave after I made a few suggestions about Godard's care. He acts as if he believes I am so eager to become the heir that I want my brother to receive poor care." His mouth straightened as his eyes gleamed with rage.

"But you left Sir Godard with him?"

"Only because he allowed the priest to return to the room, and, after a quick conversation with Father Hilaire, I knew he would make sure the surgeon did not murder my brother in an effort to save him." He took her hand and raised it to his lips. "You taste of sunshine and life."

She curved her hand around his nape as she tilted his mouth toward hers. She froze as she heard the hay behind her rustle. His eyes widened as she was torn away from him and whirled to face a man she had seen only once—the night of her arrival when they were attacked on the pier.

"Milady, I have found you at long last," crowed Jacques Malcoeur.

Something struck her head, and the world vanished into darkness as Saxon's shout rang in her ears.

Chapter 16

Saxon swallowed a curse as he was knocked from his feet while trying to get to where Mallory sprawled in the grass. How could he have been so stupid? He had warned her to be cautious, and, as soon as he was alone with her, he had been able to think only of making love with her again. His craving for her might have left her dead.

"Stay where you are, troubadour," snarled Malcoeur.

Struggling to sit, Saxon demanded, "I want to make sure she is still breathing."

The thief seemed astonished at his defiance when he was surrounded by five armed men. A quick motion sent one of Malcoeur's men to bend over Mallory. He put his hand in front of her lips and nodded.

"She lives," Malcoeur announced.

"Don't be shocked that I have no reason to believe you," Saxon answered.

"You should be less worried about the woman and more worried if you will die before your brother does. Aren't you interested in what I want?"

"I will answer that question after I see for myself that she is still alive."

"And if she is not?"

Saxon said without any emotion, "I will hold your beating heart in my hand, Malcoeur."

The thief laughed. "You? A troubadour who had to be rescued by a woman?"

"I will answer those questions as well once I have checked her myself."

"All right." He gave a magnanimous wave toward Mallory.

Not revealing that he was amazed that Malcoeur had relented, Saxon went on hands and knees to where she lay. He gently turned her over so her head was cradled in his lap. As the thief's man had, he put his fingers close to her lips. The soft, steady pulse of air allowed him to breathe more easily.

She was alive, and he needed to do what he could to keep her that way. When she groaned, he hoped no one else had heard the sound. That hope was doomed, for she opened her eyes and raised her fingers up. He guessed she was going to touch her head, which must be aching, but her hand stroked his face.

"Mallory . . ." When he was surrounded by Malcoeur's men, he could not speak his joy at seeing the life on her face and the warmth in her eyes.

She was jerked away from him and to her feet. She wobbled, but squared her shoulders when she stared at the six thieves. He started to stand, but halted when sunlight glistened off the honed edge of a sword.

"Stay where you are, troubadour," Malcoeur said before turning to Mallory. He inclined his head slightly. "Milady."

She held her head high. "What do you want, M. Malcoeur?"

"I want you to cooperate."

"Why?"

"I cannot explain that here, but I can tell you that, if you do not do as I ask, we shall kill the troubadour."

She nodded, then winced. Lines of pain cut into her face. She did not resist when a man drew her dagger from its sheath and two others grasped her arms.

The men must have been warned about her amazing skills, because the two did not release her arms until a third lashed her wrists behind her back. She did not fight them, and Saxon wondered what she was scheming. She would not go docilely with their captors unless she was waiting for the right moment to escape.

Or was she? Maybe she was in pain and wallowing in so much confusion from the blow to her skull that she could not think clearly. Saxon swore under his breath. He *would* hold Malcoeur's beating heart in his hand if she were harmed more.

Mallory looked at him, and Saxon raised his brows in an expression he hoped she would be able to decipher. He wanted her to know that he, too, would be watching for any opportunity to get away. He could not guess whether she understood or not, because she looked down at her feet. When she raised her head again, her face was as emotionless as an effigy.

"Get up!" ordered another man, prodding Saxon with his foot.

"All right."

The man tapped the lute as he had Saxon, and a discordant thud came from it.

Saxon grabbed the man's ankle and upended him. The man hit the ground hard. Standing, Saxon folded his arms across his chest and looked down at the prone man. "Be careful of my lute."

"You fret more about your lute than your lady," Malcoeur said.

He wanted to tell Mallory that the thief was trying to drive a wedge between them, but he had to trust that she would know the truth. Amazement riveted him. He had asked her to trust him, but they had never spoken of his trusting her. He wondered why.

Knowing he could not let his mind wander, he said, "The lady can defend herself, as you have learned firsthand, Malcoeur." He gave a quick glance at Mallory, who still showed no expression.

Malcoeur smiled broadly and motioned to his men.

Saxon shouted a warning to Mallory as one of the men behind her raised his fist, but he never saw which of Malcoeur's craven thieves struck him over the head.

* * *

Moonlight oozed through the cracks in the stone floor over Mallory's head. The scanty light shone on Saxon's face. His eyes were closed, but his chest rose and fell with slow regularity beneath the lute that had been placed on it when they were brought into what she guessed was a crypt. She had not seen where they went, because a sack had been placed over her aching head before she was tossed over some bony shoulder and brought to this hole that stank of damp and rot.

The space must be older than the crypt in Saint-Porchaire. The walls were uneven stone, not allowing her to find any way to get comfortable. Stone coffins were scattered throughout the space that was barely high enough for her to sit in without bumping her head on the ceiling. All the bones were not within the coffins, for she could see the dull sheen of ancient shards.

She was unsure which church Malcoeur was using as his private lair. Most of the churches were close to the city walls and the river, save for the new one being raised by the palace.

Straining her ears, she tried to hear if the thieves remained overhead. She had been able to discern their voices, but no words, after they closed the stone door, shutting her and Saxon into the burial pit. The men had been arguing with their leader, or so the raised voices had suggested.

But it was silent now. No footsteps, no voices, not even the sound of the wind. Just the moonlight that had replaced the sunshine several hours ago. Maybe the men were gone.

Good!

Bending again to the task she had begun as soon as the stone door closed, Mallory swallowed her pain as she struggled to squeeze one hand out of her bonds. She had held them at an angle when they were tied, hoping that when she moved them closer together, she would have room to escape. She had room, but not enough. Blood coursed along her wrist as she twisted it, but she could not give up.

A mumble froze her. Saxon! She called his name softly, but

he did not answer. Her head ached, so she knew what he was suffering.

They needed to get out of the crypt before Malcoeur and his men put whatever they were scheming into action. She wriggled her hands again. She smiled as her hand slid. Her own blood must be making her skin slippery. Clenching her teeth, she tugged. Pain shot up her arm as her hand inched partway past the rope. She pulled again. She wanted to shout with delight when her hand came free. She brushed aside the ropes on her other hand and dropped them on the floor.

Inching to where Saxon lay, she touched his shoulder as she whispered his name. He erupted up, reaching for his dagger. His head struck the low ceiling as she caught his lute before it could fall on the floor.

She put her finger to his lips as he began to curse. His eyes focused on her, and she saw his bafflement.

"Where are we?" he asked in a whisper.

"In an old crypt. Malcoeur and his men brought us here."

"Why?" He rubbed the top of his head.

"I don't know." She handed him the lute. "We have to go."

He gazed at her. He lifted one of her braids that had fallen down. "You are a dream come to life." He ran his fingers through the tendrils edging her face.

"Saxon, are you awake? We have to go! Now!" She leaned forward to shake him again.

He did not offer her the chance. Hooking his arm around her waist, he pulled her down to him. She started to protest, but he silenced her by capturing her lips. His tongue delved into her mouth, sliding along its slick shadows. When her hands pushed against his chest, he rolled her onto her back.

So easily she could have succumbed to his seduction, but something cracked beneath her. She shifted from beneath him. A bone? She heard another sound. She did not want to think what was sliding one stone against another. Was there someone—or something—else alive in the crypt with them?

When he started to protest, she grasped his arms and gave

him a sharp shake. "Saxon, there is no time. We have to go *now*!"

"Why?" he asked, his voice still uneven.

"I will explain once we escape. We need to go while our hearts still beat." She shoved his lute into his hands again.

Light sprayed in, blinding her. Had that scary sound been the door opening?

"You are worrying needlessly, milady," said Jacques Malcoeur as he squatted in the doorway. "I have no wish to slay you."

"That is good," she replied with more self-possession than she felt, "because I think you will soon learn that we can make it worthwhile to let us leave alive." She had had a lot of time to consider her choices while she worked to escape her bonds. Even so, her plan depended on the thief's being both greedy and rational. She was certain of the first, but not of the second.

"It will be worth much when the queen pays the ransom I shall demand for her troubadour and her lady warrior."

"You think too small, Jacques Malcoeur," she said with disdain.

"Mallory," Saxon warned in a sharp whisper.

She ignored him as she continued to lock gazes with the thief. "Why do you think only of the petty crimes you commit along the River Clain when you could have much greater rewards if you used your imagination?"

"Imagination?" Malcoeur asked, frowning. "I can imagine many things."

"Is that why you stole mail for your men to wear when they prowled the river?"

"Mail? My men have no mail. Where would they get a knight's garb?"

She clasped her hands in her lap. The shock in the thief's voice told her that he was probably being honest. But if the men in mail who had attacked them and Godard did not belong to Malcoeur, to whom did they answer?

She was not going to learn that from Malcoeur, so she said,

"As you can see, I can imagine many things, too. Thieves in mail is an outrageous idea. Can you think of something equally outrageous? Can you imagine yourself being rewarded by the king of France?"

Saxon stared at Mallory. Had she lost her mind? Other women, terrified by tales told within the palace walls of Malcoeur and his band of thieves, had fainted, revived along with promises never to frighten them so again. Had Malcoeur's ambush scared Mallory's wits from her? He could not believe that, because she had not been weakhearted when D'Ambroise sliced into his brother in the crypt at Saint-Porchaire.

But if she had not lost her mind, why was she invoking King Louis's name?

Malcoeur stared at her. "I must admit such a reward is beyond what I have ever imagined, but I am intrigued, milady. Tell me what you know." The thief smiled as he leaned toward her. He rested one arm on his knee while he lifted a strand of hair that had escaped from her braid and toyed with it.

Saxon slapped his hand away. When Malcoeur reached for his dagger, Mallory said, "Stop it, both of you! We need to be allies, not enemies."

Her mind *must* have been rattled by the blow to her skull. Allied with the thief who had tried to kill them? When she put her hand on Saxon's arm and squeezed, she did not look at him. She did not need to, for he understood she wanted him to let her continue negotiating with Malcoeur. He hated the idea, but his aching head refused to offer him another plan for escape.

"You may not know what I know," Mallory said with her quiet authority that demanded attention. "I know that none of the kings battling for control of England and Poitou and Aquitaine wishes to see the queen die. Yet, someone has tried to kill her." She smiled coolly. "Neither Saxon Fitz-Juste nor I have been able to determine the cur's identity or who is paying him to slay the queen. Perhaps it is because we know too few people capable of such a heinous act."

"But I know many." A smiled curled Malcoeur's lips.

"We can use your help, and you could use the reward the queen would offer for your assistance in discovering who wishes her dead."

"What reward?"

"A pardon for past crimes?"

"I have no need of a pardon when I have not been caught."

Saxon saw Mallory falter. She might be brilliant at persuading the thief to listen, but she remained a gentle soul, unaware how vast the depths of greed for wealth and power could be.

As if he had been privy to her scheme all along, he said, "A future pardon would be unnecessary if the queen provided you with enough gold to allow you to live in comfort for the rest of your days."

"Me and my men."

"You and your men, most certainly." He had to admire Malcoeur's loyalty to the other thieves. If King Henry the Younger had been as steadfast in his vows to his father, there would be no rebellion tearing the land apart. "We do not speak for the queen, but I can promise, if you release us now, that we will arrange for you to have a meeting with her to discuss this very matter."

"With safe passage in and out of the palace guaranteed?"

"Yes," Mallory said. "I can promise you that."

"We will need a lot of gold to live as comfortably as we wish."

"Queen Eleanor will understand that."

Saxon waited as the thief considered her unexpected offer. He had to admit that Mallory had devised a clever way to solve a troublesome problem . . . *if* the queen would issue an invitation for the thief to come to the palace and see the good sense in making such a deal.

Malcoeur nodded and moved out of the doorway, gesturing for them to come out of the low-ceilinged crypt.

Leading the way, because he was still unsure whether the thief was being honest or setting a trap for them, Saxon looked around as he emerged from the crypt. He was astonished to see half-finished paintings. They were in the small church named Saint-Jean. In front of him was the deep pool that had been used to baptize early Christians.

"Oh, my!" Mallory said from behind him, and he knew she was awed by the ancient space being redecorated with amazing frescoes.

He took her hand and kept her close as they walked around the pool toward the stairs leading up to the door. Malcoeur matched every pace, stepping in front of them at the base of the stairs.

"You have three days to obtain an audience for me with the queen," the thief said. "If you fail, I will hunt you down, and you will pay for trying to trick me."

"How shall we contact you?" Mallory asked, and again Saxon was astonished by her outer calm. In his hand, her fingers quivered as if she were ill with a fierce fever.

"Leave a message here." He pointed to an alcove to the right of the stairs. "I will find it."

"I will leave an arrow," she replied. "There will be a notch along the shaft for each hour after sunrise until the time when you are to appear before the queen."

The thief agreed and moved aside so they could leave.

Mallory remained where she was. "M. Malcoeur, if you are going to help us find the murderer, you must know what we know. Whoever it is has shown, despite awkward shooting at the queen by the river, that he is a skilled archer. When I was teaching one of my students, I—"

"That is not relevant." Saxon took her arm and tried to lead her up the stairs.

"Why do you say that?" She frowned at him as icily as she had at Malcoeur. "The murderer may have tried to deceive us with the first shots, because the arrow that matched mine flying across the field—"

"Was mine."

She stared at him, and he wished he could have found another time and another way to tell her the truth. She choked, "You are that skilled with a bow?"

"Yes."

"But why did you fire that shot to match mine?"

"I wanted to distract you."

"Why?"

Aware that Malcoeur was listening with a faint smile, Saxon knew he had to devise a tale that answered her question without revealing why Saxon had come to Poitiers. He put his hands on her shoulders as he said, mixing a bit of truth with the lies he must continue to tell her until he had completed his work in Poitiers, "Because I was afraid if you came closer to solving the mystery, you would put yourself in danger you could not escape from."

"You used the comte's colors. Why?"

"As I said, a distraction." Saxon heard Malcoeur's snicker and said, "We can discuss this later." Not giving her a chance to reply, he pushed Mallory ahead of him up the stairs before Malcoeur changed his mind and drove blades into their backs.

When they came out into the moonlight, he saw something in the grass in front of the church. She ran forward and picked up her bow and her quiver, still filled with arrows.

Coming back to him, she said in a voice so cold that he knew she had been deeply hurt by his ploy with the arrow, "We need to go quickly to the palace. You must be concerned about your brother."

He did not want to say that he had not thought once of Godard's health while negotiating with Malcoeur. He had been concentrating on protecting Mallory's life as she bargained for their freedom.

"Why," he asked, "did you speak King Louis's name to Malcoeur?"

"I wanted to shock him."

"You did. You shocked both of us."

"I was not thinking of shocking you." Her voice was clipped. "I thought you were my ally."

Instead of answering, he hurried with her along the dark streets. It must be far past the middle of the night. Anything he said now would lead to more questions he did not want to answer. She was already hurt by what she saw as his betrayal. He must avoid bringing her more pain.

Only when they had reached the moat and were crossing through the gate to enter the palace did he say, "I am sorry I tried to distract you, Mallory, in such an absurd way."

"You could have trusted me with the truth." Hurt filtered into her voice, which shook more with each word. "You are always demanding the truth from me, but this time, when you could have been honest with me, you chose to play childish games."

He wished he could see her face in the moonlight, but she was looking away from him. "I don't know why I could not trust you then."

"Because you thought I was incapable of defending myself and the queen?"

"I have never thought that."

"Never?"

Pausing in midstep, he grasped her arm to keep her from walking away. "Not for a long time, Mallory. Other women are distracted by a song or a poem or a pretty flower. I knew none of those would distract you for long, but the mystery of an unseen archer would."

Her shoulders sagged as her breath sifted past her lips. "Why do you have to make sense *now*? Why couldn't you make sense then, too?"

"I cannot answer that. All I can ask is for you to forgive me. Will you?"

She did not answer him. Instead she asked, "Why did you choose Comte du Fresne's colors?"

"When I considered who might be honorless enough to slay the queen, I thought of du Fresne and how he switches sides whenever he pleases. I had no idea he would be arriving in Poitiers at the moment I shot the arrow."

Her eyes widened as she faced him. "Do you think the comte intends to murder the queen?"

"He has shown no signs of being involved in the plot to see her dead. I have an ally watching him closely." He sighed as she had, his breath oozing out slowly. "I should have found another way to keep you from danger. You have not said yet if you forgive me."

"I have not yet decided if I forgive you."

"Mallory, this is no jest."

For a long moment, she said nothing. Just when he thought she was ready to take a vow of silence, she said, "I must forgive you, because how else can I appreciate your wanting to protect me?" She stroked his cheek, then gave it a light, playful slap. "But I do not need your protection."

He smiled as he caught her hand and, pressing his mouth to her palm, looked up at her softening smile. "But allow me the fantasy of thinking you *do* need my protection as much as I need you in my arms."

"If you must."

"I must, so let me take the arrow with the notches back to Saint Jean's church."

"*If* the queen agrees to speak with Malcoeur," she said as they continued across the courtyard where the stones had faded to a milky gray in the night.

"If?"

"She does not like being dictated to, and she will do what she wishes when she wishes." She paused and faced him. "When I first came to Poitiers, I thought the queen was perfect. She seemed all-knowing and without the conflicting passions that make the rest of us so imperfect. I was wrong. She is no goddess. She is a frightened woman who knows her sons and King Louis must not falter in their support, or she will face her husband's fury. The claim that she betrayed him because he betrayed her will gain her no clemency. We have seen that with the attempts on her life."

"So she should be eager to meet with Malcoeur before she is killed."

"As I said, I once would have agreed. Now I am not so sure."

"If we go to her—"

"No," she said, brushing his hair back from his face. "You must go to your brother and be with him. I will speak to the queen. She brought me here to help her, and that is what I intend to do."

"Whether she wishes you to or not."

She nodded. "Whether she wishes me to or not."

Chapter 17

M allory wanted to slam the door of her room, but did not. The queen might hear. She laughed humorlessly at the irony. The queen had not heeded a single word Mallory had spoken during the terse audience.

Ruby looked up from her sewing, her eyes questioning. Beside her, Chance stared at Mallory, too, as she stormed across the room and threw her bow and quiver on the bed. For once, the dog's head was down and her tail still.

"Don't ask," Mallory said, trying to keep the exasperation out of her voice as she sat on the edge of the bed. "Forgive me. I am not annoyed at you."

Rushing over to her, Ruby knelt. "Milady, did the queen not see the wisdom of your plan to protect her?"

"She is not convinced it is necessary. She believes her present contingent of guards will keep her alive. She said, 'You have been successful thus far.'"

Ruby's eyes widened, and Mallory realized her mimicry of the queen's voice had not only been in her mind. She had copied the queen's Aquitaine accent aloud.

"Milady . . ."

Coming to her feet, Mallory gave her maid the best smile she could. "Please do not tell anyone else I spoke as I did."

"I would never do such a thing, milady. You know you can trust me."

"I know I can. If—"

A furious rapping came at the door.

As Ruby went to answer it, Mallory reached for her bow and an arrow. Such a frantic sound could mean trouble, and she must be ready.

She realized how mistaken she was when she saw Father Hilaire in the corridor. The priest from Saint-Porchaire was wringing his hands, dismay on his face lengthened from his hours without sleep.

"Sir Godard? How does he fare?" she asked, even though she already knew. The priest would not be at her door unless the situation was grave.

"You must come, milady. His time is very short."

She hurried with him along the surprisingly empty hallways. The rest of the queen's household must be gathering for another Court of Love, oblivious to how a man who should have been a husband enjoying his wife was dying.

Father Hilaire opened the door and stepped aside to let her enter. Odors of infection and human waste swarmed out to surround her, but she paid no attention to them. She ran to where Saxon stood by his brother's bed where Sir Godard lay, his eyes closed, his mouth open as he gasped for each breath under sheets stained with blood.

She took Saxon's hand and whispered, "I am so very sorry."

"When will the queen see Malcoeur?" he asked, not taking his eyes from his brother.

"Don't think of that now." She put her other hand over his. "That can wait, Saxon."

"Saxon?" repeated his brother.

The priest hurried around the bed, readying what he needed for the last rites, but Sir Godard looked at his brother.

Saxon released her hand and reached out to take his brother's. "I am here, Godard."

"You must go."

"Go? Where?"

"To Father and tell him that at least I succeeded in fooling everyone." He coughed and winced. "I even fooled you, because you never guessed I was the one."

"The one what?"

Sir Godard stared back at the ceiling, and Mallory was unsure whether he even heard Saxon's question. He mumbled something before closing his eyes.

"The one what?" Saxon repeated.

"I don't know," she whispered, wishing she could offer him some comfort.

Father Hilaire began the prayers for the last rites, but halted when Sir Godard said, "Forgive me, Father, for I have sinned. It has been four months since my last confession."

"Milady, Saxon . . ." The priest looked toward the door.

Before they could leave to give the dying man the privacy for his confession, Sir Godard said, "Father, I am guilty of trying to break the fifth commandment."

" 'Thou shall not kill,' " she said with a gasp.

"Many men have broken the commandment while defending themselves in battle," the priest said.

"Not in battle," Sir Godard said. "Here in Poitiers."

Saxon went back to the bed, ignoring the shock on the priest's face. He did not care if he was intruding on a last confession. He needed to discover what his brother meant.

Before he could ask, Godard continued, his voice growing weaker as his rage grew stronger, "She does not deserve to live. She has betrayed two husbands and has turned her sons against their father. I tried to fulfill my orders to kill her, but she was saved by that harlot who has bewitched my brother. I should have . . ." He struggled to take another breath. "Should . . . killed her first. I tried. I sent a man to slay her. He pretended to be . . ." He coughed, but continued on. "He pretended to be a messenger from the French king. He failed."

Mallory put her hands over her mouth to silence her cry of dismay. Her suspicions—and Saxon's—had been right. Bertram de Paris had been the archer who fired the arrow into her room. Had he attached the note in the hope that, if he failed to slay her, he might persuade her to flee? Not because she was protecting the queen, but because he wanted to disrupt the court and hurt his brother at the same time. She had not guessed Saxon's brother—his *twin*—could be so evil.

Godard's eyes focused on Saxon, and a faint smile curved his lips. "You never suspected me, did you? I finally bested you at something, brother. You always thought you were smarter than I am, but you never guessed it was . . ."

His head rolled lifelessly to one side. Father Hilaire continued his prayers, but his voice was shaking.

Saxon walked past Mallory, who wore a horrified expression. He left the room and kept walking. He paid no attention to where he was going, and he had no idea where he was bound. He had to get away from his brother's last words.

Saxon stood alone in the moonlight and waited, as he had all day, for release from the pain and grief and anger swirling through him in a deranged, off-key melody that threatened to tear him into pieces.

During the afternoon, the sun's bright light had failed to ease the cold churning in his center while he made arrangements to have his brother's corpse taken to the chapel on their family's estate. He had hoped the task would give him some time to regain his equanimity. The priest's prayers over Godard's body had left him more unsettled and on edge, as if he had been too close to a bolt of lightning.

When the priest had suggested that Saxon return to say something to his brother in farewell, the only thing Saxon had been able to think of to say was, "I did not know."

What had he not known? He did not want to examine that question too closely. To do so threatened to create more questions that would sear him like alcohol poured on an open wound.

So he had left the palace and walked along the river. The birds lilting on the water and the laughter of two hidden lovers had given him no surcease from the memory of the hatred fired at him by his brother's eyes. Even seeking the darkness of the cave where Mallory had looked for Malcoeur had not allowed him to escape the echo of his brother's triumphant words. No music soothed him, for every note he tried to play vanished, unwilling to be drawn from his lute's strings. Everything he had believed all his life was gone.

So, Saxon had returned to the palace with the rising of the moon. He had avoided anyone else, coming to the empty top of a palace tower. He squatted down in the patch of moonlight falling through the window. With his fists against his eyes, he whispered the words he could no longer keep unsaid: "Why, Godard? Why did you hate me so much when you were Father's inestimable heir?"

A gentle hand touched his arm.

He shook it off. "Leave me alone!"

"Saxon, I can help," Mallory said softly. "Let me help."

"How can you help?" He did not look up.

"You were a baby when your mother died. It was not so many years ago for me. I remember what it is like to lose someone you love."

"I have had other people I care about die." He choked as he hunched more deeply into himself. "Godard brought the news of my foster brother's death."

She knelt beside him. "I am so sorry. I know you mourn him, and I know you mourn for Godard. You were part of three souls that came into this world at once. Now two have left, and you think you are alone." She leaned her forehead against his shoulder. "You are not alone."

"Mallory, I would be happy to *be* alone right now."

"I know."

He waited, but she did not move to leave. "Mallory, I said I would like to be alone now." He stood, and she sat back on her heels. "If you will not go, then I will."

"And go where? Where can you go to escape the grief?"

He walked away.

"You cannot escape it," she called to his back.

"How do you know?" he snarled as he kept walking.

"Because I know you are suffering from more than grief. You are feeling betrayed, and I know what it is like to be betrayed by someone you believed you could always depend on."

He halted and faced her. Tears were falling along her cheeks, but an inner strength shone from her eyes. It was a strength born of pain and perfidy and disappointment. Not from a single incident, but time and time again until she lost her ability to trust others. Yet, in spite of what she had endured, she dared to trust, for she trusted him.

She closed the distance between them and took his hands. Clasping them between hers, she lifted them up to his heart.

"Saxon," she whispered, "whatever your brother did or said or was, he was not you. He made his choices, and you make yours. That is a lesson I took many years to learn."

"He must have arranged for the men in mail to attack us." He shook his head. "I should have guessed when he was barely injured while fighting what were obviously more skilled warriors." He clenched his hands at his sides. "I wonder what sort of group would rather die by swallowing poison than chance revealing their secrets."

"We may never know."

"But Godard was right about one thing. He fooled me."

"And it feels horrible to be made a fool of." She smiled sadly. "I learned that as you have, but I learned as well that I would rather give each person the benefit of the doubt."

"You?" He grinned through his rage and grief. "You never have given me the benefit of the doubt."

"Maybe I should say almost every person." She became somber again. "Or maybe it was because of how you dared me not to like you. Although I know now it was part of your attempt to distract me from my search for the murderer . . . Oh, Saxon, I am so sorry."

He drew his hands out of hers, and her face became ashen. Did she think he was about to walk away again? Didn't she realize that he needed her now as he never had before? She had become the one bit of sanity in his life. She somehow had woven together the tough resilience of a warrior with the tender resilience of a woman.

Putting his arm around her waist, he tugged her up against his chest. He kissed her hard, wanting to drive out every emotion but his craving for her. He stretched out his other arm and found a nearby door. He pushed it open, keeping her lips captive beneath his.

He raised his head to discover it was an empty chamber. He was about to close the door when she stepped past him and into the room. She took his hand and drew him in after her. Closing the door, she slid the bolt to lock it.

"Mallory, there is no bed. Not even a pallet."

She reached behind her and loosened her gown's laces. Shrugging off her outer gown, she spread it across the floor. "There." She sat on it and crooked her finger at him.

He knelt beside her. His arm swept around her, bringing her to him again. As her breath pulsed, hot and swift, in his mouth, he relished her pliant breasts against his chest. With her, he could find joy and forget those cruel words that were his brother's legacy to him. No, he did not want to think of Godard. He wanted to think only of Mallory. He had to touch her. He had to taste her. He had to be part of her. His mind was ready to explode just at the thought of the moment when she would be all around him.

He heard material rip as he drew off his tunic, but paid it no mind. Somehow, he rid himself of his clothes and her of hers, while he kept kissing her. He drew her over him as he rested back onto the makeshift bed of their discarded clothes. With her knees on either side of him, he watched her lean down to kiss him, her breasts brushing his naked chest.

Cupping them, he slid her toward him. He ran his tongue along their downy weight before teasing the very tips. When she shivered in eager anticipation, he could feel on his stomach the increasing heat between her legs. Then she reached back to run her fingers along him, and every sensation focused on where her fingertips caressed his most sensitive skin.

He grasped her hips and raised her over him. When he drove into her, he heard her gasp. He could not even gasp. He could only feel her body closing around him like a slick, warm glove. She shifted slightly, and he opened his eyes to admire her above him. His hands slid up the sheen of perspiration on her stomach to her breasts and then back down to her waist as she began to move slowly. He gazed up into her eyes and saw her intense need building as he was surrounded by her sweetest fire. Her head went back, and her hair flowed down around them, each tress a delicious caress.

Pulling her forward, he met her mouth to mouth. She shuddered in his arms and around him. He burst within her in one perfect moment of pleasure, one perfect moment when he did not have to think about betrayals yet to unfold.

Mallory hummed lightly to herself as she leaned her bow against the wall in her chamber after spending the past two hours waxing the bow and the bowstring to keep both supple. Saxon had gone with Father Hilaire to Saint-Porchaire to finish arrangements for a memorial service for his brother in Poitiers before the body was returned to England. Sir Godard Fitz-Juste's secrets would be buried with him.

She was not sure if that was good or bad, but she guessed the surviving men who had served Sir Godard would return to wherever they had come from to find out what to do next. Telling the queen that threat was gone was impossible, because she would not reveal the truth that would heap shame on Saxon.

Or would it soon be Sir Saxon? He was now his father's oldest son, and the obligations of liege duty would be his. Would he turn his back on the queen to go and fight with his father for the older king against his sons? He must have ignored his father's wishes when he came to Poitiers, but a second son could be foolish. The heir should heed his father's wishes, even though the king's heir had not.

"Milady," Ruby said from by her door, "if you will not require anything more of me this evening, I shall retire."

Mallory smiled. The polite words were Ruby's way of inquiring whether Saxon would be helping her undress for the night. Not wanting to tell the serving woman that Saxon had already helped her undress—and dress—once already today, she said only, "Go ahead. I will—"

A woman screamed, the sound reverberating oddly both through the hallway outside her door and through the open window. Ruby gave a soft cry. Mallory grabbed her bow and quiver, pulling out an arrow, ready to set it to string, before she reached the door.

She ran out into the corridor. She paused, trying to determine which direction she should go. The woman screamed again, and she ran left toward the stairs. The sound was coming from the lower floor. A door opened almost into her face, and she backpedaled, then ran down the stairs.

Someone shouted after her, but she did not stop to answer. She had no idea who was screaming and why.

At the bottom of the stairs, she bumped into someone coming up the steps, knocking herself back against the stone newel post. Pain exploded in her hip, but she ignored it as she saw Saxon helping up the man she had struck. It was de Mauzé, one of the queen's guards.

De Mauzé spat a curse at her as he stumbled up the stairs. She ignored him as she ran in the direction of the scream. When she heard footfalls behind her, she kept running. She had hoped Saxon had not gone with de Mauzé to protect Queen Eleanor. She could use his help in whatever she was about to face.

The woman screamed more, this time in obvious pain.

Mallory paused by an open door and saw a woman bent over double on her knees. Using the tip of her bow to push the door back slowly, she scanned the room. She saw nobody else in it. Even so, she kept the arrow in her hand as she went to the woman.

Lady Elita, she realized with a soft gasp, but the tear-washed face raised toward her barely resembled that of the elegant lady she had seen. The blonde's eyes were ringed with red, and her cheeks blotched with salt. Her lips quivered as she wiped her sleeve beneath her nose.

"What has happened?" asked Saxon.

"I don't know." Mallory put her bow by the door and slipped off her quiver, dropping the arrow back into it, before going to where Lady Elita crumpled once more on the floor, her body quaking with her sobs.

Saxon closed the door behind him as Mallory awkwardly put her arm around Lady Elita and murmured soft words of sympathy. She seldom offered solace to anyone, most especially not herself. She had tried, but it was not easy for her after failing to comfort her mother when her father humiliated her again. Just as Lady Elita had tried to humiliate her.

Yet, none of that mattered when Lady Elita was shaking with uncontrollable sobs. Mallory spoke with soft compassion to the blonde and urged her to draw in deep breaths to steady herself.

She saw Saxon take a step toward them, and she frowned, motioning vehemently with her head at the door. Someone had caused Lady Elita's tears, and if that someone returned, they needed to be prepared. While he kept watch, she must discover what had upset Lady Elita and sent her screams echoing through the palace.

"Milady," she said quietly as she had before, "breathe more slowly. Doing that will help you overcome the sobs."

Lady Elita buried her face in Mallory's lap. With a sigh, she stroked the blonde's hair as if Lady Elita were a child.

"He is leaving me," Lady Elita murmured.

"He?"

Mallory heard nothing but genuine concern in Saxon's voice, and she guessed Lady Elita did as well, because the blonde raised her head and looked directly at them for the first time.

"Philippe," Lady Elita whispered.

"Comte du Fresne?" Mallory asked.

Lady Elita nodded vigorously. "He said he loved me, but now he is abandoning me without giving me the jewels he had promised." Her face hardened, and Mallory had the sickening feeling deep in her stomach that the comte's failure to give the blonde any gifts was the real reason for her tears. "He has gone from the queen's court without giving me anything."

"Gone?" asked Saxon, closing the door and crossing the room to them. "Where?"

"His estates. He learned that King Louis is ready to withdraw from battle."

"Did du Fresne leave anything behind?"

"Just some papers. Nothing I can wear to adorn my beauty. He told me he would come back for me, but I do not believe him, for I saw him riding hard to get to the French king." She wiped her eyes and nose on her sleeve and gave Saxon a smile. "That was what you wanted me to find out, wasn't it, Saxon?"

Mallory was astounded. She should not have been, but she was, by the almost instantaneous transformation. The grieving woman had vanished, and the temptress had returned. Even though her eyes were still edged with red, she was fluttering her eyelashes at Saxon.

He looked past the blonde to Mallory with an intense frown. Unsure what he was trying to tell her, she hoped it was that she should remain silent. Which was just as well, because she was speechless at the change in Lady Elita. The amazing urge to laugh overwhelmed her. Did Lady Elita think she was so alluring that no man would note how manipulative her mercurial moods were?

"Lady Mallory," the blonde said, her gaze fixed on Saxon, "need not be here, does she?"

"You seem not to need more of her comfort," he replied.

"Not of *her* comfort." She threw herself at him, wrapping her arm around his neck.

"Mallory?" Saxon asked, looking at her again.

Mallory went to the door, opened it, and picked up her bow.

Tossing her quiver over her shoulder, she paused in the doorway. She winked at Saxon, who grinned over the blonde's head. She pointed up in the direction of her room, and he nodded.

She closed the door before she released the soft laugh. She had never thought she would feel guilty for leaving Saxon alone with another woman.

Saxon opened the door and allowed himself a moment to admire how the last moonlight of the night washed across Mallory, who was asleep on her bed. Her gown was tangled beneath her, giving him a beguiling view of her lithe legs. He wished he could tear every thought but that of making love with her from his head, especially when he had no idea whether he would ever hold her in her bed again.

He thought he had closed the door noiselessly, but she sat up and called, "Saxon? Is that you?"

"Yes." He crossed the room as she lit a lamp and set it on the table. "I am sorry to wake you, but I wanted to bid you farewell."

"Farewell?" She pushed her loose hair back over her shoulders. "Where are you going?"

"To King Henry the Senior's camp."

All sleepiness vanished from her face as she sat on the chest. "So what Lady Elita said was true? King Louis is withdrawing from battle?"

"He is ready to negotiate a truce."

"And leave the young king to fight on alone?" she asked. "What happened to turn him against King Henry the Younger?"

"Nothing but the fact that his knights have been fighting King Henry the Senior's men for almost forty days. If they continue fighting beyond forty days, he must pay the knights from his own revenues, because they are not obligated by their liege vows to provide men beyond that date." Looking out her window, which gave a view of the fields beyond the river to the north, he said, "Trust King Louis to come up with the very best excuse to break off the fighting when it is becoming clear that

King Henry the Senior is the better tactician and the better warrior."

"So the queen's sons have lost." She sighed and clasped her hands on her lap. "Their father has forgiven them before for their rebelliousness. Maybe he will forgive them again."

"'Tis not the sons I am worried about. 'Tis the queen." He reached under his tunic and drew out a single piece of paper with a broken seal and handed it to her.

She regarded him with bafflement, but took the page and began to read the ornate, flowery Latin. He went to look out the window again. Maybe, by reading that one page, she would not ask the questions he could not answer without revealing that he had other pages in a pouch under his tunic. The letters between the queen and King Louis damned the queen, because they outlined her part in the plot to overthrow King Henry the Senior.

He had no idea how du Fresne had come to possess the letters, but suspected the comte had stolen the correspondence and brought it to Poitiers in hopes of having the queen pay him well to keep the letters out of her husband's hands. The changing course of the war to the north must have warned him that gold would not save his life and lands if he were discovered negotiating with the queen. He had fled to declare his unwavering loyalty to the elder king, leaving behind the evidence of his crimes.

Saxon stared up at the thin sliver of moon. King Henry the Senior had sent him to Poitiers to uncover exactly such proof of the queen's traitorous plans. There should be no reason why he was delaying his ride to the king's camp to deliver the letters.

No reason, but . . . He turned to see Mallory look up, her face as pale as the parchment. To focus the king's wrath on Poitiers meant endangering everyone within the palace, especially Mallory, who would sacrifice her life to keep the queen from being captured.

"Tell me I am mistaken that King Louis is planning to abandon the queen and her sons," she whispered.

"You are not mistaken. He believes he has no choice."

"He could offer some of his own gold."

"For what?"

"To give the young king the support he promised. After all, King Louis's daughter would, upon King Henry the Younger's sole assumption of the English throne, be queen of England."

"An England tearing itself apart. With the uprisings in the east and the forays by the Scots in the north, the whole island may destroy itself. What good will it do for King Louis to have his daughter be queen of ruins?"

She looked down at the page. "So he intends to arrange, upon hearing from King Henry the Senior, to call a truce." She swallowed hard before whispering, "We must take this letter to King Henry the Senior."

"What?" He had not expected her to say *that*.

"If King Henry the Senior is not forced to fight to the last man, he might be willing to have mercy on his wife and sons."

"I agree. That is why I have come to tell you farewell. I am leaving for the king's camp."

"Now? You cannot go now."

He frowned. It was not like Mallory to be clinging and demanding. "Dearest, I must go before more die. I—"

She put her fingers to his lips. "At dawn, it will have been three days since we told Malcoeur we would contact him about an audience with the queen. Our attempts to persuade the queen to see him have been fruitless, but—"

"There is no time for me to do that." His frown eased into a grin. "I guess I am going to have to let you prove to me that you can handle something dangerous like that by yourself."

"I will have to prove it some other time. Malcoeur will have to wait awhile longer for his audience with the queen." She stood. "I am coming with you to the king's camp."

"You are the queen's woman. You should remain at her side."

"And you are the queen's man. Don't you think that King Henry knows that? That letter requesting a *parlez* must reach the king. If you go by yourself, you may be—" Her voice caught, but she went on, "You may be stopped before you can get to him. With two of us, there is a greater chance it will reach him."

He was torn. If he told her the truth, her anger at being betrayed—yet again—would make her doubly determined to protect the queen against her husband and against Saxon. To let her travel with him was to lead her into the peril closer to where the king was seeking revenge against those who had chosen to side with his queen and their sons. And he did not doubt that if he tried to sneak away, she would follow him. The only way to protect her might be to take her with him.

Putting his arm around her waist, he drew her close. He leaned his head against her soft hair and whispered, "We will go together, but both of us must hide the truth of our allegiance."

"I will. I promise you that, Saxon."

"So do I." He had never been less sure he could keep a vow.

Chapter 18

Pulling her cloak closed around her, Mallory glared at the men pointing at her. She carried her bow as she walked with Saxon across the camp where King Henry the Senior had gathered his allies. The men seemed to find that amusing.

"Do you think he needs her to hunt his meals as well as cook them?" called one man.

"Maybe she needs an arrow to prick her, too."

Roars of laughter followed that comment. Saxon acted as if he had not heard them, so she pretended to be as deaf to the remarks that became coarser and coarser as they walked through the field. Grass might once have grown among the rocks, but now it was a mire. Mud tugged at her shoes on every step, and she wished for the horses they had ridden most of the way from Poitiers. They had traded the weary mounts for some bread and fresh rabbit, because they could not ride into the camp without garnering unwanted attention.

She almost laughed at that, but she was too tired. She was the focus of too many eyes even when she was on foot.

To avoid the lecherous gazes, she looked at the tents pitched along the riverbank. She was unsure which river it was, but the waters ran with waste. When she saw women trying to wash clothes in the water, she fought not to be sick. How could they think they could get clothes clean in water that served as a latrine only a short distance away? Some of the tents were brightly colored, but most were dreary and covered with black specks of mildew. Every breath she drew in threatened to gag her, because it reeked of the odors of unwashed bodies and spoiled food and rotting limbs and death.

When Saxon halted by a tent, she wondered how he had chosen this one out of the many scattered along the riverbank. It was little more than a pole hung between two trees with a fabric draped over the pole. Both sides were staked to the ground, so wind would not blow it away. He bent and pushed aside a flap.

"This one is empty," he said, shrugging his pack off his shoulder. He caught it before it could fall into the mud and hung it on the tent pole sticking out of the front of the simple tent. "Let me help."

She wanted to melt into his strong hands when his fingers brushed her nape as he lifted off the sack she had carried more than two dozen leagues from Poitiers. For the past three nights, she had slept in his arms, their exhaustion from their relentless journey leaving them no strength for anything else. She wanted a bath and clean bedding and his arms around her while he went with her to ecstasy.

"Where is the king's tent?" she asked, when he set her pack next to his.

"Farther up the river where the water is less soiled, I would guess." He smiled tiredly. "At least, that is where I would have my tent if I were king."

"Is your father here?"

His smile faded. "Probably, but do not ask me if I am going to seek him out. By now, he will have heard of Godard's death. Once he knows I am here, he will come looking for me, because now I am the cherished heir. What of your father? Isn't he here, too?"

"I assume so, but he will not have any interest in seeing me." She was pleased that there was no bitterness in her voice. Her father had tainted her life for too many years. She would not let that continue, for Saxon had shown her that not all men were beasts who could not be trusted. "Shall we go to the king and

be done with our business here?" She whirled to look along the
river.

Saxon jumped back as one of her long sleeves struck him
with a thunk. "What do you have in those sleeves?"

"My just-in-case."

"What is that? Arrows, as Elita had?"

She smiled. "Something I hope I will never have to use." She
folded her hands in front of her, holding her unstrung bow as if
it were a quarterstaff.

"So you intend to be mysterious, do you, woman?" he
growled as he wrapped an arm around her and enfolded her
against his chest. He pressed his mouth against the curve of her
neck before whispering against her ear, "Let us find the king
quickly. There are other things I would like to spend the afternoon doing."

"Yes, let us deliver our message and be on our way back
here."

"Deliver our message, yes."

At the odd stiffness in his voice, she drew back. "Saxon,
what is wrong?"

"Having you here," he said, releasing her. "You are right.
The sooner we are done with our errand here, the better it will
be. Let us find the king quickly."

Mallory paused only long enough to hook her quiver under
her skirt. She considered tearing the side of her gown to allow
her access to the arrows, but she did not want to draw more
attention to herself. She warned herself to be doubly alert because,
if something went wrong, she would lose valuable seconds
pushing aside her skirt to draw out arrows.

As they walked along the river, he stood between her and the
lascivious stares of the men. She tried not to hear their remarks.
They talked about her height and her body and the way she
walked. That she remained silent seemed to incite more lust in
their comments.

When one man began, very loudly, to describe what he would

do if she would lie down beside him, she whispered, "Saxon, what can I do to make them stop?"

"Be quiet, Mallory, and just keep walking."

"She would beg for more," called the man.

"And I would give it to her," another man said with a drunken laugh. "Maybe I should give it to her now." He stood and stumbled toward them.

"Keep walking, Mallory," Saxon ordered.

She was happy to comply, but the man followed them for several feet, then reached out to touch her rear end. She whirled, raising the bow to strike him.

He stared at her in wide-eyed amazement and, before she could swing her bow, tumbled backward into the river. Sputtering, he jumped to his feet and waded back to the bank.

Her arms were seized. She tried to shake the hands off her and shifted her weight to ram her foot into whoever held her.

"Enough, Mallory," Saxon said, his eyes snapping with anger.

"He—"

"Mallory, remember where you are."

"But—"

"Mallory, do I need to remind you *again* how to act?" He released her and lifted his right hand, slowly curling his fingers into a fist. "I will not hesitate to teach you a lesson."

She stared at him, appalled. She understood that he had to pretend to be a king's man, but did he have to treat her as if she had no more wits than her arrows? She answered her own question. He had to act as he did in order to show he was as coarse as the rest of the king's men.

Lowering her eyes, she said, "No, Saxon, you do not."

"Good." He grabbed her arm so tightly she winced. Pushing her ahead of him, he laughed along with the others at the soaked man.

Once they were out of earshot, Mallory pulled her arm out of his grip. "Next time, don't take to your role with such exuberance."

"I had to convince them that I would reprimand you as they would their women for such backtalk."

"Convince them, yes. Bruise me, no."

He stopped and took her arm more gently. "Forgive me, dearest. I wanted my discipline of my woman to look real. Did I really bruise you?"

As he was going to brush aside her sleeve, his face long with dismay, she drew her arm away. "I am fine. Be careful of my sleeves," she said, touching the long fabric dropping from them.

"And your just-in-case."

She smiled as he took her arm to steer her around reeking pools and half-cooked or burned piles of bones. Her expression became grim when they passed men passed out and stinking of sour wine and urine. She was amazed that *these* men were about to win the rebellion.

As they continued upriver, the smells diminished, and the ground around the tents became cleaner and more expansive. The tents showed less filth and mildew, and more women wandered among them. She saw flags denoting various families, and squires and pages tended to the maintenance of mail and weapons. As she watched them, she remembered doing similar tasks at St. Jude's Abbey.

"You are thinking of home, aren't you?" Saxon asked.

"How did you know?"

He pointed to where a flag with a single brown bear flapped in the breeze.

Her first instinct when seeing her father's battle banner was to turn and run away. She quelled that reaction as she kept walking by Saxon's side. Her father had put her out of his life when she went to St. Jude's Abbey. She must stop letting him darken hers. He was a weak man. She had discovered her own strengths, and she must never forget them. When she saw her father's page in front of the bright green tent—no, Durand must be a squire or even a knight himself now—practicing with a lance, she smiled.

"I did not expect that expression," Saxon said as they stepped beneath some trees that blocked their view of the bear banner.

"I was recalling how Durand—the man by my father's tent— always said a lance was the perfect weapon. The right length to control, but still long enough to keep out of the way of swords." She laughed. "I am pleased to see him handling one now."

"If you want to stop and speak with him . . ."

"No, we have our duty to deliver that message." She looked over her shoulder. "That is the best way to ensure that Durand lives to have a chance to use his lance in a tournament someday. He was always eager to prove himself worthy of being dubbed a knight as soon as he reached the proper age. He wanted to be a hero like the ones in your stories. Once the war is over, he can have the chance to show his prowess at tournaments."

"I hope you are right."

When he added nothing more, Mallory put her hand over his on her arm. Saxon had said little about his past or his future as his father's heir, but she knew he had suffered more than the wound that had left the scar on his side. She looked to her right and caught a glimpse of her father's flag. Maybe it was time for both of them to leave the past in the past.

Saxon did not need to point out the king's tent to her. It was several times larger than any other tent. Five smaller tents were set in an arc before it, like a fabric wall to hold back the king's foes. Horses grazed behind the enormous tent. A half dozen men were sitting and talking by a low fire, while an equal number of women were cooking by another. Nobody glanced in their direction. She found that lack of curiosity comforting.

Saxon drew her toward a table where a scribe sat behind several stacks of books and papers. His tonsure was burned a fiery red from too many hours in the sun. His bulbous nose was peeling, and she guessed it had been as scorched as the top of his head. He grunted and went back to work, clearly dismissing them.

"We wish to speak with King Henry." Saxon leaned forward

to put his hands on the table, but drew them back when the clerk regarded him with horror.

"I am Brother Reginald. I have the honor of serving the king as his eyes and ears. What you have to tell him, you can tell me. Start by telling me who you are."

Mallory stiffened, but Saxon replied calmly, "I am the son of Juste Fitz-Juste." He withdrew from beneath his tunic the page he had shown her at the queen's palace. "The king needs to see this without delay."

The clerk took it and set it atop the other papers on the table, barely pausing in the scratch of his quill across a page. "I will make sure that he sees it."

"He needs to see it now."

"The king is busy now. I will bring it to his attention when he is not busy."

Saxon stretched across the table and grabbed the scribe by the front of his tunic. "King Henry needs to see this *now.*" Shoving Brother Reginald back onto his stool, he snatched the page off the table. "Never mind. I will find him myself and make sure that he learns how you delayed him from reading the missive from King Louis."

"King Louis?" The clerk's eyes widened. "Let me see that!"

Saxon hesitated, but Mallory put her hand on his arm and whispered, "The king must see it without delay. Don't let this pompous fool's antics be the reason it takes longer for the letter to reach King Henry."

When Saxon held out the parchment, the clerk took it and began reading it. Jumping to his feet, Brother Reginald ran toward the king's tent, his long robes flapping behind him. Ink splattered across the table in his wake.

"Is that it?" she asked.

"Apparently it is for now. I assume the king will send for us if he has any questions." His grim tone had returned, but he smiled when she held out her hand and turned to walk back to their tent.

*   *   *

Mallory rolled over and winced. A rock was pushing through her cloak. Rising to her knees, she moved the cloak and pulled the stone out of the ground. She spread out her cloak again and ran her hand along it to make sure there were no other rocks waiting to poke her in the back.

Strange that she had not noticed any stones during the afternoon she and Saxon had spent within the tent. She had sensed that odd desperation he had tried to hide from her since they left Poitiers. Even teasing him that nobody in the camp would guess from this point forward that she was anything but his very cowed wife had brought only another apology for squeezing her arm too tightly by the river. Her reassurances that she would have acted the same if their places had been reversed seemed to do nothing to ease his tension. Their lovemaking had been rapturous, but she could see the worry return to his eyes the moment he drew away from her.

She had been pleased when, as they were eating their simple evening meal, a quartet of men had come to greet Saxon and express their sorrow at learning of the death of his brother. They were obviously friends, and they did not question his loyalty to the king. They seemed pleased to see him in the camp. When they had pulled out some bottles of wine, she had urged Saxon to go with them and enjoy their company. She did not add that she had some final work to do on what he jokingly called her "just-in-case."

Picking up the small rock, she pushed aside the flap on the tent. She started to toss the stone toward the river, but paused when she heard Saxon chuckle. She looked to her left and saw him sitting with his lute on his lap. Several men were with him; she could not be certain exactly how many, because the night disguised their numbers, but she heard more voices than those of the four who had come to the tent earlier.

"Fitz-Juste, it is time you returned to where you belong," said one man. "When are you going to trade your lute for the sword you once held so proudly? Or have you become too accustomed to singing songs and telling tales for women and their men who are too fearful to fight?"

"It was interesting to be within the queen's court, I must admit," Saxon answered as a flask was handed to him. He tipped it back.

Another man grabbed it from him, spilling whatever they were now drinking down the front of Saxon's tunic. Holding it up, he said, "A salute to Saxon Fitz-Juste, who persuaded the king to let him go to the queen's court when the first whispers of rebellion reached the king's ears." The man drank deeply. "I was there the day Fitz-Juste came to the king with his idea to go to Poitiers and learn what the queen was plotting with her sons and the French king. We all thought he was mad and that he would be uncovered quickly as a spy. He proved us wrong, and now he brings an end to the rebellion."

"It was nothing that any brave man would not have been willing to do," Saxon said, grabbing the bottle back and holding it high. "And it was easy to be willing when the ladies were."

Mallory heard the men cheer and laugh through the vicious fury throbbing in her head. How could she have been so stupid? Saxon had told her that he was not being completely honest with her; yet, she had let herself believe he was.

Almost blinded by her rage at allowing herself to be betrayed—again—by a man she had trusted, she threw the rock on the ground and grabbed her bow. She stood, set an arrow to the string, and fired. The arrow sliced across the strings of his lute, making a discordant sound, before embedding itself in the ground by the fire. She smiled as the men, except Saxon, jumped to their feet, looking about them in shock.

He stood more slowly and took a single step toward her before her arms were grabbed. She was shoved to the ground as her bow was ripped out of her fingers. She twisted her right arm and broke one hold on her. A foot in the center of her back pushed her savagely against the ground.

She moaned, hoping her back was not broken. She flexed her fingers and wiggled her toes. They still moved. She could breathe. That meant she could escape. When the foot in the middle of her back moved, she let it roll her over. This could be her best chance. She grasped the ankle with both hands and twisted hard.

The man toppled to the ground, just missing her. She jumped to her feet, took a single step, and halted when she saw the points of swords surrounding her. She lowered her hands, keeping her long sleeves against her skirt.

Saxon tried to push past the men, but nobody moved as a group of men strode toward them.

As the men around her dropped to one knee, Mallory dipped to the ground, too. She prayed these men were acknowledging the earl who commanded them, but knew her hopes were futile when a strong voice called, "Is the son of Juste Fitz-Juste, who brought the missive to the king, here?"

"I am here." Saxon came to his feet.

"Come forward."

He hesitated, then looked at her. "I will as soon as I collect my lady who journeyed with me."

"No!" shouted the men around her in a common voice.

"She could have killed us," snarled one of the men. He poked at her, and she fought not to cringe away when the tip of his sword cut into her upper arm. "She fired an arrow right into our midst. If the lute had not deflected it—"

The rest of his words were lost beneath other men trying to relate what had happened. Their stories were as embellished and unlikely as any tale Saxon had sung. The voices silenced in a single breath when a man stepped forward. He wore no crown or any emblem to identify himself, but when the other men scurried out of his way, kneeling once more, she knew he was King Henry, the sovereign king of England and Wales and Ireland and his ancestral lands on the continent as well as lands brought to him in marriage.

She stared at him, the man who had vowed to be faithful to

Queen Eleanor. His hair was graying, but his shoulders were not stooped. On his face, wrinkled by time and the rough life he had led, were the remnants of the handsome young man who had won a duchess's heart and gained him the lands that stretched from Anjou in the north almost to the Pyrenees.

"Did you shoot the arrow?" he asked as he walked toward her, the swordsmen backing away like fearful mice.

"Yes." Mallory held her head high. She would not speak falsely to the king.

Saxon stepped forward, edging around the crouched men, and said quietly, "She made a mistake, your majesty. Those unfamiliar with a bow can send an arrow flying in error. No one was injured, so what damage has been done?"

"Do you know this woman?"

"Yes, your majesty."

"Did she come from Poitiers with you?"

"Yes, your majesty."

"From the queen's court?"

Saxon hesitated for only a moment, but it was time enough for Mallory to answer, "Yes, your majesty, I was at the queen's court."

"Did she send for you to join her in Poitiers?" the king asked.

Revealing that the queen had journeyed to St. Jude's Abbey might make the king angrier, so she was pleased she could answer honestly, "No." She swallowed hard, fighting for each breath as his stern gaze locked with hers.

"No?" His brows lowered. "But you serve her with your bow, don't you?"

Again she did not hesitate. "Yes."

A stricken expression swept across Saxon's face as the king pushed past him and continued toward her. Saxon started to follow, but was halted by a bare sword. He reached under his tunic. He withdrew his hand with nothing in it when his arm was tapped by the flat of a sword carried by another of the king's men. His mouth tightened, but he remained silent.

She knew he was enraged that she had let her pain blind her to good sense. Just hours before, she had vowed to set her past aside, and it had roared back into her life to betray her as thoroughly as Saxon had. How could she be angry at him when *she* had betrayed herself?

"I don't believe the arrow was sent flying in error," King Henry said as he paused directly in front of her. "I believe it was carefully aimed by this expert archer."

She said nothing. He had not asked her a question. Until he did, she would say nothing and wait for the chance to explain without betraying the queen. But what could she tell the king that would not reveal the truth?

The king asked, "You were trained in St. Jude's Abbey, weren't you?"

"Yes, your majesty."

He blinked twice at her quiet answer. Had he expected her to lie? She knew the importance of being honest, for she had suffered from too many of Saxon's half-truths.

"If you are from St. Jude's Abbey, you serve the queen."

"Yes, your majesty."

"Why are you here?" He put his face close to hers and snarled, "Are you spying for the queen?"

"No, your majesty."

"Why are you here?"

"To deliver the message of King Louis's desire to arrange for a truce with you."

"Delivering the message is why Saxon Fitz-Juste is here. Why are *you* here?"

Mallory faltered as she had not before. She had been honest with King Henry. To repeat the exact same answer would suggest she thought him incapable of comprehending it when she first spoke the words, so she said, "I came with Saxon because we believed two of us traveling with the information had a better chance of reaching you than one of us alone."

"Are you admitting to betraying the queen?"

"No, your majesty. I came here in hopes of bringing a quick end to the rebellion and to beg your mercy for the queen."

The king scowled at her, and all the tales she had heard of his savage temper flooded into her mind. He seized a sword from one of the men. When he put it against the side of her neck, she looked past him to Saxon. She wanted her last sight to be his face.

"Mallory . . ."

Did he say her name, or was it no more than her heart seeking his?

She gasped when King Henry lowered the sword and drove its tip into the ground between her toes. He turned his back, gesturing to his men. They rushed forward to take her by the arms. She kept her elbows close to her, so they could not sense the weight holding down her sleeves.

As the king walked away, Saxon once more tried to push forward to reach her. He was seized, too, and shoved to follow the king.

"No!" she shrieked.

"Shut up, woman," snarled the man on her left.

"Don't let the king slay him! He has done nothing wrong!"

The men laughed, and the one on the left said, "Don't worry about Fitz-Juste. The king knows exactly how well Fitz-Juste has served him."

"Worry about yourself," added the man on her right, "and take this time to make a list of your sins, so you can make a final confession."

She pulled her gaze from Saxon, who was being herded along the river, and stared at her captors, horrified. "But the king did not slay me. He—"

"Will not allow a traitor to die so easily." The man on her right laughed again. He put his hand around her throat and forced her to look at him as he growled, "Soon you will be praying that he had sliced your head off here tonight."

Chapter 19

Saxon sat on the ground near the king's tent. He was waiting for a chance to speak with the king, as he had for the past five hours. The sky was a bright blue, and the birds were singing their exultant songs in the trees.

He leaned his forehead on his drawn-up knees and tried to imagine what he should do next. He always had had an answer for any puzzle. He was the smart one, the capable one, the one who tried harder because he was the second son. Now his cleverness had misled him, because he had been certain he could protect Mallory in the king's camp. Instead he betrayed her, hurting her until she had reacted in pain. She had been foolish, but she had had a good reason.

He reached under his tunic and drew out the packet of letters that he had found with King Louis's request for a *parlez*. Could he buy Mallory's life with them? If he burst into the king's tent, demanding a chance to show he truly had brought Mallory here because he feared for her life when King Henry turned his fury on the walls of Poitiers, would the king give him Mallory's life in reward for delivering the letters between his wife and her former husband?

"Here you are," came a familiar voice.

Saxon stuffed the letters back into their hiding place as he stood to face his father. Juste Fitz-Juste's face showed that he had heard of his elder son's death, because it had deep lines that had not been there when Saxon left for Poitiers almost a year ago. His shoulders were bent as if he wore his mail tunic beneath his dark blue surcoat with the white lion's head and crescent moon.

"Good morning, Father," he said.

His father cleared his throat before saying, "You are the heir now, Saxon. It is your duty to swear your allegiance to the king and gain your knighthood."

"I understand that."

"King Henry will expect you to denounce the woman you brought with you from Poitiers."

"Lord de Saint-Sebastian's daughter?" He should not be using such a tactic with his father, but he would do whatever he could to gain allies for Mallory.

"The earl has many children."

"His legitimate daughter, I should have said. She was cloistered when her mother died and he took another wife."

His father choked out, "Legitimate?" Recovering himself, his father sighed. "That is too bad. Having you marry an earl's daughter would gain our family some of the prestige we hoped to obtain with your brother's wedding." He shook his head. "How could the fool not see what was about to unfold?"

"He was so besotted with the idea of marrying Lady Violet that he worried more about the wedding than the woman. Do not blame Godard for being shortsighted. Even *I* did not see it."

"But you were not the heir then! He was!"

Saxon swallowed the words he must not say. His father could not see beyond his assumption that his heir was the smartest and fastest and best at everything.

Keeping his voice even, he said, "Godard is dead, Father, but Mallory is still alive."

"Mallory?"

"Lady Mallory de Saint-Sebastian."

His father clapped him on the shoulder. "As I said, that is a shame. Such an arrangement would have served us well."

"It does not need to be a shame. Help me persuade the king to release Mallory unharmed."

"Are you insane?" His father frowned as he had when Saxon was a child. "That would chance our family losing the king's favor. I will not risk that for a woman. You are my heir now, Saxon. It is time for you to act like my heir and heed your father about what is best for our family and lands."

Saxon was about to argue further when a man pushed out of the king's tent and called his name. With a nod toward his father, he went to the king's tent.

"Saxon," shouted his father.

He paused in the doorway to see his father hurrying after them, slipping off his surcoat. He handed it to Saxon. With a nod, Saxon pulled it on over his mud-stained tunic. His father held out his arm, and Saxon grasped it in acknowledgment of his father as his liege lord.

His father stepped back as Saxon ducked to go into the tent where the king was conducting his day's business. Boards on the ground kept the mud and stones at bay. A simple bed and a wooden chest with little ornamentation were set to one side, and Saxon realized the king slept in the tent.

Looking to the other side of the tent, he saw that the king sat at a table, with Brother Reginald bending over one shoulder and pointing to something on a scroll set in front of the king. The scribe seemed accustomed to the sharp questions fired at him and answered in a voice too low for Saxon to hear. The king affixed his seal to the scroll and handed it back to Brother Reginald, who scurried past Saxon and out of the tent.

Only then did King Henry acknowledge that anyone else was within the tent. Closing the box of wax, he stood and came around the table. His expression did not change when his gaze focused on the surcoat Saxon wore.

"I am sorry," King Henry said, "to hear of your brother's death."

"Thank you, your majesty." Saxon could not help wondering if the king would have spoken those trite words if he knew Godard had tried to murder Queen Eleanor. Or had the king sent Godard to do such a heinous deed? He could not ask that question, and it was better to allow the plot to die along with his brother.

"Saxon Fitz-Juste, you have served me well, as your family has since I took my place as England's king."

He bowed his head. "It has been our honor to serve."

"You spent several months at the queen's court, and your reports were precise, but short. I trust you will have other information to share with us as we reach Poitiers's city walls."

"I will answer whatever questions I can."

"Good." The king eyed him up and down again. "You are now your father's heir, and your oath of allegiance to me shall be given again at your knighting ceremony."

"I look forward to it, for I hope to continue to serve you as I have during the past year."

"Hope?" The king sat on the chest by his bed and crossed his arms in front of him.

Saxon recognized that pose, for he had copied it. The king was trying to appear at ease, but he was watching Saxon, appraising every motion and considering every word for a meaning beyond the obvious. King Henry was the veteran of many battles—both on the battlefield and in castle halls—and he was an opponent never to be underestimated.

Opponent? He never had imagined he would attach that word to the king's name, but King Henry could not be his ally when he held Mallory under a death sentence.

"I hope you will offer me another chance to serve you," Saxon replied when he realized the king was waiting for him to answer.

"In spite of your appearance in my camp with one of the queen's ladies." King Henry stood, pacing the tent.

"Yes." He smiled. "She is just a woman, your majesty."

The king rounded to glare at him. "Just a woman? Have you forgotten, Fitz-Juste, that 'just a woman' fomented this rebellion?" He did not give Saxon a chance to answer as he went on, "I am very aware of what the queen's ladies residing in St. Jude's Abbey are capable of, for two of them have served me well in protecting my kingdom." He held up his hand to keep Saxon from speaking. "But I now realize that they have been trained to follow the queen's orders and no one else's. They will follow those orders to the death, if necessary."

"Is it necessary?"

"How can you ask such a question, Fitz-Juste? When they were just a curiosity, called out from behind their walls to protect the throne, I was willing to abide with the queen's women. Now one has proven to be a traitor to the throne. The Abbey must be closed, and the women behind its walls—and here—dealt with."

Saxon clasped his hands behind his surcoat, listening as the king ranted. King Henry would not heed anything Saxon said about sparing Mallory's life. The king was going to make an example of Mallory, because he could not do so with the queen.

His arm brushed the packet of letters. If he revealed what was hidden beneath his tunic, would King Henry accept the correspondence in exchange for revoking Mallory's death sentence? He was acting as if he had no more sense than his brother! To speak now of what he carried would guarantee Mallory's death as well as his own. The king would see him as a traitor for failing to deliver the packet into Henry's hands as soon as Saxon arrived in the king's camp.

There must be some other way to gain her freedom. The king was furious with her, but not as angry as he had been at other times, when it was reputed he rolled about in the rushes and snarled like a beast. The Plantagenet temper was fearsome. Not even the bravest knight in his realm would dare to rouse it. If the French king had not filled the young Henry's ear with nonsense, King Henry and his sons would be allies instead of adversaries.

A commotion sounded outside the tent. Scowling even more fiercely, the king went to the doorway. He moved back out of the way as several men entered, pushing someone ahead of them.

He drew in a sharp breath when Mallory fell to the floor

with a thump. Her cheek was red where she had been struck, and the right shoulder of her gown was torn.

"What is this?" King Henry asked.

"She tried to escape," said a man who was wiping blood from his nose. Beside him, another knight turned to spit a broken tooth outside the tent. "We caught her."

"Get up," ordered the king.

Saxon did not wait for permission to go to Mallory and help her to her feet. He put his hand on her arm as she struggled to her knees, but she knocked it away. He must persuade her to heed him. Her life—and the lives of those she considered sisters—depended on her listening to him and trusting him . . . at least once more.

"Mallory, you must understand why I did what I did," he said, not caring who else listened.

"No, I do not need to understand it. I need only to understand that you lied to me to get what you wanted."

"That is not what it was."

"Then what was it? Did you laugh about how concerned I was that I might fail the queen?"

"I got no amusement out of your anxiety for the queen's safety." He caressed her cheek. "I was worried about *your* safety."

"I don't need you worrying about me, Saxon Fitz-Juste! Nor will I be lied to by you. I can go home and have my father lie to me."

As she started to stand, he caught her by the shoulders and found her lips easily, for he had hungered for them during the long hours of waiting to speak with the king. The thrill of the flavors of her skin taunted him to forget everything else—including the king—and help her flee.

She eased away as he released her, and he saw pain on her face. She wanted him, but she did not dare to trust him any longer. In his head echoed the words they had spoken in Poitiers.

"Mallory, please trust me."

"*Trust you?*"

"*I will explain when I can.*" He folded her hand between his. "*Just trust me now.*"

She yanked her hand away. "*Do you know how many times my father said those exact words to my mother? I would trust him as soon as I would trust you.*"

"*I am not your father, Mallory. I have not betrayed you.*"

"*Yet.*"

She had been right, and now she was going to have to pay for his perfidy. She stood. She wobbled a bit even as she raised her chin in silent defiance.

"Milady," King Henry said, wearing a faint smile, "I have been clement with you because one of your number may have saved my life, but my patience with you is growing thin."

"I understand that, your majesty," Mallory said, her voice as defiant as her pose. "I understand as well that—"

"Mallory, silence," Saxon hissed and frowned in her direction. She clamped her lips closed, but he did not allow himself to relax. Any other woman, even the ones at the queen's court who claimed to be better than men, would accept such a glower as a warning to be silent and remain that way.

Mallory would not.

"Take her back to the tent, and double the guard there," the king said as he turned toward his table, obviously ready to bring the discussion to an end. He gave Mallory a cool smile as he sat on the bench behind the table. "Bring her back at sunset. I will be finished with my day's work, and I will have the time to obtain the information I need from her to put an end to St. Jude's Abbey."

"No!" she cried. Rushing toward him, she dropped to her knees. "Your majesty, I beg of you, do not fault the Abbey for my mistakes. I will tell you everything I know if you will spare the Abbey."

"Not your mistakes, Lady Mallory, but the queen's, and you will tell me everything you know about them at sunset." He picked up a scroll and unrolled it.

Saxon was frozen with shock when Mallory rose slowly. No tears brightened her dull eyes. No emotion was visible on her face. She walked across the tent as if all life had left her. When she passed him, she did not glance in his direction. She simply kept walking. He was unsure whether she would have walked right into the tent's wall, because she was steered away when one of her guards took her arm and pushed her out of the tent.

He wanted to follow, to urge her to believe it was still possible to save her life and to save her beloved Abbey, but the king had not excused him.

As if Saxon had spoken aloud, the king looked up and said, "I have a task for you, Fitz-Juste." He held out a scroll that was closed with his seal. "You are believed to be the queen's ally, so if you chance to meet anyone who follows her and my rebellious sons, you can persuade them that you are one of them. That should grant you passage to where King Louis awaits my answer." He motioned for Saxon to come forward. Slapping the scroll into his hand, he smiled coldly. "You will take it to him."

"It is my honor to serve, your majesty," he said, stuffing the scroll beneath his tunic next to the packet of letters.

"The journey is short, so you should return within three days."

"Three days are nothing, your majesty. If I could beg a boon—"

"If you are asking me to delay Lady Mallory's questioning, do not. You saw her. She is ready to tell me whatever I wish to know."

"You will not be certain if she is lying or telling the truth. I can confirm that for you, and save you much time and possibly men on your way to Poitiers."

King Henry smiled icily. "You may have more of your father about you than I had guessed, Fitz-Juste. Very well. It seems I would be wise to delay her questioning until your return."

Saxon bowed his head and went out of the king's tent. He spoke to no one while he went to the river and stared along it. Once he would have believed the king without question, but that was before he had come to see that nothing was as simple and straightforward as the stories he had sung for the queen's court. If it behooved the king to question Mallory and execute her before Saxon could reach King Louis and return, King Henry would not hesitate.

He listened to the river as it flowed over rocks and slipped beneath plants. Each motion created music. With a curse, he drew off his lute. What music could there be in his life if Mallory were dead? He should throw it into the river.

He lowered the lute to his side. He would not accept that her death sentence was inevitable. Nothing was inevitable until it had happened. There might be a way to save Mallory's life. He shrugged his lute back over his shoulder. Drawing out the scroll, he slapped it against his other hand.

What had Mallory said her father's squire's name was? Dennis? Donald? No, it was Durand. The lad wanted to be a hero. Saxon was about to give him his best chance . . . and, he hoped, Mallory hers.

Chapter 20

Mallory winced as she pulled her torn sleeve over her shoulder. She wanted to transfer what was hidden in the drooping fabric to her other sleeve, but one of her guards might try to come in again and chance to see what she was doing. She doubted any of them would try to sneak in and force her beneath him, not after her single encounter with their leader in the tent.

She wiggled her toes. She had been afraid she had broken one on that beast's hard head. He had thought she would be willing to entertain him to while away the time until the king sent for her. She had changed his mind for him with a sharp kick to the head. While he had been senseless on the floor, she had relieved him of her dagger, which he had taken earlier.

He had stumbled out, bragging how she had worn him out to the point that he was reeling. She had not paid any attention to how he persuaded his fellow guards to stay out of the tent. Whatever lies he had told served her purpose, because none of the other men had entered the tent yet. She guessed from their loud voices that they were enjoying wine that they had stolen from some new knight's tent. They were laughing about how the knight owed them for some bet he had wagered and lost.

She watched the shadows lengthen as the sun dropped toward the western sea. Trying to flee while it was light would be stupid. She had not managed to slip away before dawn, and now there were four men watching the tent.

Shifting her feet, she moved them again quickly when her

leg was pricked by a feather on one of her arrows in her hidden quiver. Her bow had been taken from her, but they had not searched her to find her quiver, believing her assertion that she had had only one arrow. She had to be grateful that the men considered her, as a woman, incapable of having the good sense to carry more than a single arrow.

Or maybe they were right. If she had had any sense, she would not have let her anger at Saxon explode. For so many years she had held her fury with her father deep inside her. Why couldn't she have restrained it one more time?

The answer was simple: She could not restrain it because she had opened her heart to Saxon, allowing herself to love. She had thought any ability to love had died along with her mother. By releasing that love, she had lifted the lid on a Pandora's box of darker emotions, and, like a boiling pot covered too long, that slight crack had let everything spew out.

Now she had doomed St. Jude's Abbey. Each time she closed her eyes, she could not help thinking of these coarse men over-running the gardens and stealing everything of value, including the innocence of the sisters, who believed that by hard work and generous spirits they could serve the Abbey and the queen. It was all about to be destroyed.

She had sent Fleurette D'Ambroise to the Abbey. Would the girl get there before the king's men, or would she arrive to find St. Jude's Abbey in ruins?

Her hands fisted on her knees. She had to find a way to send a warning to St. Jude's Abbey. If she were recaptured after that and put to death, she could die knowing the Abbey had a hope of survival.

But whom could she trust to take such a message to the Abbey? Not her father, who would say she was receiving the punishment she was due for not obeying him. Durand? He had been a warmhearted lad. Would he do her such a favor? She sighed. He would not want to risk infuriating her father.

Closing her eyes, she wished she could trust Saxon to take the warning to the abbess. He had kept the truth about the

Abbey secret in Poitiers . . . or so she assumed. She could not be certain about anything.

Except that she wished he were with her in the tent, to hold her and comfort her and let her tell him that she loved him. Even when she was furious with him for betraying her trust, she could not dampen her love for him. It made no sense, but she had to wonder if everything in the world must make sense. She hated what he had done, but she loved the man he was—loyal and caring and imaginative and sensual.

So she sat and waited for sunset. The shadows slipped from one side of the tent to the other. As it grew darker, she wondered why the king was delaying her execution. She could not keep from envisioning what was to come. How long would she be tormented before she was given surcease in death? And would Saxon come to watch her die?

"Or save me," she whispered. How ironic that she was discovering now that she wanted a chivalrous knight like the ones he sang about at the queen's court. Hadn't she learned that only a dolt would believe such a man existed?

"I would be glad to try," an answering whisper came from behind her.

She pulled her knife and whirled to face a man in a dark surcoat decorated with a beast's head and a crescent moon. Her arm was grasped, and she was pushed down onto the ground. His thumb dug into her right wrist, and her abruptly numb fingers dropped the knife beside her. She stared up at him, shocked that she recognized the firm length of his body.

"Saxon!" she whispered.

She framed his face and brought his mouth to hers, wanting to believe the impossible was possible. He was with her; she was in his arms.

Then, with a curse that would have shocked even Jacques Malcoeur, she shoved him away.

He put his hand over her mouth. She could not see his features in the darkness, even when he moved close enough to whisper in her ear.

"Say nothing, Mallory," he said as he slipped his hand under her arm to help her sit. "We have little time to sneak you out of here."

His voice ricocheted through her like a barrage of arrows bouncing off frozen ground. It warmed her from her ear to the tips of her toes that curled up within her shoes. Even her blazing rage melted within the more potent heat of his touch.

He lifted the back of the tent and motioned for her to crawl out on her belly. She wanted to ask how they would elude the guards, but his hand was still over her mouth and he was gesturing emphatically toward the cloth wall. Knowing she had to take the chance of trusting him once more—because he would not have skulked into her tent unless he truly wanted to help her—she dropped to her stomach and inched out of the tent.

Mud splattered her face and slithered up her sleeves as she pulled herself out. She remained close to the ground, waiting for Saxon to follow. He did and, putting his fingers to her lips once more, took her arm. She stood along with him and edged through the darkness.

When they reached the trees along the riverbank, he paused. She started to ask him what had happened to the guards, but he pulled her to him and claimed her lips. She eagerly surrendered them to him.

"I am sorry, dearest," he whispered as he drew back too soon. "I have been a fool not to be honest with you. I feared that if I were honest, then you would despise me for having been false before."

"I don't know if anything would have been different," she answered as truthfully. "I still would have insisted on coming here in the hope that I could protect the queen." Her voice broke. "Now I may have destroyed both her and the Abbey."

"Don't worry about them."

"Saxon—"

"Worry about getting yourself to safety. You cannot help them if you are dead."

Mallory nodded, even though she doubted he could see her

motion in the darkness. When he released her, she was surprised that he reached down to the ground. He picked up a stick and held it out to her. Not a stick, but her unstrung bow. She took it as he drew another bow from behind a tree and shrugged a filled quiver over his shoulder. She tried not to think of him sending those arrows into the king's men, because she knew he could fire with deadly accuracy. She followed him through the shadows, glad that the sliver of the moon's light was almost as faint as the stars'.

Time and again, they paused, not even daring to breathe as several of the king's men went by, some mounted, most on foot. Dozens of questions taunted her: Where were her guards? Why hadn't she been taken before the king at sunset, as he had ordered? Where were they going? She asked none of the questions as she kept pace with him, wondering where they were bound and how long it would take before they reached safety. She hoped the moonlight would not reflect off the moon sewn on his surcoat as they passed a small cottage.

Shouts sounded behind them.

"Run!" Saxon ordered.

She already was. Gathering up her filthy gown, she raced with him among the trees. Her breath pounded hard against her chest with each step. She could not outrun men when she was wearing a long gown and had a quiver lashed to her leg.

Looking through the trees, she saw another small building. It might be a cottage or a barn. She paused and listened. Her heart thudded in her ears, and she held her breath as she strained to hear through the darkness.

She heard horses. She ran toward what must be a barn. Saxon glanced back and saw she was not behind him. She waved to him, and he hurried to meet her.

"Horses. Ride." She panted on each word.

"Good idea."

"Go and get them."

"Mallory—"

"Go! I will be right with you."

She strung her bow, then leaned it against the barn's wall. She saw lanterns weaving through the trees and knew the king's men would be there quickly. Pulling her dagger, she slit the side of her gown to give her access to her quiver. Next, she slashed her long sleeves off. As they fell heavily to the muddy ground, she knelt and cut the fabric. She pulled out the pieces she had hidden within it—the wooden box, several other pieces of wood, the ten thin shafts that now were fletched and had small arrowheads on them, and two lengths of bowstring.

Trying not to be distracted by the lights visible through the trees, she took one piece of wood and bent it like a bow. She tied the longer string to each end. She hoped she was not making a mistake in the dim light as she put the other partially bolted pieces together, lashing the box to the top of a long, narrow piece of wood after setting the ten small arrows within the box, one on top of the other until the box was full. Where was the top? She could not find it amidst the mire. No matter. She twisted the screws holding the firing mechanism to the box.

She hefted it and dropped to one knee. It was heavier than she had guessed, because she had used hollow reeds when she had made a similar weapon at St. Jude's Abbey.

"What are you doing?" asked Saxon as he appeared out of the darkness. He was leading two horses through the mud, which silenced their hoofbeats. His strung bow was draped over his shoulder. He dropped the horses' reins and drew off the bow. Pulling out a handful of arrows, he drove their tips into the ground so he could grab them quickly to fire one after another.

"Put your arrows away," she ordered.

"What?"

"Put them away. The king's men do not know that you are helping me. Let them think I am alone . . . until we need to reveal the truth."

"Mallory, you do not need to try to protect me. As soon as your guards awake by the tent, they will realize the wine they drank was drugged. They will learn who arranged for it to be given to them, and the king will soon discover I did not go to King Louis as he asked."

"What are you talking about?"

"I will explain later."

Sounds of their pursuers erupted from under the trees. She rose off her knee to squat. She shifted her weapon onto her knees. Putting one end of the long board against her stomach, she balanced the bow section in front of her.

"What in the name of all that is unholy is *that*?" He gasped.

"Nariko calls it a *chu-ko-nu*."

"Nariko?"

"My instructor at the Abbey." She quickly checked its simple firing mechanism. "It is a crossbow from the distant East. She learned how to make it from her father, then taught me. It can fire ten arrows in very quick succession."

"How quickly?"

"In less than half a minute."

"You are jesting."

She looked up at him and smiled. "No."

"That is amazing! Why have I never heard of such a weapon before?"

"It is from the East, far beyond Outremer. We . . ." She raised the crossbow. "They are almost here. Have the horses ready. We will have only seconds to go after I fire."

He shoved his arrows back into his quiver and grabbed the horses' reins again. "Ready."

As the men, almost a half dozen, rushed out from under the trees, she pulled the lever over and over. Each time, an arrow flew from the small box. They arched through the dark, thin silvery lines that vanished among the trees.

"The arrows are too small! They will not halt anyone," he said in a sharp whisper.

"But they will confuse our pursuers. They will think they are riding into an ambush with many archers."

Shouts as the men raced back under the cover of the trees told her that she had guessed correctly.

"Let's go," she called. "We have baffled them once, but we will not be able to a second time with this weapon."

She paused only to unstring her other bow and to hide the now useless *chu-ko-nu* under a bush, drawing leaves over it, so nobody would find it. When Saxon tossed her up onto the horse's back, she gave a shout to the horse. It galloped across the field, clearing the low wall at the far end easily.

She looked back to see Saxon racing to catch up with her. The faint light glowed on the images on his surcoat and the pale gray of his horse. He could have been one of the courageous heroes in his stories, but she knew he was much, much more.

As he drew even on his horse, he pointed to the west. "We can reach the sea and find a way across the Channel—"

"No, we have to go to Poitiers. I vowed to protect the queen. I have not been released from that vow."

He took her face in his hands. "Dearest, you must think of your other vow. The one to St. Jude's Abbey. You must warn them of what has happened, so they may be better prepared if the king turns his fury on the Abbey."

"I can take the queen to the Abbey, and there we will protect her."

"You are few in number compared to the legion the king can raise against the Abbey."

"We are vowed to protect the queen, and not a woman within the walls will renege on that pledge."

"Then not a woman within the walls will be suffered to live if the king attacks."

Mallory turned away. He was right. King Henry had shown himself to be merciless in the destruction of fields and villages in his path. He had ordered her torture and death, even though she had been willing to tell him everything to save the queen.

Quietly, she said, "Once I reach the queen's palace, I can send word to St. Jude's Abbey. It is the best I can do."

"Your best is usually more than enough."

She reached out to run her fingers along his strong arm. "I hope you are right."

*   *   *

Saxon kept his sword at the ready as he went with Mallory into the palace's great hall. Rumor had followed them back to Poitiers, and it was said King Henry had already gone to meet with the king of France. That was probably true, because King Henry was an able administrator, and he would want to bring an end to the war on the continent as swiftly as possible so he could return to England to subdue his rebellious subjects there and beat the Scots back north of the border. It was whispered as well that King Henry intended to raze Poitiers as heartlessly as he was destroying the villages and fields to the north. Saxon ignored those terrified stories. The king would not destroy the city he had helped strengthen with new city walls and repairs to its churches.

But Saxon realized most people believed the rumors. From the moment they had entered the city through the gates, which were open and unguarded, and walked along the almost empty streets, he knew what they would find in the palace.

It was deserted.

The walls of the great hall had been stripped bare of their tapestries. The ropes that had held them in place were tangled on the stone floor. The windows were shut, making the air in the large room stagnant. Shadows gathered near the closed doors. The benches at the raised table were tipped onto their sides. A single shoe sat in the middle of the long floor.

He climbed the steps to the closest hearth and bent to touch the ashes. A bit of warmth remained in their depths. Standing, he said, "They could not have left more than a day ago."

Mallory leaned her strung bow against her foot. When she stood in the middle of the floor, awash in the day's last light reflecting with black-blue fire on her hair, he could understand why her abbess had suggested her to guard the queen. She looked as if she could defeat an army by herself.

"But we did not see them on the road."

"They may have headed in a different direction. The queen has many allies to the south in Aquitaine."

"She did not go south," said Jacques Malcoeur as he emerged from the shadows by a door at the far end of the hall.

Saxon was amazed at the common thief's appearance. He carried a tarnished sword, and two daggers poked through a silk sash at his waist.

"What are you doing here, Malcoeur?" he asked.

"When you did not leave the arrow to let me know when to meet the queen, I came looking for you." His eyes flicked from Saxon to Mallory and back.

Saxon's thumb stroked the hilt of his sword, and he wished he had his bow, which he had left with the horse in the courtyard. He could not reach Mallory before the thief could. As he came down the steps, he forced himself to a pace that matched the thief's. He did not want to panic Malcoeur.

Mallory did not move to raise her bow or reach for an arrow. "You have found us, M. Malcoeur. What now?"

"I found the queen first," Malcoeur said, pausing an arm's length from her. He lowered his sword. "She was readying to leave. When I explained why I was in the palace, she told me to guard it until she returned."

"She may not return," Mallory said. "King Henry may reach Poitiers first. Take what you can find of value, M. Malcoeur, and get out while you can."

"She is right." Saxon came to stand beside her. "Take what you can while you can. The king's forces may not be far behind us."

The thief gulped and nodded. He turned to run out of the room, almost striking a woman entering.

With a gasp, Mallory ran to hug Ruby. "What are you doing here? You should have gone with the queen!"

"I knew you would come back and would want to know where Queen Eleanor went." The serving woman whistled, and Chance bounced into the room, excitedly bouncing around all three of them.

Saxon bent to calm the dog. "Malcoeur said she did not go south."

"No, she has headed north with her most faithful retainers. The comtesse remained a short time longer, then left this morning at dawn."

"Where is the queen bound?" he asked.

"I heard she is going to the château of her uncle, Raoul de Faye."

"In Faye-la-Vineuse?" He straightened and swore vehemently. He looked at Mallory and saw she was considering her next options. To tell her that she risked her life on what might be an already lost battle would not change her mind. Her curt answers to Malcoeur had been filled with the fervor of a knight recalling his sword-sworn oath. "There was talk in the king's camp that the king intended to punish the queen's uncle for rising up against him. She may be riding directly toward the king's men. Who is with her?"

Ruby counted off the men on her fingers as she said their names: "De Mauzé and de Matha and Mangot and le Pantier."

"Those are the four men who traveled with you, Saxon, and the queen to St.—to England." Mallory faltered, and he knew she wished she could speak honestly in front of Ruby, but what the serving woman did not know might be the very thing that protected her when King Henry arrived in Poitiers. "We must go after them."

He seized her shoulders and shook her gently. "Mallory, you must flee! The king has put a death sentence on your head."

"Milady!" moaned Ruby.

Mallory said, "I vowed to protect the queen, and I shall."

"The king's allies will be looking for a woman carrying a bow, and I have no doubt King Henry has offered a generous reward to be paid when you are brought back to him. You will be worthless to the queen if you are dead."

She faltered, and he fought the yearning to pull her against him as he soothed her disappointment. She wanted to rescue the queen, to prove she was worthy of being one of St. Jude's Abbey's ladies. But she had to admit he was right. The king's men would be almost as eager to find her as they would the queen.

Ruby said into the silence, "Let me get you something to eat. You must be hungry."

"Very." Saxon gave the serving woman the roguish smile he had each time he had come to Mallory's door.

Slapping his arm playfully, Ruby flushed as she looked at his surcoat. "Forgive me. I should not have—I mean, you are now a knight."

"Not quite." His smile grew chill while he walked with her and the dog toward the door. "Possibly never, for the king will not forget how I assisted Lady Mallory to flee."

"You must tell me about it while I bring you your meal," the serving woman said.

"It is quite a tale. Isn't that true, Mallory?"

When she did not reply, he turned to see Mallory had not moved. He went to her, put his arm around her shoulders, and led her out the door. Never again would he be able to sing a song about a broken heart without envisioning her face at that moment.

Chapter 21

Mallory stepped up onto the sill of her bedchamber. Both doors were bolted, and Ruby slept on the floor in front of hers. Mallory had offered to take the last watch before dawn, and Saxon had fallen asleep in a chair by the other door, exhausted after their long journey back to Poitiers. She was tempted to tumble back into the bed and surrender to slumber herself.

She had worked too hard, distracting Saxon and Ruby with half-truths as she gathered what she needed. Under the bedcovers, she had hidden the length of rope that once had held a tapestry. It was at least ten feet in length, and she hoped it was long enough. Clothing she had found in an overlooked chest and put beneath her bed. She had seen Jacques Malcoeur and his men piling their plunder in one corner of the garden, but she had said nothing as she slipped by in her search for boots. She never found a pair that fit her, so she would have to wear her shoes. In the fletcher's room, she had been luckier, and she refilled her quiver with arrows as well as wrapping more in a sack. Those had gone under the bed with the clothing until the time was right.

And it was right with the others asleep. She blinked several times to wash fatigue from her eyes. Taking care not to strike her bow against the sill and wake Saxon or the maid, she put an arrow to the string. She quickly calculated how sluggish the arrow would be with rope tied to it. The other window was not far, but the impact must drive the arrow deep into the wooden shutters closed on it.

Leaning out the window and hoping that the vibration of the bowstring would not rouse Saxon or Ruby, she let the arrow fly. It struck the shutters, but lower than she had hoped. She looked back, but neither of the sleepers stirred.

Chance raised her head, but put it down on her paws when Mallory motioned to her.

Mallory released two more arrows that were lashed to the same piece of rope. They hit within inches of the first arrow. Sitting on the sill, she put her bow around her left shoulder and checked that the strap holding her quiver was firmly on her right. She tugged on the sack of extra arrows at her waist. It was tied snugly.

She could not hide any arrows in her sleeves, because she was wearing the clothes she had hidden under the bed. Maybe the clothing had been meant for one of the princes, but it fit her well enough. The tunic hung halfway down her thighs, giving her a sense of some modesty. She had braided her hair and shoved it beneath a cap, hoping it would stay in place long enough for her to reach the queen.

Telling herself not to fret about such foolish things, she swung her legs out the window. She gave the rope a pull. She could not guess if it would hold while she swung down to the ground, but she had to take the chance.

She gripped the rope and pushed herself off the window. She felt the rope give and knew the arrows would break quickly. She slid down so fast that her hands were seared by the rough hemp. Then she was falling. She rolled as she struck the ground, and the rope and broken arrows fell atop her.

Mallory swallowed her moan as she sat. She had fallen no more than a few feet, but every inch of her was jarred. Looking up at the window, she held her breath. If Ruby or Saxon had heard her fall, they would come looking for her.

Seeing neither of them, she stayed close to the wall and the deepest shadows as she hurried toward the stable. She must find a horse that could carry her the eight leagues to Faye-la-Vineuse at top speed. Any minute lost could be the one that meant the queen's death.

"Where is she?" Saxon demanded, holding his sword to Malcoeur's chest. Dawn's first light inched across the courtyard. "If you did something to harm her . . ."

The thief gulped hastily and shook his head. "I did not harm her. We were busy all night gathering this." He made a curtailed motion toward the stacks of clothing and furniture in one corner of the courtyard.

"Did you see her?"

"No." He choked again, then gasped, "I swear. I did not see Lady Mallory."

Saxon lowered his sword. Kicking at the rope he had found under Mallory's window, he scowled at the shattered arrows that had given her just enough support to escape undetected. "She could not just disappear."

One of Malcoeur's men inched forward. "Milord . . . Sir, there was someone else in the courtyard last night."

He recognized the man as the one who had been sitting on the wharf and singing the night Mallory arrived in Poitiers. "Who?"

"A boy."

"What was he doing?" Suspicion seeped into Saxon's mind.

"He took a horse and rode away."

"Did he have a bow?"

The man's brow furrowed. "I think so."

Saxon kicked the rope across the courtyard as he snarled an oath. "She must have changed into boy's clothing."

Ruby gasped from where she was sitting on the steps behind him. "She would not do such a thing! It is heresy for a woman to wear men's clothing!"

"Do you think the mere threat of excommunication would keep Mallory de Saint-Sebastian from doing whatever she believed she needed to in order to fulfill her vow to protect the queen?" He strode toward the stable.

"Where are you going?" Ruby called.

"Where do you think?" He touched the packet of letters under his tunic, knowing that if the king's men found them, the queen and her followers could meet a painful death. He could not leave them in Poitiers. Maybe they would still have some use. "I am going to Faye-la-Vineuse to save Mallory and the queen . . . if I still can."

Mallory heard a horse riding hard behind her as she turned her own steed onto the road leading up the hill toward the small village of Faye-la-Vineuse. Ahead of her on the hilltop, the lights from the château were earthbound stars across the otherwise black landscape. Rain poured as if all of the heavens were weeping for Queen Eleanor, whose fate might have already been decided. She hoped that was not so, that there was time to persuade the queen to flee across the Channel to St. Jude's Abbey.

Leaning over her horse, she called, "Just a little farther, and you can rest. Just go! Go as fast as you can!"

The horse went more swiftly along the road edged on both sides by fields. One side had been harvested, but the other was laced with grapevines growing in straight lines as they had for hundreds of years.

Less than a dozen houses and an equal number of trees stood near the walls of the château. It was little more than a fortified house, for the outer wall was the building's wall. Across the road, a small church was only a single story tall as it clung to a sharp drop into the valley on the other side. She did not see where the River Vincuse was, but it must be nearby to give the village its name.

She jumped off her horse as she heard another come to a stop behind her. She reached for an arrow, but did not draw it out of the quiver when her name was called. She peered through the rain.

"Did you really think I would not give chase?" asked Saxon as he lashed his horse's reins to a low branch. Water dripped from the leaves, but he shook it off as he walked toward her.

"I had hoped you would stay safely in Poitiers."

"While you risked your life? That was not likely."

"You are the king's man, Saxon."

"As are the ones I saw coming in this direction just before dark."

She could not halt the frisson of fear trickling down her back. "All the more reason for you not to be found here. I cannot ask you to break your vow to the king further."

"And what of my vow to you?"

She stared at him. "What vow have you made to me?"

Before he could answer, the door to the château opened, splashing light out onto them. Two men rushed out, swords drawn.

Mallory raised her hands to show she had no weapon at the ready. "We are here to see Queen Eleanor."

"Why do you think she is here?"

Instead of answering, she said, "Tell the queen that Lady Mallory de Saint-Sebastian is here with information she needs to hear immediately."

"Where?"

"Right here." She pointed to herself.

"*You* are a lady?"

She pulled off her cap and let her soaked hair fall over her shoulders. "I am Lady Mallory de Saint-Sebastian, and I have an important message for the queen. It is vital that she hear it without delay."

The two men glanced at each other, then motioned for her and Saxon to come inside. One led the way while the other stood back to follow them. If they did not do as he wished, he could spit them with his sword like pieces of meat.

Mallory was pleased to feel Saxon's hand in the middle of her back as they walked into the château. The first man took a brand from the wall, and she hurried to keep up with him because there was no other light in the narrow hallway.

She said nothing when they were led into a room where the queen sat with the four guards she had brought with her from Poitiers. The men were huddled close together by the hearth, where a fire could not banish the dampness. They were talking too low for her to hear.

Going to the queen, she dropped to her knees. "Your majesty, I come with the warning that you must leave this château now! The king is closing in on Poitiers, and he will be here soon."

"Who are you?" Queen Eleanor asked.

She raised her head. "Lady Mallory de Saint-Sebastian, your majesty."

"Lady Mallory is dead. It is said my husband ordered her death."

Grasping the arm of the man holding the brand, she drew it closer. "I am alive, and I am here to bring you to safety at St. Jude's Abbey."

The queen stared at her. "You *are* alive."

"I am."

"And dressed in men's clothing." She stared past Mallory, and a small smile tipped her lips.

"We must leave for England straightaway!"

"England?" The queen stood and shook her head. "I am going to France, where I still have allies."

"France?" Mallory jumped to her feet and glanced at Saxon. "It is too dangerous. The king's army is between here and the French border."

"But the king will be looking for his wife." Queen Eleanor plucked at Mallory's wet sleeve. "Not for a man riding with comrades away from the fighting. Your disguise is inspired, Lady Mallory. Thank you."

Mallory stared at the queen's back as Queen Eleanor called to her guards, asking them to find her men's clothing that she could wear. They quickly gathered clothing for her out of their own travel sacks. The queen took the garments and went into an adjoining room to change. Mallory started to follow, but the queen stated that she could change on her own. Wanting to urge the queen again to reconsider and come with her to St. Jude's Abbey, she said nothing. Until now, she had not realized how much alike the king and queen were. Both chose to listen only to what they wanted to hear.

Whirling, she said, "Saxon, we have to do something!"

"Wait here," he replied. He went to the queen's four Poitevin guards. Squatting by them, he began to draw a map in the dust on the floor, quietly outlining a route that would lead them away from the king's army.

She went to the window and looked out to see that the rain was easing. Lights flickered to the north across the fields, and she realized the king's army was even closer than she had guessed.

She heard Saxon mention her name to the queen's guards. The men looked at her and smiled and nodded. He shook their hands as he stood and crossed the room to where she leaned on the window.

"There," she said, pointing. "The king's army."

"I know how close the king is, as the queen's men do, so they understand the importance of following the directions I gave them."

"The king will never forgive you for this."

He smiled and put his arm around her waist. "Let me worry about the king, dearest."

The queen came back into the room. The tunic she wore dropped to the tips of her shoes, looking not so different from one of her gowns. She crossed the room and held out her hand to Mallory.

Dropping to her knees, Mallory bowed over it.

Queen Eleanor put her hand on Mallory's head and said, "You have once more proven the value of St. Jude's Abbey, Lady Mallory. Take a message to your abbess that I may not be able to contact her again for some time, but St. Jude's Abbey must continue to be ready to serve England's queen."

"I will tell her." She did not add that she was unsure if there would be an abbey much longer. She hoped the king would not send men to raze it.

Turning to Saxon, the queen smiled. "You have served me well, too. I hope I may hear your tales told again." She took Mallory's hand and placed it on Saxon's. "I give my lady into your keeping, Saxon Fitz-Juste. See her safely home."

"I vow to do so, even if she hates having anyone watch over her."

"She *is* a lady of St. Jude's Abbey." She looked at her guards. "Come. We must leave posthaste."

Mallory came to her feet as the queen went out of the room, so regal and feminine in every motion that she wondered if anyone would believe Queen Eleanor was a man. Her guards and the two men who had brought them to the queen's chamber followed.

"I wish," Mallory said into the silence when the footfalls had faded, "that she would have come to St. Jude's Abbey."

"She knows that to go there now would mean its being the focus of the king's fury." He pushed away from the window as the sound of horses being ridden away reached into the room.

"But she would be safe, and the Abbey may be doomed anyhow."

"No, the Abbey is safe." He reached under his tunic and drew out a soaked sheaf of papers. Going to the fire, he dropped them on the flames. The papers sizzled and steam rose from them before the fire began to nibble on their edges. "And so is the queen."

"What do you mean?"

He pointed to the pages, which curled before disintegrating in the fire. "There now is no proof that the queen ever contacted her previous husband for help against King Henry."

Mallory dropped to sit where the queen had been, too shocked to speak.

He faced her. "Among du Fresne's papers, I found correspondence between Queen Eleanor and King Louis. I believe du Fresne brought it to Poitiers in hopes of persuading the queen to pay him to destroy it."

"But he fled, fearing that one of the kings would discover he had stolen the letters."

"Yes."

"You could have shown them to King Henry and been richly rewarded."

"I considered it, but the reward I wanted he would not have given me, even in exchange for the letters." He knelt beside her and folded her hands between his. "He was determined to make an example of you and St. Jude's Abbey."

She closed her eyes and leaned her forehead on their joined hands. "He still will."

"No, he will not." He released her hands and put one finger beneath her chin, tipping her face up toward his. "He will be so grateful to you and to the Abbey, where you were trained to see the obvious solution to a problem, that he will forget his rage."

"I don't understand."

He smiled gently, and her heart began the wild rhythm it beat only when she was within his arms. "I told the queen's guards that you came here dressed as you are to persuade the queen to do the same. As well, I told them that you had mapped out the route they should take, a route that will lead them directly to where some of the king's men can find them."

"What?" She jumped to her feet. His hand on her arm halted her from racing down the stairs to her horse.

"Listen to me, Mallory."

"The queen—"

"Listen to me, Mallory." He spun her to him. When she yanked her arm out of his grip, he cupped her face in his hands. "Mallory, listen to me. *Trust* me." His voice dropped to a desperate whisper. "Trust me once more, please. I know you have every reason not to trust me."

"You have sent the queen into the hands of her husband. If he loses his temper, he could have her killed." Tears filled her eyes, distorting his face. "I promised to protect her. I cannot fail her and the Abbey."

"Trust me, Mallory. Trust me enough to heed what I have to tell you."

She swallowed the sobs welling up in her throat. "I will try."

"What I have done is aimed at saving the queen. Mangot, de Mauzé, de Matha, and le Pantier know that the only way to keep their own heads firmly on their shoulders now is to turn the queen over to the king privately. He will not slay her. To do so would bring the fury of Europe and the church upon him. Don't you see? It was the only way to save you and the Abbey and her."

"Yes, I see that." She stared at him, then whispered, "I never thought we would have to betray our oaths of service to keep her alive."

"I know how difficult this is for you, Mallory, for you have suffered too many betrayals in your life, including the queen's when she plotted against her husband."

"I believed she was perfect. Have I been blind not to see the truth?"

"Vows cannot be blind, dearest, nor can we be blinded by our attempts to obey them." He drew her back to the window, where the faint moonlight glittered on the wet road. "I told you outside that I had made you a vow."

"You did not tell me what vow that was." She was surprised she could grin as she added, "A vow to undermine everything I tried to do to protect the queen?"

He did not smile as he drew her into his arms. "I vowed that I would love you forever."

"You did? When?"

"The moment you stole my heart." Finally he laughed. "I think it was when you hit Malcoeur over the head with a plank from the quay."

"The night I arrived in Poitiers? You hid that vow well."

"No, I showed you in every way I could, which proves that the only thing that truly blinds us is love. I would not have made the mistakes I did at the king's camp if I had been thinking clearly instead of being blinded with love for you. I was so happy that you were with me that I forgot myself in that joy."

"Can I blame my own errors on being blinded by love, too?" she asked, suddenly laughing as she had not guessed she would again.

Putting her arms around his shoulders, she leaned into his kiss, hoping it would be only one among a lifetime of kisses.

Epilogue

". . . and Garwaf saw his wife and her new husband come to the king's tournament. As a wolf, he tried to bite the knight, and no one in the king's court could understand why the previously gentle wolf had become vicious. When Garwaf's traitorous wife was presented to the king, the wolf leaped up and bit off her nose.

"The knights were about to fall upon the wolf and slay it, but the king's wisest man urged the king to spare the wolf, saying that it had never been savage to anyone but the knight and his lady. He begged the king to question the lady to discover why the wolf was seeking vengeance on her and her husband.

"It did not take much torture for the lady to reveal the truth of how she had betrayed her husband and had his clothes stolen to leave him in the guise of a wolf the rest of his days. The king had the clothing brought to him and placed them in a private chamber with the wolf, because he knew no lord would wish for his king to be a witness to such a transformation. When the king went into the room an hour later, there was Garwaf as a man. There was much rejoicing, and Garwaf's lands were returned to him. The scheming lady and her knight were banished. It is said she gave the knight many children, and not a single daughter had a nose."

Saxon put down his lute and smiled at the young girls sitting around him. The refectory of St. Jude's Abbey with its long tables and simple benches was decorated with autumn flowers, and the girls wore matching ones in their hair. By the door, the abbess sat, smiling. Beside her stood the woman who had been introduced to him as Nariko. Her hair was as long and sleek and black as Mallory's, but her eyes had a slant above her high cheekbones that he had never seen on another face.

"Tell us another story, Lord Fitz-Juste," asked the girl he had once called Lady Fleurette. She now proudly answered to Sister Fleurette and was reported to be one of the best students in the archery classes. She seemed to be adjusting to her new life with an ease he wished he could with his.

Since he had been knighted and raised to the rank of baron by the king at Chinon, where the queen was being kept prisoner while King Henry brought his sons to heel, he had been approached by those who wished to gain a share of the king's favor that had been heaped on him. All these sisters asked was another story, which he gladly offered them, for the life of a jongleur felt more comfortable to him than the life of a peer. The title of baron and lands in both England and north of Poitiers had been given to him in gratitude for bringing a quiet, bloodless end to the rebellion.

"Just one more tale," begged Sister Fleurette.

He glanced at the abbess, who nodded. "Which story?" he asked the girls.

"The one about Lady Mallory!"

He was not surprised. He had already sung the story a dozen times in the two days he had been at St. Jude's Abbey, coming to bring the king's message that his gratitude extended to leaving the Abbey intact as long as the abbess did not contact Queen Eleanor.

Lifting his lute, he began to sing of the lady archer who had played a part in saving a king's kingdom and a queen's life. His voice faded when a shadow crossed the open doorway just as the bells in the chapel began to ring. He set the lute on a bench beside him and stood to go to where Mallory was entering the refectory.

She was dressed in a simple dark green gown that clung to

her magnificent curves. Her hair washed down around her shoulders from beneath a circlet of flowers. She had never looked more beautiful than on this day when she was about to become his wife.

One of the girls jumped up and ran to give her a handful of the flowers decorating the chamber.

Mallory took them, bending to give the blond girl a kiss on the cheek. "Thank you, Sister Isabella."

He reached out and took her hand as he led her to the abbess. Kneeling with Mallory, he whispered, "I ask for you to give this lady of St. Jude's Abbey to me so she may become my wife."

The abbess put her hands on their heads. "The love between two hearts that beat together is one of God's greatest gifts to His children. Lead us, milord and my daughter, to the church, where we may witness and celebrate the joining of your lives together."

Rising, Saxon guided Mallory out the door. Once they were far enough ahead of the others, he said, "I was wondering if you had changed your mind. I had time to sing the whole tale of Garwaf, the werewolf, and I was starting another song."

She adjusted the flowers on her head, which were tipping toward her right ear. "These silly things kept falling off, but I secured them as best I could with some thread from one of my arrows, which I will have to refletch. I think they will last until we finish speaking our vows." She put her other hand on his arm. "Which song were you singing to them?"

"Why do you have to ask?" He chuckled. "The song of the maiden archer Mallory de Saint-Sebastian, who met her match in the greatest archer of all time."

"You?" She faced him and brushed her lips against his, not able to wait any longer to taste them.

He laughed as he pulled her closer to him. In the moments before his lips found hers, he whispered, "No, my dearest lady, not me. Cupid."

Look for the next exciting
Ladies of St. Jude's Abbey book

Rock the Knight

Coming in January 2007

"Why are you standing in the rain, milady?" Jordan le Courtenay asked in lieu of a greeting.

Lady Isabella regarded him with bafflement. "I said I would wait here."

"That you did, but it was not raining then."

"I said I would wait here," she repeated as if he had no more sense than one of the spring blossoms bobbing beneath the rain along the priory's wall. "I need to speak with you. I was sent to find you to seek your assistance."

"Who sent you?"

"I am here on behalf of Queen Eleanor."

He frowned at her. "Do you expect me to believe that?"

"Yes."

"Why?"

Confusion again was on her face as she drew her hood back up over her blond hair. "Because I have just told you that I am here on behalf of Queen Eleanor. You have no reason to accuse me of lying."

"Nor do I have any reason to believe you."

"True." A hint of a smile tipped one corner of her expressive mouth, and he fought his own that wanted to respond to that charming motion. "However, milord, if I wanted to fill your head with lies, I could have done so in the shelter of the priory. I would not have waited here in the rain."

"Unless you wanted me to believe you were being honest when you were not."

She laughed, and he wondered if the storm had been swept away by sunshine and a rainbow. Everything seemed abruptly alive with light and color.

"Lord le Courtenay, we can stand here for as long as you wish and debate what I might have done if I had come with lies. However, the truth is that I have been honest with you. I have been sent by Queen Eleanor to find you, and it would behoove you to believe the word of a lady in her service."

He hated to admit so quickly that she was right. Unless she made the queen appear out of thin air—an unlikely event—she could not prove she was speaking the truth . . . and he could not prove she was not.

"Even if you are an emissary of the queen, why did you come to speak with me?" he asked.

"Because you are the nephew of the abbess of St. Jude's Abbey."

He nodded to keep her from guessing that he had not expected to hear her speak of his aunt. He had seldom seen Aunt Heloïse, for she had been named as abbess of St. Jude's Abbey before he was born. Four times she had come to his father's estate of La Tour du Courtenay, staying less than a fortnight each time. He recalled her smile, because he had noticed, even as a child, that her eyes remained intense and gauging the reaction of everyone around her. When he had mentioned that to his father, he had been told that he should not expect an abbess to react as others did.

But she had acted in a very familiar way. She had, at that moment, resembled his father when the earl had some important matter on his mind.

He knew an abbess had all the responsibilities of her abbey to consider, including the spiritual well-being of everyone who lived within its walls. In that, her duties were not so different from those of a lord who held a fief on behalf of the king.

"Why did the queen send you?" he asked. "Is something amiss with my aunt or her abbey?"

A faint smile once more eased the tension on Lady Isabella's face. "The abbess told me before I left the Abbey that you would be concerned about her, and she said as well that I should assure you posthaste that she is well."

"You were at St. Jude's Abbey?"

Her smile wavered, and she bent to pick up her satchel as she said, "Surely you know that the Abbey welcomes any visitors who travel past its walls."

"If my aunt is well, why are you here?"

"As I told you, I am here to seek your help."

"Mine? For what?"

She drew her cloak closer as the breeze freshened with a chill that had not been banished with winter. "May we walk away from the priory, milord? What I have to say to you should be heard by no other ears."

"Even monks?" He laughed coolly.

"No other ears." She started to walk toward the trees and did not turn to discover if he followed.

Jordan pulled his own cloak more tightly to him as he turned into the wind and the driving rain. His horse whinnied a protest, but turned away from the prospect of seeking dry shelter. Ahead of them, Lady Isabella had bent her head only slightly, as if she were indifferent to the discomfort of the storm. As he caught up with her, matching her paces, he waited for her to speak.

Even though she did not glance in his direction, she clearly realized he walked beside her, because she said, "The task I was given—and for which I need your help—sounds quite simple. Queen Eleanor entrusted some papers with the erstwhile Bishop of Lincoln, and, now that the bishop has assumed his new duties in Rouen, she wishes to have the papers retrieved and delivered to her."

"Why would the queen need to send us to retrieve papers from the cathedral? She could petition the current bishop—"

"There is no bishop in Lincoln now."

He wanted to fire back that he knew there was no bishop and that she should not interrupt him when he was about to suggest that the queen could petition whoever had served as the bishop's assistant at the cathedral. He swallowed his retort when they stepped out from beneath the trees. Ahead of him was the burial mound. It appeared even more pitiful and lonely in the downpour. He turned to tie his horse again, not wanting anyone to see his pain.

"Who lies there?" Lady Isabella asked, her voice gentling from its assertive tone.

"My most trusted friend."

"I am sorry." She was silent a moment as they paused by the grave, then asked. "Why does he lie here in an unmarked grave on unconsecrated ground?"

"The brothers within Kenwick Priory denied him burial inside their walls because he died during a tournament."

For the first time since they had walked away from the priory's gatehouse, she looked at him. Her eyes were narrowed, and he guessed she was appraising him anew. "During a tournament? What a shame for a man to lose his life so worthlessly!"

"It was a waste. If I had been here, I would have tried to persuade him not to accept the challenge to ride in order to gain a woman's hand. No woman is worth a man's life." He watched her closely as a delicate fragrance drifted from her, tempting him to imagine what hid beneath her cloak instead of waiting for her reaction to his derogatory words.

Again she did not speak for a long minute as she stared at the grave; then she whispered, "I agree."

"You do?" He was astonished. His disparaging comment about a woman's value would have gained him rebukes from his sisters. And he could not imagine her brothers accepting such an implied insult without demanding a chance to regain their honor through personal combat.

"There are enough men dying in wars. More should not die simply to gain a woman's admiration." As she raised her head to meet his eyes, her hood slipped back again to reveal her hair that framed her face in a golden cloud. He barely noticed that as she caught his gaze with her intense one and whispered, "What the queen has asked of us could prevent another war from erupting here in England and on the continent."

"How?"

"I don't know, because that was all I was told. It was enough for me to offer my service. Is it enough for you, milord?"

"It is," he said, glancing at the unmarked grave. An end to battles between the king and his sons that left good men dead? Was it even possible? He must find out. "It is more than enough. Tell me how I can help you, Lady Isabella."

About the Author

Jocelyn Kelley has always had a weakness for strong heroines and dashing heroes. For as long as she can remember, she's been telling stories of great adventures. She has had a few great adventures of her own, including serving as an officer in the U.S. Army and signing with a local group of Up with People. She lives in Massachusetts with her husband, three children and three chubby cats. She's not sure who's the most spoiled.

Learn more about Jocelyn and her future books at www. jocelynkelley.com.